I0762932
THE GREAT GREEN
HIGH KHETARA
THONIS
BUBAS
PERSET
THE RED DESERT
LOW KHETARA

PRAISE FOR *HIS FACE IS THE SUN*, THE FIRST NOVEL IN THE THRONE OF KHETARA TRILOGY

INSTANT *NEW YORK TIMES* BESTSELLER

INSTANT AMERICAN BOOKSELLER ASSOCIATION BESTSELLER

JUNIOR LIBRARY GUILD GOLD STANDARD SELECTION

YALSA BEST FICTION FOR YOUNG ADULTS LIST,
TOP TEN TITLE FOR 2026

★ "[An] immersive must-read."

—*Publishers Weekly*, Starred Review

"An entrancing, epic first novel in a trilogy built around an actual ancient Egyptian prophetic text."

—*Shelf Awareness*

"An engrossing political fantasy with myriad twists and turns."

—*Kirkus Reviews*

"Betrayal, murder, magic, and a monster combine within a desert setting for an ancient Egyptian–inspired *Game of Thrones* feel."

—*School Library Journal*

"[An] epic start to a brand-new series. With sibling rivalries, court intrigue, secrets, and betrayals, there's so much to love."

—*B&N Reads*

"A bold and opulent fantasy that glimmers with magic and intrigue!"

—Emily Thiede, author of *This Vicious Grace*

"Captivating. A love letter to fans of Egyptian mythology."

—Aimée Carter, international bestselling author

"I can't recommend this one enough!"

—Kamilah Cole, bestselling author

"A world of beauty, intrigue, and hard choices."

—Patricia C. Wrede, *New York Times* bestselling author

"A brilliant tapestry of an ancient fantasy realm brought to life. This Egyptologist wanted the story to go on and on."

—W. Raymond Johnson, PhD, former director of the Epigraphic Survey/Chicago House, Luxor, University of Chicago

"Beautifully written and a total page-turner."

—Ann Dávila Cardinal, author of *You've Awoken Her*

SHE KNOWS ALL THE NAMES

THRONE OF KHETARA SERIES

His Face Is the Sun

SHE KNOWS ALL THE NAMES

THRONE OF KHETARA
BOOK TWO

MICHELLE JABÈS CORPORA

Cover design by Erin Fitzsimmons/Sourcebooks

Internal design by Laura Boren/Sourcebooks
Map and chapter header art by Gerralt Landman

Published by Sourcebooks Fire, an imprint of Sourcebooks
1935 Brookdale Rd, Naperville, IL 60563-2773
(630) 961-3900
sourcebooks.com

Cataloging-in-Publication Data is on file with the Library of Congress.

Printed and bound in Canada.
FR 10 9 8 7 6 5 4 3 2 1

TO MY AGENT, ALLISON HELLEGERS:
Who made me believe

AND TO ISIS:
Queen, Mother, Magic-Maker—
Thank you for giving me the names
And blessing me with the wisdom and resilience I needed
To write this story

PROLOGUE
WINGS

If only he'd been looking up at the world instead of down at his feet, he'd have seen it coming.

The ibis had been poking about in the dense papyrus thickets, dipping his needle-sharp beak into the river, *quick-quick*, hunting for fish. He was a disheveled bird, his moon-colored body and jumble of black tail feathers giving the impression that he cared very little about appearances.

But he *did* preen. Every morning.

Besides, he looked no different from his brethren. His flock was scattered around him, loping through the water with deliberate strides, their red-ringed eyes focused on the slippery morsels that darted beneath the surface. They'd had poor hunting the previous day, and so they were particularly hungry—and particularly careless.

They neither heard the rustle of men in the thicket nor felt the water tremble with the men's approach.

Then: a splash. Close. Very close.

The ibis raised his head, his long, slender neck bending into a question. He murmured, low and wondering, before another splash turned his wonder to alarm.

Fly away! Fly away! the ibis opened his beak to cry.

Too late. A guttural call broke the silence, and as the flock opened its wings in unison to take flight, a net fell upon them, dragging them back down.

Panicked, the ibis flapped and struggled as the net drew tighter and tighter still, until he found himself pressed up against the other birds in a writhing mass of flesh and feathers. Terror turned the voice of the collective into a cacophony of individual cries. The ibis kicked against the birds below him, while the claws of the birds above dug into the tender skin of his face and neck. He felt the net rise into the air, carried through the marshes by unseen hands. Soon, the green smell of the water was replaced by dust and heat. The ibis grew so exhausted he could no longer move, and was pummeled down, down, into the belly of the net.

Over the frightened yelps of his brethren, the ibis heard a man speak.

"Did you hear what happened?" the man said. "One of the fishermen told me."

The other man grunted and spit on the ground. "Better not to speak of it."

The first man, ignoring his companion's advice, continued. "He said he'd arrived from south of Bubas and saw something strange flowing downriver. Never would have believed it if he hadn't seen it with his own eyes. What do you think it means?"

"That's for the priests to decide. We have our work; they have theirs."

"I think it means change is coming to Khetara," the first man said, undeterred. "Just as the pharaoh said it would! Don't you remember his speech? 'The forgotten floodgates of power'? 'The currents of war'?"

There was a pause. "Perhaps."

The ibis was pressed against one of his flock mates, and felt his heart racing beneath wet plumage. A moment later, the net was set on hard, sandy ground.

"You don't agree?" the first man asked.

"I agree that the sooner we process these birds, the sooner we can go home."

With that, the net loosened. There was a cry and flapping of wings as a bird was pulled out, and then a sharp *snap*.

The ibis's own heart quickened with horror.

"How can you be so cynical?" the first man asked as another bird was lifted from the net. "Everyone I know is excited about King Meryamun! He has great plans for the kingdom! All of Thonis is suffused with hope!"

"Hope and foolishness are neighbors, my friend," the second man said. "It is all too easy to enter the wrong house."

Snap.

Suddenly, the struggle to reach the opening of the net reversed, and the captured birds began fighting to get away from the men's grasping hands. The ibis found himself being shoved to the top, until he could see the growing pile of limp feathered bodies on the ground nearby.

"Pah!" the first man scoffed, reaching for the bird directly above the ibis and pulling it free. "Our entire business is based on hope! Hope that our mummified ibises will cure our customers' ills, grant their wishes, and bring Thoth's favor upon them in the Duat. Without hope, people wouldn't buy, and we would have nothing."

"Perhaps the new king will rule as he claims," the second man said. "Perhaps this omen is a good one. But hope is a poor replacement for preparation. Keep your eyes open, my friend. The gods help those who help themselves." The ibis watched as the man snapped his flock mate's neck with one swift motion and tossed its corpse onto the pile.

He felt the shadow of death fall over him.

Then a new scent met his nostrils, riding the wind. It was bitter and strange—and it gave the ibis courage.

The man reached back into the net, groping for a throat to squeeze.

Not today! the ibis crowed with a surge of ferocity. *I will not die today!*

He stabbed his beak into the flesh of the man's palm—once, twice, *quick-quick*. Blood fountained from the wound, and the hand jerked away. The man loosed a string of curses, and before his companion could close the net, the ibis launched himself into the air.

The strange-smelling wind lifted him up, away from angry words and reaching hands, away from his doomed brethren. He wheeled south, the mouth of the river and the green sea at his back, flying past farms and villages until he reached a great white city.

The ordeal transformed the ibis's hunger into near starvation, and he knew he wouldn't be able to fly much longer without stopping for food. Below, he saw a lush walled garden with a pond at its center. The garden lay in the shadow of a massive structure, and although the ibis could see many people flowing in and out of it, the garden itself appeared to be deserted.

Even better, he could see the silvery flash of scales beneath the pond's surface.

When he got closer, however, the ibis saw that he'd been mistaken. There *was* someone in the garden.

A girl and a cat were hidden among the rosebushes by the

pond. The girl was reedy, hairless, and plumed in blue. Her bare feet were in the water, and she was muttering quietly to herself, over and over, like birdsong. Powerful energy emanated from her. Dangerous energy. It didn't carry the lethal intent of the men who had captured the ibis's flock, but it held dark portents. As if sensing the bird's presence, the girl looked up. Surprisingly, her face was kind.

The striped cat looked up at him too, the pupils of her golden eyes widening. And although she looked old, the ibis could see the cat's teeth were still as sharp as ever.

Death had nearly gotten him once already. It would be foolish to tempt fate a second time. The ibis clacked his beak in frustration and turned away.

He sailed past the garden and the buildings teeming with life and crossed to the other side of the river, the quiet side, where stone giants rose from an ocean of sand. The ibis had no strength left to hunt. He needed to eat and not become food for another. But where could he find an easy meal?

Movement attracted his attention. A single line of men, laden with goods, marched from a sailboat down into a valley inland from the river. The salty smell of fish wafted up from them, so the ibis decided to follow. With any luck, he could snatch up a bite or two without being noticed.

Sailing past the line of men, the ibis dipped down into the valley and alighted on a flat-topped acacia tree. From that vantage point, he could see many people at work, talking among themselves, piling food and all manner of strange things, and going in and out of a hole in the valley wall like ants. Strangest of all were the bald men huddling over a great many human corpses, efficiently disemboweling them one by one before filling them with white sand.

One of the men overseeing the gruesome work caught the ibis's eye. He was birdlike himself, his nose beakish, his plumage as dingy and plain as the ibis's own. Even his nest of black hair was reminiscent of the ibis's tangle of tail feathers. The birdlike man walked to one of the bald-headed ones and said, "How much longer? We must get through the mummification rituals today, or these people will not be ready for the funeral. My father will be laid to rest in fewer than seventy days; his court must be prepared to join him in the tomb."

The bald man wiped perspiration from his brow. "Apologies, Prince Bakenamun. We were not expecting these..." He paused. "These sacred dead. There are so many of them, and you know the rituals take time. We are going as quickly as we can."

The birdlike man blinked, his irritation changing to remorse. "Of course, of course. It is I who should apologize. You and the other priests are doing your best; I should not have addressed you so sharply. We are all...*adjusting* to the new king's doctrine." He frowned. "But where is Montuhotep? Should he not be here supervising your work? I have been busy inside the tomb, directing the painters and engravers."

The bald man cleared his throat. "The master says he is ill. He has taken to his bed, and I do not know when he will be well enough to attend to his duties here."

The birdlike man ran a hand through his unruly hair, making it even messier. "For the love of Amun, must I do everything?" he muttered.

While they spoke, the ibis noted the other men had lain down their burdens and were returning to the boat, leaving the food unattended. This was his chance!

Fluttering down from his perch, the ibis landed before a delicious-smelling package tied with twine. He deftly untied the rope with his beak and pulled back a corner of the fabric to reveal a treasure trove of dried fish. He was about to grab as many as he could carry when he was startled by a voice behind him.

"Lost your flock, have you, Sacred One?" the birdlike man asked, having left the bald-headed men to their work.

The ibis froze on the brink of flight, his hunger battling with his fear. But the man didn't lunge or try to kick him away. Instead, he said, "Go ahead. Take the fish." A sad smile touched his lips. "I know it's not easy being alone."

Unable to believe his luck, the ibis scooped four fish into his mouth and launched into the air, his wings beating hard to accommodate the extra weight. Once he cleared the valley wall, he found a safe place to land and gobbled up the fish, *quick-quick*, before another animal could get a whiff of them.

He felt better almost immediately.

But in place of his hunger came sorrow. The birdlike man was right. He was alone.

What was the ibis without his brethren? They had acted as one organism, moving in a comfortable ritual that repeated over and over, day after day. He had no idea what to do or where to go now that his flock was gone.

His sorrow sharpened into despair.

Perhaps it would have been better to die with them.

Not true. Not true. If he was his flock, and his flock was him, then within himself the ibis held all that remained of his brethren. He must live on, so that they too could live. He would find a new flock—*yes, yes*. Then all would be right again.

With this in mind, he took to the air once more, heading for the river, scanning the skies for birds in flight. *I am alone now, but it will not always be so, not always,* the ibis assured himself.

As he traveled south, he glanced down at the river and saw an unusual sight. Men, women, and children had gathered along its banks and were staring at the water. Some were silent. Others exclaimed in wonder and dismay. It was only when the ibis coasted out of the glare of the sun that he saw what they were seeing.

Usually blue-green in color, the river was turning crimson. The red waters flowed north, powerful, ominous, and very, very wrong.

A whisper of the ibis's earlier terror returned.

Over the amalgamated shouts of the people, one woman's voice climbed the western wind and reached him.

"Beware!" the woman cried. "The Great River of Khetara has turned to blood!"

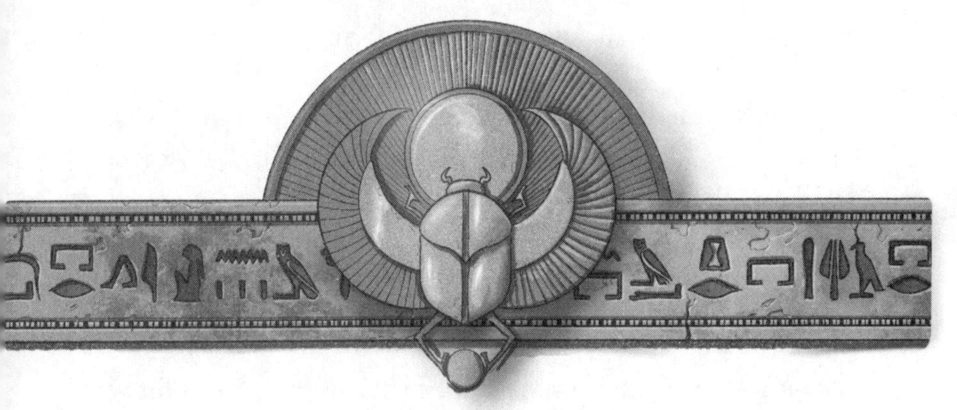

1
KARIM

Karim died young, violently, and with much left unfinished.

The manner of his death surprised him, but it really shouldn't have. There had been many indications of its coming: the wrongness of the dark tomb he'd found in that valley, its unfathomable riches, the blood, the broken and dying boy he'd left behind.

And the creature he'd awoken.

It had pursued him across the desert, relentlessly, like the wind. He'd stabbed it, burned it, impaled it on a tree—and still it came. The creature wanted something. Karim had thought it wanted the amulet he'd stolen, but no.

It wanted *him*.

He had been the one to summon it, after all. Summoned his own demise, like a mouse blundering into a viper's den. Just as the painting on that temple wall, the Oracle of the Lamb, had predicted he would.

Dying wouldn't have been so terrible if he'd done it with a clear conscience. However, Karim's death not only marked the end of his life—but also the beginning of another's.

The forgotten king.

Setnakht.

The undead pharaoh needed Karim's heart—the heart of an acolyte—to truly live again. Once he'd gotten it, Setnakht was free to finish the work he'd left undone when he'd died a thousand years ago.

The Oracle of the Lamb gave hints about where that work might lead. To a river of blood. To chaos, sorrow, and ruin. To a kingdom forever broken. And it was Karim's still-beating heart, savagely ripped from his chest, that would enable Setnakht to bring those ill portents to pass.

Karim had never meant for it to happen. None of it.

I'm sorry.

Those had been his final words, the words of a man who, in his last agonizing moment, recognized that his sacrifice hadn't saved the people of Khetara and the Red Lands as he'd intended.

In fact, he had doomed them all.

There had been pain, unfathomable pain. A lurch that shook his body to the core, and then—

Silence.

The quiet fell over him like a thick blanket, blotting out sound and light, erasing the weight of his body and the sensation of his breath, which he'd never quite noticed until it had gone. Karim's consciousness hovered in the darkness.

There was nothing, nothing, nothing.

And then there was light.

The light did not originate from any specific point—it simply came into being, like an idea. It engulfed him, and Karim could sense something, or many somethings, within that light. Slowly, the shapes became defined.

A man's silhouette, visible but ethereal. The man's voluminous robes swirled, their many folds billowing as if underwater. Karim studied the contours of the man's face, and a name formed within his consciousness.

Father.

The man smiled and opened his arms, and in that single gesture Karim felt the radiating power of his father's love. He willed himself closer, and soon other figures began to emerge from the light. His grandmother, who had died when he was young; warriors from his tribe who had been killed in battle. They were all intensely present, and yet their forms were as diaphanous as clouds.

Then he saw Djet.

The boy was as plump and full of youthful exuberance as he had been that fateful day in the valley. It gave Karim great comfort to see him like that, not terrified and bleeding from a dozen wounds.

Like his father, Djet looked happy to see him and gestured for Karim to join them, to move deeper into the world of light.

Karim could see his own hands now, still gossamer like mist, but growing sharper with every passing moment. He reached out to Djet, to his father.

I'm home. The thought was a balm to all his guilt and shame.

Then another figure emerged from the light. It towered over the other apparitions, dark and imposing.

Pasenhor?

The old priest of Khnum approached like a thunderhead. His presence was jarring, discordant—as if he did not belong in that place and yet had come through sheer force of will.

It's not finished, thief.

Karim heard the priest's voice, though his lips didn't move.

Can you not hear her calling you?

Pa's piercing eyes willed him to listen and remember, though Karim very much wished to forget. He wanted to join his tribe and let go of all that had come before.

Listen!

The priest's command brooked no argument. Karim listened.

"Your story is not finished!"

The voice came from another world, catching hold of him like a rope around his chest, pulling him away from the light.

"I need you!" the voice said. It was both familiar and unfamiliar, like two voices speaking at the same time.

Karim fought the pull of the voice, his ephemeral hands grasping at the priest but finding nothing but air.

Pa regarded him without sympathy. *Gather your flock, Karim of the Red Lands. Go out into the wilderness, find those who are lost, and bring them home. The oracle demands it.*

No... Karim begged as the light dimmed and darkness closed around him once more. *No!*

The figures from his past faded from view save the priest, who stood against the light like a monolith, his voice loud in Karim's mind. *Your story is long—too long, perhaps. But it must be told nonetheless.* The priest chuckled, heavy with irony. *You see? I was right. You're a thief of time, after all.*

Karim cried out as he was dragged through thick darkness, down, down, down to the heavy weight of earthly things, to breath and heat and hunger, to yesterday's memories and tomorrow's obligations.

And though he fought the chains of his mortal body with all his strength, with four words, the mighty voice locked him back into his flesh with a finality that made the earth around him quake.

"Come back to me!"

Karim opened his eyes and gasped. Above him, the cloudless sky was pink with the first blush of morning. He blinked once, twice. His memories of what lay on the other side of death slipped away like grains of sand, until all that remained was a faint sense of having lost something precious. His mind was jumbled, confused. Only a moment before, he'd been in the grip of the monster.

But Setnakht wasn't looming over him.

The valley was quiet.

I'm alive, Karim thought. *But how? The last thing I remember was…*

Seized with terror, Karim probed his chest where Setnakht had ripped into him. He expected to feel torn flesh and exposed bone—but the skin was unbroken.

Unbroken, but changed. He tilted his chin to inspect the raised scarring that spread over his left breast. To his amazement, the scar formed a recognizable design. A design drawn onto him as if by a divine hand.

A scarab.

Deep within him, his heart—feeling heavier somehow—began to race.

What sorcery is this? he wondered.

He sat up. If he needed proof that his recollection of the attack was genuine, his singed, blood-soaked robes were more than enough evidence. He winced as he peeled them off and dropped them into an evil-smelling heap.

Setnakht did *take my heart. But what happened after that? I died… So how am I still here?*

He scanned the area. Sitamun was lying on her back an arm's length away. She was unconscious, but thankfully looked unharmed. He put his palms on the ground, bracing for the pain that was sure to accompany his attempt to move toward her. Over the past couple weeks, not only had his chest been torn open but he'd also been kicked, slashed, burned, and slapped.

Suffice it to say, there was rarely a time when movement didn't come with a fair measure of discomfort.

To Karim's great surprise, however, he felt no pain. It was as if every wound he'd suffered had vanished with the dawn.

As the shock faded and his awareness returned, Karim noticed other differences in his body. A lightness. A prickling sensation that coursed through him, energizing him despite the horrific ordeal he'd just experienced. And through his eyes, the valley around him looked brighter, clearer, and more colorful than it had ever looked before.

Karim breathed, and the air was sweet.

He hadn't simply been resurrected; he'd been remade.

Nearby, Sitamun stirred and groaned, distracting Karim from his frenzied thoughts. At the sound of her voice, a memory from beyond struck him like a lightning bolt.

Hers was the same voice that had reached him in another world.

Called to him.

Commanded him.

Dragged him back to his broken body and somehow mended it.

With new eyes, Karim saw the same radiance—the same half-remembered, divine light that had filled that place between life and death—emanating from the princess like a beacon.

It was her! Karim realized. *Her voice! Her command!*

Sitamun struggled up onto her elbows and took in her surroundings. When she saw him sitting there, staring at her, her eyes widened in astonishment.

"Sitamun," he whispered hoarsely. "What have you done?"

The princess blinked. Her mouth opened, then closed.

Karim waited, expectant, growing more irritated with each passing second. "Well?"

"You're…alive?" Sitamun finally blurted.

"Yes, I'm alive!" Karim sputtered, clambering unsteadily to his feet. He was covered in gore and wearing only a loincloth, but he didn't care. "*You* brought me back!"

"I *did*?" Sitamun said, bewildered. Following his lead, she stood up, wobbled like a newborn donkey, and collapsed. Karim caught her before she hit the ground. He led her to sit on a boulder, and the clouds in her eyes cleared. She beamed at him with childlike triumph. "I did!"

Karim squatted in front of her, amazed at how lithe his body felt. But no, no, he couldn't think about that now. "I need to understand, sena. How did you do it?"

Sitamun's expression turned to horror. "That…thing," she said, her lip curling in disgust. "He tore you apart! He ripped out your heart! There was so much blood! So much…blood…" Her eyes rolled up into her head, and she sagged.

"Stay with me, sena! Stay with me!" Karim said, shaking her and patting her cheek.

Sitamun sat up and slapped his hand away. "I'm fine!" she announced. After a few deep breaths, she continued. "That monster put your heart into his own chest, and it…it healed him. Wove his body back together like threads on a loom—most of it, at least. I thought he would find me and kill me too, but he left. When I finally got up the courage to come out, I saw you, and…" The next words were choked with emotion. "I didn't know what to do. You were dead, and I was all alone. So I started wrapping you in your robes, to bury you, but then a blue amulet fell out of your pocket."

The scarab amulet from Setnakht's tomb, Karim thought.

"It had a message on one side written in the gods' words," Sitamun went on. "*This is the heart of a king.*" I read it, and something came over me. It was as if I suddenly understood what I needed to do, like I'd been possessed by some kind of spirit." She shook her head. "I'm not explaining this very well."

"Keep going, sena," Karim urged.

"I told you that the kingdom still needed you. I told you to come back."

Karim shivered, the hazy memory of her command reverberating through his body.

"And then I put the amulet inside your chest."

Karim lurched backward. "You *what*?"

Sitamun looked up at him, her eyes haunted.

"That stone was a heart," she explained. "Or at least, it had the potential to be. The word is the deed, remember? From my lips to the gods' ears. Somehow, by saying it, I made it happen. I made it true."

Karim touched his chest with a trembling hand. He didn't want to believe it. But the scarab-shaped scar, the heaviness in his chest, and the supernatural lightness of his body forced him to accept what the princess was saying. He felt good, *too* good. He had enough energy to climb out of the valley and race to the horizon, to swim straight across the river, to fight a dozen men with his bare hands—and yet there was a burden on his soul that frightened him. Suddenly, he felt like a trapped animal.

"What did you do to me? What did your Khetaran magic turn me into?" he asked.

Sitamun's brow furrowed. "What are you talking about? I saved your life! You haven't changed. You're still you!" Then she focused on his eyes and grew pale. "Aren't you?"

Karim half growled, half shouted something unintelligible and began to pace. "Just like a Khetaran, hey? You want something, you take it. Did you ever stop to think that maybe I didn't *want*...whatever this is? That I didn't want to come back?"

The princess stood to face him. She wore a simple white dress that clung to her curves in a way that would have been distracting if Karim hadn't been so mad.

"Unbelievable!" she said, throwing her hands in the air. "You go on and on about this oracle and how it's our destiny to save the kingdom, and then when you're *brutally murdered* and by some miracle I bring you back—*this* is the thanks I get?"

Instantly they were both yelling at each other. Karim told the princess exactly what he thought of her and her cursed, nonsensical kingdom, and Sitamun used some particularly colorful language—including comparisons to a variety of farm animals and assorted vermin—to describe what she thought of him. They were shouting at each other, red-faced and gesticulating wildly, when a dog barked.

Sitamun froze.

Whatever insult Karim had been about to volley next never left his lips. He turned to see a pointy-eared shadow rising from behind one of the boulders nearby.

"Behkai?"

At the sound of his master's voice, the big black dog came galloping toward them. He crashed into Karim at full speed, his tail a blur of motion, his massive paws planted on Karim's shoulders as he licked his face with unbridled joy.

"Ugh! Behkai! Stop!" Karim cried, trying and failing to push away the amorous snout. "I know, I know. I'm alive! I, too, am surprised!"

Panting and drooling, Behkai then directed his affections to the princess, licking and nuzzling her hand.

"What a good boy," she said, bending to kiss him on the head.

"Hmph," Karim grumbled. "She gets the royal treatment, I get assaulted." He squinted at the dog. A patch of white fur in the shape of a man's hand covered the left side of Behkai's face. Even his eye had turned a cloudy, blue-white color. "What's that?"

"Behkai tried to protect you and the monster touched him," Sitamun replied. "A burn, perhaps?"

"Doesn't seem to hurt him," Karim said as he gently stroked the white mark. The dog squeezed his eyes in pleasure, pushing his head against Karim's hand. "Been through a lot, haven't you, boy?"

"We all have," Sitamun said.

Karim gazed up at her, saw the pain in her eyes, and sighed. The anger had gone out of him.

The princess bit her lip, then asked, "Why wouldn't you want to come back?"

Karim ran a hand through his curly brown hair. "I didn't have to face the consequences of my actions if I was dead. Now I do. That is more curse than blessing. Already I have the deaths of two innocents on my conscience. Who knows how many more there will be?" He stabbed his chest with one finger. "It was my heart that gave Setnakht life! Mine! Whatever disaster comes, comes because of me! Do you have any idea what that's like?"

Sitamun's nostrils flared, and Karim remembered everything she had confided in him. The death of the little girl. The murder of her father. The twisted machinations of her brother and his rise to the Khetaran throne. And Sitamun's involvement in it all.

"You know I do," she said softly.

Karim shook his head and looked to the horizon. The sun sat upon it now, a great golden ball perched on the edge of the world. The heat of its early-morning rays filled him, as it did for all Red Lands tribesmen, with the need to move forward.

"What now, hey?" he asked. "You'll make your way to Bubas and try to raise an army?"

"No," Sitamun said. "I'm going with you. To Perset."

Karim's eyes bulged. "You are?"

"Yes." The princess sailed past him and plucked her black

travel robes from the ground where they'd fallen. Squinching her nose in distaste, she vigorously shook the sand from the fabric before swinging it around her shoulders. "Now that I've seen what this Setnakht can do, it's obvious that even a great army may not succeed in defeating him. Not without more information about the heka used in his resurrection. He has a plan, that's clear, and if we're to have any hope of stopping him, we must have one too. And as you said yesterday, this lost city of Perset may be the only place to find answers." She sniffed. "So, let's go. We have a lot of ground to cover."

Karim, shocked and delighted at this unexpected turn of events, hardly knew what to say. "Well…good!"

Behkai looked back and forth between them with intense anticipation, mouth open, tongue lolling.

"Yes, she's coming after all," Karim told him. "I hope you're happy."

To his credit, Behkai seemed very happy.

Sitamun waved a hand toward the campsite. "Gather our things, will you?"

Karim scoffed. "Who died and made you god?"

The princess rolled her eyes and began climbing out of the valley, Behkai trotting at her heels.

"Hey!" Karim shouted, scrambling to locate something to cover his nakedness. "Where do you think you're going? Wait for me!"

2
RAE

Rae held the scrap of papyrus in her shaking hands and began to read aloud.

"'A letter from Raetawy to her mother,'" she recited haltingly. "'How are you, Mamet? I hope your life with our ancestors in the West is joyful and free of suffering.'"

She sniffed and glanced up at the makeshift shrine. In spite of repeated warnings from Menk and Omari, Rae had snuck back to the farm and salvaged her mother's sculpture from the scorched remains of their house. Everything else had been stolen or burned, but the small stone statue had fallen off its pedestal out of sight and had been left behind by the nomarch's men. It was chipped and blackened when Rae found it, but she'd washed away the soot in the river and found that the damage wasn't too bad.

The sculpture was a bust made in her mother's likeness, with long black hair flowing in thick waves over both shoulders, and her round, smiling face painted in yellow ochre. Her name in the gods' words—along with a wadjet eye of Ra—was written in black along the front. Some of the paint had washed away, but she could still read her mother's name. *One day*, she'd thought, *when this is all over, I'll make it look new again.*

She'd brought the sculpture back to the ruins of the old palace, where she and the other Horizon rebels had been staying. The brewer's murder had triggered a citywide search for Rae and all her associates, and Rahotep's palace turned out to be an ideal hiding place. It was situated on the southern edge of Sakesh, just north of the farms and not far from the banks of the Iteru. The place was considered bad luck and full of mutu—so most Low and High Khetarans alike did their best to avoid it.

Rae had found a small room with a window overlooking the river, cleaned it up, evicted several scorpions, and made it her own. When she'd returned there with the sculpture the night before, she'd set up her mother's shrine using some broken bricks as a makeshift pedestal. "Don't mind the mutu, Mamet," she'd said to the shrine, adding a chunk of dried fish and some water in a potshard as offerings. "The spirits here have a right to be angry."

Rae hadn't slept. Instead, she spent the night writing the letter by candlelight.

Her mother had died not long after the Great War, when Rae was only a baby, so she had no real memories of her. But her father had reconstructed her through stories—recollections of her kindness, her strength, her sense of humor—until her mother's shape had been built into the landscape of Rae's mind like a temple.

Since her father's abduction, that temple had been the only place she found refuge.

Rae sniffed again, her lower lip trembling as she read the letter to her mother's shrine.

"'I miss you,'" she said. "'I would say that I wish you were here, but you are safer where you are than in Sakesh. Life is not good here. There is hunger and drought, and the High Khetarans rule over us and take what little we have for themselves.

"'I joined a group of men to fight for our freedom, and the resistance was going well until we were betrayed by one of our own. People died. Some of them by my own hand. And Yati"—she gasped, hardly able to go on—"Yati was taken, and the farm was burned.'"

She paused to dash hot tears of shame from her eyes.

"'It was my fault. It was my fault and I am going to do everything I can to get him back. I write this letter, Mamet, to ask you to please watch over Yati, wherever he is, and keep him safe until I find him.'"

She glanced out the small window, where the first light of dawn pierced the horizon.

"'I'm sorry I let you down,'" she said, unable to meet the painted eyes of the sculpture. "'Forgive me.'"

Rae folded the letter and set it in front of the shrine with the other offerings. She stared at it in silence as the sun rose at her back.

Rae tore a piece of bread off the loaf, shoved it in her mouth, and chewed mechanically. It was stale, but she hardly noticed.

"One of the fishermen generously offered the use of his largest skiff for our journey to Thonis," Menk was saying. "It's large enough to carry five. He also said we can take some of his old fishing equipment. We can wrap your supplies and weapons inside the fishing nets so they won't be seen. As Rae suggested—the simpler the disguise, the less likely you'll be stopped and searched."

Rae took another bite of bread. The Jackal had given her the idea to disguise themselves as fishermen. After all, if he'd had some fishing equipment with him, or had been properly attired for the job, she would never have given him a second glance. Remembering the Red Lands tribesman and his satchel of treasure, she thought: *Isn't it strange that I'm going downriver to Thonis, just as he did? I wonder where he is now.*

She sat at the remains of an old banquet table in a large chamber of the palace, breaking the fast with Menk, Omari, Baki—and Mamet Mut. After taking control of the Horizon rebels two nights earlier, Rae's first order of business was to bring the head weaver into their inner circle. The stout woman took to rebellion with her signature gusto, offering a host of ideas, strategies, and information. Menk was impressed, and maybe a little infatuated. Every time she spoke to him, his tremendous ears turned pink.

While Menk explained that everything would be ready for their departure the next day, Rae felt Mamet Mut's probing gaze upon her. The older woman leaned over the table, her generous bosom nearly upsetting a bowl of lentils.

"You haven't touched your beer this morning," the woman whispered. "Nor anything except that piece of bread. You need your strength, Raetawy. It's hard enough for these men to take orders from a woman without her looking like a boiled chicken. Eat! Drink! Get some color in your cheeks!"

Rae grumbled and reached for her cup of beer, but when the cloying, sweet smell hit her nostrils, she nearly gagged.

That *smell.*

It immediately sent her back to the brewery. To the night she confronted the brewer with his treachery and thrust a dagger in his gut. The smell of the beer recalled it all: the rage, the sound of the brewer's cup shattering on the floor, the sight of all that blood pouring out of him—

Rae groaned softly and pushed away the drink.

Menk stopped midsentence, and Omari looked over at her.

"You all right, Ay?" he asked.

Rae cleared her throat and sat up straight. "Fine," she replied. She reached for the water jug and poured herself a cup. "It all sounds good to me, Menk. We'll leave first thing in the morning."

"Have you decided who you're taking with you?" Menk asked.

Rae nodded. "It will be me, Omari, Buto, the potter's son, and Kay, the fisherman. Buto is a pain in my ass, but he's young and strong and a good fighter—as is the potter's son. And Kay is dependable and will help ensure that our disguise is convincing. Not a bad one to have in a brawl either."

There was flash of movement at the door. Rae glanced up, but saw no one. *Somebody is eavesdropping.* She had a good idea who it might be.

"Wise choices," Menk said. "Mamet Mut, Baki, and I will remain here with the others to continue our canvassing and surveillance efforts."

"Because the plan will be fluid once we arrive and set up in Thonis, we'll need to relay messages back here to Sakesh," Rae said. "Menk, do you think your pigeons can make the trip?"

Menk nodded. "They've carried messages to Thonis and back before. They can do it again."

"Good," said Rae. It was only after her rise to leadership in the Horizon that Rae found out about Menk's flock of trained birds, which were about to become extremely useful. "Now, if we are successful—"

Mamet Mut quirked an eyebrow at her.

Rae cleared her throat. "*When* we are successful in recovering our people," she corrected, "we will need a safe way to transport them home. One skiff will not be enough for the return trip."

Baki spoke up. "It will be my mission to devise a plan for your safe passage back to Sakesh." The shepherd had been quiet for most of the meeting but seemed to jump at the undertaking. Rae suspected he was still eager to repay her for taking a beating from the nomarch on his behalf.

There was only one more point to discuss. No one had spoken of it yet, as if its mere mention might bring greater misfortune upon them. But Rae was never one to hold her tongue.

"And what of the river?" she asked.

Her question was greeted with silence.

"Menk, you were obviously down at the riverbank this morning, speaking to the fisherman. Tell me: What of the river?"

Menk scratched behind one of his enormous ears and spoke. "The Iteru appears to have returned to normal after yesterday's... phenomenon. Though none were yet brave enough to enter its waters—at least not while I was there. I'm sure that will have changed by now. Even one day without the river is too much."

Rae toyed with the golden swivel ring she'd gotten from the Jackal, spinning the rectangular bead that had a different symbol on each face. Snake. Feather. Eye. Scarab. Snake. Feather. Eye. Scarab. She'd gone down to the riverbank the day before, as soon as news of its transformation reached her. It was an extraordinary sight—the entire river had turned the color of blood.

Most people were too superstitious to get close to the water, but Rae was curious. She'd bent to dip her fingers and found the water oddly thick and foul-smelling, but it lacked the copper tang of blood. Still, after several people were sickened by drinking river water that morning, a wave of panic had engulfed the city. *Just what we need,* Rae had thought bitterly. But hearing the water had returned to normal, she hoped the crisis—*that* crisis at least—had passed.

She stopped spinning the golden bead, leaving the Eye of Ra facing up.

What did it mean, the river turning red? What are the gods trying to tell us?

Perhaps the answer could be found in Thonis.

"We should get on with our preparations," Omari said, brushing breadcrumbs from his hands and pushing back his chair.

"Yes, yes, much to do," Mamet Mut agreed.

After some final words, the inner circle dispersed, leaving Rae alone with the unappetizing bowl of lentils. Sighing, she stuffed a couple of spoonfuls in her mouth, drained the rest of her water, and went to have a conversation with the eavesdropper.

"Why were you spying on us, Tam?"

Rae found Tamerit in the storage room, stooping to take inventory of the food supplies, fishing equipment, and weapons that they'd set aside for the journey to Thonis.

Tam stilled, then straightened. Instead of her usual formfitting kalasiris dress, she wore a coarse, belted tunic, and her tightly curled black hair had been pulled into a messy bun at the nape of her neck. After a long pause, she resumed her work, not sparing a single glance in Rae's direction.

"I wouldn't have to spy on you if you'd invited me to the meeting," she said.

Rae sighed and rubbed her temple with one hand. "You're a member of the Horizon now. You and the other weavers. Isn't that enough? We have to keep the inner circle small, so—"

Tam whirled to face her. "Leave the potter's son. Take *me* to Thonis."

Rae stared at her in disbelief. "Absolutely not," she blurted.

Two circles of color appeared on Tam's cheeks. Like a raging bull, she marched over to glare up at Rae, unfazed that Rae was a head taller.

"Why? Because I'm not a 'good fighter'? You don't know what you'll find when you get to the capital. How do you know I wouldn't be a vital part of the plan? Because I'm not a man? Even after everything that's happened, you're still as bad as they are!"

"No!" Rae exclaimed, her own anger rising. "That's not why! I don't want you to come because..." She faltered.

"Well?" Tam's gaze was searching. Then her expression softened. "Oh. Oh, I see. You're afraid."

"Of course I'm afraid!" Rae exclaimed, a little too loudly. She glanced over her shoulder, but no one else seemed to be around. She lowered her voice and tenderly cupped the back of Tam's neck with one hand. "I can't lose you too."

Tam covered Rae's large hand with her smaller one. "This is war, Raetawy. You know that I'm no safer here in Sakesh than I would be in Thonis. If you let me join you, at least we'd be together."

Rae pursed her lips. She knew the mantle of leadership would be heavy, but she hadn't realized how difficult it would be to separate her emotions from what was good for the collective. Tam was right—the weaver did bring a different set of skills to the group. Unlike Omari, who was as intimidating as an ox, and practical Kay, Tam was clever, persuasive, and had the ability to insinuate herself into any group of people.

Like a spy, Rae thought. *A spy* would *be useful in Thonis...*

She hated placing Tam in danger, but the weaver made a good point. Staying in Sakesh wasn't safe either. Rae growled in frustration. "Fine," she said helplessly. "The gods forgive me. The potter's son is out. You're in."

Tam's face lit up. "Thanks be to Ra!" she cried, then threw her arms around Rae's neck and kissed her.

Rae felt a rush of unexpected pleasure. She'd wondered if she'd ever be capable of that kind of joy again, but there it was. Tamerit gave it to her as if it were the easiest thing in the world.

What began as a kiss quickly evolved into more.

Suddenly, desperate to eliminate any space between them, Rae stumbled forward, knocking over several baskets of fruit in the process, until she had Tam's back pressed up against the stone wall. Rae's mouth roved over Tam's neck and collarbone, while the weaver began pulling at Rae's tunic, trying to remove it.

"Someone might see," Rae protested, weakly.

"They all left. There's no one here," Tam replied, breathless, her lips at Rae's ear, her tongue darting, searching.

Rae allowed Tam to unbuckle her belt and slip off the tunic, casting it to the floor. Tam's own tunic had fallen off one shoulder, sending Rae into a frenzy of desire. Standing there in nothing but her loincloth, Rae kissed the weaver's smooth, copper skin—but froze as Tam's fingers touched the scars on her back.

"Don't," she said. She'd removed the bandages the day before, although she'd kept the arrow wound she'd sustained from the ambush wrapped. After taking them off, she'd managed to get a glimpse of her back in an old bronze mirror. It looked...bad.

"Don't," she repeated quietly.

Tam cocked her head. "Let me see." Her voice was the coo of a mourning dove.

Rae took a step back, flushing. "It's horrible."

The weaver reached for her hand and held it firmly. "Let me be the judge of that."

With a shuddering breath, Rae turned. Folding her arms over her breasts, she winced as Tam's gentle touch traced the lines of scarring where the nomarch's flail had torn into her flesh. Rae listened for a response—a gasp of horror, a cluck of pity—but Tam was silent.

After a moment, Rae felt the weaver's lips on her skin, feather-soft, anointing each scar with a kiss.

She recoiled. "What are you doing?"

Tam said, "Don't you see? These scars—they're evidence of

your courage. They inspired a rebellion. I'm sorry they cause you pain, but you shouldn't be ashamed of them. You shouldn't be ashamed of anything."

Rae turned back around and gathered the weaver into her arms. When she spoke, her voice was husky. "Baki said that son of a dog gave me fifty lashes, did you know that? He counted." Rae brushed a coil of hair away from Tam's face and gazed deeply into her eyes. "I would take a hundred more, for you."

The weaver's brow furrowed, a dozen emotions crossing her face. "Rae," she whispered, and then leaned in until their lips met once again.

They were entwined together when a voice called from outside the door. "Ay? Is that you? I wanted to ask—"

Rae and Tam flew apart. Rae dove for her clothes on the floor, but it was too late.

Omari stood in the doorway, staring at them in open-mouthed shock as Rae held the tunic over her bare chest.

"I-I thought you'd left," Rae stammered, her cheeks burning with embarrassment. "I didn't know… We were just…"

Omari put up his hands to silence her and shook his head. "I'll come back later." His expression was unreadable, and before Rae could stop him, he'd turned on his heel and was gone.

With a deep sigh, Rae leaned against the stone wall and gently slid to the floor, her head in her hands. "That is *not* how I intended for him to find out about us."

Tam sat down next to her, plucking a couple figs from a basket and popping one in her mouth. She shrugged. "Oh, I don't know. It's not like you were going to tell him."

"I was! At the right time!" Rae retorted.

Tam rolled her eyes. "Sure you were. What are you so worried about? You said there was no spark between you. That you two are simply friends. So, what is it? Do you think he won't look at you the same way now that he knows you prefer the company of women?"

Rae buried her knuckles in her eyes until she saw stars. "No...Yes... I don't know. When we were kids, we swore never to keep secrets from each other—and this seems like a big secret."

Tam snuggled up next to her, the soft roundness of her body so comforting that Rae had little choice but to relax. "You're allowed to have a private life," she said. "Besides, I'd wager there are things Omari keeps from you too."

Rae nodded.

Tam kissed her on the cheek and helped her pull the tunic back over her head. "Come on. No more fun for today. We've got a lot of work to do to prepare for tomorrow!"

The two of them finished inventorying the supplies, and Rae was grateful for the distraction. She told herself that Tam was right, that Omari was probably just embarrassed to have interrupted them and wouldn't mention it again. That all would go on unchanged between them.

She told herself that and almost believed it.

3
NEFF

At home in Bubas, Neff used to sit with her father in their market stall every day, waiting for customers to approach with their problems. Her father listened attentively to their stories, then offered the appropriate product: *This spell scroll will make her fall in love with you! This one will cure your headache! If you burn this wax figure of your rival, he will suffer a terrible end!*

In this way, Neff became accustomed to reading people—to knowing who was desperate enough to accept an inflated price, who needed extra encouragement to close the deal, and who was only speaking to them out of curiosity and never intended to buy anything.

As it turned out, being an adviser to the king of Khetara wasn't much different.

It was late morning, two days after the coronation, and Neff sat on a plush ebony- and cypress-wood chair next to Meryamun in the throne room. The palace had been a hotbed of activity ever since Amunmose's death, with viziers, merchants, priests, and government officials all vying for the new pharaoh's attention. They came to Meryamun with their own specific predicaments and schemes, intent on proving that theirs were of greater importance than all others.

Dutifully, the king deliberated before dispensing a decision in each matter. And despite knowing the kind of man the young pharaoh really was—one who would assassinate his own father and slaughter two dozen innocent people who were loyal to the former king—Neff was impressed at his cunning and intelligence as a leader. Occasionally, he asked for her advice on a matter but, more often than not, he seemed quite capable of handling everything himself.

"We have received word from several nomarchs, in both the north and the south, that they continue to face resistance in collecting the king's tax," a squinty-eyed vizier was saying. He was the last to present his report that morning, the others having paraded in one by one to offer grim tidings—inevitably followed by subtle reminders of the "agreements" that were made preceding Amunmose's death.

So the viziers did *know about Meryamun's plan to poison his father,* Neff had realized. It made sense, of course. She'd heard rumors that Amunmose had despised the viziers and rarely heeded their counsel. They were probably happy to be rid of him.

For his part, Meryamun skillfully circumvented their attempts to secure funding for the new supply ship one wanted, or the exclusive trade agreement for another's eldest son, or whatever lucrative prize they'd demanded in exchange for keeping their mouths shut about a few poisoned honey cakes. He did this with a combination of flattery and distraction, and he did it well. Each man left the throne room feeling pleased with himself, yet also entirely unsatisfied.

This last vizier was a small, fastidious man who looked as if he'd gone straight from wearing the sidelock of youth to old age, content to skip all the foolishness in between.

The vizier went on. "Not only has there been a decline in food production throughout the kingdom this season, there has also been a reduction in productivity due to workers sickened by the annual plague. Put simply, my king, the current strategy is lacking and has been for a long time. The problem, however, is this: We cannot lower the tax without imperiling the power of the crown, but we cannot keep the tax as is without risking civil war."

Neff could tell that Meryamun appreciated the vizier's frankness. He did not simper before the throne, nor complain about the state of the kingdom. He merely presented the facts.

"A conundrum, isn't it, Sabni?" Meryamun said. He wore a red and black striped headdress beneath a gold circlet that featured a cobra rearing on his brow. He was bare chested aside from a beaded collar. His elaborately pleated schenti was embroidered with green serpents with red malachite beads for eyes. Neff had yet to see him wear the same outfit twice.

"It is, indeed, my king, a conundrum," Sabni replied.

"Tell me, my friend, what is it you require in return for your continued allegiance?"

The vizier blinked. "Nothing, my king. My allegiance has no price."

"I see. You were the last to accept the proposal regarding my father, were you not? Why is that?"

Sabni paled. Neff was amazed that Meryamun would so brazenly discuss his father's assassination—then again, the only other people in the room were two of the king's personal guard.

Even if there were others, Neff thought, *what could anyone do about it now?*

It was a question that kept her up at night.

To Neff's surprise, instead of begging for mercy, Sabni spoke as plainly as the king himself. "It wasn't that I didn't agree with your reasoning, my king. It was simply that I am a servant of the pharaoh, and therefore I find any act that goes against him—no matter how ineffectual he may be—distasteful."

Meryamun leaned forward, his voice low. "You're no traitor. Is that what you're saying?"

The vizier swallowed and chose his next words with care. "In the end, my aversion to the plan was irrelevant. The decision was made, and you became the new pharaoh. Therefore, my service now extends to you alone."

Meryamun nodded appreciatively. "I like you, Sabni. You look like a goat, but you have the heart of a lion. Here's what I want you to do—craft a message and get the scribes to write a copy for every nomarch in High Khetara. Gather enough messengers to deliver the scrolls as quickly as possible."

"What's the message?"

Meryamun smiled, and Neff's blood went cold. "You will name the other viziers as enemies to the crown, guilty of corruption and gross malfeasance over a number of years both before and during my father's decline. You will instruct the nomarchs to tell the people of their cities and villages that exposing the viziers' crimes was the first act of my reign, and that they will be punished to the full extent of Khetaran law. Corruption of any kind will not be tolerated."

Sabni attempted to hide his shock but he didn't do a very good job. "W-what punishment?"

"Execute them. Publicly."

"All of them?"

"Except you, of course." Meryamun laughed. "Don't look so terrified, Sabni. It brings out the goat in you."

"But...but why?"

Meryamun's lip curled. "Because no one likes a traitor."

The vizier nodded and wiped the perspiration from his brow. His lips moved soundlessly, committing the king's message to memory.

"Anything else for the scribes?" he then asked.

"Yes. You will also mention the dangers the kingdom faces from outside forces: our enemies to the west and the Tashans to the south. The decline of our military over these past seventeen years has allowed those kingdoms to go unchecked, and they no longer respect our sovereignty. Even now, they are making plans to invade our borders and threaten the Khetaran way of life. Which is why we need the people's cooperation to save our kingdom from ruin."

Sabni's brow furrowed. "Is it true that the Tashans are on a war footing? I had thought our recent meeting with their delegation was fruitful."

Meryamun chuckled. "Oh, Sabni—soon you will understand the nature of my relationship with the truth. She is my mistress and becomes whatever I need her to be."

"It will be done, my king," Sabni said. "Within days, all Khetara will hear of this news."

The vizier bowed his head and began to back out of the throne room. He'd made it halfway before he stopped. "Apologies, my king. What of the tax?"

The young king tapped his lips with a long, gold-ringed finger. "Wait two weeks. Then raise it."

With a final bow, Sabni turned and exited.

As soon as he was gone, Meryamun slumped in his throne and glanced over at Neff. "You see, little priestess? From under the ground it comes… No more meetings until this afternoon. Wine!" He shouted the last in the direction of the open door, then turned back to her. "I've been meaning to ask, have you received any divine insight about my dear sister?"

"There's still no word of Sitamun?" Neff said, tempering the curiosity in her voice. She didn't want Meryamun to think her too interested in the princess's fate. He had no knowledge of the Oracle of the Lamb, nor of Sitamun's involvement in it, and Neff wanted to keep it that way. The oracle placed her and the errant princess on the same side of a coming battle, which surely meant that Meryamun was destined to be on the other.

"She's proven herself to be surprisingly difficult to find," Meryamun replied with a hard smile. "Though perhaps my surprise is unwarranted. Sita was always more clever than she let on."

Neff shook her head. "I am sorry, my king. I have prayed, but the gods have been silent."

"Hm," Meryamun mused. He reached forward and adjusted the strap of her dress, his fingers lingering on her collarbone. Neff forced herself not to recoil. "Perhaps there's something we can do to...*encourage* them to speak. Yes?"

Neff didn't like the sound of that. But before he could continue, he seemed to remember his refreshments hadn't arrived.

"I said *wine*!" he shouted.

An instant later, a young woman dashed into the room, nearly upsetting the tray of fruit, cheese, and fresh bread she balanced on one hand. In the other, she carried an alabaster wine jar that sloshed dangerously with each step. Several attendants carrying fans hurried in after her.

"Apologies, my king," the maidservant said breathlessly. "We were preparing the midday meal. We came as quickly as we could." She set the tray on the small table next to the throne and raised the wine jar to fill Meryamun's cup. Her hands shook.

"Ach!" Meryamun leaped to his feet. "You've spilled it on me, you stupid girl!" He brushed at the drops soaking into his clothes.

The maidservant stepped back, her eyes round with fear.

"Guard!" Meryamun growled.

One of the guards strode past the cowering young woman to the dais where Neff and the king sat beneath a blue canopy.

"Take this useless creature and beat the pretty off her."

"Yes, my king."

Neff's pulse began to race. It wasn't the first time she'd witnessed how quickly Meryamun's temper could flare, nor how devastating the consequences could be for anyone in its path. *Do something,* she told herself.

Taking a deep breath, Neff laid a hand on the king's arm.

Meryamun's body stilled, and his head tilted toward her.

"There are so few servants left in the kitchens," she said. "It would be a shame to lose another—clumsy as she might be. I'm sure she won't be so careless again, my king."

Meryamun sighed. "I suppose you are right." He nodded toward the guard, who was in the process of dragging the poor maidservant from the throne room.

"Let her get back to work," he called out. "I want my meal on time."

The guard, who didn't seem to care one way or the other, dropped the young woman like a sack of onions and returned to his post. The maidservant, her eyes blurry with tears, scurried out without another word.

Neff sagged with relief. She'd begun to learn, through trial and error, that Meryamun's anger could vanish as quickly as it came, if given the proper direction. Another bit of her father's wisdom came to mind. One time, when a shipment of papyrus arrived damaged, instead of tossing out the stained, poor-quality scrolls, her father diluted some ink, altered his handwriting, and advertised the resulting scrolls as "artifacts from an ancient temple" for double the standard price.

After they sold the last one, he'd said, "Remember, my girl, everything that happens, good or bad, is an opportunity to get what you want."

Neff saw an opportunity.

"My king," she said. "Perhaps it's time to add more servants to the palace staff. The kitchen isn't the only place that could use more hands. More attendants, messengers, and litter bearers would be useful as well. I'm sure you yourself probably require more—"

"Hands?" Meryamun said into his wine as he sipped it. He glanced wickedly at her from the corner of his eye.

Neff blushed.

Meryamun drained his cup and sighed. "It's true. I've been so caught up in bureaucracy I haven't spared a thought for the administration of the palace. I'll get good old Sabni to put his mind to—"

"Sabni will be busy with the scribes," Neff broke in. "Perhaps you and I could go into the city and handpick the servants ourselves. We could make an announcement, and those interested could come see us to apply."

Meryamun scoffed. "That is highly unusual. The king, out in the streets?"

"Ah, but that's exactly why we should do it. Your father rarely completed the Shemsu Hor—it would be the first time many Khetarans actually saw the pharaoh with their own eyes. We'd get the staff we need and further endear you to the people, all in one afternoon."

"It isn't a bad idea. And you would help me choose, using the wisdom of the gods?"

Neff bowed her head. "Of course. Everything I do, I do in your service."

She sent a silent prayer to Bast. *Let him say yes!* The fact was, she couldn't disrupt Meryamun's plans alone. If she could exert some influence on who entered the royal service, perhaps she might begin to build a coalition of allies within the palace. Commoners who could be convinced to help her take down the king. The people she chose would surely be more amenable to such a plan than servants hired by the vizier.

Meryamun considered and said, "As you wish, Nefermaat. My head guard will arrange it. Maybe then it won't be so difficult to get a drink around here."

Neff sent her thanks to Bast—and her father—and smiled.

"Nefermaat?"

Neff stopped outside her chambers and turned to see who'd called her name. Queen Bintanath stood in the corridor, wavering like a reed in the wind. She wore a simple white kalasiris and yellow mourning cloak. Her only ornament was an obsidian vulture collar, its black beaded wings wrapped around her bony shoulders. Neff had overheard some of the servants say that the queen had undergone a sudden change since her husband's death—that overnight, she had transformed from an imperious and demanding force to a ghost. A mutu that haunted the palace halls.

"That's your name, isn't it?" the queen asked.

Neff crossed her hands in a sign of respect. "It is, my queen. We met when I first arrived at the palace."

"You're a seer."

"Yes, my queen."

Queen Bintanath looked at her intently, as if she were grappling with a decision, before saying, "You will come to my quarters when your schedule allows. I wish to use your skills." And with a swirl of yellow, she turned back the way she had come.

Neff kept her composure until she was safely inside her

chambers, the curtain pulled shut over the doorway. She leaned against the stone wall and covered her face with her hands.

I can't do this, I can't do this, I can't do this...

Maintaining a close relationship with Meryamun was already hard work. Now she had to worry about the queen mother too? Not to mention Master Montuhotep, who was probably scheming away at the temple, planning his revenge on Neff for usurping his position at the king's side.

The moment she was alone, the dam holding back all her feelings burst, flooding her with fear, despair, and worst of all, breathtaking loneliness.

It had been frightening enough at the Temple of Amun, surrounded by strangers and strangeness, but there she'd had Kenna. The young prince had been a bulwark against the crushing isolation. At the palace she had no one. No one to talk to, no one to guide her, no one to protect her from the multifarious dangers lurking around every corner.

Something soft brushed against her ankles.

A black-striped cat stared up at her with golden eyes.

"Maiow," the cat said.

Neff's heart warmed.

Well, almost no one.

At first, Neff assumed the cat was only visiting, but after a day or two, it had become clear that she had come to stay. Neff was delighted to have the company and had arranged a pillow and bowl of fresh water for her new friend near the window to make her feel at home.

"Hello in peace, Cat," Neff said, kneeling to stroke her. The cat was old and had probably lived at the palace longer than Neff had been alive, so naming her felt presumptuous. In the end, Neff thought it best to simply keep calling her "Cat."

The cat arched her back and rubbed her face against Neff's leg.

"I'm very glad to see you. Oh! Did we get another delivery?"

Neff hurried over to the table in the center of the room, where dozens of scrolls and oddments lay arranged in neat piles. They were all supplies the Heka priests had brought for her, at the king's command. A new batch of items had arrived every day since her initial request to learn the secret art of magic. She got the sense the priests were loath to relinquish their monopoly on such knowledge, so were releasing it in a trickle instead of a gush. Perhaps they hoped the king might change his mind—though Neff would ensure that he wouldn't.

That day's delivery was particularly interesting. There was a small ibis figurine—an animal sacred to Thoth, the god of writing, wisdom, and magic—which was a perfect focus object for certain spells.

How funny that I saw one perched on the garden wall this morning! she thought.

There was also a very old figurine of a woman holding a double-headed snake staff, which she found fascinating, though she wasn't sure of its purpose. Finally, there was a twine-wrapped bundle of papyri that included a variety of spells and instructions on the application of heka.

Neff picked up the bundle, intending to bring it to the window to read while enjoying the tray of food that had been left for her midday meal, when something slipped out and dropped to the floor.

She bent to retrieve the dark-colored scroll, which looked older than the others. Instead of the usual white clay seal, the dark scroll's seal was black.

Could they have included this by accident? Neff wondered.

She carried the scroll to the window, ate four grapes in quick succession, then gently pried open the seal. The cat leaped onto the sill to join her, sniffing at the food before delicately stealing a chunk of roast duck for herself. Neff unrolled the papyrus, secured the four corners with smooth stones, and began to study it.

Although she was still learning to read the gods' words, she knew at once that the scroll was part of a larger work and therefore incomplete. Some text was written in red ink—those words, she'd learned, were instructions to the priest on how to properly cast the spell—and the rest was written in black. That portion was the spell itself. All heka was achieved through a combination of object, word, and action; a priest needed all three for the magic to work.

"'A spell to summon Medjed,'" Neff read from the heading. She looked up at the cat, who was eyeing the plate of cheese. "What's a Medjed?"

The explanation was probably on another scroll. *A scroll I don't have,* Neff thought, after a cursory glance through the other papyri. Her curiosity piqued, she read on.

The instructions were as follows: *Take four ostrich feathers and burn them in a green vessel. Turn the bowl three times eastward and one time westward while you speak the words. When you have finished speaking, blow the ashes into the air.*

Neff furrowed her brow. She'd learned that burning an object reduced it to its essence, and applying breath had one of two purposes: either to dispel something, like a demon or disease, or to give life. She had the feeling this summoning spell intended the latter.

She didn't understand the significance of turning the bowl. She knew that the living world was to the east—which was why all Khetaran cities were built on the east side of the river—and the Land of the Dead was in the west. But how did that affect the magic?

She read on.

Ho, Medjed! the spell said. *You of the House of the Lord of*

Silence! I call to thee, O smiter! O guardian of the lost! I call you to my side. Protect me with your terrible eyes that see yet are unseen. Come to me, and punish those who would do me harm!

Thoughtful, Neff turned to eat her meal before the cat took it all for herself. Tearing the fragrant flatbread into pieces, she ate them one by one with the squeaky white cheese, then washed it all down with sweet beer.

Medjed must be a minor deity. I could certainly use a guardian, especially a magical one. No, she couldn't risk it. It was too dangerous to attempt such a spell without reading the supporting text.

But what if the supporting text doesn't exist? Or the Heka priests won't let me see it? They probably didn't even intend to share this one!

She looked at the engraved bowl of grapes.

A green vessel.

Neff glanced across the room, where a tall vase sat in the corner, filled with gifts Meryamun had offered her. "To honor your name, Nefermaat," he'd said.

Written in the gods' words, her name was made up of two symbols. A heart and an ostrich feather.

Neff counted the ostrich feathers in the vase. There were seven.

The last grape slipped through her fingers and rolled across the windowsill. The cat batted it to the floor.

I have everything I need to cast the spell, Neff thought in disbelief. *It's all right here.*

Perhaps it was meant to be.

"Well, what do you think, Cat? Shall we summon a god?"

It didn't take long for Neff to assemble the items. She set the bowl with the four ostrich feathers on the floor by the window and brought a lit candle to stand beside it, along with the spell scroll. She held the engraved hippopotamus tusk in her right hand. The wand, something every Heka priest needed in their tool kit, served to focus her power.

Neff listened for any sound outside her chamber. It wouldn't do to be interrupted while attempting to cast the spell.

The corridor was silent.

Am I really doing this? It was awfully reckless—but then again, her situation was desperate. Besides, it might not work. Even some of the simple spells she'd attempted had no effect, and this one was obviously much more advanced.

Just try, she told herself. *What's the worst that could happen?*

Kneeling in front of the bowl, Neff quieted her thoughts and picked up the candle. The cat watched from her pillow, her tail flicking with interest. Neff dipped the flame into the bowl and waited for the feathers to alight. They began to smolder, then burn. Neff set the candle down and began turning the smoking bowl. As she did so, she spoke the words, making sure to enunciate each one clearly.

"Ho, Medjed! You of the House of the Lord of Silence!"

Three revolutions to the right—

"Come to me, and punish those who would do me harm!"

And one to the left.

Finally, Neff set down her wand and took the bowl of ashes in both hands. She inhaled a deep, deep breath, and blew the ashes toward the open window.

A cloud of black particles billowed into the air and hung there for an instant before the breeze pulled them out and away. Neff watched the cloud dissipate, the bowl still raised to her lips. She waited in anticipation.

Moments passed.

Nothing happened.

Neff sighed and set the bowl down.

She cleaned up the items, rerolling the scroll and setting the green bowl back on the tray with the remnants of her meal. She moved slowly, heavy with disappointment. Aside from a couple small victories, her attempts at casting spells had been largely unsuccessful. She'd been trying to teach herself the art of heka, but clearly the knowledge was meant to be passed down from master to apprentice, much like everything else in the priesthood. But even with the king's urging, she knew the Heka priests wouldn't agree to mentor her. They'd say they were too busy or would sabotage her education somehow.

She needed help, but aside from the Heka priests, who else in the kingdom had the ability to teach her?

Then she knew.

"Of course! Why didn't I think of it before?"

Pulling on her sandals, she made for the door. She'd have to hurry if she wanted to get back to the palace in time to join Meryamun for his afternoon audiences. And she'd have to take the long way to avoid being seen.

"I'll be back, Cat," she said.

The cat didn't seem to hear her. She was staring at a space a few feet in front of the window, her pupils wide and dark.

Neff shook her head. *Cats are so strange, always looking at things that aren't there.*

Pushing through the curtain, she slipped down the corridor with the wind at her back.

4
SITA

Where do the gods end, and I begin?

Sita contemplated the question as she and Karim walked to the river, with Behkai leading the way. After packing up and leaving the valley, they decided to make a quick stop to bathe before starting their journey into the desert to find the lost city.

"I'm filthy, and you…" She scowled, giving the tomb robber an appraising look. He was absolutely covered in gore. "You need to be *boiled*. Twice."

"Come on, it's not *that* bad," Karim said. He sniffed his armpit, then gagged. "Fine, sena, have it your way. We'll have a bath. My robes could use a wash as well."

It didn't take long to reach the river. They waited for a trading ship to pass before approaching the riverbank, which was thankfully shielded from view by a thicket of reeds and some squat palm trees.

"Turn around!" Sita commanded as she set down her pack and removed her belt.

Karim rolled his eyes and obeyed. "Hurry up, will you?"

Feeling both embarrassed and exhilarated, Sita stripped off her dress and loincloth and stepped into the river. She gasped. *So cold!* She dipped her head under the water, and the temperature that had chilled her became refreshing. She broke the surface, slicked her hair back from her face, and began scrubbing her body clean.

"No peeking!" she said.

"I'm *not*!" Karim protested, although she could have sworn she saw his head turn.

When she was done, she got out, squeezed the water from her hair, and quickly washed the dirt and bloodstains from her kalasiris before slipping back into it. The wetness turned the white dress nearly translucent, but that couldn't be helped. "All right. Go ahead and do your business so we can get going."

"Has anyone ever told you that you're very *pushy*?" Karim said as he turned toward her. His gaze dropped to her chest before refocusing on her face.

Sita crossed her arms, cheeks reddening. "What are you looking at?"

"Only what I'm being shown, Princess," Karim replied, his eyes full of mischief. With that, he shouldered out of his robes and took a running jump into the river.

"Ugh!" Sita cried, covering her eyes with both hands. Obviously, the thief didn't care about modesty.

She heard him splashing around, humming to himself.

What a dog, she thought.

Then, after a long moment, she spread her fingers and peered through them.

Karim stood waist-deep in the water, his arms up, his hands working through his brown curls. The water clung to the dark hair on his scarred chest and slid in rivulets down his stomach and the V-line of his pelvis.

Suddenly, she felt as if she were transported back to the pleasure garden, peering through the poppy flowers to watch something private.

You're as bad as he is! Sita scolded herself. She looked away and moved up the bank to wait for Karim to finish washing himself and his clothes. The sight of the scarab scar on his chest—shaped exactly like the amulet she'd placed inside him—brought her back to the question that she'd been asking herself since the thief's miraculous resurrection.

Did I *bring him back? Or was I simply a vessel for the gods' will?*

The quandary left her quiet and thoughtful as she and Karim filled their waterskins and made their way east toward the open desert. Neither of them said a word until they were out among the dunes, having left all vegetation behind.

"Your lips are silent, sena, but your face speaks," Karim said.

Sita startled. She hadn't noticed him watching her.

He went on. "Are you worried we won't be able to find Perset? Or that we'll perish in the attempt? There's an oasis marked on the map near the lost city, so as long as it's still there, we should be able to find it."

"No, it's not that," she said. She paused, searching for the right words to explain. As if sensing her unease, Behkai trotted to her side. She reached down to scratch between his tall, pointed ears. "The oracle you told me about, the Oracle of the Lamb—you really believe it's true?"

Karim sighed. "It is a source of extreme confusion. On one hand, the oracle is Khetaran doctrine, and I have no faith in such things. On the other, I cannot deny what my own eyes have seen." His gaze flicked to hers with a subtle wariness. "I cannot deny that it was through Khetaran magic that I stand here and speak to you now." There was a bitterness in his tone that made her sad and angry at the same time.

She quickly suppressed those feelings. *You cannot blame him for being upset when his faith is thrown into question.* She thought about what he'd told her about the ancient oracle, about its omens of death and destruction, and her own role—along with Karim, a priestess, and a warrior—in that dark future.

"How about you, hey?" Karim asked. "Do you believe?"

Sita shook her head. "It's complicated. I don't think you'd understand."

Karim bristled. "Why? Because I'm an uncivilized Red Lands tribesman and not an educated Khetaran like you?"

"No! It's not that at all! It's..." She dropped her head back and stared at the wide-open sky. "I'm the daughter of a pharaoh, all right? Up until a few days ago, every detail of my life was decided for me. When I ran away, it was the first time I took control of my own destiny. But if this oracle is real, then it means I was *meant* to run away. It means leaving the palace, meeting you, even bringing you back—all of it was decided a thousand years ago. If everything I do is predetermined by the gods, then do I really have a say in anything? Do my choices even matter?" She clutched the Isis knot and scarab pendants hanging at her breast, the last remnants of her old life. "If the hand of a god guides me, am I truly free?"

Karim didn't respond right away. He stared at the rolling dunes stretching out before them, his eyes narrowed in concentration. "Have you ever made a plan, sena?"

Sita thought about all the parties and banquets she'd

organized, and the fowling days out on the river. "Many times, yes."

"And did each detail always happen as you intended?"

Again, Sita recalled musicians who fell ill, tardy guests, strong winds that blew her specially prepared party food into the river.

"Of course not. There are too many variables. You can't control everything that happens." She blinked. "I think I see where you're going with this."

Karim gave her a little grin. "Just because a god—whether it be mine or yours—has a plan, doesn't mean it always comes to pass. We can *choose* to walk the path set out for us, or we can choose not to. Or maybe something completely out of our control alters the entire situation, hey? None of that changes the fact that *there was a plan.*"

Sita nodded. The thief's logic was sound. "You really think we get to choose our fate?"

Karim shrugged. "I think we get to choose whether we follow the path set out for us, Sitamun." He paused. "And I think we get to choose with whom we share that journey."

Had he moved a little closer to her? Or had she suddenly felt his closeness?

"Perhaps you can call me Sita," she said. "Sitamun is so formal, and we're going to be spending a lot of time together."

Karim's eyes twinkled. "Very well, Princess."

They walked in comfortable silence after that, Sita occasionally reaching down to give Behkai a pat on the rump, and Karim scanning their surroundings as he consulted the old map he'd stolen from the Temple of Amun.

Sita's muscles ached, and blisters grew on the backs of her ankles where her ornate sandals rubbed her raw. Like herself up until that day, her shoes had been built for looks, not work. When the pain became too much to bear, she kicked them off and walked barefoot. The sand between her toes was soothing, and the glorious, golden expanse all around them distracted her from dark thoughts.

Every once in a while, she stole a glance at her companion. His boyish, rugged face. His dark eyes that flashed when the light hit them just right. *Only two days ago, he was a stranger, and now…* What was he? A friend?

Not like any friend I've had.

The men in Sita's life treated her much like one of the decorative statues she'd seen in the Thonis marketplace: as something to be bought and sold. *Or prey to be hunted,* she thought, remembering Mery's hand on the back of her neck.

She shivered.

Even Femi, like all the other servants and courtiers, had treated her with deference.

Not Karim.

He'd argued with her! Called her names! Although none of them, she admitted, were nearly as bad as the ones she'd called *him*. And he seemed to have no interest in the value of her station. On the contrary, he had nothing but disdain for the Khetaran throne. Karim was, without a doubt, the most difficult, peculiar man Sita had ever met.

She watched him throw a tamarisk branch for Behkai to fetch, howling with laughter when the dog lost his footing and tumbled down a dune.

A friend, she thought again. The idea filled her belly with a warm, fluttery feeling.

She wondered how she might describe him to Nebet, while her attendant brushed out her hair at night like she used to do. *He's insolent, abrasive, unapologetically rude,* and *a criminal,* she imagined saying.

Karim caught her looking at him. "What?"

"Nothing."

You're being stupid again, Sita told herself. *Letting yourself be fascinated by a man totally unsuited for you.* It was true, of course, but with only sand and sky to look at for hours on end, Sita couldn't help filling her mind with silly, impossible thoughts of him.

When, later that evening, they came upon a gathering of rock formations, they decided it would be a good place to bed down for the night. Sita surveyed several options before choosing as their campsite a natural arch that allowed them a view of the entire landscape and provided shelter from the elements. After eating a small meal from their provisions, they both fell into a deep sleep, exhausted by the day's travels.

They got an early start the next morning, taking small sips from their waterskins before wrapping dark scarves around their faces, donning their hoods, and setting off. They talked about trivial things—the heat, the herd of twisty-horned addax they saw in the distance, the food they wished they were eating. Barely a day had passed since they'd begun their journey, but already Sita had started to adapt to her new environment, shedding her old self like a snakeskin. She was still hot and sore, but the strenuous activity also made her feel strong. Perhaps Karim was rubbing off on her. Like the twisty-horned addax, the thief was at home in the desert.

The two of them were arguing about the best way to eat fava beans when Sita spotted a strange vision up ahead.

"Is that…a girl?" she asked.

Karim squinted at the distant figure, putting a hand to his forehead to block the sun. Dumbfounded, he said, "It appears so, sena. But where would a child have come from? None of the Red Lands tribes venture into the eastern desert. It's too close to Khetaran trouble."

"I don't think any of our trade routes go this way either," Sita added. She studied the small form walking toward them, dressed in brown, wide-sleeved robes, her dark hair blowing in the wind.

She doesn't look more than eight or nine years old, Sita thought.

The girl carried a beautifully woven cloth bag slung across her chest, so full that it was nearly bursting at the seams. She was focused on the ground in front of her and didn't seem to have noticed their approach.

"Greetings to you, young sena!" Karim called out, waving a friendly hand at the girl. "What are you doing out here, hey? It's not a safe place for someone like you!"

The girl's head jerked up, her concentration instantly replaced by wide-eyed terror.

Undeterred, Karim soldiered on. "Do you want to come over here and pet my dog?"

In response, the girl turned her back and ran in the opposite direction.

"Brilliant move, genius," Sita said, tearing off her hood and scarf.

The tomb robber threw up his hands. "What? What did I say?"

Sita sighed and took off after the girl. Not only was the child in danger, she might also have vital information about the place they were looking for. "Wait!" she called out. "Please, we only want to help you!"

The girl glanced back at her—surprised, perhaps, by the female face and the strength of Sita's command—and tripped over the uneven ground. Before she could recover, Sita caught up with her and grabbed her arm.

"Leave me alone!" the girl yelled. When Sita wouldn't let go, the girl punched her in the stomach.

Sita doubled over, the wind knocked out of her, but she managed to hold on to the writhing child long enough for Karim to join them.

He clicked his tongue. "Now, now, young sena," he said, suppressing a laugh, "that's no way to treat a lady."

Sita grumbled at the amusement in his voice. "You find this funny?" she said.

Karim tugged his own hood and scarf down and shrugged. "A little."

The girl seemed to recognize that violence wasn't going to get her out of her predicament. She stopped struggling and stood there, panting, eyeing them both with suspicion.

"I'm going to let go of you," Sita said softly. "Don't run, all right? We truly just want to talk." Slowly, she released her grip.

The girl didn't move.

Sita blew out her cheeks and bent slightly so that she was face-to-face with the child. She had gold-green eyes, like one of the palace cats. "Now then, my name is Sita, and this is Karim. What's your name?"

The girl folded her arms and said nothing.

Sita narrowed her eyes, then reached into her belt and pulled out her waterskin. "Here," she said, handing it to the girl. "Have some. You're probably thirsty."

This time, the girl didn't hesitate. She grabbed the waterskin and guzzled half of it before Karim could leap forward, shouting, "Hey! Hey! Not so much, young sena! If we don't find an oasis to refill those waterskins, we'll all die out here!"

Sita swatted away his concerns and dropped to one knee in front of the girl. "Better?"

The girl nodded. She bit her lip, then whispered, "Aya."

"Your name is Aya?"

Another nod.

"Well, Aya, like my hairy friend said, this isn't a safe place for a young girl to be walking alone. Where is home?"

Aya set her mouth and shook her head.

"Are you lost?"

Aya shook her head again.

No, not lost. She just doesn't want to tell me where she came from. Is she afraid of going back? Or is there another reason?

Sita frowned. "Did you run away?" she asked.

Aya didn't reply, but her eyes were suddenly suffused with tears.

Sita reached out to push a lock of hair from the girl's face. She was glad Aya didn't recoil. Something about her reminded Sita of Maet. *If she had lived, she might have grown to be like this girl. Headstrong, feisty...* The thought brought a fresh wave of sorrow upon her.

"Let us help you, Aya," Sita said, laying a hand on the girl's shoulder. "I understand, wanting to run away. I'm running from something too. But it doesn't solve our problems, you know. We can't run forever. Eventually, we have to go back home."

"Sita..." Karim said.

"One minute," she replied, not looking at him. Her gaze was locked on Aya's young, frightened face.

It hurts, See-see.

I'm scared, See-see.

Sita's heart lurched with the memory.

"Sita..." Karim said again.

"Give me some time, will you?" Sita snapped. "I know we need to find the city, but we can't leave her here. I *won't* leave her here. Do you understand?"

Karim's voice became frantic. "For god's sake, woman, turn around and look!"

Confused, Sita did as she was told. At first, she couldn't comprehend what she was seeing. Above and beyond their position, the sky was bright, blue, cloudless. Behind them, however, a wall of thick, yellow clouds reached from the horizon to the zenith.

Clouds that churned, flowing over themselves like a charging, living creature. Sita had seen similar phenomena before, but never so immense.

"Is that—?"

"A sandstorm," Karim finished. "Big one. We have to find cover. *Now!*"

Grabbing Aya's hand, Sita scanned the area for any landforms. There were some boulders in the distance. The three of them and Behkai began to run.

Sita pulled Aya along with her, though with her short legs the child had a difficult time keeping up.

"Faster, Aya!" she yelled.

The wind was picking up, throwing sand into their faces. Sita glanced back. The storm was gaining, blocking out the sun, barreling toward them with terrifying speed.

"The map!" Karim yelled.

Alarmed, Sita watched the ancient papyrus sail by, the thief chasing after it.

"Leave it!" Sita shouted over the roaring wind. "It's not worth your life!"

"I can't! We'll never find Perset without it!" Karim shouted back. The map dropped to the ground and rolled wildly over the dunes, the thief in hot pursuit.

Sita shook her head and focused on running. The boulders were still so far away, and the storm was nearly upon them.

Sita's lungs burned with exhaustion. Aya was crying, slowing down, barely able to continue. Behkai galloped at her side but kept looking back, probably torn between staying with her and going to help his master.

We're not going to make it.

Sita stopped. She squinted into the yellow maelstrom and watched helplessly as it swallowed Karim whole. *"No!"* Sita screamed in horror, but the storm had grown so loud that it stole her voice and filled her mouth with sand.

He can't be gone! I just got him back!

There was no time to mourn. They had mere seconds before the storm overtook them. Dropping to her knees, Sita pulled on her hood and shielded Aya's face with her headscarf. Then she gathered the young girl and the dog into her arms and prayed.

"Hear me, O Isis," she murmured as the world around them shrieked and turned black, stinging them with a hundred thousand thorns. "Great Mother, goddess of magic, queen of the throne. Hear me and strengthen me with your blood and your spells and your words of power."

Aya wailed in her arms.

Sita thought of Maet, the girl she couldn't save, and a thunderous determination overtook her.

Not again! she vowed, her teeth gritted against the howling wind. *It will not happen again!*

"She will be protected!" Sita screamed.

The storm crashed over them.

5
NEFF

The embalmer sat at the long table at the back of his workshop in the Temple of Amun, carefully inscribing sacred words onto a roll of linen wrappings. As usual, he wore a simple white tunic, and his hair was a wild nest. His hair was the only feature that separated him from the other priests, who shaved themselves bald in their daily cleansing rituals.

The embalmer, to whom the rules didn't always apply, had never had the patience for such things.

His hand paused halfway to the inkpot.

"Come in, Nefermaat," he said without turning. "I can tell from your heavy breathing that you've run the entire way here."

Neff entered the room and sagged against the wall. "How did you know it was me?" Kenna seemed to have an almost supernatural talent for observation.

"It was either you or a very overworked dog," he said and faced her.

Neff scowled. "Very funny."

A silence fell between them. Neff toed the ground with her sandal, feeling awkward. The last time they'd seen each other was at the coronation, and they hadn't spoken. Kenna had been rightfully hurt by Neff's choice to leave the temple in favor of living at the palace with Meryamun, but she'd tried to give him a sign that there was more to her decision by handing him a small pomegranate. They'd shared one together in the temple gardens the day the prince had offered to be her honorary brother. She thought he'd understood what she was trying to tell him—that she was still loyal to him, still his little sister—but she didn't know for sure if he'd gotten the message.

Is he still angry at me?

As if reading her mind, the young prince said, "I assume you've come to explain why you'd leave your duties at the temple to spend your days ministering to my brother." He spoke the last word with distaste, with the undercurrent of what Kenna really wanted to call Meryamun: a murderer.

"Yes and no. I don't have that much time right now, but I promise to tell you everything as soon as I can. I came to ask for your help. I need you to teach me how to practice heka."

Kenna's eyebrow lifted. "I heard the priests have been sending you materials. Mery must really trust you if he's given you access to such forbidden knowledge. You've been ordered to use its power for the crown, is that it?"

"That's what your brother thinks, but it's not what I truly aim to do. I want to learn so I can use heka against him. That's why I left the temple. I didn't want to, but you're right, Meryamun trusts me. Sitting by his side, I have a chance at stopping him."

The cynicism dropped from Kenna's birdlike, angular face and was replaced with dismay. "You did this to undermine him? To sabotage the king? I took your pomegranate as a sign of peace… not a clue to some kind of fledgling conspiracy!"

"I am only following the path the gods laid out for me in my visions. It is what I am meant to do."

The piety in her voice unsettled the young prince. She could see the war going on behind his eyes—he was a man of faith, but he'd also been at the receiving end of his brother's wrath.

"He'll kill you if he finds out the truth."

"I know."

Kenna rubbed his face, smearing ink onto one cheek, then leaned against the table, looking pained. "You shame me, little sister. You've more courage in one finger than I have in total."

Neff dropped her head. "That's not true."

"It is."

"So...does that mean you'll help me?" she asked hopefully.

Kenna took up a cloth and began meticulously cleaning the ink from each finger, oblivious to the streak of black across his face. Neff watched him, suppressing a smile. When he finally answered, she saw a glint of excitement in his eyes.

"When do we start?"

The next day, Neff and Kenna sat on the floor of the Horus Room, cross-legged like children, with a dozen papyri scattered around them. The subterranean chamber had been emptied and abandoned since Amunmose's court was poisoned there, so Neff thought it the ideal place to conduct their lessons. It was an eerie room, the air heavy with phantoms, but Neff needed to be certain that they wouldn't be caught. Besides, if any spirits still lingered there, Neff imagined they'd be pleased to see someone working to defeat the man who'd ordered their deaths.

They'd been practicing for more than an hour when Kenna said, "It's all well and good to learn the correct inflections and movements—but what do you know about heka itself? About its origins?"

Neff set down the papyrus she'd been studying. "Is that important?"

"Of course it's important!" Kenna exclaimed. "One cannot build a sturdy house without a strong foundation." He clasped his long, thin hands and straightened. "Where do you think magic comes from, Nefermaat?"

"The gods?"

"Not exactly. Heka is older than the gods—in fact, it was magic that brought them into being. Like us, the gods are subject to heka, which permeates every creature, every rock, everything in our world. When a priest invokes the gods in his spell, he is simply calling out the heka within them to work upon the heka within the magic's recipient. Heka is not outside nature; it *is* nature."

Thoughtful, Neff leaned her chin on her fist. "I've read spells that call to heka in the invocation. 'Hear me, O Heka…' But isn't 'heka' just another word for 'magic'?"

"Heka is magic, but he is a god too. Have you ever seen a picture of his divine form?"

Neff shook her head.

"Let me see what I can find…" Kenna rifled through the pile of scrolls he'd borrowed from the House of Life to further her education. "Ah! Here we are." The prince pulled a papyrus free and unrolled it.

Along with some text, the scroll featured an illustration of a figure wearing a complex triple-feathered crown and the sidelock of youth. He was naked and had one finger raised to his lips in a gesture of innocence. Neff gasped. "He's a child!"

Kenna's eyes crinkled with the hint of a smile. "He is. It's his title, in fact. Heka the Child. Where else could magic live but within a pure, wondering heart? Another reason why Montuhotep was a fool to treat you the way he did. A high priest should know not to underestimate the divine power of the young."

The idea of a child god filled Neff with a glittering excitement. "Tell me more," she pleaded. "Tell me everything."

Kenna explained the inherent duality of magic, its darkness and its light. He taught her about "encircling," and how it can be used to either protect or control, and about saliva as both a creative tool and a curse. He also gave her some practical instruction about protection spells.

"If a threat is on the horizon, armor yourself against it by preparing a spell and wearing it on your person," Kenna told her. "The trick is that the spell must be *very* specific to the exact nature of the threat in order to safeguard you from it."

Neff nodded and scribbled notes on some papyrus scraps she'd brought. They were about to move on to another topic when the Medjed scroll caught Kenna's eye.

"What's this? I don't think I've seen it before."

"The Heka priests may have put it in my delivery by accident. It's really old—part of a longer work, I think. It has to do with an obscure god named Medjed. It doesn't work, though."

Kenna looked up sharply. "And how do you know that?"

Neff froze, realizing her mistake. "Um..." She shrunk back and squeaked, "Because I tried it?"

"You did *what*?"

"Nothing happened. I promise!"

Kenna rubbed the hooked bridge of his nose with two fingers. "Nefermaat, I know you are eager to learn, and that your intentions are noble—but you cannot experiment with magic that you don't understand!"

"I'm sorry!" Neff wrung her hands, feeling sick at the thought of disappointing the prince. "I just...I feel so alone at the palace, and so scared. I thought this Medjed could be my guardian. But like I said, nothing happened. Nothing good and nothing bad either."

Kenna sighed, and his next words were soft as goose down. "I don't blame you, little sister. If anything, I blame myself for not being there for you."

"You're here now."

Their eyes met, and Neff could have sworn she saw Kenna's glisten.

He sniffed, immediately back to business. "Besides, I probably would have done the same thing. It *is* curious, this scroll..." He dipped his head to study the faded text. "The name Medjed is familiar, but I simply can't remember where I've read it before." He shook his head in irritation. "It will come to me in time. It always does."

Neff returned the ancient scroll to its container and was moving on to the next one when the air in the room shifted. There was someone behind her! She gasped and whirled around, expecting the worst—

Except no one was there.

Kenna had jumped to his feet beside her, alarmed. "What? What is it?"

Neff scanned every shadow in the Horus Room and found nothing. "I could have sworn I felt something moving behind me. I guess I'm nervous about being caught. If Meryamun finds out what we're doing..."

"You're right. We've been away long enough already. We should get back before we're missed. When shall we meet again?"

"I'll try to send a message. Your brother has agreed to bring in some new servants from the city, so I'm hoping to befriend one of them. If I gain their loyalty, they can pass communications between us."

"You'd trust someone you just met with such a task?"

"We can't do this alone, my prince. I must have faith that the right person will cross my path."

"Very well, little sister. I'll await your message."

The two left the chamber and parted ways—Kenna taking a secret corridor, and Neff sneaking back through the hall that led up a set of stairs to the palace proper.

Neff made her way toward the stairs, unable to shake the feeling of being followed. *I must steady my nerves before I rejoin the king for his afternoon meetings*. She took a deep, cleansing breath.

A muffled cry sounded from somewhere nearby.

Neff stopped, listening.

Then she heard a familiar voice, though it was too far away to make out the words. The voice was coming from a hallway that led in the opposite direction from the stairs. Curious, Neff slowly made her way toward it. Luckily, the seldom-used corridor was deserted.

Light flickered from a chamber halfway down the hall. As she approached, she was able to make out what the voice was saying.

"I liked that sound you made, Femi. I liked it very much. Do it again."

A grunt of pain followed, but no cry.

There was a rumble of amusement. "You still have fight in you, hmm? After all the threats and beatings and starvation, you still resist. That's beautiful. I mean, look at you!"

Pressing herself against the wall by the doorway, Neff craned her neck and peered inside.

In the middle of the room, a young man with short, dark hair was tied to a tall wooden post, his wrists bound above his head. He was naked save for a loincloth, and his muscular body was marred by lashes and dark purple bruises. There were deep cuts along his lower ribs, his groin, his feet, and under his armpit, and thin curtains of blood cascaded from each one.

His face, however, was unmarked.

The king stood in front of Femi, a dagger dangling from one hand. Perspiration shone on his bare chest, and his face was bright with exhilaration. As Neff watched, he stepped close and dipped his face into the curve of Femi's throat. "I'll be honest," he said, lightly tracing a line down Femi's torso with the point of his knife. "I didn't understand what Sitamun saw in you at first. But I see it now."

Femi closed his eyes and grimaced.

"I remind you that you can stop this at any time. Say the word and I'll call the guards to cut you down and bandage your wounds. You could be in a soft bed, eating meat and drinking wine within the hour—with me. You'd like that, wouldn't you? To serve once again at the pleasure of the king?" He licked his lips. "All you have to do is tell me where she is."

Neff put a hand over her mouth. Ever since the coronation, Meryamun had behaved as if Sitamun's absence was inconsequential—as if her departure was due to her grief over their father's death, and that her return was imminent. But as the days passed with no sign of her, his explanation became less and less believable. That morning was the second time in two days that he'd asked her to pray to the gods for a vision about Sitamun.

He's getting desperate, Neff thought. *His guards must have been torturing this man, trying to pry information from him about the princess.* So far, it seemed that Femi hadn't offered any answers, but seeing what they'd done to him, Neff had to wonder how much more suffering the young man could take.

"As I've said before, my king," Femi said, breathless. "If I knew how to find her, I would tell you." He cried out as Meryamun pressed his thumb into the gash in his ribs. "She didn't tell me where she was going, I swear it! *On Amun, I swear it!*" His face contorted with agony as the king pushed harder, forcing a fresh stream of blood to pour from the wound.

Neff had to look away.

When she turned back to them, Femi's body had gone limp and hung from the bindings around his wrists.

The king cradled the man's pale face in his palm, tilting Femi's chin toward him. "Hm! I was certain that my guards simply didn't have the stomach for real torture, and that I needed to do the job myself. Perhaps I was wrong. I've carved you up like a bull for a banquet, and still you give me nothing. If I didn't know better, I'd say you were telling the truth."

The king frowned at the bloody smear he'd left on the man's cheek. He took up a clean cloth from a table nearby and blotted the stain with it. "I told them to spare your pretty face, you know. You should thank me."

Femi's eyes fluttered, and a pink bubble of spit appeared on his lips as he struggled to breathe.

Neff was so horrified by the scene before her that it took several seconds for her to register the tug pulling her away from the door.

Thinking that she'd been caught, Neff's heart nearly leaped from her chest. But when she turned to see who had discovered her—again, there was no one there.

What is going on? she thought, her pulse pounding in her ears. She'd *felt* the pressure of someone gripping her shoulder.

Wait. What was that sound?

Footsteps. Coming down the stairs at the other end of the dark corridor. They were coming her way.

Neff scanned the area in a panic. There was a large, lidded basket by the door. She quickly climbed in, hiding among a bunch of soiled linens that stank of sweat and blood, and sealed herself inside. Holding her breath, she peered through the weave of the basket.

The head guard appeared in view. He stopped inches away from the basket to announce himself at the chamber door.

"My king," he said.

"What is it?" Meryamun replied.

"You are needed upstairs. Vizier Sabni has completed his initial task and is requesting further orders."

"Very well. I'm done here. This man knows nothing of my sister—aside from what he learned in her bed."

Neff's senses sharpened. If Femi was Princess Sitamun's lover, then he could be a valuable ally. According to the oracle, she and the princess were meant to work together in some way.

And as my father always said: The enemy of my enemy is my friend.

The head guard cleared his throat. "What shall I do with him then?"

"Leave him here for now; I may want to play with him some more later. As far as Sitamun..." There was a pause. "How long did the Tashans stay in Thonis after the banquet that night?"

"I believe they remained in the region for several more days, my king, visiting with physician priests and conducting trade deals at the marketplace."

"So, it's possible they were still close the night Sitamun disappeared."

"It's possible, my king. The ambassadors did not offer a specific schedule for their departure."

Meryamun lowered his voice, so that Neff had to strain to hear him. "She *was* getting cozy with Prince Harsi at the banquet..."

"Do you have additional orders for me, my king?"

"I do. Gather some men, take my fastest ship, and track down the Tashans. If my sister is hidden among them, bring her back."

"And the rest of the delegation?"

There was a pause. "Kill them."

"My king?"

"Kidnapping my sister is crime enough to warrant execution, wouldn't you agree?"

"Yes, my king. However, if they *don't* have the princess…"

"If they don't, spare one, and bid him return to Tash with a message. Khetara has a new pharaoh. One who knows full well that many years have passed since Tash has offered fealty to the region's sovereign kingdom. They can consider the blood of their ambassadors as payment overdue." The guard began to step away when the king stopped him. "Either way, bring me Prince Harsi. Alive. He may prove useful."

"Understood, my king. We will do our best to reach the Tashans before they cross their borders."

Meryamun sucked his teeth. "What have I told you about calling defeat to your door? You are the hand of Pharaoh! Go now, and see that it is done."

"Yes, my king."

The guard departed, and Meryamun followed shortly after. Neff waited until their footsteps had faded to silence before emerging from the basket. She was about to follow—worried that the king would summon her and find her missing—but stopped in front of the chamber door. Femi was still. Looking at him hanging like a butchered animal in a slaughterhouse, she felt like crying.

His head lifted at the sound of her approach, and his eyes widened in surprise.

Without a word, Neff picked up a piece of sharpened obsidian, not unlike the kind Kenna used to make incisions during the mummification ritual. She turned to Femi, and his nostrils flared, uncertain of her intentions.

Neff held up a hand to indicate peace, then reached up to place the obsidian in his hand.

He regarded her with interest. "Who are you?" he whispered.

"Someone who could use more friends," she answered.

Femi's fingers closed around the blade, hiding it from view. He pressed his lips together and nodded.

Neff gave a small bow and slipped out of the room.

As she climbed the stairs to the main floor, Neff's thoughts turned once again to the force that grabbed her right before Mery's guard appeared. *Like a warning.* It was the same sensation she'd had in the Horus Room, as if someone else had been in there with them.

You're jumping at shadows, Neff told herself as she made her way through the palace. *Stop being childish and focus on the trip into Thonis to help the king choose the new servants.* Kenna and Femi were valuable allies, but with Meryamun torturing innocent people and stoking a war with Tash, the situation was getting worse by the day. She needed to gather as many conspirators as she could.

Meryamun took down a king with a combination of cunning, strategy, and a multiplicity of well-placed pawns, each with their own role to play.

If Neff was to have a chance at defeating him, she needed to do the same.

Your brother isn't the only one teaching me how to beat you, my king, she thought as she reached the throne room. She still couldn't shake the sensation of something trailing in her wake, but as she pushed through the doors, it was almost a comfort to feel as if she weren't going alone.

6

KARIM

He almost had it.

The errant map fell to the ground, rolling against a rise in the desert, and Karim dove for it. He dimly heard Sitamun shouting for him to stop, but he ignored her. Without the map, they were lost. *Got it!* he thought as his fingers closed around the scroll.

That's when the sandstorm hit.

The force of it took his breath away. It was like being struck by a solid wall rather than a million tiny particles. He fought to cover his face with his robes as the sand stung his eyes and flew into his nose and mouth.

I must get to the princess! he thought, struggling to keep his footing and failing. He couldn't see her, the dog, or the little girl. He couldn't see anything at all.

The storm pounded him mercilessly, and he was reminded of the beating he'd received from Babu, except this was a hundred thousand Babus pummeling him with fists made of earth and air.

As he did before, Karim curled up on his side, trying to shield himself from the blows.

The barrage seemed to go on forever.

At one point, the dune beside him toppled, and Karim found himself nearly buried in the sand. Panicked, he tried to rise, but the storm shoved him back down.

He sat on the ground, trying to stay upright as more and more sand blew over him, covering his feet, his ankles, his waist. It happened so quickly that by the time he realized he was trapped, it was too late to free himself. He strained, reaching up to push away the avalanche of sand, but it kept coming. Soon it was up to his chest, his neck.

He opened his mouth to take one last gasping breath before it buried him completely.

"Karim!"

The voice was muted, distant. Suspended in darkness, Karim couldn't see, couldn't move, couldn't breathe, and yet, he could hear that voice.

Sitamun.

It was as if time had stopped.

"Karim, where are you?"

Was she getting closer or farther away? She sounded desperate.

His left hand, at least part of it, was above the surface of the sand. He could feel a hot breeze blowing across his skin, and the sun beating down on it. Not knowing what else to do, he wriggled his fingers. Then he snapped them.

He felt the earth tremble with the approach of galloping feet. A moment later, something cold and wet sniffed at his hand. A dog started barking.

"Behkai! What did you find?"

There was more pounding followed by a small quake of someone falling to their knees. A smooth hand slipped into his and squeezed.

"Hold on! I'm going to get you out of there!" Sita scrabbled at the sand, digging furiously.

As the sand loosened around him, Karim was able to move his arm, then his shoulder, until—with the princess's help—he heaved himself up and out of the shallow grave.

Karim knelt on the ground, tearing his robes from his face, then fell on all fours and began coughing and vomiting sand, so much sand that he wondered if he'd ever get it all out.

Sita stood beside him, panting. Behkai whined and pawed the ground, as if eager to lick Karim's face but uneasy about the foul-smelling stuff pouring out of him.

Finally, Karim stopped retching and took a long, ragged breath. He expected his eyes to be swollen and his lungs to burn, but after a little while, his breathing normalized and the pain faded. He sat back, wiping the trail of spittle from the side of his mouth.

Sensing his opportunity had come, Behkai leaped forward to offer an abundance of moist canine affection.

"All right, all right," Karim said after allowing the dog to have his moment.

Sita was covered in sand, her black hair wild and windswept. "Are you all right? I thought I'd lost you!"

Karim nodded and staggered to his feet. "I think so, sena," he said, shaking the grit from his robes. "We're lucky the storm blew by so quickly. If I'd been buried down there any longer, I don't think I would have made it."

Sita stared at him. "The storm went on for an hour, maybe more. When it finally ended, I searched everywhere for you. I'd nearly given up when Behkai found you."

"That can't be. It had only been a few minutes when the dune collapsed on top of me. There's no way I was under there for an hour. I would be—"

Their eyes met.

The word hung unspoken between them.

Dead.

Sita swallowed. "Perhaps I was wrong about the time. Perhaps it only *felt* like an hour."

"Perhaps."

Karim wanted to believe her. He wanted to believe it had only been a few minutes. However, the position of the sun said otherwise.

Choosing not to go further down that unfathomable line of thinking, Karim turned his mind to another burning question. "How did *you* survive? Did you make it to shelter before the storm hit?"

Sita bit her lip. "Not exactly."

Karim waited for her to continue. "Well?"

"I don't know!" She threw up her hands. "It was as if there was this barrier around us. The storm raged, but somehow it didn't touch us. I don't understand it."

"It didn't touch you? Is this more of your Khetaran magic? Did you do something? Say something?"

"I suppose I did. I was worried about the little girl, so I—"

The little girl! Karim had forgotten all about Aya. "Where is she?"

Sita's shoulders fell. "Gone. She must have run away when I went looking for you."

Karim reached back into the hole and pulled out his pack. He rooted around in it. Everything was accounted for, except—

He slapped his forehead. "The map! I had it in my hand!" He fumbled in the hole, trying to find it. After sifting through the sand for several minutes and finding nothing, he stood and began to pace. "What will we do now, hey? If the map is buried or flying on the western wind, how will we find the lost city? We don't know our way around this region."

Sita squinted into the distance. "We don't, but Aya does." She pointed, and Karim turned to see a set of small footprints leading southeast. "Maybe the storm convinced her to return home. If we follow and track down her tribe, they might be able to tell us how to find Perset."

As if he understood her words, Behkai trotted over to the footprints, marked the scent, and took off in Aya's wake.

Karim hesitated.

"Unless you have a better idea?" Sita asked.

Karim swept an arm toward their new path and tipped his head. "Lead on, Princess."

Sita snorted, and they forged ahead.

She didn't ask Karim any other questions about how he'd survived being buried alive, and he didn't interrogate her about how she'd magically shielded Aya and Behkai from the storm.

But as he walked, Karim could think of nothing else.

In more ways than one, he feared where their untrodden path was taking them.

First, the wind took the footprints. Then it took the scent. Frustrated, Behkai snuffled at the ground and began to wander in ever-widening circles.

"Now what?" Sita asked, her cheeks pink with exertion.

Karim stopped and put his hands on his hips, scanning the horizon. Up ahead, the rolling dunes were interrupted by a collection of towering landforms. Most had sheer faces that would be impossible to scale, but one landform—a spire, like a finger pointing to the sky—featured a small plateau about halfway up the summit. "If I climb up there," he said, "I'll have a better view of the area."

Sita stayed with the dog while he went on his mission. He made quick work of the peak, his body feeling surprisingly hale given the fact that only a couple hours earlier he'd been vomiting up piles of sand. Reaching the plateau, he stood and looked around. From that vantage point, Karim could see far across the desert in all directions. He turned southeast. There were no structures in sight. No oasis either, which didn't bode well. Their water supplies were already low. A little farther south, though, he noticed something odd about the land. It looked…red.

Could it be a trick of the light?

He leaned forward, trying to get a better view, and put his hand on the wall of the spire to steady himself. As he touched the rock face, the world shuddered—and Karim had the sensation of falling backward, even though he hadn't moved at all.

Then, everything changed.

The sun was low on the eastern horizon, and a morning chill hung in the air. A man stood beside him, pointing out landmarks in the distance. Below, at the base of the spire, he could see a large caravan—servants, pack animals, men in white robes surveying the land and noting details on rolls of papyrus. They were clearly Khetaran, but their style of clothing was unrefined, the colors muted.

Karim couldn't move or speak, only watch as the scene played out before him.

"There are several areas of interest in this region," the man said. "Particularly to the south. There are no landforms to speak of, and the ground is relatively flat. Most importantly, we've discovered a water source nearby. It's the perfect location for development."

"And what is that area there?" The voice came from Karim's throat, though neither it nor the words were his. A bejeweled hand that also wasn't his pointed south.

"That is the Red Desert, my king. It is not large, but the sand there is heavy in minerals that give it that color."

Karim felt a rumble of approval in his chest. "Then that is where we build. For Set is the red god, and my city shall be his House."

Karim gasped as he tumbled forward in time. The world righted around him, the sun dropping west, the afternoon air hot and dry, just as he had left it.

He stared at his hand that had touched the spire. The vision had left him breathless. It was like he'd been thrust inside someone else's memory, someone who had once stood in that very spot, steadying himself on that same stone.

Not "someone," Karim thought. *Him.*

Karim ran a finger along the scarab-shaped scar on his chest, fearing afresh the consequences of what thrummed beneath his skin.

This is the heart of a king.

Sita was dozing in the shade of the peak when he returned, Behkai curled beside her, keeping watch.

"Wake up, sena," Karim said. "We don't need Aya's tribe after all. I can see the lost city. It's south of here."

The princess's face lit up in a way that made Karim's traitorous heart leap. "That's wonderful! Let's go!"

He hadn't really seen it, of course. But fear had grabbed hold of him and Karim dared not speak the truth. If he and Setnakht were connected in some way, how deep did that connection go? If Karim could see the pharaoh's memories, did that mean the monster could see his?

Karim rubbed his hand on his robes, feeling as if he had touched something foul, and together, he and Sita set off toward the Red Desert.

It was early evening by the time they reached the place where the sand gradually turned from gold to red. They hiked up a steep rise, pausing halfway to catch their breath.

Sita was drinking from her waterskin when she stopped and cocked her head. "Did you hear something?"

Karim listened. "Not me, sena. It's probably another herd of addax passing through."

They pressed on. When they finally arrived at the top, rosy-cheeked and streaming with sweat, Karim peered over the edge of the ridge and was faced with an extraordinary sight.

Below them, built at the bottom of a vast, crescent-shaped valley, was a crumbling Khetaran city. It looked to be about the size of a large village, but in its heyday, it must have been as glorious as Thonis itself. About a hundred mud-brick houses—many in various stages of collapse—congregated around what had once been a lengthy courtyard, which over a millennia had become a wilderness of palm trees and overgrown shrubs. The courtyard led through several gateways, their doors long since broken and turned to dust. Beyond the final gateway was a grand, flat-topped structure supported by towering columns that still retained the shadows of once-vivid paintings. A palace, perhaps, or a temple.

Or maybe both.

Alongside the palace, Karim spied a cluster of verdant trees and ground cover surrounding a dark, telltale glitter.

An oasis! That must be the water source the man spoke of in my vision.

A massive statue stood guard to the left of the palace's arched entrance. Even from a distance, Karim could see the statue had suffered significant damage from the elements. Its arm, held out in a welcoming gesture, was severed at the wrist, and one of its tall, blunted ears had fallen from its head. Still, Karim had no trouble distinguishing who it was.

"A red desert for a red god," he said, echoing Setnakht's words.

Sita clasped her hands in amazement. "The House of Set," she exclaimed. "I can't believe we found it!"

Behkai's tall ears perked with interest, and he sniffed the air before loping down the other side of the ridge toward the abandoned city.

"Hey!" Karim called.

Sita lifted her robes to follow, her eyes sparkling with excitement. "Come on! What are you waiting for?" She dashed down the hill, leaving a cloud of red dust in her wake.

Karim shook his head in annoyance. "Oh, nothing," he muttered to himself, trudging after them. "Nothing at all, sena. No reason to worry about traps, curses, venomous snakes…"

"Hurry up!"

"…unstable rocks, scorpions…"

It was cooler at the bottom of the valley, where the vegetation breathed moisture into the air, and the landscape shielded them from the khamsin wind. It was quiet too. Eerily quiet.

The mud-brick houses at the outskirts of Perset were the worst off—most were nothing more than a few crumbling walls, and none still had a roof. But as they got closer to the city center, the condition of the structures improved significantly. There, some of the homes were nearly whole and looked quite habitable.

"It's incredible that no one has settled here," Sita remarked. "Perhaps the remote location has allowed it to be overlooked by travelers."

Karim was inclined to agree. "If we hadn't been searching for it, we might have walked right by." He gazed around in wonder. "What the Anen wouldn't give for a place like this! A city with ready-made homes and an oasis, safe from raiders and prying eyes!"

Behkai walked with his nose to the ground, unusually alert.

Then without warning, he looked up, barked, and took off between the houses at a sprint.

"Hey! Don't run off!" Karim called, before being distracted by something on the ground ahead.

At first, he thought it was an animal, but as he got closer, Karim saw it was a brown blanket writhing in the breeze. He bent to pick it up. Confused, he asked Sita, "Does this look a thousand years old to you?"

She shook her head. "Behkai?" she called, a note of alarm in her voice. "Behkai! Come!"

Karim examined the blanket. It was soft and small, as if for a child. "Someone must have found this place before us, sena."

In the distance, Behkai yelped.

Karim and Sita froze.

When the dog didn't return, Sita whispered, "I think they're still here."

Karim dropped the blanket with a curse and tore off after Behkai. *If anyone's hurt that fool dog, I'll kill them myself…*

Sita trailed behind him, hurling quiet recriminations at his back. "Will you slow down? You told me *I* was being reckless, and now you're running straight into a trap!"

Karim didn't slow but was forced to stop at a crossroads. Half a dozen tumbledown houses were tightly clustered around a courtyard that was littered with scrub bushes and fallen rocks. Behkai could have gone in any direction.

"You check over there, and I'll go—" Karim started, but when he turned to face the princess, she wasn't there. "Sita?"

Nothing.

"Sita!"

His heart raced. Someone was picking them off one by one. He stood at the center of the courtyard, turning in circles, attempting to catch sight of what hunted them before it got him too.

He heard a soft rustling to his left. A shadow moved. He whirled but saw no one. The sound came again, behind him this time. He turned, feeling like a cornered beast.

"I have gold, priceless artifacts," he said to the empty courtyard. "Release the girl and the dog, and they'll be yours. Or else—"

Something shot out of the shadows and struck him behind his knees, sending Karim crashing to the ground. When he looked up, a tall middle-aged woman stood before him, the shaft of a spear gripped in her hand. She was barefoot and wore a short gray schenti and sleeveless tunic. A single braid of silver hair hung over one shoulder, and her weathered, olive-skinned face regarded him with the calm passivity of a hunter. Between the color of her hair and the strange lightness of her eyes, she reminded Karim of a ghost.

"Or else what?" a man's voice said.

Karim scrambled to his feet. A moment later, an older portly man with a thick beard and dark hair stepped out from behind one of the houses. He was unarmed, but his glare was weapon enough.

"Or else I won't stop until you've paid for what you've done," Karim said grimly.

Suddenly, others materialized from a dozen hiding places: from behind boulders, from atop half-caved roofs, from inside ancient homes. They were mostly men, but there were a few women too. Karim was surrounded.

"All of us?" the old man asked.

Anger—and that new uncanny energy inside him—made Karim brave. "I'll fight until my last breath," he declared.

The old man narrowed his eyes, then loosed a dry chuckle. "This shrub has thorns, does he not?" Some of the others tittered in response. "Put away your prickles, sen. The girl and pup are alive and well."

A young man emerged from the crowd, dragging a furious Sita along with him. She was bound and gagged, but otherwise unharmed. A woman led Behkai by a rope looped around his neck. The dog, unlike the princess, looked utterly carefree.

"Why didn't you bark?" Karim huffed at the dog.

"I gave him a big piece of meat," the woman answered.

Karim sighed. He was relieved, but still uncertain about the situation they'd bungled into. *Who are these people?* he wondered. The lilt in their voices was familiar, as was the expression the old man had used.

Put away your prickles, sen.

"You're Red Landers, aren't you?" he said.

The old man crossed his arms.

Karim took that as a yes. "But no tribe settles this far east. The Anen would have heard of you. I would have known—"

"No, you wouldn't," the old man broke in. "We've lived in this city a long, long time, sen. And we've gone to great pains to erase ourselves from memory."

Much like Setnakht, Karim thought. *I wonder if they know anything about him*... "But why? Why would you want to be forgotten?"

The question brought forth a wave of bitter muttering from the crowd.

"Why?" the old man repeated. "Because our ancestors grew tired of the raids, the uncertainty, the constant fear of death. So they journeyed across the Iteru and beyond the reach of the river people and happened upon this place. We never went back. No one returned to the Red Lands to tell the other tribes what became of us. Perhaps they thought we perished in the desert."

A name bobbed to the surface of Karim's mind. "You're the Hudjefa, aren't you? I've only ever heard of you in the old stories."

"All the better for us," the old man said with a hard smile. "We left the outer edges of the city empty, reserving the homes at the center for ourselves. That way, our sentries have time to alert us to any intruders who might stumble in. Although you two are the first in many years."

"What happened to the other intruders?"

"They were scoundrels and brigands, their only intent to kidnap, steal, and destroy. We dealt with them in the only language they understood." He eyed Karim meaningfully. "Why are *you* here, sen?"

Karim raised his palms in a gesture of peace. "We came only to explore this place, hey? To search for information about the people who built it. If you give us a few hours to look around, we promise to leave and never return."

The old man glanced at Karim's pack, bursting with treasures. "Those don't look like the possessions of a simple explorer, sen. Those look like the spoils of a thief."

Karim opened his mouth to deny the claims, but he couldn't because they were true.

A hairy brute with a scar across his cheek stepped forward, a stone mace gripped in one hand. "Enough talk, Elyas. Don't give the sheep a name, lest you pity them when it comes time for slaughter."

Sita shouted into the gag, struggling in her captor's arms.

"Wait a minute," Karim said, his pulse racing once more. "I thought you said we were safe here!"

Elyas looked pained.

"They're no different from the others," the brute said to the old man. "It doesn't matter that he's a Red Lander, nor that the other one's a woman. They both have mouths to speak. Either one of them could condemn us all."

"That's not true!" Karim protested. "I swear on my life we won't speak a word to anyone!"

"Elyas..." the brute urged.

The old man sighed. "Zev is right," he said. "All it would take is one slip of the tongue, and you could bring destruction upon our heads. I am responsible for the lives of these people, and I cannot allow that to happen."

The crowd drew back, seeming to not want to be a part of what was coming.

Karim couldn't believe his ears. "You wouldn't kill us in cold blood. You wouldn't!"

Elyas gazed at Karim with regret. "You should never have come."

The brute with the mace approached him, and another man came up behind Karim, tied his wrists behind his back, and forced him to his knees.

"Please, sen," Karim begged. "Don't do this. Can't you see that we are all brothers?"

Elyas looked away.

Behkai began to bark, straining at the rope around his neck, and the shadow of the mace fell over Karim's face as it was lifted high in the air.

"Wait!"

A small figure pushed through the crowd and appeared at Elyas's side. "Wait," she said again. "Sabba, tell Zev to stop!"

Karim squinted at the girl. "Aya?"

Elyas wrapped a protective arm around the girl's shoulders. "How do you know my granddaughter's name?"

Zev, the brute with the mace, hesitated. Elyas gestured for him to stand down while he waited for Karim to answer.

"We came across the girl in the desert," Karim said hurriedly. "She was alone. She wouldn't say what she was doing, but we guessed that she'd run away from home. Not long after we found her, we were caught in a powerful sandstorm, and if it wasn't for her"—he nodded at Sita—"your granddaughter would have been lost."

Elyas's brow furrowed. "Is this true, Aya?" he asked the girl.

Aya dropped her head and nodded.

"You told me you were out exploring. Why would you run away?"

The girl didn't reply.

Elyas grumbled into his beard, clearly disconcerted by this new development.

"Elyas?" Zev said impatiently. "What say you?"

All eyes turned to the old man. After a long moment, he shook his head. "I cannot condemn those who have delivered my beloved from the jaws of death. The mark on my soul—on all our souls—would never be erased. We shall not be defined by such an act. They will be spared."

The crowd seemed to exhale with relief. While his wrists were unbound, Karim sent thanks to whatever gods happened to be listening. Sita tore the gag from her mouth the moment she was released and ran to him. For an instant, Karim thought she might embrace him—but she stopped short, awkwardly patting him on the shoulder.

"I'm…glad to see you're all right," she said.

Karim regarded her—filthy, windblown, breathless. She was so different from the prim woman cloaked in black whom he'd met at the Thonis market not so long ago. He felt a burning desire to touch her, to wrap his arms around her waist and pull her close. "You too, sena," he said instead.

"But what will we do if they return west and tell everyone about us?" Zev shouted over the chatter. "What if they come for us with an army? What then? Are their lives so much worthier than ours?"

Elyas held up a hand for quiet. "I said their lives were spared. I did not say they were free."

Sita turned to the old man. "What do you mean, not free?"

"I mean, dear girl, whomsoever comes to this city stays here. You're one of us now. Today and for the rest of your days."

7
RAE

"What's going on up there?" Tam asked, craning her neck to view the front of the crowd.

"Nothing yet," Rae replied. She peered over the heads of the people in front of them, who'd assembled in the courtyard before the towering palace gate.

The five designated members of the Horizon had arrived in Thonis two days earlier, after a swift and uneventful journey down the Iteru on their fishing skiff. After making camp on the riverbank, they'd spent the rest of the day doing reconnaissance around the outskirts of the palace, where they suspected the Low Khetaran prisoners were being held. It took the whole afternoon and evening to get their bearings, but on the second day, they'd had a breakthrough.

Rae and Tam had been at the Thonis market with Omari and Buto, trading the perch and mullet that Kay the fisherman had caught along their journey for more supplies, when representatives from the palace came to announce that the king would be selecting a limited number of citizens to fill positions in the palace. It would be menial work—servants for the royal kitchens, attendants, messengers—but the men made it clear that serving the pharaoh in any capacity was a great honor. This created a good deal of excitement in the crowd, which erupted with chatter when the men departed.

"Choosing servants from the common folk!" Rae overheard an old woman exclaim as she served up stewed lentils from a bubbling pot. "My, my! This new king certainly is different!"

Rae was thrilled by the news. "This is our chance!" she told the others. "If we get jobs inside the palace, we can locate the captives and devise a plan to free them."

Omari crossed his arms and glanced around the busy marketplace. "There will be a lot of competition for those positions."

Rae followed his gaze. Although it was far larger and more opulent than the Sakesh market, even the pharaoh's capital city wasn't immune from the ills plaguing the rest of the kingdom. Beggars lined the streets, and vendors haggled with customers for a fair price that most could no longer afford. On the surface, Thonis glittered. But Rae had known enough strife in her time to see it lurking beneath the surface, like a crocodile in still waters.

"We only need one of us to make it," Tam said then. "Whoever doesn't can stay with Kay, gather information from the outside, and help get messages back to Sakesh."

From the moment Rae had invited Tamerit to join them on the mission, the weaver had made herself indispensable, offering efficient solutions to problems, charming the High Khetaran vendors at the market, and maintaining optimism and pluck despite the grim circumstances of their situation. Rae glanced over at Tam, standing on her tiptoes, the morning light shining on her black curls.

Every day, every hour, Rae fell a little more in love with her.

Now the two of them stood with Omari and Buto near the front of the gathered crowd, waiting for the king to arrive and begin the selection process. Kay had stayed back with the boat to catch more fish to trade.

Buto dipped his head to Tam. "I can put you on my shoulders, if you want to see better." Then he added, "And later, we can do it again lying down…hmm?" He waggled his eyebrows.

Tam snorted. "Generous, but no."

Omari's face reddened. "Shut your fool mouth," he barked, giving Buto a shove.

Tam put up a hand to pacify them. "Be at peace, Omari. He was joking around. Right, Buto?"

"I'm only trying to lighten the mood," Buto said.

"This isn't a game!" Omari snapped. "We need to focus!"

Rebuffed, Tam and Buto turned back to the gates and were silent.

Rae studied Omari with concern. He'd been unusually quiet throughout the whole journey, and he hadn't said a word about having seen her and Tamerit kissing back in Sakesh. No questions, no teasing…nothing. Then again, they'd been busy, distracted by more important matters. Still, it wasn't like Omari to lash out. Was he actually angry at Buto? Was the pressure of the situation getting to him? Or was he mad about something else entirely?

You should talk to him.

When would they have time alone for such an uncomfortable conversation? Besides, Omari wasn't her lover. Did she really owe him an explanation?

No secrets, remember?

Her inner battle was interrupted by the sound of the palace gates opening.

The crowd quieted. King Meryamun, flanked by palace guards dressed in scarlet schentis and Eye of Horus collars, strode into the courtyard. The young pharaoh was a vision of gold and glory, of glossy black hair and burnished copper skin.

Rae imagined that the High Khetarans must be pleased to have such a man for their king—particularly after Amunmose, who wasn't known for his good looks. The pharaoh's shining appearance didn't impress Rae, though. She recalled the fire that consumed her home, the way it glowed and shimmered in the night. It had been beautiful too.

She clenched her fists and buried her rage deep, where no one would see it.

Meryamun stood with his arms folded over his chest, critically appraising the crowd. It was then that Rae noticed the girl standing at his side, appearing somewhat out of place.

She wore a white dress belted in gold and had short blue-black hair that looked like a very expensive wig. Her hair and heavy makeup aged her, but given her diminutive size and spindly limbs, she was probably no older than thirteen. Despite being dressed like a princess, Rae saw that the girl had a wedjat eye tattoo on each side of her chest.

The mark of the holy.

A pungent, smoky breeze blew across the courtyard, bringing with it a sense of mystery. Rae wondered how such a young girl could find herself both marked by the priesthood and a breath away from the pharaoh.

"Kneel before your king!" one of the guards commanded, and the crowd was quick to obey.

Rae's jaw tightened. She sank to her knees with a curse on her tongue, and the other rebels followed suit.

King Meryamun gave no preamble; everyone knew why they were there. "If you are older than twenty, you may go," he declared.

About two dozen people rose to their feet and departed, silent and downcast.

"If you cannot read the common script, you may go."

Others withdrew, including Buto. He gave them a helpless shrug before exiting. Luckily, both Omari and Tamerit knew enough from their training as merchants to pass muster. Only about thirty people remained.

The king began walking through the crowd, assessing each person with a piercing gaze. He waved away a woman with burn scars on her arms, and two young men whose clothes were ragged and unclean. Finally, he stopped in front of a woman and smiled. "You'll do," he said.

The woman stood, bowed, and moved to stand next to the guards. The king continued, plucking people from the crowd like blooms in a garden. Rae quickly noted a pattern—he was choosing the loveliest faces. *To match the rest of the furniture,* Rae thought bitterly.

Then Meryamun was upon them. Rae's entire body tensed in anticipation.

"Mmm," the king mused, studying Omari. "He's a brute all right. Quite an impressive figure." There was a long moment when Rae thought Omari would be chosen, but then the king shook his head. "Tempting, but no. Only a fool brings a wild bull into his house."

Rae's hopes began to fade as a scowling Omari rose and left.

What will we do if this plan doesn't work? How am I going to save my father?

The king stopped in front of Tamerit, and Rae was suddenly overcome with a new worry.

"Oh, yes. I like this one," Meryamun said to the nearest guard, his voice soft and eager. "She's perfect for the kitchens. And perhaps other activities as well."

Tam rose to her feet, and Rae's vision narrowed as a hot, angry flush rose up from her chest, screaming for release. *Don't you touch her, don't you touch her…*

Beneath her, the earth seemed to tremble, though it must have been her imagination.

"And what do we have here?"

Rae glanced up. The young pharaoh stood over her. She straightened, contorting her face into what she hoped was a pleasant expression. "My king," she said, reluctantly bowing her head.

"Another rare specimen," Meryamun said. Rae remained still, trying not to recoil as his gaze roved over her body.

You must impress him, she told herself. *If he doesn't choose you, Tam will go into the palace all alone. Into our enemy's house. And perhaps into a monster's bed.*

The king lifted the Sekhmet amulet from Rae's chest and regarded it with interest. "The Lady of Slaughter, hmm? You do look fierce. I don't know that I've ever seen such arms on a woman before." He ran his tongue along his teeth, considering. "You've got fire in your eyes. I like that. However, it seems equally unwise to invite a lioness into my house as a bull." He dropped the amulet and started to move on.

No. No!

Without thinking, Rae reached for his arm. "Wait," she said.

The guard was upon her in an instant, his blade loosed from his belt. "You dare touch the pharaoh?" He seized her by the wrist and didn't let go. "You'll not leave this place with a hand that has defiled the king."

Surrounded by guards and the cowering crowd, with Tam looking on in alarm, Rae's stomach twisted. She clenched her captured hand and thought of her father, what he'd lost, and how hard he'd fought to protect her from the same fate.

The guard placed the edge of his khopesh against her skin, taking aim before the blow.

Rae shut her eyes and whispered to the heavens. "Hear me, Ra, Maker of Hours, Lord of Days, hear me and cast your light upon me. Burn away the fear in my heart, and watch over me so that I may see you again tomorrow..."

She waited for the swish of the blade, for the bite of pain, but it didn't come. Confused, she cautiously lifted her head. The guard had lowered his weapon and waited while Meryamun conferred with the young girl she'd seen accompanying him.

"You want *this* one?" the pharaoh said. "Why her?"

The girl's narrow face turned to Rae. There was something strange about her, something almost feline, that sent a frisson of unease up Rae's spine. When the girl spoke, her voice was high and sweet, but the words were carefully chosen, as if spoken by one much older than she.

"The gods have shown me visions of this lioness. It is no accident that she has been placed on our path. As Bast sent me here to serve you, my king, so did Sekhmet send this woman to serve me. Bast and Sekhmet are but two sides of the same goddess, one is incomplete without the other."

The king didn't look entirely convinced. "She disrespected the crown, Nefermaat. That cannot be overlooked."

Nefermaat approached and gestured at the guard to release his grip on Rae. Kneeling, she and the girl were almost eye to eye.

"What is your name?" Nefermaat asked.

Rae's mind raced. *I dare not speak the truth. If they are interrogating Father, he may be forced to give up my name, and then they'd know my identity. They'd know I've come for him.*

Rae blurted out the first name that came to mind. Her mother's name.

"Ahura."

Nefermaat drew back, as if stung. Her eyes suffused with sudden tears, but the girl recovered quickly from whatever had unnerved her. "Why did you ask the king to wait, Ahura?" she asked.

"Because of my father," Rae replied. "He is suffering greatly, and my only wish is to work in the palace so that I may help him."

It was often easier to lie by telling the truth, if only part of it.

Nefermaat turned to the king. "You see? This woman's family, like so many others in Khetara, are in dire circumstances, and she only wishes to serve the crown and to relieve her father's pain. Is that disrespect demanding punishment? Or courage deserving reward?"

King Meryamun chuckled, gazing at the girl with obvious adoration. "You are as cunning as you are wise, little seer. Already you have learned much from me—namely, doing whatever it takes to get what you want. Very well, you may have this wild creature as your pet. But I warn you, if you cannot control her, I'll put her down myself."

Nefermaat bowed her head. "You are most generous, my king."

The guard jerked Rae to her feet and shoved her toward the other chosen few. Tam was immediately by her side, the weaver's hand invisibly slipping into hers and squeezing it tightly.

Rae breathed a sigh of relief, feeling slightly dizzy. *It's all right. You're together. It's going to be all right.*

The king finished his selection, and soon the chosen were ushered toward the gates and the palace proper. Rae nodded to Omari and Buto on the perimeter. Omari raised a hand in salute, but even from afar Rae could see the bitterness in his expression. *He wishes it were him instead of me.*

Though she could understand his frustration, there was nothing to be done. Each of them had a role to play, and they didn't always get to choose which one.

As she passed through the gates into the palace courtyard, Rae wondered about the young seer who had plucked her from the hands of fate and convinced the king to accept her. *What could have made her to do such a thing?* she wondered. *Did she truly have a vision that predicted my coming?* She couldn't help but wonder what else such a vision might have shown the girl.

Rae pushed the thoughts from her mind and urged herself to focus. *All that matters now is that I'm in.* She was one step closer to saving her father, and she would do whatever it took to succeed.

This is war, she reminded herself.

The new servants moved aside so that the king's palanquin could pass. The girl sat at the king's feet like a cat and met Rae's eyes as they went by. Rae gave her a small nod in thanks.

She returned it with an enigmatic smile.

I appreciate your help, Nefermaat, Rae thought grimly, *but you might live to regret it.*

8
WINGS

The ibis flew south, following the river, searching for a new flock. He passed thousands of birds along the way: crowned hoopoes sunbathing on the riverbank; long-legged snipe wading through the water; orange-faced vultures scowling up at him as they huddled over the dead, cleaning up what others had left behind.

He thought he saw other ibis, but it was only a mustering of storks. They glared haughtily when he approached, and once he realized his mistake, he took flight—*quick-quick*—before they could peck him to pieces.

It was discouraging, yet the ibis felt that he had no other option but to continue. So he'd fish at dawn, fly all day, then stop for the night. Sometimes he'd roost with herons, who were a quiet sort and didn't mind his company, but often he slept alone.

Sometimes he was awakened by the *kroo kroo* of a nightjar. Sometimes he'd dream. Of fish, mostly, but occasionally of being back in that terrible net. Of the racing hearts of his doomed brethren, their warm bodies pressed against him as they were carried to their deaths. Those were the worst nights.

One morning, the ibis was fishing in the shallows when he saw a man approaching the riverbank on the other side. The ibis had flown far south, and wasn't near any human place, so he assumed the man must be a traveler. He was a big, bald man, and he wore blackened rags that smelled like smoke. He appeared to be hurt, as the ibis noticed half a dozen open wounds on the man's body. He saw exposed sinew and bone, but somehow no blood. The injuries didn't seem to bother the man. He strode briskly and without a hint of pain.

The ibis watched with interest as the man walked straight into the river, not pausing once as his head disappeared under the surface of the deepening waters.

Strange, very strange, the ibis thought. Alarmed, the bird took flight and alit upon the branch of a nearby sycamore tree to observe from a safe distance. About five minutes later, the man emerged near where the ibis had been fishing, rising slowly out of the water, seemingly unfazed by his journey across the river bottom. He stopped to wipe the algae from his body on the riverbank before continuing west.

What kind of man is this? the ibis wondered. Curious and weary of his own aimless wanderings, the bird followed him.

The man walked for so long that the ibis considered returning to the safety of the river. In the end, he kept on. *I've come all this way, yes-yes, I'll see whatever there is to see.*

Desert gave way to a large, craggy valley. The valley walls were honeycombed with holes, and old bones and broken things were scattered everywhere. It smelled of death and violation.

The man walked directly to a wall where there stood an enormous stone. With a mighty heave, he threw the door wide, exposing a gaping tunnel behind it. Then the man disappeared into the dark.

The ibis was curious, but not *that* curious. He did not follow. He waited.

When a figure finally emerged from the tunnel, it took a moment for the ibis to recognize it as the same man. His rags were gone, replaced with glittering bronze plumage inlaid with red and blue stones, his bare feet now booted in black. As the man cleared the tunnel, the wind caught his crimson cape and tossed it into the air behind him like a long, extravagant tail.

The man looked up at the sky and seemed to study the position of the sun before lifting a bronze helm and placing it on his head. It was a strange object, with two tall ears and a protruding snout that cast the man's eyes in shadow.

The ibis was even more confused than before. What kind of a man felt no pain? Walked through the river without surfacing to breathe? Opened cliffsides and transformed like a butterfly within them? *Is this even a man?* he wondered. *Or another being entirely?*

The armored man turned back to the tunnel and beckoned. "Come," he said. His voice was deep, resonant, strange. "Come into the light."

From within the darkness, a creature emerged. A creature so forbidding that the ibis nearly left his perch on the valley wall and fled, *quick-quick,* away from the ghastly sight.

But he didn't. He stayed. He wanted to see what would happened next.

"You have rested peacefully at my side all these years, imi-ib," the man said, stroking the creature's back. It made a dry, nickering sound that sent a shiver through the ibis. "And I have wakened you for a great and holy purpose. You were once the wind that carried me swiftly across the Two Lands. So you will be again."

The creature responded with a harrowing cry, and a crawling blackness erupted from it, spreading from its feet across the ground like a plague.

That was enough for the ibis. He took flight, wheeling around to head east, back to the river. He was frightened and hungry and alone in a world that no longer made any sense.

I should not have come here. If he had been with his flock, they would have known better. The group always chose the best way, the safest way.

But they are all dead.

The thought was sobering.

For the first time, the ibis considered that the choice of the many was not always the best one.

I have seen the man and the creature, and still I remain. Perhaps I will see other wondrous things, and perhaps I will survive them too.

Heartened by this new idea, the ibis dove into the marshes among a gaggle of geese and began his search for a meal.

The fish tasted particularly good that day. He ate his fill, imagining where the wind might take him next. *I am free, and I am alive,* he thought, splashing through the crystal waters.

I am alive.

I am alive.

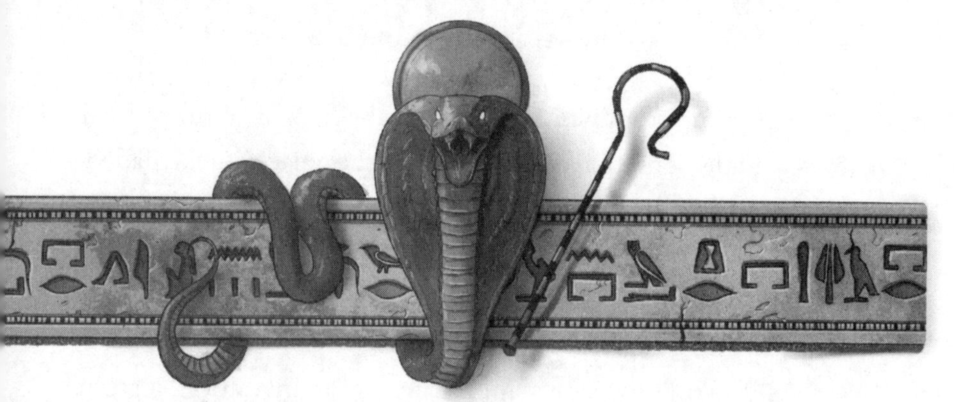

9
SITA

"Sitaaaaa!"

The voice woke her from the seventh sleep. "Coming, Mother," she mumbled, rolling over and pulling the blanket tighter around her shoulders. She didn't want to get up. Not yet. She'd wait until Nebet came in with her morning meal, then she'd get dressed and take the food to the pleasure garden to eat. She'd have plenty of time before she had to meet her tutor for her lessons—

Sita blinked at the dirt floor and became aware of the thin rush mat beneath her, the light pouring through the window of the dusty mud-brick house, and the sounds of men and bleating sheep outside.

Oh.

She groaned as it all came rushing back.

The escape from Thonis. The journey through the desert. The sandstorm. The lost city and the Red Lands tribe living there.

You're one of us now.

Sita sat up from where she lay on the floor. She rubbed her eyes, and the sensation of being back in the palace quickly faded.

"Sitaaaaa!" the voice called again, not her mother, but a visitor at the door.

Next to her, Behkai rose and stretched his long black body before trotting eagerly to greet them.

As if taking the dog's appearance as an invitation, a stout elderly woman marched in, laden with parcels.

"Nice boy. Good boy. Now move out of my way, will you?" she said, trying to get past Behkai, whose curious snout found its way into the baskets she was carrying. "Ach! No! Get!"

The woman turned to Sita, exasperated. "Well? Raise yourself from bed and help me, you lazy girl! Before your guard dog eats your breakfast."

Sita scrambled to her feet and pulled Behkai back by the scruff of his neck. "Sorry, Miri."

Elyas's wife had been the first in the tribe to introduce herself to Sita and Karim, and she had taken responsibility for their care. Clearly, she was grateful for what they'd done to protect her granddaughter. She set them up with a house, showed them where to get water for drinking and their washbasin, and made sure they each had a woven rush mat to sleep on.

Sita noted that the house Miri chose was in the center of the community, where there were always many eyes to watch them. The Hudjefa didn't trust her and Karim not to sneak off in the night, despite the fact that they'd never survive the journey back without provisions or a map. They had no choice but to stay long enough to secretly gather supplies and look for an opportunity to escape.

For the time being, though, they were safe. Knowing this, she and Karim had decided they might as well use the time to explore the city and see what they could uncover about Setnakht.

The old woman set down the baskets and began unpacking a stack of flatbreads, a jug of fresh sheep's milk, and some dried dates. "You and your husband had better hurry. They'll be expecting you both in the bakery for the day's work. Where is he?" She looked at the solitary rush mat and quirked an eyebrow at Sita.

"Um," Sita began, but Karim's appearance on the ladder from the roof saved her from having to explain. He wore only a loincloth, and Sita couldn't help but watch the muscles in his back contract as he climbed down to their level.

"There you are!" Miri exclaimed.

Karim ran a hand through his mussed, wavy hair and stretched like the dog. He gave Behkai a pat on the rump and looked between the two women with apprehension. "What? Were you looking for me?"

Miri put her hands on her hips. "Yes, I was looking for you, sen—why are you sleeping on the roof and not next to your wife?"

Sita and Karim's eyes met. They'd lied and told Elyas and the others they were married so the tribe would allow them to live in the same house and not think their traveling together was suspicious. The tribe had been universally shocked at the concept of a Red Lander and a Khetaran being wed—for they could tell right away that Sita was one of the river people. But Sita had woven a story about how they'd met at the marketplace, how Sita had shown Karim an old Khetaran map in hopes that he could lead her through the desert to find where it led, and how they'd fallen in love and gotten married along the way. That same map, Sita claimed, had eventually brought them to Perset. The tribespeople, particularly the women, had been so riveted by her tale of adventure and romance that they didn't think to question its validity.

Sita knew telling the Hudjefa they were husband and wife was a strategic move, but keeping up appearances had proven to be a challenge.

Miri stood with her hands on her hips, waiting for an answer. "Well?"

Karim frowned at Sita, eyebrows raised, as if to ask, *What do I say?*

Sita subtly shook her head. *Say something, you fool, or else I will!*

"She snores," Karim blurted, at the exact same time Sita said, "He snores."

Sita glared at him.

Karim shrugged.

Miri guffawed and patted Karim's cheek with affection. "Then perhaps you should both consider putting wax in your ears rather than distance between you." She made to leave, telling Sita as she passed, "If I had one like him, I wouldn't allow a little snoring to keep *me* away. But I'm an old woman who's been married for forty-three years. What do I know?"

Miri left with their thanks. When she was gone, Karim leaned against the doorframe and grinned. "Apparently, I'm quite the catch, sena."

Sita rolled her eyes. "What you are is late for work. Come on. We have to eat and get going if we want to finish in time to do more exploring before dark."

In the two afternoons they'd spent scouring the city, they hadn't found anything of note, but they still needed to search Setnakht's palace. Sita was certain that if they were going to find something important, it would be there.

She cleared her throat, working to keep her gaze level with Karim's. "Maybe you should get dressed first?"

Karim looked down at himself as if only just realizing he wasn't wearing any clothes. "If you prefer, sena," he said with a smile.

Sita was in the bakery grinding wheat when it happened.

The warm hum of women's chatter was interrupted by a chorus of shouts from outside. Sita followed the other women to the door to see what all the commotion was about. She saw the brute Zev running down the street toward them, carrying a young man in his arms. A boy of about fifteen ran beside him, his face creased with worry.

"Elyas!" Zev bellowed. *"Elyas!"*

Karim appeared at the bakery door, a large bundle of wheat on his back. "What's going on?" he asked.

"I think someone's hurt," Sita replied, and ran to meet them.

The young man Zev carried was as pale as death, his one leg soaked in blood. Through the mess of flesh, Sita could see the sharp end of a bone poking through the skin.

"What happened?" she asked Zev as he continued shouting for aid.

"Find Elyas, woman, if you want to be useful! Otherwise, get out of my way!"

The young man groaned, his eyes fluttering as he fought to remain conscious.

"Please, let me help," Sita said.

Zev's nostrils flared. "You will not touch him, Khetaran. Elyas may have spared your life, but that does not mean you are one of us. Not to me."

"What's going on here, Zev?" Elyas hurried toward them, walking as quickly as his elderly legs could carry him.

Zev turned to the frightened young man at his side. "Tell him, Amal."

Amal wrung his hands. "I-I..."

"Speak, boy!" Zev roared.

"Sami and me were f-fooling around on the roof," Amal

sputtered. "We were jumping from my house to his, a-and when Sami jumped, he..." The words died on his lips.

Elyas examined the terrible wound, his expression darkening. "Bring the boy inside, Zev. Amal, find Sami's mother at the oasis. She will want to be with him."

Amal hung his head, then took off running.

Sita followed Elyas and Zev into one of the houses, which had been set up as a kind of infirmary with rush mats and simple linens for bandages.

"Put him there, Zev," Elyas said. "Then go get Miri. Tell her to send the others for fresh water and to come right away. We must try to stop the bleeding..." He shook his head, dropping his voice to a whisper. "Even if the boy survives the night, he'll never walk again. But we must try, for his mother's sake."

Sita glanced at Sami. Zev had lain him on one of the mats, and the boy had grown quiet, too quiet. His lips were open, his face gray. Something stirred in her, a force powerful and bone deep. She touched her carnelian Isis knot amulet.

The blood of Isis flows through your veins, my girl.

Isis. The goddess of magic. The Great Mother.

She Who Knows All the Names.

"Let me help him, Elyas," Sita said softly.

The Hudjefa leader's brow furrowed. "Help him? What do you know of medicine, sena?"

"I am no priest, but I know some Khetaran healing techniques, and people come from all over the region to learn such wisdom. At least let me try!"

Zev reared toward them like a cobra, ready to strike. "Elyas, you mustn't entertain the whims of this woman! She is a stranger! She hides the truth from us, I know it. I can see it in her eyes!"

Sita felt a sudden fury well up inside her. Every second they wasted arguing brought Sami closer to death. *"You will allow me to help this boy!"* she commanded. The air inside the infirmary vibrated with the strength of her voice, and the two men fell silent.

"Please," she added softly.

Elyas narrowed his eyes, studying her with newfound intensity. "Who are you?" he whispered.

"Do you want me to answer the question, or do you want me to save Sami's life?"

Elyas swallowed. Zev's jaw tightened, but he said nothing more.

After a long moment, Elyas stepped back, allowing her passage to the injured boy.

Sita rushed to Sami's side and fell to her knees before him. The wound looked bad, but then again, she'd brought Karim back from the dead. Why shouldn't she be able to heal a broken leg?

Because I don't know how this magic works yet, she thought. *I have no talisman this time, and I cannot rely on divine intervention.* She thought back to her years of lessons with her tutor, lessons that covered everything from religion to taxes to history, and medicine too. Her tutor didn't go into depth about the wisdom of the priesthood, but she knew enough. And she'd witnessed the physician-priests treat injuries and illnesses of all kinds at the palace. *Medicine is half method and half magic," she remembered her tutor saying. "Sometimes only one is necessary, but you often need both.*

Method and magic, Sita considered, then came up with a plan.

"I need more linens," she said. "Plenty more. And half a dozen thin pieces of wood, about three hands' breadths in length. If you don't have any, cut down a tree and have the carpenter make them to those specifications. I also need your sharpest copper needle and some strong linen thread. Get them from the weavers. I've seen the girls using them. Are there any red poppies growing by your oasis?"

Elyas blinked rapidly, bewildered by Sita's list of demands. "I believe so. Why?"

"Have someone gather the seeds of the blossom and boil them. Add some onions too. When it cools, bring the potion to me."

It was then that Miri, Sami's mother, and several others arrived with water and dismay. Elyas quickly repeated Sita's commands while she took up a bandage and used it to apply steady pressure to the wound. Sami's mother was crying, and Sita heard her ask Elyas, "You trust this stranger with my son? You think she can save him?"

Sita listened for the old man's answer.

"I trust that the Lord has put her in our path for a reason," Elyas said.

"A Khetaran?" said a man. "But they believe in false gods, sen. Why would the Lord bring one of them to us?"

Elyas shook his head. "I don't know. But I feel great stirrings in my spirit telling me to trust this girl. I only hope they have not led me astray."

The group seemed to accept this, and all departed to complete the tasks set out for them. Having managed to stanch the bleeding, Sita was using fresh water to clean the wound when Karim arrived.

He took in the scene before him and rubbed his stubbled face with one hand. "What are you doing, Sitamun?" he asked.

Sita faced him, her expression fierce and radiant with purpose. "What I should have done back in Thonis. What I neglected to do for too long."

Karim's eyes shone with an expression she was afraid to interpret. With a nod, he said, "I shall leave you to it." Then he departed.

Alone with her patient, Sita put a hand on Sami's chest and began rocking back and forth, chanting words that seemed to come to her on the breeze, from the heavens to her lips. "You will be well," she began. "You will survive this day, and you will walk through the streets with your people once more. You will run to your mother, and she will lay a thousand kisses upon your brow. The word is the deed.

"The word is the deed.

"The word is the deed."

Sita remained by the boy's side, tending to his wound until the sun dipped below the horizon. When the work was done, there was nothing to do but wait. Exhausted, she lay down on a rush mat beside her patient and closed her eyes.

Sleep didn't come.

Instead, she listened to the women who had assisted her throughout the day talk outside.

"She moved the bone back into his body," one woman said. "And then sewed the wound shut like a hole in a dress!"

"That sounds like torture. What of Sami? How did he bear it?"

"That's the strangest part. He was as peaceful as a lamb. The girl said it was because of the poppy brew she gave him; it takes away the pain for a time. Can you imagine? Sami lost a lot of blood, but she says if he survives until morning, he may recover."

"What do you think of them? Sita and her Anen tribesman?"

The other woman sighed. "I think they bring changes with them, as all new things do. But whether those changes are good or bad, I cannot say."

Sita stared at the makeshift splint she'd assembled with the materials they'd brought her. At Sami's relaxed, sleeping face. There was still no color in it, but that would come. Isis willing, that would come.

She must have dozed off, because when she woke again with

a need to make water, the infirmary was suffused with thick darkness. Sita stumbled to her feet and groped her way to the door.

"Oh!"

She nearly jumped out of her skin when she bumped into someone just outside the house. "By Amun, you frightened me," Sita said, putting a hand to her chest. She squinted at the face of the visitor and saw it was the tall gray-haired woman who'd caught her and put Karim on his knees when they'd first arrived in Perset.

The woman regarded her but said nothing.

She was a formidable figure, with steely eyes and simple garb designed for movement, not fashion. The woman seemed an unusual choice for a warrior, but a warrior she was. Sita vividly recalled running through the streets to find Behkai, when the woman dropped out of the air, soundless, effortless, and caught her with the ease of a leopard pouncing on a gazelle. So much had happened over the past several days that Sita hadn't thought about the woman since that encounter. *Who is she, I wonder?*

"Did you need something?" Sita asked.

The woman shook her head.

Sita waited for more of a response, but none came.

"Well then, how can I help you?"

The woman waited, as if Sita might make the connection on her own. When Sita remained confused, the woman made two fists and crossed them in front of her chest. She bumped her wrists together twice.

She doesn't speak, Sita concluded, and tried to guess at the meaning of the gesture. "You're...stopping something?"

The woman circled one hand, as if to say, *Keep going.*

"You're protecting... Oh! You're protecting Sami and me! You're standing guard!"

The woman nodded.

There was something about her—perhaps it was her gray hair or her quiet strength—that reminded Sita of Nebet. She thought of her beloved attendant back in Thonis with a pang of desperate longing. A childlike desire for Nebet's work-roughened hand on her cheek. She thought of the grief Nebet must feel, not knowing if Sita was alive or dead, and wished she could send her a message on the western wind.

I'm all right, she'd say. *I'm safe.*

When Sita returned from relieving herself, the woman hadn't moved from her post. Sita stopped to lay a hand on her arm before returning to the shadowy infirmary. "Thank you," she whispered.

She slept soundly until morning.

When Sita opened her eyes, blinking into the bright sunshine, Sami was looking back at her from his mat.

"Hello," he said. "Is there anything to eat?"

Sita scrambled to his side and lay a hand on the boy's forehead. It was cool and dry. She checked the splint to see if the wound had bled through the padding, but it too, was dry.

"How do you feel?" she asked him.

Sami struggled up on an elbow, wincing as his leg shifted slightly. "Hungry."

Sita smiled. She laughed. "You're hungry," she said, giddy. She stood and ran out of the infirmary in bare feet, her hair a wild tumble. She found the silent woman where she'd left her, and Sita enveloped her in a sudden embrace.

"Did you hear?" she said as the woman awkwardly patted her on the back. "He's hungry!" She shouted the news to the still-quiet houses, to the sleepy faces that appeared to see what all the fuss was about.

Sami's mother came rushing into the street, her face haggard with exhaustion. "Is it true?" she asked, fear and hope intermingling in her voice.

Sita nodded, and the woman broke into tears of happiness. Soon, others gathered and joined her in expressing their relief. The women from the bakery, Zev and Elyas, Miri and Aya all came to gawk at Sami, who was alive and awake and asking for his breakfast.

Sita had seen so much death, so many horrors. But on that day, she had wrested a boy from the jaws of fate. Pulled him back from the brink and into his mother's arms. When she'd saved Karim, she'd wondered how much of his resurrection had been her doing and how much had been the machinations of the gods. With Sami, she knew for certain her actions had saved his life.

The knowledge gave her a new and wonderful feeling. A joy borne of the marriage of power and purpose.

"The Lord has smiled upon our people today!" Elyas announced to the gathered throng. "Tonight, we celebrate!"

The people cheered, thrilled to be treated to a feast instead of a funeral.

Sita spied Karim nearby, leaning against the side of a building with his arms crossed, watching her. Their eyes met, and he grinned, then shook his head, as if to say, *Princess, what will you do next?*

The other young women came for her at sundown. Already dressed in colorful robes and dresses, they pushed a protesting Karim out of the house he and Sita shared and deposited heaps of clothing onto the floor. Laughing and arguing among themselves, the women went through half a dozen dresses before they found one that fit Sita to their satisfaction—a flowing henna-red gown tied at the waist with a black sash embroidered with geometric patterns. Then they gave her a hairbrush and a pot of coconut oil to bring out the luster in her hair.

The air vibrated with excitement and good cheer, reminding Sita of the night of the Bast Festival. Of being dressed by her attendants in her chambers at the palace, and the anticipation she'd felt as she prepared for the impending celebration. She'd felt such joy that night! Such freedom! She hadn't felt the same way since. Mery had made sure of that.

Sitting there, in that faraway place, surrounded by women who didn't even know her true name, she felt that joy again. It was a different kind of emotion, though. Wrought not from the thrill of rebellion, but from conquest over adversity. From the simple miracle of doing what she believed was right.

She thought of Sami, alive and in the arms of his mother. Finally, there was something to celebrate.

Someone handed her a brass mirror, and Sita held it up to see her reflection in the dying light. Despite the brushing, her hair flowed in unruly black torrents. Her skin was sun-drenched, unadorned, and yet it glowed with vigor and good health. The woman in the mirror looked nothing like the person who fled Thonis. She was a stranger.

What had she said to Femi in the pleasure garden, right before she left him and her old life behind?

I don't even know who I am away from this place.

She touched the mirror, feeling the weight of the burden she'd been given, and for the first time, recognized she had the strength to carry it.

Then go and find out, my princess.

Sita smiled at the stranger in the mirror, and the stranger smiled back.

I do not know you yet, but I would like to, she thought.

Suddenly, the women started clapping and laughing. Sita set

down the mirror and turned to see the cause of their mirth. Karim stood in the doorway, having been dressed in a beetle-green robe that was open-chested and belted with leather. His wavy, dark brown hair shone in the gloaming, and his eyes sparkled with mischief—that is, until he saw her.

"Your husband is here to take you to the feast!" one of the women said gaily and pushed Sita toward him.

Sita stumbled into his arms, and they stood there together, awkward and unsure.

Sita blushed under Karim's gaze. "Why are you looking at me like that?"

"How am I looking at you?" he asked, his voice soft.

It was an expression she'd seen once before from Femi, and it frightened her. "I-I don't..."

"Come on now!" one of the women crowed, "It's time to go!"

They herded Sita and Karim out of the house and into the flow of Hudjefa making their way to the city's central courtyard. Her words unfinished, Sita allowed herself to be swept along by the crowd, Karim close by her side.

The night was filled with the sights and sounds of jubilation. People carried platters of roast mutton and onions, still-steaming flatbread wrapped in cloth, bowls of tart yogurt and butter, and bulging sacks of plump brown dates. They carried instruments too: reed flutes, a lute played with a bow, and drums of all sizes, which they played as they walked.

By the time Sita and the others reached the courtyard, a great bonfire was burning. Men fed the fire with gathered brush until it glowed bright and hot and the flames rippled in the easy evening breeze.

Elyas and Miri came and led them to where Sami had been placed on a bed of blankets to enjoy the festivities. His mother embraced them both, heaping blessings upon them until they were pulled away by others offering plates of food and cups of date wine.

Sita declined the wine. For once, she did not want to dull her senses, did not need drink to keep her mind from descending into darkness. *I want to remember this*, she thought. *I want to remember everything.*

They were seated next to Elyas, and as Sita began tucking into the delicious meal, she noticed the silent woman standing at the edge of the firelight.

"Who is she?" Sita asked the old man.

Elyas swallowed the bread he was chewing and replied. "Ah, that's Dumiya. She kept an eye on you last night, did she not?"

Sita nodded. "Does she ever speak?"

"Not once in all her life," Elyas replied. "She makes herself understood in her own way. She is a force to be reckoned with, that one. At a young age, Dumiya decided it was her job to protect our people, and no one—not her grandfather, nor her father, nor myself when I became leader of the Hudjefa—could tell her otherwise. She has been watching over this city ever since." He paused, thoughtful, and took a drink of his wine. "She is the best of us, I think."

Many came to greet them as they finished their meal, seemingly eager now to know the new faces among them. Even Zev raised his cup to Sita across the firelight. The children capered about with Behkai, who managed to glut himself with so much roast meat that he had to lie down.

Once everyone had finished eating, the dancing began.

The people clapped in time with the drums, and the lute player started up an energetic melody that got everyone on their feet. As Sita and Karim watched, the community made a circle around the bonfire and began to sing.

"As the sun rises, we rise," they sang, "As the flowers grow, we grow!"

Aya dashed out of the crowd and grabbed Karim's hand. "Come on, sen!" the little girl cried. "Dance with me!"

Elyas laughed and urged him on, so Karim allowed himself to be dragged into the fray. Sita clapped and watched him move, clumsy at first, until he picked up the basics of the dance. Aya shrieked with delight as he swung her around and around as they circled the fire under the moonlight.

"Tomorrow is not promised," they sang as the music played on. "Tomorrow is not certain!"

Then Karim was in front of her again, his face aglow, his skin glistening with sweat. "Dance with me," he said, panting.

Sita's breath caught in her throat as again, she saw passion in his eyes.

It's this place, she thought. *This moment. No more than that.* Being among those people in that long-forgotten city was almost like living another person's life. It was easy to forget what existed outside that valley, to forget the tragedies that had brought them there, seeking answers. *You drowned yourself in oblivion before,* she told herself, *and you vowed never to do it again. You cannot delay much longer, no matter how good it feels. You must finish what you came here to do.*

"There is only tonight!" the people sang.

She looked at Karim's open hand, reaching out to her.

Perhaps just for one night...

She lay her hand in his.

Karim grinned and pulled her to her feet, into the music, into the crush of joyous movement, into the heat. They moved together in a blur, her fingers laced into his, singing and dancing as sparks flew up from the fire to meet the stars.

"There is only tonight!"

She fell against him, her head light and dizzy despite not having had a drop of wine. He caught her in his arms, and her hand fell upon the scarab-shaped scar on his chest. She felt his heart beating wildly beneath her fingers, the heart she'd impossibly turned from stone to flesh. Close now, so close, her breath mingling with his, mingling with the smoke and the wind, she met Karim's gaze. His eyes glinted with that otherworldly light, and she was lost. Everything faded away—the pain of the past and the uncertainty of the future—as he threaded his fingers through her hair and pulled her toward him.

Their lips met as the song reached its climax, and the fire crackled and burned.

"Only tonight!"

10
RAE

Rae's arm muscles trembled under the heavy burden, threatening to give out. Clouds of hot steam buffeted her face, and a clamor of angry voices assaulted her ears. *For the love of Ra,* she thought, *put me out of my misery.*

"More?" she asked as the palace cook ladled soup into a bowl and set it on the already crowded breakfast tray Rae carried.

The shiny-faced cook glared at her. "You are here to work, not to speak," she said. "You're lucky I'm trusting you to serve the pharaoh's favorite. At first I was sure you'd either drop it all or steal it. Now, stay right there. A bit of melon and mint salad should do it..."

She shuffled away, pushing past the bakers toiling at the mouths of clay ovens and cooks stirring fragrant, steaming pots nestled in embers. It was hot and loud and chaotic, but even Rae had to admit the royal kitchens boasted a truly mouthwatering smell.

Not that she'd gotten to enjoy much of the food herself.

Rae grunted, shifting her grip on the tray. *It's criminal how much these High Khetarans eat. This one meal could feed an entire Sakeshi family for a whole day.* She studied the bowl of soup. It was thick and green, and gave off a bitter, but not unpleasant, aroma.

"What is this?" she asked.

The cook returned with the fruit and set it on the tray. "Didn't I *just* tell you to stop asking questions? Your mind is like an empty room, girl!"

Then the cook sighed in resignation. "The soup is made with jute mallow leaves, garlic, and coriander. Very tasty, very healthy food. The little seer has taken a liking to it, so she gets a bowl every morning. Happy now?"

"Delighted. Can I go?"

The cook pointed a finger at her and said, "Spill a drop of it and I'll have your hide. I don't care how big you are."

Muttering a litany of curses under her breath, Rae shuffled out of the kitchen into the open corridor leading to the palace proper. She paused, letting the fresh cross breeze dry the perspiration on her brow. Her muscles relaxed a bit, though she still didn't feel at ease.

As soon as she, Tamerit, and the other new arrivals had been brought into the palace, she'd been ushered into a bathing chamber with the other women, ordered to strip, and then instructed to wash herself until the head attendants were satisfied. After she'd nearly scrubbed her body raw, she'd been fitted with a long white kalasiris made of linen so fine that even Tam was impressed. Soft as it was, it drove Rae to distraction, as it was so tight that she was forced to take mincing steps everywhere she went.

The kingdom for a tunic! she thought. She could hardly walk in the dress, no less run, fight, or any other useful activity.

Not that she expected to be doing those things anytime soon.

It hadn't taken long for Rae to recognize she wasn't cut out for the life of a spy.

She was accustomed to danger. She'd faced it back in Sakesh, time and time again. Sought it out, even. But that danger was straightforward—it was fists in an alleyway, a whip at her back, arrows in the night.

The risks of the king's palace? Those were different.

There was no fighting, no violence, no pain—aside from the frustration of dealing with the royal cook. And yet, danger was everywhere. Hidden in every glance, every word, every decision she made.

It was awful. She'd take a fistfight over courtly intrigue any day.

While she paused to catch her breath, two maidservants exited the kitchen carrying their own breakfast trays. One looked to be about Rae's age, the other slightly older. Rae followed at a short distance behind him, hoping to catch a bit of their conversation.

"Still no word of Femi?" the older one asked.

The younger maidservant sighed. "No. His wasn't among the bodies taken across the river to be interred with King Amunmose. So, I have to believe he still lives. I have a theory he's being kept down in a subterranean chamber. One of the cooks told me that in addition to the gruel for the rebels, the pharaoh's head guard told her to make up a tray of bread and beer. I think that food is for Femi."

"What makes you say that? Why would the king keep Femi prisoner?"

The young woman's expression darkened. "Because of *her*. Sitamun."

Rae had been so spellbound by the conversation that she'd almost let the jute leaf soup spill into the fruit salad. She steadied the tray and continued.

"The princess?"

"Femi was bedding her before she disappeared. The king must think he knows where to find her."

The princess is missing? Rae filed the information for later use. *I wonder where she got off to?*

The older maidservant looked both scandalized and delighted. "Femi and the princess? Together? Are you certain?"

Scowling, the younger woman said, "I'm certain. Before Sitamun took him into her bed, he'd been in mine. Something happened the day of the Bast Festival. We'd met in the pleasure garden that afternoon and all was fine, and then…then it was over, and the only star in his sky was Sitamun." She paused. "I still care for him, though. I still want to know if he's all right."

"Of course you do," the older woman said sympathetically. "Amun willing, you will see him again." Then they turned down a corridor toward the ladies' chambers.

Rae stopped tailing them, having learned exactly what she needed to know.

Gruel for the rebels, she thought. *So they're keeping the prisoners underground. That's where I'll find Father!*

Rae cast an eye over the green soup. She'd managed not to spill any, but it was getting cold. She'd better hurry.

Her mind whirling with plans, she made her way to the young seer's room.

Nefermaat was sitting at a low table surrounded by piles of papyri when Rae arrived.

"Oh good, you're here," the girl said with a smile, then pushed some of the scrolls aside to make way for her breakfast.

Rae blinked. Nefermaat looked very different than she had that first day in the courtyard. She was wearing a simple white shift—not unlike Rae's own—and no jewelry except for the Bast collar she'd worn before. Her face was free of makeup, and shockingly, she was *bald*.

So, it was *a wig.*

Stripped of all her finery, Nefermaat looked to be barely more than a child.

Rae let her guard down, just a little.

A golden cat with black stripes rose from her spot in a sunbeam and padded over, clearly interested in sharing the girl's meal.

Nefermaat chuckled as the cat snagged a chunk of cheese from the tray. "I should ask Cook to bring you your own plate," she said with obvious affection. Primly, the cat carried her spoils back to the sunbeam to eat. Nefermaat glanced at Rae. "How about you? Have you eaten yet? I'm happy to share my breakfast, if you'd like to sit."

The girl's guileless expression was enough to melt the stoniest of hearts.

Still, Rae was no fool.

There's more to this Nefermaat than what she seems, she thought. A young girl didn't get to be both a priestess and the pharaoh's favorite by being a simpleton. *She is close to Meryamun, so it would behoove me to get close to her too. Who knows what she might tell me, if she let her own guard down?*

Rae bowed her head in reply to the invitation. "Thank you, Priestess. I would like that."

"Call me Neff," the girl said, and gestured to the cushion across the table.

Rae sat, feeling unusually nervous as she watched the girl pile bread and cheese, fruit, and a slice of some kind of egg dish onto a plate and hand it to her. Once Neff started in on her soup, Rae began to eat.

As expected, it was the best meal she'd ever eaten. The egg dish, cooked with an abundance of onion and parsley, was particularly good. Rae nearly asked for seconds but reconsidered and stayed quiet. As if reading her mind, the girl cut another piece and slid it onto Rae's plate.

"So, Ahura," Neff said casually. "Tell me a little about yourself. You're not from Thonis, are you?"

Rae froze, a chunk of bread lifted halfway to her mouth. She was starting to regret using her mother's name as her alias, and she hadn't bothered to come up with a backstory for the person she was pretending to be. Hadn't Tam recommended she do that?

She shoved the food in her mouth, using the time she spent chewing to come up with an answer. "I'm from Bubas, actually," she said. *It's the nearest High Khetaran town,* she reasoned. *Besides, I bet this highborn girl rarely sets foot outside the palace, so she probably doesn't know much about the villages anyway.*

"Bubas, you say?" the girl replied with interest. "Is that where your father lives? When we met, you said you needed this job to help him."

Rae nodded, hesitant to elaborate. She sensed that this girl was clever enough to ensnare her if her web of lies became too tangled. Instead, Rae said something that was undeniably true. "I love my father. I would do anything for him."

The girl regarded her with dark, bottomless eyes. "I feel the same about mine." She dipped a piece of bread in her soup and ate it. "What about your mother? Does she need help too?"

Rae's eyes dropped to her empty plate. "My mother is dead. She died when I was very young."

"I'm so sorry," Neff said softly.

She means it, Rae thought, taking in the seer's solemn face. *Who is this girl?* She wasn't at all what Rae expected from the villainous, bloodthirsty king's closest confidant.

Neff reached for her cup of beer. "You know, Ahura is my mother's name."

Rae suddenly went cold. "It is?"

"I haven't been able to see her since I came to the palace," Neff went on. "Every night when I go to sleep, I wish she was here with me, telling me not to forget to wear my sandals and to look out for scorpions. When you told me your name in the courtyard, I knew you were sent for a reason. I knew that the gods had given me a sign we were meant to be together."

Rae had a strange sensation of arriving at a place she'd been before, whether in dreams or in a story the gods had been whispering in her ear from the moment she was born.

The river will get its way, in the end.

"I thought you'd had a vision," Rae said, shaken.

"I did—but I was only guessing that it was about you. The messages of the gods are not always easy to interpret. Do you think I guessed right, Ahura?"

"I…I…" Rae stammered.

Crash!

Both Rae and Neff looked to the window ledge. The striped cat had knocked over a wooden cup full of reed pens, scattering them to the floor. The cat didn't seem interested in the pens, though. She was focused on something in front of her. She pawed and hissed.

Except nothing was there.

"What's wrong with your cat?" Rae asked, grateful for the interruption. She shivered and glanced about the room, suddenly overtaken by the sense that they were being watched.

"Oh, nothing," Neff replied, rising to collect the pens. "Cats are Bast's creatures, and they share of some of the goddess's powers. They protect us, bring us good luck and pleasure, and have the power to…" The girl's expression turned distant, like she'd remembered something very important. "To see things we can't," she finished.

"What kind of things?" Rae asked.

Neff peered at Rae as if she'd only just remembered she was there. "I'm sorry. It's gotten late. I must finish getting dressed and attend to my duties. You can remove the tray."

There was a formality to the girl's voice that hadn't been there before, reminding them both that they were not friends, but servant and master.

"Of course, Priestess," Rae said, quickly getting to her feet.

Neff's forehead crinkled.

"Of course, Neff," Rae corrected herself, hoisting the significantly lighter tray off the table. "Is there anything else?"

The young seer paused. "There is, actually. But first I must ask… Can I trust you, Ahura?"

A prickle of unease ran down the back of Rae's neck. Why was Neff asking her that question?

Perhaps I'm not alone in my lies, Rae thought. Nefermaat, she was certain, was keeping secrets too. But did the girl suspect Rae's true intent? If she did, it didn't show. Still, Neff was a royal priestess—a *seer*. Surely she knew danger when it was right in front of her, sharing her meal!

Her game doesn't matter, so long as it doesn't interfere with mine, Rae told herself. *Just play along.*

"You can trust me," Rae answered.

Neff nodded. "Good. I need you to take a message to Prince Bakenamun at the Temple of Amun. You are not to hand it to anyone but him." She bent to retrieve a small scroll sealed with wax and held it out to Rae.

"I was told to take care of your laundry after delivering the morning meal," Rae said, hesitant.

"The laundry can wait until your return. No one will trouble you about my dirty clothes."

Balancing the tray on one hand, Rae took the scroll and bowed her head. "It will be done," she said.

With several more awkward bows, Rae exited the chamber. She took a moment to scan the corridors for guards and—finding none—hurried back to the kitchens to drop off the breakfast tray. She could have sworn that she'd felt a presence in that room, someone watching them while Neff assailed her with questions. *Maybe the cat was onto something, after all.*

Hurrying as quickly as she could in her tight dress, Rae nearly walked right past Tamerit as the weaver was leaving the kitchens carrying two jars of wine. She'd seen her that morning in the maidservants' quarters where they both slept, but because other people were always around, they hadn't had the opportunity to exchange information since the day before.

"It's so good to see you, Tam—I mean, ah…"

"Herit," Tam prompted.

"Right." Rae was having the worst time remembering to use the aliases.

Tam rolled her eyes. "Any news?" she whispered.

"Yes! I found out where they're keeping the prisoners!" Rae said proudly.

"Oh! Good!"

Rae's shoulders slumped. "You knew already, didn't you?"

"I found out yesterday. It's helpful information, though. Really it is!"

"Don't patronize me."

"I'm not!"

Rae raised an eyebrow.

Tam shifted the conversation. "Don't you want to hear what I've learned?"

Rae wanted to be annoyed but couldn't manage it. She'd never seen Tamerit so excited, so *alive*. Apparently, the subterfuge that made Rae's skin itch made Tam feel right at home. Rae wanted to kiss her. "Tell me."

Tam's eyes darted back and forth, ensuring no one was within earshot. Then she proceeded to share all she'd heard from the other servants—about Amunmose's personal guard and servants' death at the hand of the new king, the princess's flight, Queen Bintanath's strange behavior in the aftermath of the coronation, and the many theories as to why the Iteru had temporarily turned the color of blood. It spilled out of the weaver in a great torrent, and Rae struggled to absorb everything she was told.

"All this you learned since *yesterday*?" Rae asked.

Tam nodded. "Nebet is especially happy to speak with me. She's been quite lonely since Sitamun left."

"Do you know *all* their names?"

Tam looked offended. "Of course I do!"

By the gods, Rae thought miserably, *I am terrible at this.*

"And," Tam added, almost as an afterthought, "I've received an invitation. Well, more of a summons, I suppose."

Rae felt a twinge of apprehension. "An invitation to...?"

"To a party of some kind." Tam bit her lip and looked away. "In the pharaoh's chambers."

A rush of heat flooded Rae's face. "What?" she exclaimed, too loudly.

"Shh!"

Other servants passed by carrying bowls of fruit and gave them a curious look. Tam smiled and nodded hello. The two women greeted her—by name—and continued on.

"Keep your head, will you?" she whisper-shouted at Rae. "This is exactly why we came here! Who knows what kind of secret information I might glean from being close to the king?"

"Too close, in my opinion..." Rae muttered.

"I can handle myself. Or don't you trust me?"

Rae closed her eyes, willing the fury building inside her to recede. She took several deep, cleansing breaths, then replied, "I trust you."

What she didn't say was: *It's the king I don't trust. It's everyone in this accursed palace I don't trust.*

"Good," Tam said. "I'll go to the party tonight, and you find that chamber where they're holding the prisoners. We'll figure out what to do next in the morning."

Before the weaver could resume her duties, Rae reached out with her free hand and grabbed Tam's wrist. "Please be careful."

Tam—or, rather, "Herit"—gave her a single crisp nod and departed.

A party, Rae thought as she stepped back into the hot, steamy kitchens.

Without thinking, her hand curled into a fist.

11
RAE

Rae was still brooding over Tam's party invitation when she reached the Temple of Amun's towering gate. *Focus!* she told herself. She was about to deliver Neff's message to Prince Bakenamun, and if he was anything like his wicked brother, she needed to keep her wits about her.

She squinted up at the temple. Like everything else in Thonis, it was so magnificent that it made Sakesh's Temple of Ra look like a hovel in comparison. The Low Khetaran priests kept up their duties as well as they could, but their numbers were small and their offerings meager at best.

Not that Ra's House had always been that way. Before the Great War, it had been an awesome place, full of light and bedecked in gold, as befitted the falcon-headed sun god. At least, that's what Rae's father always told her.

Father.

It was torture, being so close to him, yet not knowing for certain that he was alive and unharmed.

I'll see him tonight, she thought with hope in her heart. *And then I'll find a way to get him home*. Hovel or not, the Temple of Ra was a holy place, and she would make sure her father saw it again.

Squaring her shoulders, Rae approached the guard standing at the temple gate.

"Greetings to you," she said with a stiff bow, "I have come with a message for Prince Bakenamun."

"I'll take it," the guard said, and offered her an open palm.

"I've been ordered to deliver it directly to him."

"By whom?"

"That isn't your concern." Rae took a step closer to the man so that they were eye to eye. "Now, are you going to inform the prince of my arrival, or do we have a problem?"

For one thrilling instant, Rae thought the guard might put up a fight—but he was either too lazy or too gutless, because he huffed in annoyance and strode away. Rae was almost disappointed. It felt good to throw her weight around again. That, at least, was something she excelled at.

A few minutes passed before the guard returned with a very small, very strange man at his side. *This is the prince?* Rae thought in confusion. He barely came up to her shoulders.

Prince Bakenamun peered up at Rae over a beakish nose, his unruly nest of black hair making him appear as if he'd just rolled out of bed. He looked nothing like the king. It was a wonder they were brothers at all.

The prince dismissed the guard, who plodded to the other side of the gate, clearly put out over the entire situation.

"You're Neff's girl, are you?" Bakenamun asked.

"I am."

He studied Rae with such intensity that it made her uncomfortable. He seemed to take in every detail of her face and body—but not in a lewd way. From the way he looked at her, she may as well have been an interesting plant.

Only when his examination was complete did the prince speak further. "Fascinating," he said simply. He cleared his throat. "You have a message for me?"

Rae handed him the sealed scroll.

"Very good," the prince said, tucking it into his tunic. "I have something for you to take back to Nefermaat as well." From his belt, he pulled a black leather cylinder, which Rae assumed must contain another scroll. She was about to stick it in her belt when the carnelian amulet on its lid gave her pause. It was a red lion, not unlike her own amulet.

The symbol of Sekhmet.

Sekhmet was a fierce protector, but she was also famously brutal. According to the doctrine, the lion-headed goddess had once nearly destroyed the entire world in a fit of rage. She was vengeance personified. She was the Lady of Slaughter.

Why would young Nefermaat need a scroll such as this? Rae wondered. *And why would the prince give it to her? Are the two of them colluding on a secret plan of their own? That would explain why Neff questioned my allegiance before sending me on this errand.*

"Do you miss it?"

The prince's question snapped Rae out of her reverie. "Miss what?"

"Working on the farm."

Rae went rigid. *How could he possibly know?*

"The tan lines, the state of your hands—everything about you gives it away," the prince said casually, reading her thoughts. "I'm curious what brings a young woman of your obvious skills and unusual stature to a position serving in the palace. Pardon me for saying so, but you seem ill-suited for the job."

Rae considered her next words carefully. Like Nefermaat, the prince had an uncanny ability to see to the truth of things. "I did it for my father," she said.

Her answer seemed to sting the prince. "I see."

Does he mourn his own father? Rae wondered. She didn't like to think of Amunmose as a real person with grieving children, and yet Bakenamun's pained expression forced her to.

The prince held up Neff's scroll. "Thank you for this," he said thickly, and turned away.

Rae hurried back to the palace, chilled by the encounter. One more trip to see the prince, and he'd have her whole life story figured out! She'd have to do her best to avoid him.

She touched the Sekhmet scroll at her belt, wishing it was the sekhem scepter instead. Ever since she recovered it from the House of the Medjay, the weapon had become part of her, and she felt naked without it. She knew it was safe at their camp by the river, but her fingers itched to grip something real, something more than all the secrets and intrigue she found herself handling in the palace. A force was building inside her, like water behind a dam, demanding release.

Not yet, she told herself. *Soon, but not yet.*

After delivering the scroll to Nefermaat's chambers and assisting with the midday meal, Rae searched the palace for the entrance to the subterranean level while delivering clean linens. It was a massive building, so it took her the better part of the afternoon to locate the proper stairwell. As she walked by, she noted the single guard, and a shadowy corner behind a column where she could conceal herself to keep watch. When the guard inevitably left his post to make water that night, she'd make her move.

The rest of the day flew by. Between all her household duties and dealings with the bad-tempered cook, Rae barely had a moment to sit down. *I wish I were back in the fields*, she thought wearily. At least the zebu didn't complain about the quality of her work.

That evening in the maidservants' chambers, she noted how many women—Tamerit included—didn't return from their duties. How seven beds remained empty, even after thick darkness fell.

Some of the other women whispered about it, but none of them whispered to her. Unlike Tam, she hadn't made any friends. Trying not to think about what might be happening at the party, Rae lay down, closed her eyes, and pretended to sleep.

She waited until every last candle had been blown out, until the sounds of shifting bodies had mellowed to soft, rhythmic snores. Then, she rose on silent feet, changed her clothes, and slipped into the dim corridor and through the quiet palace halls. She'd spent the evening planning her route, setting out the loose black dress she'd acquired so that she'd be less visible, deciding how she'd deal with the guard if he refused to leave his post. She was ready for anything.

Rae reached the end of a corridor. To the right was the path to the stairwell leading underground. To the left was the king's chambers.

She paused, listening as the lilt of music, peals of laughter, and feathery, hair-raising cries of pleasure floated into her ears like an intoxicating breeze.

Rae's carefully laid plans suddenly vanished from her mind. All she could think of were those sounds, and whether Tamerit was the one making them.

The voice of reason pleaded with her. *Father is waiting for you!*

The roar of the lion was louder.

She turned left.

Rae intercepted one of the seven missing servants on her way to the king's chambers. The young woman staggered, carrying a blue long-necked wine jar painted with lotus flowers.

"Why don't I take that?" Rae said, reaching out for the jar. "You look like you've had enough for one night."

"Hey!" The servant wrenched the jar to her chest. "I didn't see you at the party. Were you even invited? Only the king's *favorite girls* were invited." She hiccupped.

"Yes, well, he saved the best for last," Rae said.

"Maybe the *biggest*..."

Rae drew herself up to her full height. "You say that as if it's a bad thing."

The servant shrunk under Rae's imposing gaze and released the jar. "I'll go to bed."

"Good idea."

When the servant had scurried off, Rae hefted the jar into her hands, took a deep breath, and strode to the pharaoh's quarters.

The two guards at the door gave her a strange look when she appeared, but when they saw her carrying the blue lotus jar, they waved her in.

The air inside the chamber was so thick with incense it made Rae's eyes water. She glanced around the semidarkness, trying to get her bearings. The room was immense and loud and filled with flickering firelight.

And hot. By the gods, it's hot.

Then she saw—really *saw*—what was going on.

A sea of hands, glistening skin, open mouths, dark hair tossed to the beat of drums. Women dressed in transparent linen shifts and revealing bead-net dresses and almost nothing at all, each holding blue cups in the shape of lotus flowers. Men in thigh-length schentis, chests heaving with barely controlled breath, lotus cups gripped in their hands, too, rested on couches and chairs and mats on the floor, their eyes dark with intensity. Couples danced to the music, their bodies so entangled that they appeared as a single insatiable creature.

Rae's head swam. A rush of heat bloomed in her belly, making her feel simultaneously embarrassed and exhilarated. She stood rigid, the wine jar held in front of her like a shield, her mouth dry, unable to move, unable to tear her gaze from the scene.

Then she saw the pharaoh.

King Meryamun reclined in a cushioned, low-backed chair, chatting amiably with another man, who sat opposite him. Half a dozen women attended to them both, bringing trays of fruit and rubbing their feet and shoulders with oils. With a jolt, Rae recognized the woman rubbing the pharaoh's feet. As if sensing that she was being watched, the woman turned. When she saw Rae standing there, her heavy-lidded seduction turned to fury.

What are you doing here? Tam mouthed.

Rae's heart began to race. *This was a mistake. I should never have come. I have to leave before—*

"Who is that?"

The king had noticed her.

"Ah! Nefermaat's pet, come to play?" he called out. "I don't remember inviting you, but seeing as you've brought more of my special wine, I'll allow it." He beckoned her forward, and Rae had no choice but to obey. She approached them, skirting dancing girls and couples on the floor as she went.

"Get her a cup, will you?" King Meryamun said to Tam. "If she's to join the party, she must do so properly."

Tam bowed her head and handed Rae a lotus cup. Nervously, Rae poured herself wine from the jug she was carrying.

"Go on," he said. "You're late. You'll have to catch up with the rest of us."

The king watched as she lifted the cup to her lips. Rae had

never had wine before. Was it supposed to smell like flowers? Eager to stop being the center of attention, she gulped it down as quickly as she could.

Meryamun licked his lips. "Good. Have another and then you can attend to my friend here. Wouldn't you like a rub from this great strapping girl, Harsi?"

The other man glanced up at her but said nothing.

While she gulped down another cup of wine, Rae took notice of Harsi's unusually long schenti and green sash, of his square jaw and deep brown face. *He's not Khetaran. Tashan, maybe?* She'd seen similar sashes on men riding boats downriver from Khetara's southern border. *But why does he look like he's been in a street fight?* Even in the dim firelight, she could see the skin beneath one of Harsi's eyes was swollen and purpling and the knuckles of both hands were riddled with cuts.

The pharaoh grinned, toothy and dangerous. "Now, don't be boring, my prince. Don't you like the party? I threw it just for you. To get your mind off the unfortunate loss of your companions." He nodded at Rae.

Mute with helpless rage, Rae sank to her knees, took the Tashan's foot into her hand, and began massaging it.

"See? Isn't that nice?" Meryamun said.

Harsi stared at him but didn't reply.

Meryamun rose from his chair and approached, as languid as a panther. Watching him, Rae began to feel lightheaded. *What was in that wine?*

The young king sauntered behind Harsi's chair and bent over him, hands on the Tashan's shoulders, lips at his ear.

"You want to kill me, don't you?" Meryamun murmured, soft and sensual. "You'd like to put a knife in me, or even better, wrap your fingers around my throat and squeeze. I don't blame you. Revenge is infinitely more satisfying than a foot massage."

He glanced down at Rae and tutted. "The lioness doesn't look like she's enjoying it any more than you are. Though I can't imagine why—you're quite the handsome specimen. Not good enough for my sister, but then, who is?

"I must say, I was quite disappointed when my men failed to find her with you. I would have been forced to punish her severely, but at least I'd have her back. Where is that girl?"

He sighed. "Still, you're not a bad consolation prize. With you as my guest, I'll have Tash prostrate at my feet soon enough."

Listening to this speech, Rae felt chilled. *If Meryamun is willing to murder Tashan ambassadors on a whim, what will he do to the people of Sakesh?*

She needed to act. To get out of that room, find her father, and return home. But her mind was softening like butter, and though she strained to keep hold of it, her grip on reality loosened with every passing second. She began to breathe faster as a wave of unwanted yet unstoppable euphoria crashed over her.

The king noticed.

"You see, Harsi?" he said. "The blue lotus tames everyone, even the lioness. You should have some too." He lifted the wine jar, filled the prince's cup to the brim, and then held it to the Tashan's lips.

It was only when Harsi began to struggle that Rae saw the prince's wrists were tied to the arms of his chair.

"Drink," Meryamun ordered, tilting the cup until red rivulets spilled from the corners of Harsi's mouth. "Drink..."

Rae's head lolled. Suddenly, she was on her back on the floor, with no memory of how she got there. Above her, the ceiling was painted with stars that glittered, and it felt as if everything in the room—the air, the music, her dress—was made of warm honey that dripped over her body and blocked out every other thought.

Tam's face appeared before her, a constellation of stars shining around her head like a halo. "For the love of Ra, why did you drink so much?" she whispered.

"Thought I had to… Didn't you?" Rae's words were slurred. She reached out to touch Tam's hair, and its softness was almost too much to bear.

"I pretended to drink, then spit it into a potted plant," Tam replied.

A shadow fell over them.

"Is this why you weren't interested in the good prince?" the king asked Rae. He reached down and tangled his fingers in Tam's curls, then closed his hand into a fist.

Tam's nostrils flared with pain.

"Well," he went on, releasing her. "You have excellent taste. Please, don't let me stop you. I'll be right here, watching." He resumed his seat in the chair, and the other women fell over him once more, their hands on his shoulders, his chest, offering plump figs and dates to his lips.

The stars on the ceiling were so bright and golden and beautiful they made Rae want to cry. Some small part of her understood what was going on and roared because she too wanted to put a knife in the king, wanted to tear him apart and taste his blood…

But then the violence melted into desire and made her dizzy. She could see the anxiety in Tam's face, but Rae couldn't feel it within herself. All she could feel was the fire on her skin where the weaver's body melted into hers.

"What…what do I do?" she gasped.

Tam pressed her lips into a thin line, and Rae could see the weaver's fear twisting itself into resolve. Gently, Tam cupped Rae's face in her hand and pulled her closer.

"I'll tell you what to do," she whispered. "Forget about the king. Forget about the man tied to the chair. Forget the other people around us. Just look at me, do you understand? Look at me, and forget everything else."

Rae nodded. Then, starving, desperate, she dove headfirst into her lover's arms.

12
KARIM

Karim swung his scythe across the stalks of grain, and they fell at his feet with a satisfying swish.

I could get used to this. He thought of Raetawy, the farm girl he'd met on his journey downriver, to whom he'd given the red lion amulet. He remembered the golden fields of wheat behind her and wondered if she took the same pleasure in harvesting. It was certainly quieter and sweeter-smelling than being a shepherd.

Safer than tomb robbing too.

Karim couldn't blame the Hudjefa for wanting to protect their life in that secret, fertile valley. The oasis provided rich soil for growing grain and vegetables, and there were date palms and fig trees in abundance, likely the progeny of those planted by the ancient city's architects. Knowing what he did about his own people's struggles for survival in the Red Lands—the constant travel, the fear of nighttime raids, the reliance on the herds to provide everything from food to clothing to barter—he could understand the tribe's decision to cut themselves off from the outside world to preserve their way of life. Not that Karim wanted to be trapped in Perset indefinitely, but...

The idea *was* tempting.

He thought of Sitamun. Her smile as they danced in the firelight. The curve of her back against his hand as he held her. The exhilarating softness of her lips as they kissed.

How wonderful it would be to forget everything outside the valley, as the Hudjefa had done! What a relief to cast off the burden of the past, to be tomb robber and princess no more, and start life anew in that hidden paradise!

He swung the scythe again and again, allowing his mind to fill with pleasant, preposterous thoughts.

"Karim-sen! Why are you still working? It's time to eat!"

The voice pulled Karim from his daydreaming. Young Aya stood beside the field in a long brown dress, her dark hair untamed.

"Oh! I must have lost track of time," he said, lowering the blade.

"Sita sent me," Aya went on. "She made bread and wants you to have some. It's a bit burnt, but she seems very excited about it. She says if you don't come soon, she'll feed it to the dog, because 'at least Behkai will appreciate it.'"

Karim smiled. "Did she now?" *That woman is taking this ruse of being married quite seriously*. "I shouldn't keep her waiting then, hey?"

Together, they made their way from the field toward the houses. As they walked, Aya regaled Karim with stories about what colors her friends liked, how horrible it was the time she ate a rotten fig, and why snakes "aren't actually so bad." The girl had been spending more and more time with him and the princess since Sami's miraculous recovery, helping around the house, playing with Behkai, and talking. She talked so much, in fact, Karim wondered if she ever stopped to take a breath. He didn't mind, though. Aya reminded him of his sisters when they were little—though he tried not to think of them too often. The shame of not going back for them and his mother, of abandoning them after his fight with the other Jackals, was too painful to contemplate.

It was one more memory from his past that he almost wished he could forget.

"Zev still doesn't like you, you know."

Karim turned to Aya, who had become very serious. "No? I'm not surprised. Zev doesn't seem to like much of anything."

"He says you and Sita are pretending to like it here, and that one day you'll run back home and tell on us." She kicked a rock and watched it skitter down the path. "Are you really going to run away, Karim-sen?"

Karim tried to disguise his discomfort. That was, in fact, exactly what he and Sita were planning to do. Since the day they'd arrived, they'd been slowly collecting supplies, as well as using every free moment to explore the ruins. So far, other than a few choice artifacts that they'd found inside Setnakht's palace, they hadn't discovered anything useful about the ancient pharaoh. Karim knew that soon they'd need to cut their losses and make their way back to Khetara—but the thought of doing so became more difficult with each passing day. They'd made friends in the city, had lived and worked alongside their neighbors. Sita had saved a life. Strange as it seemed, Perset had begun to feel like a second home.

Instead of answering Aya's question, Karim asked one of his own. "You know, you never told us why *you* ran away. Why we found you alone in the middle of the desert."

"I wanted to see," Aya replied.

"See what?"

Aya threw up her hands. "Everything! I want to have adventures! But Sabba says we mustn't leave the valley because there are mean people who want to hurt us. He doesn't even like it when I explore the city! All because I got bit by a scorpion one time. The day I ran away, I'd found something out by the palace. I tried to get someone to come look at it, but they were all too busy."

Karim stopped short.

There it was. That familiar tug, like a rope around his chest pulling him toward secrets buried and forgotten.

Aya went on, bouncing on her heels beside him. "I was so mad that I got my bag and left. I wanted them to miss me and feel bad about ignoring me." She bit her lip and peered up at Karim. "But after you and Sita found me and the storm came, I got scared. So I ran home while she was looking for you."

"Aya," Karim said slowly. "What did you find out by the palace?"

The little girl beamed. "Something *wonderful*."

Karim swallowed, his instincts tingling. As surely as the sun rises, he knew that whatever Aya had found would bring an end to his life in Perset. Whatever it was would change everything.

Karim ought to have been thrilled. They'd been scouring the city for something, anything to aid them in the battle against Setnakht, and Aya may have found it.

And yet, all Karim felt was dread.

He thought of Sita waiting for him in the house they shared, delighted to have baked a loaf of bread with her own hands. The princess had changed so much since they'd arrived. She worked long shifts in the bakery, as if every bowl of flour she ground was atonement for her past. She'd begun to teach the other women basic techniques for treating wounds and other ailments, so they too could have the power to heal. Every day, Karim saw her light—hidden for so long—shine a little brighter.

He felt it too. Even now, knowing the answer to their prayers might be buried nearby, he longed to go home to Sitamun. To finish his work in the fields, then return to luxuriate in the lie they'd built together. The lie that had become so comfortable that it felt almost like the truth.

Karim scolded himself for such selfish thoughts. *Wake up, you fool. You have slept on your task long enough. You cannot escape who you are. Neither can the princess. What we have is fleeting. It blooms only here, only now, and never again.*

"I'm sorry no one listened to you before," he said to the little girl. "But I'm listening. Will you show me?"

Aya squealed in delight. "Yes!" She took his hand and tugged him toward the distant ruins.

"Right now? What about lunch?"

"Let her give it to the dog. Come on!"

Karim allowed himself to be dragged down the path, feeling like a boat that pulled anchor and was being swept away by a fast-moving current.

As he went, he mourned the bread that he'd never get to taste.

After a short walk, Aya led Karim to a large open area west of the palace. Unlike the verdant land on the east side, which was close to the oasis, nothing grew there except scrub bushes. In fact, there wasn't much to see besides some broken stone archways and pillars, which lay half buried in the sand.

Overwhelmed with excitement, Aya released Karim's hand and dashed through the ruins.

"Look! It's over here!" she exclaimed.

Karim jogged up to her, amazed. The sand had been cleared away to reveal a huge black granite statue, which must have stood at the height of three men before it fell onto its side and was buried over time.

How in the world did Sita and I miss this? he wondered. They'd been so focused on searching the palace, they hadn't considered looking that far afield.

"Isn't she pretty?" Aya asked, sweeping her fingers across the statue's serene face.

It was a statue of a kneeling woman with one hand raised, her palm facing toward her in a mysterious gesture. She wore a pillar-like crown on her head, topped with what appeared to be a basket.

"Can you read what it says?" Aya asked, pointing to a line of Khetaran writing engraved on the statue's back.

"No, but Sita can. We must fetch her right away. But first I want to check something."

Standing beside the statue, Karim turned in a slow circle, surveying the open land around him, noting the placement of the ruined archways, the crumbled pillars. Then, without warning, he dropped to the ground and lay flat on his belly.

"I want to try!" Aya said and flopped down next to him. She was silent, staring off into the distance before spitting sand out of her mouth and asking, "What are we doing?"

"The people who built Perset probably chose this location because the valley is flat, hey?" Karim said.

Aya nodded. "If you built a house on a hill, it would fall down!"

"Right. And as you can see from this angle, the land around us is very flat. But you can also see that this area we're in is lower than the ground around it."

"You mean… The ground fell down, like the statue?"

Karim got back to his feet and brushed the sand from his clothes. "Exactly, young sena! That would explain why the arches and pillars collapsed. If the land beneath them sank, it would have caused them to topple."

"But why would the land sink?" Aya asked.

Karim smiled, smelling smoke and honey on the wind. "Because there's something built underneath it."

Aya's eyes bulged. "So...what I found...it's good?"

His sorrows momentarily forgotten, Karim grasped the girl by her shoulders and declared, "Aya-sena, it is incredible! You are a genius!"

"I am?" the girl asked, confused and delighted. "I am!"

"Now, go quickly and fetch Sita. Tell her to bring a chisel, my bow drill, and a torch. And Aya, let's keep this discovery to ourselves, hey? I don't want the whole tribe descending upon us until we know what we're dealing with."

"I am a genius!" Aya said, by way of agreement, and took off running.

Allowing that invisible rope to lead him, Karim wandered the area before stopping in a place that felt different than the rest. Falling to his knees, he pushed his fingers into the hot sand, searching for the prize that would lead to all other prizes, the gateway to triumph or ruin or both.

Searching for a door.

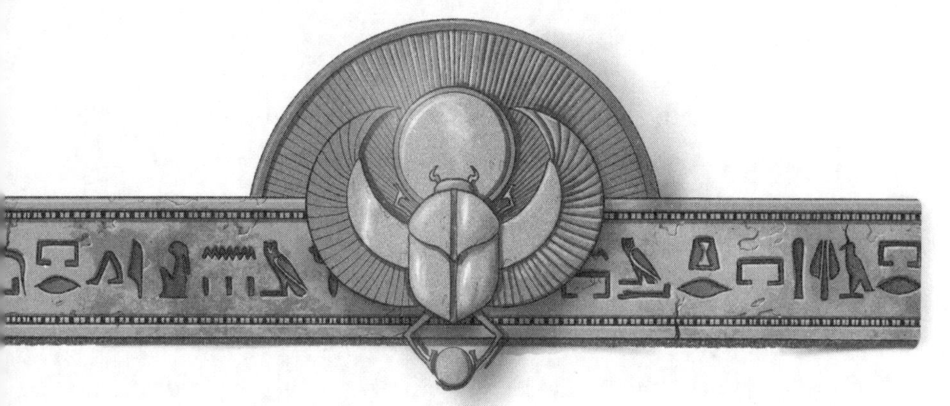

13
KARIM

Karim was still working in that same spot when Sita arrived, weighed down like a donkey with tools and supplies.

"Is it true? Did you and Aya really find something?" she asked, pink-cheeked and panting.

"It's true!" Karim said, getting to his feet. "Here, let me help you with all that." He lifted the packs from her shoulders and set them on the ground. "Where is the young sena?"

"I sent her to fetch a jug of fresh water. I thought we'd need it."

"Right. Well, I'm glad you're here."

Unexpectedly alone with the princess, Karim wasn't sure whether to kiss or embrace her or do nothing at all. Had she only kissed him that night because it was expected of a husband and wife, and because everyone had been watching? It had felt real... but maybe Karim had been imagining something that wasn't really there.

Sita looked away, suddenly very concerned about the state of her hair. Finally, she broke the tension and said, "Show me this great discovery of yours!"

Karim led her to the half-buried statue.

Sita identified the figure straightaway. "That's Nepthys, goddess of the night and childbirth. You can tell it's her because of her distinctive headdress—a house with a basket on top." She smiled faintly, then added, "Supposedly, she is the goddess who named my brother Mery."

"Is that so?" Karim asked, unconvinced.

"If you believe the stories. But why include a statue of her here? I thought Setnakht worshipped Set alone, forsaking all other gods. Unless…"

Sita squatted behind the statue, squinting at the words written there. "'Nepthys,'" she read. "'Lady of the House. Sister of Isis. Mother of Anubis. Beloved of Set."

"She's Set's wife!" Karim exclaimed.

Sita nodded. "That must be the connection. Do you see the position of her body? Kneeling, with one palm facing herself? That's the traditional gesture of a mourning woman. It makes sense to see Nepthys depicted this way, because among her other titles, she was also a protector of the dead." Sita stood, and her brow furrowed. "But what dead is she protecting? There are no tombs here."

Karim grabbed Sita's hand and pulled her toward the place he'd been working. "Ah, but princess, I think there are."

When Sita saw what he'd uncovered, she gasped. "Is that—?"

"An entrance to an underground structure? Yes, I think it is. And if I'm right, it's big. Very big."

Sita knelt in front of the large rectangular stone that was set into the ground, and traced her fingers across the writing engraved there.

"'All that begins starts in darkness; and all that ends returns there. Night is the mother of all things. May I ever rest in her arms, among the imperishable stars.'" She turned to Karim. "This sounds like a prayer for a mortuary temple. It's one thing to dig out a valley wall for a tomb, but quite another to erect an entire temple underground. It's impossible, isn't it?"

Karim took up a large copper chisel and held it out to her. "Only one way to find out."

Sita bit her lip, hesitating.

Karim chuckled. "Your gods led us here, sena. I think they'll forgive a bit of heresy, just this once."

Sita suppressed a smile and took the chisel. "You know, you're pretty smart…for a dog."

"I'm going to tell Behkai you said that," Karim replied. "He'll be very upset with you."

"No, he knows I hold him in high esteem."

"He'll drool all over you."

"Only because he likes me."

Karim raised an eyebrow. *Something else the dog and I have in common.*

Sita smirked. "So? Where do we start?"

Using his hammer, Karim helped Sita wedge the chisel between the slab and the top of the stone structure. After that, they were able to insert another chisel into the opening, and they worked together to raise the slab enough to slip a rope underneath it. Then, with the slab propped above its frame, they dug in their heels and heaved at the rope, pulling with bursts of force until the stone slid aside, revealing a dark portal beneath.

Dripping with sweat, the sun beating down on his head, Karim dropped the rope and squatted to peer into the abyss. "There are stone steps leading underground. At least we won't need ropes to lower ourselves inside." He stood and slung his pack of supplies over one shoulder.

Sita didn't move. She stared down into the hole, her face unreadable.

"Are you all right, sena?" Karim asked.

Sita swallowed, then bent to retrieve the other pack. "I'm fine. Let's go."

Using his bow drill, Karim lit the torch and took the first cautious step down. The torchlight illuminated the stone steps ahead, but he could not see where they led.

They descended slowly, and before long, the square of daylight behind them shrank to a pinprick.

It was all so familiar: the cool darkness, the quiet, the muted aroma of old and forgotten things. It made Karim think of his life before—his family, his tribe. Djet. Suddenly, he felt as if the boy was at his side again, whispering excitedly in his ear.

What do you think is in there, hey?

"Answers, I hope," Karim murmured.

"Did you say something?" Sita asked from behind him.

"Just talking to myself." He squinted into the gloom. "I think we're close to the bottom. I see a landing ahead."

Once he reached the landing, Karim stepped out into an open chamber. Although it was difficult to see beyond the small circle of firelight, the shadows of monoliths loomed above him. Karim could feel the vastness of the space in the air, could hear it in the way his breath broke the stillness. A chill ran up his spine.

He swept his torch around him and saw what looked like two parallel trenches built into the stone floor, each about a hand's breadth wide, that ran straight into the darkness ahead. Each trench was filled with what appeared to be animal fat, with a thick rope set along the middle, as if placed there while the fat was liquid hot.

In all his travels, Karim had never seen anything like it. *Could it be what I think it is?* he wondered. Curious, Karim lowered his torch to the tip of one rope and set it aflame.

The effect was instantaneous.

Karim laughed, delighted, and lit the second channel.

Twin trails of fire blazed forward from where Karim and Sita stood, racing into the distance, illuminating everything along the way.

They were standing at the end of an enormous columned hall, the ceiling so high above them that it remained lost in darkness. Every surface boasted pictures painted in red and black and gold: sharp-beaked vultures, sycamore trees, and dark-eyed women who watched Karim with eerie intensity. Many of the columns were cracked and leaning, and bits of loose stone littered the ground. It was as Karim had thought: Over time, the underground structure had shifted and sunk, causing the earth above it to sink too. Arched doorways—so many that Karim lost count—ran along both sides of the hall.

Sita gasped and raised a hand to her mouth. "By Amun, I've never seen its equal."

Karim whistled. "I'm accustomed to cramped tombs with no more than four chambers. There must be hundreds of rooms in this place! It would take days, perhaps weeks, to explore each passage. What are we going to do?"

Sita shrugged. "What else? Start at the beginning." She strode past him toward the first door on their left, inspecting the wall paintings as she went.

Karim meant to follow her, but he found himself rooted in place. A strange, familiar sensation overtook him, just as it had on that plateau in the desert. As if instructed by an unseen force, he fell to his knees, leaned forward, and touched his forehead to the ground.

Faintly, he heard Sita call to him. "Come over here. There's something you should see..."

Karim sat up, and time shifted. Around him, the broken

columns were restored, and the fire burned more brightly, filling the hall with dazzling light. Red-robed priests flowed in and out of the archways carrying all manner of items, and the chamber echoed with hymns chanted in the name of Set. Karim could hear the words being spoken on his own lips, though not with his voice, and when the hymn was finished, he felt himself rise to his feet. He towered over the priest standing beside him.

"Is the temple to your satisfaction, my king?" the priest asked.

Karim heard himself say, "It is as I envisioned. Tell me: How many of my acolytes perished constructing it?"

The priest pressed a finger to his mouth. "At least a hundred, my king. Perhaps more. I'd have to refer to my records to be precise."

The deep voice said, "Make sure they are all entombed here, in the arms of Mother Night. They died in her service and shall be rewarded in the Duat. Save the largest chamber for my beloved. For as Set tore his betrayer into fourteen pieces, so the seventh door to the seventh door shall lead to the house of my queen."

Sita's voice sliced through the vision like a knife. "Karim! Are you coming?"

Karim heard that deep voice say one final prayer as the scene vanished around him. "May she live forever in the West."

Karim gasped. He was prostrate on the floor, bathed in a cold sweat, his heart hammering.

Sita stood over him, concerned. "What happened? Are you hurt?"

Karim stumbled to his feet. "No, sena. I..." He hesitated. He hadn't shared the vision he'd had in the desert. He'd been too afraid.

But he couldn't keep the truth to himself any longer.

He pressed a hand against the scarab-shaped scar on his chest. "The amulet...my heart...I think it's imprinted with Setnakht's memories. When I stand in certain places, places where he himself stood long ago, I can see what happened there through his eyes."

Sita stared at him. "That is powerful magic."

Karim licked his lips. "It is as if I am in his body, watching events from a thousand years ago."

"How many times has this happened?"

"Twice. The first was back in the desert, which is how I knew where to find the lost city. And again, just now."

"Why didn't you tell me?"

The hurt in her eyes stung him. "Because…because…"

"Because you don't trust me?"

"No!" His voice echoed in the cavernous space. "I do trust you," he added quietly. He wanted to say that he was afraid the revelation might change the way she looked at him, that she might see the seed of evil sprouting in his soul and recoil, but he couldn't form the words.

Seeing the anguish on his face, Sita softened and placed her hand on his. "I was the one who put that amulet inside you. Whatever burden that act placed on your shoulders is mine to carry too."

Karim nodded, warmed by her words.

"So tell me, what did you see?"

He described the vision to her, doing his best to repeat Setnakht's conversation with the red priest word for word.

Sita scoffed. "Ignoring the fact that Setnakht completely misinterpreted the story of Osiris, what he said is extremely useful. He said that his queen was to be entombed here. If anyone knew Setnakht's deepest secrets, it would have been his wife. We have to find her."

"The seventh door to the seventh door," Karim said.

"Exactly!"

They hurried to the nearest doorway, and Sita noted the little arch and five slashes carved into the stone wall beside it. "The doors are numbered. This one is fifteen. We need to find the one marked with a seven."

"Here!" Karim called after a few minutes of searching.

Together, they entered the dark passage, the firelight from the hall fading behind them. Karim held his torch high as they came to the first doorway. Sure enough, it was marked with one slash.

"This place is a maze," he said as they progressed deeper into the temple, counting the doors as they went.

"Amun help us if we get lost," Sita said, and slid a little closer to him.

After what seemed like a long time, they finally reached the seventh door. The darkness behind and beyond them was so thick, it was almost palpable. Karim thrust his torch through the doorway, hoping Sita wouldn't notice the way his hand shook. It was all too reminiscent of Setnakht's tomb. The stale air. The weight of the earth pressing down upon him. The oppressive silence. He could almost feel a presence moving in the shadows behind them, breathing, waiting for the right moment…

Stop it, you fool!

Sita stepped into the chamber ahead of him, holding a candle aloft. She turned in a circle and frowned. "There's nothing here."

"Nothing?" Karim followed her inside. The room was indeed empty. It wasn't a particularly large room, although it did have an array of paintings on its walls. Karim sighed in frustration. "Perhaps Setnakht changed his mind and put her somewhere else."

"What should we do now?"

"I don't know…"

Karim moved to study one of the images. It looked like a family portrait. There was a man and a woman facing each other, painted in the same strange style as the figures he saw in

Setnakht's tomb. The man was clearly the pharaoh himself. He wore a crown with a serpent at his brow, and Karim recognized the familiar symbols for Setnakht's name below the image. The woman must be his queen, but she wore no crown. Instead, she was bald and had little eyes on each side of her chest, much like the young seer at the Temple of Amun.

"Setnakht's wife was a priestess," he said. "And I think they had a son." He pointed to the small, naked figure in the woman's arms.

Sitamun squinted at the writing below the woman's picture. "Her name was Queen Anet. No mention of the child's name."

"He had everything," Karim said bitterly, gesturing toward the idyllic family scene. "A wife, a son, riches beyond measure, a kingdom at his feet. Was that not enough?"

Sita's expression was solemn. "In some men, power creates a thirst that cannot be quenched, no matter how much of it they drink. Perhaps Setnakht was such a man." Her eyes darkened. "My brother is one too." She moved to the center of the room, shining her candle onto the paintings around her. "What I don't understand is: There are images of the queen all over this chamber, which leads me to believe your vision brought us to the right place. But where is her tomb? Where are her grave goods?"

The ground beneath Karim's feet trembled, and a sudden grinding sound filled the air. In the space of an instant, a black hole opened in the stone floor where Sita was standing.

The princess shrieked and was gone.

Karim leaped toward the hole and stared over the edge, screaming her name. "Sita! Can you hear me? *Sitamun!*" He squinted into the blackness, begging every god who would listen to spare the princess's life.

In the gloom, he spied a pinprick of light.

The candle!

Somehow, the flame hadn't gone out.

He heard a soft groan.

"Sitamun!"

"I'm...I'm all right."

Karim nearly collapsed with relief. He dropped down on his belly next to the hole and lowered his torch into it. A weak tendril of firelight reached Sita's upturned face. She blinked up at him, a slash of blood across her cheek.

"Trapdoor?" Karim asked.

"Trapdoor."

He watched as Sita pushed herself out of the rubble and onto her feet. She hissed, then leaned against the wall of the pit. "I twisted my ankle in the fall."

"Is it broken?"

There was a pause. "No, I don't think so."

Karim pulled the rope from his pack. "Hold on. I'll pull you out." Grasping one end, he tossed the rope into the pit.

The princess strained to reach it. "It's too short!" A note of panic entered her voice. "I'm trapped, and no one even knows we're here..."

"I'll get help!" Karim exclaimed. "I know the way out. I'll run back to the village and get Elyas. We'll bring a longer rope and get you out of there. All right, sena? I'll be back as soon as I can. I promise."

Are you really doing this again? Leaving someone you care about alone in the dark?

First there was silence. Then Sita said, "All right."

Her voice was calm, but Karim could hear the terror working to claw its way out.

Feeling sick, Karim turned away from the hole and ran.

14
NEFF

Neff sat in the banquet hall, partaking of a midday meal with the pharaoh and a congregation of palace officials and priests. Attendants laden with platters and water jugs filed in and out, while other servants stood nearby waving ostrich feather fans, ensuring that a steady breeze cooled the stifling air.

She picked at her bowl of stewed fava beans, anxious to return to her chambers after her afternoon duties were complete. She was desperate to open the scroll that Ahura had delivered the day before and see what Kenna had sent her.

She glanced around the table at the serious-faced men, men including Sabni and the new viziers he had appointed. As Meryamun had commanded, the old viziers had been named traitors to the crown and executed, their bodies thrown into the river to be carried out to sea, for traitors were never to know the comfort of a tomb or the promise of eternal life. To Neff's eyes, the new men seemed no different from the old ones, aside from having a much healthier fear of their young king.

The new viziers said many things, but none of them included the word *no*.

Neff pushed her plate away. She had no appetite.

Nearly every minute of every day, she was surrounded by people, and yet she'd never felt so alone.

"More water?"

Neff turned to see Ahura standing beside her carrying an alabaster water jug. She had dark circles under her eyes, but she managed a tight smile.

"Yes, thank you," Neff replied.

Ahura bent to refill her cup, spilling a little on the table. Then the attendant nodded and moved on to the next guest.

Watching her, Neff thought that perhaps she had acquired a new friend.

When she'd met Ahura in the courtyard that day, it had felt just like when she'd met Karim. Like fate had placed her in Neff's path. Karim had described the fourth person in the Oracle of the Lamb as a tall, strapping farm girl from Sakesh. Ahura certainly fit the physical description, and Neff doubted her claim about hailing from Bubas. If she was indeed a Sakeshi, why had Ahura come to the palace and assumed a false identity? Neff knew from her audiences with Meryamun that Sakesh was the heart of the southern rebellion. Did Ahura have her own plans to disrupt power in the kingdom?

Neff had to believe that her new servant could be trusted. After all, if the gods hadn't meant for them to meet, why would they have sent a woman with her mother's name?

You may doubt yourself, the High Priestess of Bast had told her, *but never doubt the goddess. You are on this path because she deemed it so. Stay on it, no matter where it leads.*

Neff took a deep breath and forced herself to eat, using a piece of spiced flatbread to scoop some fava beans into her mouth. *I need my strength to get through the day.*

"Montuhotep!" sounded the king's strident voice. "You're late."

Neff looked up to see her old master, the high priest of Amun, enter the chamber. He was pale, his shoulders hunched, a shadow of the powerful, self-assured man she'd met when she first arrived in Thonis. Back then, he had been the one to sit at the king's right hand.

Their eyes met, and Neff saw a flash of hatred pass over his face as he took a seat at the other end of the table.

"Forgive me, my king," Montuhotep said. "I was caught up in the preparations for your execration ritual."

"Execration ritual?" Sabni asked, a bite of baked egg halfway to his mouth. The small man looked to Meryamun. "I had not heard about this, my king. Curses?"

Meryamun tutted. "Don't be grumpy, Sabni. I have entrusted you with the management of my viziers. It doesn't mean you oversee *all* my affairs. As a healer has his pills, ointments, *and* heka to cure the sick, so a king needs an army, a strategy, *and* magic to defeat his enemies. Sematawy knew this, but like so much of his wisdom, it was forgotten. The kingdom my father bequeathed me is plagued with rebellion and has lost the respect of the neighboring kingdoms. If I am to heal Khetara of these ills, I need heka on my side as well as bows and arrows. This execration ritual will give me just that: a curse upon each and every enemy of the crown."

"My priests have commissioned all the clay pots that you need," Montuhotep broke in, apparently not wishing his accomplishments to be forgotten in the exchange. "And they are working on the wax figures as well. I have also personally spoken to the man in charge of the fortress, and he is honored you've chosen that location for the ritual."

Meryamun turned to the high priest. "And what of the Sakeshi dogs? I want them out of the palace as soon as possible."

"It won't be much longer, my king. They too must be prepared for the ritual."

The king's smile sent a shiver up Neff's spine. "Of course they must. They're the main event."

"*Ach!* You stupid girl! You are spilling everywhere!"

Neff turned to see Ahura recoil from one of the viziers, whose robe was soaked with the water she'd poured into his lap.

Ahura blinked at him, distracted. "I'm sorry…" she said and left the room in haste.

Meryamun leaned over and whispered in Neff's ear. "Your maidservant is about as graceful as an ox. One more misstep, and I'll be forced to have her thrashed. Perhaps that might teach her some manners."

Neff nodded. "I'll speak to her, my king. May I be excused? I have arranged to go to the queen's quarters for a dream reading."

"You may little seer. Perhaps your auguries will do my mother some good. She hasn't been herself since Father's death, though I would have thought my ascension to the throne would lift her from her doldrums."

Neff noted bitterness in his voice.

"Women become so tiresome when they grow old," Meryamun continued with a sigh. "Their irrational ravings, their dismal moods—yes, go and fix her, Nefermaat, would you? You'd be doing me a great service if you succeed."

Neff found the queen sitting by a window in her chambers, clad in a yellow dress.

Yellow for mourning.

Queen Bintanath didn't turn when Neff announced herself. She simply raised a hand to beckon her inside.

"Forgive me for not coming to you sooner," Neff said as she approached.

"Sit."

Neff swallowed and took a seat on the long, cushioned bench next to the queen, who stared into the desert, unblinking. Blousy curtains danced in the breeze from the open windows, which looked upon the women's pool and the desert beyond. A falcon cried out, circling in the azure sky, but otherwise, there was perfect silence. Many palace occupants, their bellies full from the midday meal, spent the hot afternoon hours dozing.

Neff glanced at Queen Bintanath, uncertain how to introduce the topic of dreaming. The queen was slender verging on gaunt, and she wore none of her usual regalia—not even a wig. Neff couldn't help but notice a thick line of gray at her hairline. For someone who was notoriously meticulous about her appearance, her uncolored roots seemed like yet another sign that the queen was unraveling.

"Those are very pretty bracelets," Neff ventured, indicating the three lengths of twisted linen the queen held in her hands. Each was simple but elegant, strung with carnelian and gold beads.

"They're not bracelets. They're necklaces. Given to my three children the night they were born." Her voice was dry, like the breeze. "I gave birth to them in this very room, on the night of a terrible storm. The three dancers who attended to me tied these around my babies' necks. I saved them as keepsakes." She lay the necklaces along her palm and touched the golden beads. "That was so long ago. It almost feels as if it happened to someone else."

"My mother gave me a doll when I was born," Neff said. "I keep it in a special box at home."

The queen turned to look at her. "And where is home?"

"Bubas."

Queen Bintanath snorted. "I should have thought my son would know better. Hanging jewels on a village girl doesn't make her any less common."

Neff winced, but then she remembered her father's advice. *Sometimes a customer will test you simply to see how much you can handle. A true businessman doesn't allow his feathers to be ruffled. He keeps his eye on the prize.*

Neff raised her chin, mirroring the queen's own rigid posture. "I wouldn't be here if you hadn't summoned me, Queen Bintanath."

The queen's lips didn't move, but the corners of her eyes crinkled with approval.

"Quite right," she said. "I wanted to see for myself if the stories about you are true. I was never satisfied with Montuhotep's predictions. One got the feeling he was simply saying what one wanted to hear, regardless of what the gods were telling him."

Neff cringed, recalling the false message she'd given King Amunmose before his death—a message that failed to reveal he was being slowly poisoned by his favorite son. *This time will be different*, she vowed. *This time I'll tell the truth, no matter how harsh it might be.*

She took a deep breath and allowed her mind to soften. "Please, my queen. Tell me of your dream."

Fiddling with the three necklaces, the queen turned back to the quiet desert and began. "In the dream, I'm out there, among the dunes. I'm alone and wearing a long black cape made from vulture feathers.

"I walk toward the horizon, where a blue-winged sun rises over Thonis. There should be a cobra on each side of it, but there is only one, a red cobra. As I watch, the red cobra slithers to the center of the sun, as if resting upon its brow. The sun's rays grow hotter and hotter, until they are so hot the cape upon my back bursts into flames. My skin blackens and peels away. The light becomes so bright that it fills the world, and then..."

The queen blinked. "Then I wake up."

Neff felt her mind sink into the world of the dream, into the darkness at the center of the light. She saw the desert. The winged sun. The red cobra. She saw the woman caped in vulture feathers.

Except the woman was not Queen Bintanath. She was the goddess Nekhbet, the vulture-headed protector of the kingdom, the crown, and all its children—alive and dead.

The Mother of Mothers.

Neff waited for the blazing sun to burn Nekhbet as it had in the queen's dream. Instead, the goddess walked to the horizon and wrapped her heavy wings around it. She was so small, and yet Nekhbet was somehow able to enfold the sun in her arms, casting the world into darkness.

Through the darkness came a message, whispered on the wind.

When the vision faded, Queen Bintanath was watching Neff with a mixture of amazement and fear.

"So it is true," she whispered. "My husband was quick to fall for a young, pretty face, but Mery is different. He was right about you. That was no act. You are touched by the divine." She leaned forward and seized Neff's wrist, holding her firmly. "Tell me, child: What did you see? What message do the gods have for me?"

Neff's pulse began to race. *Say it!* she told herself. *Come what may, you must tell her!*

When she spoke, her voice was steady.

"It is not so much a message as it is a question, my queen. Do you protect the crown or the one who wears it? Beware, for if you fail to do the former, the latter will come to destroy all that the light touches. Sanctify yourself in the truth; wrap your arms around that which burns this kingdom until the fire has gone out. Only then will you find peace."

The queen blinked, seemingly unable—or unwilling—to comprehend the message. Her lip curled. "Say that again."

Neff's body began to shake. *She'll have me killed, my throat cut...*

She began again. "D-do you protect the crown or the one who wears it? Beware, for—"

"Again!" the queen raged. She stood and snatched a ceramic cup from the side table, hurling it against the wall. It exploded in a shower of shards and bloodred wine.

Neff didn't flinch or cower. She spoke slowly and clearly, her hands folded tightly in her lap. "Wrap your arms around that which burns this kingdom until the fire has gone out. Only then will you find peace."

A palace guard appeared in the doorway. "Queen Bintanath, is everything all right?"

The queen kept her eyes on Neff. "Leave us!"

The guard hesitated before bowing his head and making his exit.

The queen's face twisted into a mask of fury. "How dare you make these insinuations!" she snarled, gripping Neff's wrist so tightly that it hurt. "How dare you suggest I am living a lie, that I don't have the kingdom's best interests at heart! I don't need some skinny, impudent little whelp like you to tell me how to...how to..."

Neff didn't move. She felt sick and dizzy with fright, and the pain in her wrist brought tears to her eyes, but she didn't make a sound. A single tear broke free and rolled down her face.

Queen Bintanath saw it, and her fury drained away. She released her grip on Neff's wrist and took a step back. Already, a purple bruise blossomed there.

The queen sank onto the bench.

Neff cradled her wrist in her hand and took a shuddering breath. "I-I only did what was asked of me, my queen. To deliver the message I was given."

Queen Bintanath dropped her gaze to the three small necklaces still clutched in her hand. One for Kenna, one for Sita, and one for Mery.

After a moment she spoke, her voice soft and strange. "You think you're ready to be a mother. You think that when the children come, the wisdom of the world will wash over you, and you will know what to do. You'll know what is right. But you don't. You don't."

The queen fell silent after that. Neff remained in her seat, tense, counting the droplets of wine splashed across the floor in front of her. After what felt like a long while, she decided it was safe to rise. She bowed to the queen and dismissed herself from the room.

You did what you set out to do, she told herself as she hurried to her own chambers. *You told her the truth*. It was a relief, after so many lies. Though she feared what calamity that truth might bring.

The cat greeted Neff at the door, yowling and winding around her ankles. She leaped onto the table as Neff collapsed onto a stool and poured herself a cup of water with shaking hands.

"Hello, Cat," Neff said after gulping down her third cup. "How is your day? Better than mine, I hope."

The cat purred and swept her tail across the black leather cylinder marked with the sign of Sekhmet. Reaching for it, Neff carefully removed the scrolls from the container, unrolled them, and weighed down the corners with small stones. Kenna's letter to her, written on a scrap of papyrus, lay on top.

Nefermaat, the note read, *I cautioned you about using powerful magic when we last met, but perhaps I was wrong. Perhaps the time for caution has passed. When you told me about this Oracle of the Lamb, I confess I found it difficult to believe. I am a priest, but I am also a man of logic and reason, and the oracle defies both. How can the future be both predetermined and dependent upon our actions?*

After much thought, however, I have concluded that the world is so complex, it encompasses all possibilities, including one in which you are at the center of a cataclysm. You have endured great hardship in a short time, made greater by the fact that you are only a child, and yet these trials have strengthened you.

I have taught you many things, little sister, but I think you have taught me more. You may not be of royal blood, but like the children of pharaohs, your power is innate. You need only use your education—and your faith—to meet this challenge. The rest is up to Heka.

Enclosed here is the set of scrolls that I discovered in the secret wall that day in the House of Life. I trust you will use them wisely when the time comes.

With Amun's blessing,

"Your brother and loyal friend,

Kenna.

Neff set the letter on the table, pride and longing like a double-edged blade in her heart.

As if sensing her anguish, the cat bumped her head against Neff's hand. "I'm all right, Cat," she said, sniffing. "Now, what's this?"

She examined the top scroll. Unlike Kenna's letter, it was written in the gods' words, so it took her longer to decipher.

"The Book of the Red Lady," she murmured. "The Red Lady," she knew, was one of the goddess Sekhmet's various titles.

"These look like spell scrolls," she went on, both for her own benefit and the cat's. Sekhmet was not often invoked in the magic used by priests of Amun. Wondering what kinds of spells they might be, Neff began translating the headings of each one:

To Enthrall a Man.

To Make a Man Blind to His Brothers.

To Loosen a Bowstring.

To Have Power over the Winds.

Neff felt the blood drain from her face. Aside from the life-giving spell she'd been working on with the twig, and the spell to summon Medjed, these were by far the most powerful spells she'd ever seen. What's more, they were malicious.

Dark magic.

No wonder they were hidden inside that wall. In the wrong hands, spells like these could be incredibly destructive. In the right ones, though…

She studied the lists of ingredients marked in red ink and blew out her cheeks. Some of the items would be hard to get her hands on. *But not impossible.* Still, even if she got what she needed, there was no guarantee she'd be able to cast the spells correctly.

Kenna wouldn't have given this to you if he didn't believe, a voice within her urged. *The potential for failure is high, but the consequences of not trying at all are much worse.*

Neff heard a hiss. The cat stood with her back arched and hackles raised. As she had so many times before, the cat was staring into the middle of the room, focused on something that wasn't there.

Or was it?

Neff recalled telling Ahura how cats are capable of seeing "the unseen," and how it reminded her of the Medjed spell. The spell had called him a guardian with "eyes that see yet are unseen." When nothing happened after she cast the spell, she'd assumed it hadn't worked.

But what if it had? What if Medjed had been with her ever since, and she just didn't know it?

She stood, trying to pinpoint exactly where the cat was staring. "Erm…hello?" she said, tentatively.

Nothing happened.

She went to the window and gathered a handful of sand that had blown in overnight and hadn't yet been swept out by the servants. Then she threw it up in the air.

The sand drifted to the floor in a cloud, but Neff could have sworn she saw some of the grains create the outline of a form about half her size. When the sand had settled back to the ground, she also noticed that it neglected to fill two small areas with very recognizable shapes.

Feet.

Neff went rigid with shock. *By Amun, something really is there!* She grabbed a length of white linen she'd used to dry herself after her bath that morning. Biting her lip, she flung it over the same spot.

The cloth floated down onto the invisible object, giving form where none had been, making it look as if a small child hid under the white cloth.

Neff's fear intensified. She dashed behind the table and hid.

What will it do now that I've discovered it?

The cat didn't seem to understand the gravity of the situation. She padded over to Neff, rubbed her chin against the table leg, and meowed, as if to say, *See? I told you so.*

Trembling, Neff peered over the tabletop.

The diminutive figure, seemingly having registered the cloth, turned left, then right. It didn't appear to be angry or frightened, simply confused.

Gathering her courage, Neff popped up her head. "Hey! Medjed!"

The figure stopped. Was it looking at her? She couldn't tell.

"Are you…are you going to hurt me?"

Medjed shook its head.

"Are you meant to be my guardian?"

Medjed nodded.

So it was Medjed who must have been in the Horus Room with us, and who alerted me about the guard in the corridor! Neff thought. *It's been following me all along!*

Relieved, Neff stood and slowly approached the little figure. "So, the spell actually worked! Does that mean I'll be safe from harm when you're around?"

Reluctantly, Medjed shook its head.

Neff crossed her arms. "What kind of guardian are you if you let bad things happen to me?"

Medjed shrank.

"No, no, I'm not upset," she said, eager not to hurt its feelings. "I'm only trying to understand. I suppose my parents were my guardians, and they couldn't always stop bad things from happening to me either." She thought of that last morning in Bubas, of her mother's stricken face when Neff boarded the ship bound for Thonis. "Will you at least *try* to protect me?"

Medjed nodded.

"That's good enough, then."

The little guardian returned to its former height and moved closer. The cat, no longer perturbed by Medjed's presence, batted at the floating cloth in high amusement.

Neff regarded the cloth critically. "If you wear this shroud when you're out, people will definitely ask questions. But when we're alone, it makes it easier to talk to you. You just need one more thing…" Turning back to her table, she picked up a black ink palette and a reed brush. "Now, don't move," she instructed.

Medjed was still.

Leaning forward and with the tip of her tongue sticking out between her lips, Neff carefully painted two simple eyes and eyebrows onto the cloth. When she was done, she stepped back to check her work.

"There!" she said, setting down the brush. "Now I can see which way you're facing. It will be much easier to talk to you properly. See? "

She pointed at the brass mirror on the wall. Medjed turned toward it—and jumped.

Neff giggled. "Good, isn't it?"

Medjed cocked its head to the side, uncertain.

"Well, I like it, anyway." Neff smiled at the creature, amazed that she had summoned it into existence all by herself. *Maybe Kenna's right. If I can call Medjed, I really can cast spells! Even powerful ones! My studies must be paying off.*

She turned back to the magic scrolls and thought of Meryamun's plans for conquest and domination. So many had already died by his hand, and more would surely follow. The lamb in her vision warned her about the blood to be spilled, about the sorrow and ruin that would come to the children of Khetara.

Neff thought of her parents and her friends in Bubas.

She thought of Kenna.

The time for caution has passed.

Resuming her seat at the table, Neff spread a fresh sheet of papyrus in front of her and turned to the Book of the Red Lady.

"Medjed," she said, "Please go outside and keep a lookout. Warn me if anyone is coming, all right?"

Medjed nodded, then slipped out from beneath the cloth, leaving it to fall to the floor in a heap. Seizing her opportunity, the cat walked over to the fabric, turned in a circle, and lay down on it to sleep.

Satisfied, Neff returned to her work. *To Enthrall a Man,* she read, making a note on her papyrus. *Take a lock of hair from the man you wish to enthrall and soak it in blood from your own hand for one night. Fasten the hair to a waxen figure inscribed with the man's name and burn it in sacred fire while speaking these words…*

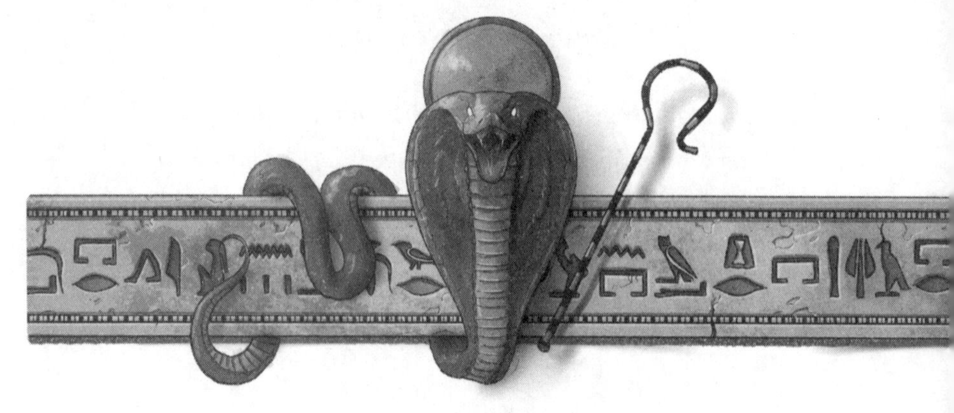

15
SITA

Sita sat at the bottom of the dark pit, gripping her candle like a lifeline. Karim's rapid footsteps had faded into silence, and the only sound that remained were her own panicked breaths.

He'll be back soon, she assured herself. *He promised.*

She sat uncomfortably on the pile of rubble, leaning her back against the wall of the pit. Rocks poked her, and every time she shifted, a bolt of pain lanced up her leg. She'd told Karim that it wasn't broken, but something in her ankle had snapped on impact.

She didn't want him to worry.

Or maybe she didn't want to admit to herself that in an instant, all her plans had been dashed.

If her ankle was broken, how would she escape Perset and make the journey across the desert back to Khetara? Stopping both Mery and Setnakht already felt like an impossible task, and now this…

I am a fool, she thought miserably. *How did I ever think I could succeed?*

Sita sat up and gritted her teeth against the pain.

Stop thinking and focus on the candlelight. Wait for Karim to return.

She stared at the flame, doing her best to steady her breathing. At first, the light was still, but after a while it began to flicker.

How is there a breeze down here? She squinted into the darkness, but the candle only illuminated a small area around her. For all she knew, the pit might lead to a tunnel. If she were able to walk, she could explore her surroundings, but that was out of the question.

The breeze flowing toward her strengthened. It carried a scent as strange and familiar as a forgotten dream.

The flame guttered.

"No! Please!" Sita cried, shielding the candle with her hand.

The light went out.

Darkness swept in, thick and stifling and complete. She dropped the candle and wrapped her arms around herself, a hysterical moan of terror rising in her throat. Whether her eyes were open or closed made no difference at all.

Suddenly, it was very hard to breathe.

Don't think, don't think, don't think—

The weight of the darkness pressed inward, growing heavier, crushing her. She felt her body disappear into the void, piece by piece—first her feet, then her legs, then her hands and body and neck, until she was only a mouth struggling to breathe and a mind drowning in despair.

There, in the pit, she'd fallen into the very place where she'd buried all her guilt and shame. With no love or light to drive them away, they threatened to consume her whole.

In the darkness, she heard Maet's mother crying over her daughter's body.

She saw the dead on the floor of the Horus Room.

She felt Mery's breath in her ear and heard the words that turned her world upside down.

Just as Osiris had his sister-wife Isis and Set had Nephthys, so will I have you.

Little by little, the memories began to tear her apart.

"Please," she said, sending a prayer into the endless silence. "Someone help me."

She could pray all she wanted, she knew no one was coming. It might be hours before Karim returned. Until then, she was alone with her thoughts. Alone with her demons.

Then—deep within the murk, she saw a pinprick of light, orange and dancing.

Was she imagining it?

Sita struggled to bring it into focus. Was it very small, or simply far away?

The light grew and grew, bobbing gently like a butterfly, drawing closer.

As her eyes grew accustomed to the radiance, she saw a hand below the light, holding it aloft.

Sita's heart soared. *There* is *a tunnel down here—and someone's coming!* The figure approached, and she watched in amazement as the one shape revealed itself to be two.

The women walked in silent symmetry. They were long and lithe, with shining hair that was either black or blue, Sita couldn't tell. The one carrying the torch had sand-colored skin and eyes like a cloudless sky, while the woman beside her had midnight eyes and skin as brown as the richest earth from which all green things grow. There was a contrast in their manner, too. Where the woman carrying the torch smiled brightly, the second was somber, and kept her hands clasped in front of her as if in prayer. Despite these differences, however, their faces were exactly the same. Sita knew at once—as one recognizes one's self in others—that they must be twins.

"Who are you?" Sita asked when they stopped in front of her.

The bright one dipped her head in greeting. "We are here to help, Sitamun."

"Did Karim send you?"

The somber one gave a small smile, as if enjoying a private joke. "We were sent, yes."

In any other situation, Sita would have noticed how their gowns—one white, one black—looked more like fine Khetaran kalasiris than the simple, embroidered dresses of the Hudjefa. She would have wondered how the women knew her full name, when she'd only introduced herself to the tribe as Sita, or how they'd arrived in that tunnel, so far below the temple floor.

Yet Sita did not question the two women, as one does not question the events of a dream.

"Can you walk?" the bright one asked.

Sita shook her head. "I think my ankle might be broken."

"Let me see," the somber one said. She kneeled to examine Sita's injury. In the torchlight, Sita could tell that her foot was horribly swollen, purple-yellow bruises already appearing on one side. Did it look crooked as well?

She swooned.

"Do not be afraid," the woman said softly, and she took Sita's ankle into her hands.

Sita sucked her teeth, anticipating more pain—but it didn't come. The woman stroked and prodded her foot, yet Sita felt only a cool, relaxing sensation.

"My sister knows much about the body," the bright one explained. "She and her son work with the dead, which actually teaches one a lot about life." Her voice was bell-like and danced like the flames of the torch. "Her talents are often overlooked, misunderstood. She doesn't like to brag, but she's quite the gifted healer."

The somber one gave her companion a wry but loving grin. "My sister brags enough for the both of us."

Sita's eyes suddenly welled with tears.

The woman stopped her prodding. "Have I hurt you?"

"No," Sita murmured to her, then looked up at the bright sister. "What you said reminded me of my brother."

"Your brother," the somber one echoed, continuing her ministrations. "Tell me about him."

"He works with the dead too."

Overlooked. Misunderstood.

"He's brilliant. Though I don't know if anyone's ever told him so." Sita frowned. "I have failed a lot of people, but I fear I've failed him the most. I have not seen him for who he really is."

The somber sister considered Sita. Up close, her face was as smooth as if it were carved from obsidian. "Did you ever think that, perhaps, your brother feels the same way about you?"

Sita scoffed. "He thinks I'm a silly girl—silly and weak."

"Are you?" the sister with the torch asked.

Sita didn't answer.

The kneeling woman released Sita's ankle. "Many think that you must shine a light to see clearly. But some things can only be understood in the dark. Perhaps you'll know yourself better before you leave this place, Sitamun." She stood and reached for Sita's hand. "Now get up."

Sita blinked at her. "But my ankle..."

The woman cocked her head, birdlike. "Is there something wrong with it?"

"What do you mean? It's—" The words died on Sita's lips as she looked down. Her swelling and bruising were gone.

It can't be...

Tentatively, she flexed her foot. There was no pain. She tried putting a little weight on it.

It was as if the injury had never happened.

"Come along now," the sister with the torch said merrily. "Mustn't dawdle!"

Sita rose to her feet, perplexed. "But how—?"

"As I said, my sister has quite a gift!"

Sita stared at them in wonder. *Quite a gift indeed! She'd put Khetara's greatest healers to shame.*

She followed the two women as they retraced their steps through the tunnel.

"It's not often that I meet another set of twins," Sita said as they walked. "You are twins, aren't you?"

"We are," the somber sister replied.

"My brothers and I are triplets, but everyone always says Mery and me might as well be twins, we're so alike. That used to make me proud. Now..." She trailed off.

"What is he like, your brother Mery?" asked the bright sister.

Sita ducked under a sunken stone in the ceiling. "Charming, fun, passionate..."

"Ah!"

"...selfish, manipulative, ruthless, cruel..."

"Ah."

"No one in the world was closer to him than me. If anyone should have known what he was capable of, what was truly in his heart..." She wasn't sure why she was opening up to strangers, but shock and fear had made her honest. Plus, they were very good listeners.

"He did bad things, your brother?" the bright sister asked.

Sita swallowed. "Unimaginable things."

"And you fear if this evil exists in him, it must exist in you?"

"I suppose I do," she replied.

"It does."

Sita didn't know how to respond. She stopped and leaned against the wall, momentarily short of breath. "W-what?" she finally said.

"People often make assumptions about us," the bright sister went on. "They believe I am the benevolent one. But I have wrath. I can manipulate and deceive. I have punished those who have not given me shelter, and I have stolen secrets from my own father in his time of need."

"Others believe I am mournful," the somber sister added. "Yet I also bring comfort. Joy. I have nursed the children of strangers and given guidance to the lost."

The sisters then began speaking in tandem, first one, then the other, like the recitation of a poem written long ago.

"The existence of evil does not negate the potential for good."

"Nor does the existence of good negate the potential for evil."

"Within the vastness of your soul, there exists all things."

"Just as the earth contains wonders and horrors in equal measure,"

"The brightest sunlight casts the deepest shadow."

"And in profound darkness, the smallest star can be a beacon."

The flow of words made Sita feel lightheaded, but she kept walking, so as not to lose the women in the dim, winding tunnel.

"Perhaps you and your brother *are* the same," one sister said, Sita couldn't tell which. "Perhaps you are capable of unimaginable things too."

Sita shivered, uncertain how to reply to such strange tidings.

"Where are you taking me?" she asked after they had walked a while in silence. "Is this another way out of the temple? Karim will wonder about me…" Before either woman could answer, the tunnel walls caught Sita's attention. "Wait! There are paintings here. This is Queen Anet, Setnakht's wife!"

Sita stopped to point at a picture of a familiar bald-headed woman. In the image, the queen held a staff entwined with two serpents and stood in front of a falcon-headed god on a great golden boat. "This is Ra on his solar barque, on his nightly journey through the underworld," she said, fascinated. "Queen Anet goes before him, walking on water, almost as if she is protecting him."

She squinted at the image of a red fish below the queen's feet. "My tutor told me about this. The name Anet..." She paused, then snapped her fingers. "Yes! Anet is a sacred fish who, along with her brother Abtu, alerts Ra and protects him during his journey." She regarded the ancient queen with new eyes. "She must have been a powerful priestess to have been given that name."

The two women listened, their expressions patient and knowing.

"This is the way to her tomb, isn't it? Her actual tomb. Perhaps Setnakht wanted to ensure that it wouldn't be found by tomb robbers, so he installed traps and a hidden door in the room above leading down to this tunnel."

The somber sister patted Sita on the shoulder. "You took... the hard way."

Sita sighed. "Don't I always?"

The woman shrugged. "I would rather wield a tempered blade than one that has never endured the flames."

Sita's cheeks reddened.

"Instead of focusing on your shortcomings," the bright sister commented, "remember your strengths. The word is the deed. What you say, what you think, becomes your reality."

Sita stopped. "What did you say?"

The Hudjefa wouldn't know such words.

They'd reached the end of the tunnel. The two women stood beside each other in the archway ahead, one bathed in the torch's firelight, the other cloaked in shadow.

"The word is the deed," the women repeated in unison, the sound reverberating through the space.

The somber sister smiled and turned her back. "You can find your own way from here, Sitamun."

"What?" Sita said. "You can't leave me. What if I get lost?"

The other woman turned away too, a mirror of her sister. "You won't. You're exactly where you need to be."

With that, she hurled the torch into the chamber.

Sita cried out, shutting her eyes against the sudden brightness.

When she opened them again, the women and the torch were gone. The chamber beyond was aglow with firelight. The room was large, and half a dozen burning braziers lined its stone walls.

"Hello?" Sita called, her pulse racing.

Where had the sisters gone? Was she dreaming?

She touched the tunnel wall, felt its solidity beneath her fingers.

No. This is real.

There, in the middle of the illuminated chamber, she saw a magnificent sarcophagus carved of red granite, with the recumbent form of a woman on its lid.

Sita's breath caught in her throat. *Queen Anet's tomb. This is it!*

She took a few tentative steps inside. The floor was littered with stone shards, many of them vibrant with color. The wall on the left had been reduced to rubble, as if someone had taken a hammer to it. Sita bent to pick up a large piece, squinting at the painted fragment.

It was a rendering of a lamb, its head raised heavenward, its mouth open, a bloody wound staining its wool red.

The lamb, a voice in her mind whispered.

Sita dropped the fragment. It clattered on the ground.

Shaken, she turned to the back wall. The paintings there were undamaged and featured engravings that were finer than others she'd seen in the temple. The central image was another scene of Queen Anet and her king—but this was no family portrait. In it, the queen, dressed as a priestess, knelt before Setnakht and offered him two symbols enclosed in a shen ring, indicating the gift was both protected and eternal. The first symbol was a rolled scroll, tied at the middle, and the second was the symbol of a seated god with the head of an ibis.

"The Book of Thoth," Sita murmured. She'd never heard of it.

Queen Anet gave the book to Setnakht. I wonder what was in it…

Sita turned back to the sarcophagus. The carved-stone woman lay with her arms crossed over her chest, a beatific expression on her face. Images of Nepthys were engraved along the lower half of her body, while lotus blossoms and a large winged scarab decorated her arms and chest.

Sita wondered again about Queen Anet's grave goods. The chamber contained no baskets, chests, or artifacts of any kind—save one. A long twisted piece of driftwood lay along the sarcophagus as if the stone woman was holding it.

That must be the queen's staff pictured in the paintings, Sita realized. Except if this was Queen Anet's staff, it was missing an important element. Two, in fact.

I wonder what happened to them?

The silence was broken by a fearsome hiss. The sound was very loud and very close.

Sita froze. She scanned the room, seeking its source.

Then she saw them—two cobras, slithering toward her from either side of the sarcophagus. One was a deep wine color with a black band across its throat, and the other was entirely black.

They moved toward her in silent, sinuous harmony, each one as thick as her arm and four times as long.

Sita watched them, transfixed. She knew she should back away, but she couldn't move. The snakes raised up their heads until a full third of their bodies had lifted off the ground, and their hoods spread wide.

She broke into a cold sweat as the red cobra slithered before her, so close she could see the firelight reflected in its eyes. It tasted the air with its forked tongue.

Flick.

Flick.

Sita stared, afraid to look away.

She blinked, and the cobra lunged, though it was so fast she swore she'd imagined it.

She felt a tingle at her wrist. Without moving her head, she glanced down at her bare arm. Two puncture wounds, small and clean, dotted her skin.

Nebet's constant warning filled Sita's mind. *The serpent's kiss is as quick as lightning—and just as deadly.*

Almost instantly, the tingle became a searing agony. She fell to her knees and onto the dusty ground as the pain traveled up her arm and spread through her body like fire consuming dry brush.

Gasping, moaning, Sita turned her gaze back to the two cobras. The red cobra remained close, rearing, hissing, while the black cobra lurked behind it, still and watchful. They didn't seem interested in attacking her again. Perhaps they knew one bite was enough.

As poison flooded her veins, Sita was overcome with another sensation.

Despair.

She was going to die, having failed her kingdom and everyone she'd ever loved.

She thought of the oracle and all its divine portents. How could the gods have been so wrong about her? How could they not have seen the path of her life lead to a meaningless death?

How foolish she'd been, allowing herself to be delayed in Perset for so long, when she should have been raising an army to remove Mery from the throne! How selfish to fall into a happy rhythm—not to mention the arms of a man—and forget the suffering that lay outside the lost city!

You thought you'd changed after leaving Thonis, but you haven't. You're still weak, still a coward.

She had tried so hard to deny her demons. But still they came for her. Despite her struggles to live in the light, Sita was destined to die in darkness, alone but for the hatred she felt for herself.

The pain was cresting, and Sita knew that death would soon follow. She cursed the two strange women for abandoning her. Perhaps if they had stayed, she could have avoided this fate. She recalled their strange talk, their mysterious pronouncements.

Perhaps you and your brother are *the same.*

Sita almost smiled at that.

Mery would never take a snakebite lying down. He'd grab the snake by its throat and bite it back.

Tears pricked Sita's eyes, and she gasped as that one simple thought unearthed a secret she'd kept hidden, the most terrible secret of all.

A sob escaped her throat.

Despite everything that had happened, everything Mery had done—

"I still love him."

Without meaning to, she'd whispered the words aloud. And like a spell, her words invoked the voices of the two sisters. They echoed through the chamber, speaking in tandem with each other and with the slowing pulse of her heart.

Will you cling to the light?

Or embrace the darkness?

Will you accept the shadow within?

Or remain forever fractured?

She thought again of Mery.

My twin.

Being compared to him used to make her proud. Used to make her feel like she too was like the sun—brilliant, radiant with power.

Now the thought filled her with horror.

My mirror.

Her brother knew they were the same. One soul reflected upon itself. That's why he wanted her at his side, to act as the other edge of his sword. One edge to cleave, to shape the world in his image—and the other to bathe in the blood of his glory.

After the Bast Festival, she'd learned to hate herself because every time she saw her reflection, it reminded her of him.

Sita felt the venom spread into her lungs, her throat.

He and I may be alike, but I would never do what he did!

It was in that moment of defiance that Sita recognized where she and Mery diverged.

Mery had chosen to poison their father, to let Maet die, to massacre the innocent—and Sita had chosen to defy him.

Our stories are not defined by our demons, said the voice of her conscience or a goddess or both. *They are written about the choices we make when we are left alone with them.*

Choose, said the light.

Choose, said the darkness.

Is the truth a poison?

Or a cure?

Will you fight?

Or will you die?

Sita only had a few breaths left before her end. Only a few moments before the choice was made for her.

She gasped. “I choose to fight!”

The word is the deed.

Her next breath came a little easier.

The two cobras remained motionless before her, watching, waiting. The voices in her mind came as if from the serpents themselves. *Tell us your name, child of Khetara!* they commanded.

“I am Coward! I am Fool!” Sita cried, her body still glittering with pain. “I am the One Who Faces the Storm! The One Who Defies Death!”

Her legs returned to her, and she struggled to her feet.

“I am Betrayer, Healer, Lover!”

She lurched toward the sarcophagus, and the two cobras slid back, allowing her to pass. The flames in the braziers seemed to burn brighter.

“I am the Candle in the Darkness, and the Shadow in the Dawn!”

She reached for the wooden staff and closed her hand around it.

“I am Sitamun, Princess of Khetara—and I am not finished!”

With that, she swung the staff from its seat. It struck the floor with a thunderous boom that shook the earth around her.

Then, like two obedient servants, the cobras slithered up the length of the twisted wood, winding around it and each other until they reached the crest. There they froze, alive no longer, but sculpted of red copper and black iron, entwined as one.

Queen Anet’s staff was whole once again, and Sita herself—free of pain—felt complete for the very first time.

For she had many names, and she finally knew them all.

"Sena! I'm coming!"

The shouts were so muted that if the silence hadn't been total, Sita never would have heard them.

Karim! she thought.

She rushed out of Queen Anet's tomb into the dark tunnel, which grew darker the moment she entered it. Puzzled, she turned back. The burning braziers in the tomb had gone out. There was no fire, no heat. Even the potent, acrid smell of smoke that had filled the chamber was gone. The only light shone from the serpent staff, which glowed faintly in the gloom. Full of wonder, Sita ran her fingers along the spine of the black cobra, and could have sworn she felt it breathe.

I believed in stories once, she remembered telling Karim long ago, perhaps in another lifetime.

"I'm sorry I lost faith," she whispered, reveling in the way her hand fit perfectly into the twists of the wooden staff. She gripped it tightly. "It won't happen again."

She rushed back to the pit, and she was waiting there when Karim's agitated face appeared high above.

"Sena!" he exclaimed when he saw her peering up at him. "Zev and I have come to rescue you!"

"Zev?" Sita said, surprised.

"He says he is the strongest man in the tribe and would have taken offense if I had brought anyone else!"

"Didn't you think he might take this opportunity to kill us both?"

There was a pause. "I did not consider that, no!"

Zev's head popped over the edge next to Karim's. "I can hear you, you know," he grumbled. "And I'm not going to kill you, though you deserve it for all the trouble you've caused. Still, Elyas would be...displeased."

"Well, that's comforting," Sita replied. "Now will you please lower the rope? I'd like to get out of here."

Karim looked surprised, but he tossed the rope down to her. "What about your ankle, sena? I assumed one of us would have to come down and carry you out."

"No need," Sita said. She lifted the staff over her head and secured it into the back of her belt before grabbing hold of the rope. "I'm stronger than I thought."

"What is this accursed place?" Zev asked as they trekked to the main hall.

Karim's eyebrows raised when he saw the serpent staff Sita carried, but he was wise enough not to ask questions in front of Zev. The staff's light had vanished once she climbed out of the pit, as if it knew it was no longer needed. *Later,* Sita had mouthed, and Karim nodded in assent.

"It's a temple for the dead," Sita answered. "An underground necropolis built by the people who lived in this city a thousand years ago."

Zev eyed her with his usual suspicion. "First you mend a broken leg, and now this. You know too much to be some simple Khetaran commoner. You may have the whole tribe fooled, but not me. You've been lying to us since the moment you arrived."

Sita nodded, unbothered by the accusation. "You're right, Zev. We have."

Karim stopped short. "Sita!"

She put a hand on his shoulder. "We cannot remain here any longer, Karim. We've learned all that we can from this place. We must tell the Hudjefa who we really are and demand our immediate release. No more waiting. No more lies." She turned to the other man. "I apologize for our deception, Zev, but it was not without cause. You did try to kill us. It didn't seem wise to reveal my true identity."

Zev's hand went to the dagger at his belt. "Who are you?"

Sita drew herself up. "I am Sitamun, Daughter of Amunmose, Princess of Khetara. And if you value the lives of your people, you will not stand in my way."

Zev's hand dropped back to his side. "A princess…" he murmured in disbelief. "But why—?"

Sita pushed past him and strode toward the steps leading up to the surface. "There's no time to explain. Already too much has been wasted."

Karim hurried forward as they began to ascend the stone stairs. "What happened to you down there, sena?" he whispered. "You seem…different."

"Not different," Sita replied. "I am finally myself."

Karim nodded. He clearly wanted to know more, but he didn't press her. "Why the sudden urgency?"

Sita recalled the ruined wall painting inside the tomb, the stone fragment bearing the image of the lamb. She was no seer, but she knew an ill portent when she saw one.

She was about to answer him when a scream came from the surface.

Sita and Karim looked at each other with dread.

They ran the rest of the way without waiting for Zev to catch up. Sita tore out of the stone portal into the scorching light of day. It was so bright and sudden that, at first, she couldn't see a thing. She blinked rapidly, and out of the white radiance, she glimpsed a small figure dashing toward her, shouting her name.

Aya.

In her haste, the little girl tripped over the hem of her robes and went down in a cloud of sand. Sita was upon her in an instant.

"Aya!" she exclaimed, pulling the girl to her feet. "What's wrong?"

Aya's face shone with terror, and her voice was high and thin. *"Something is coming!"*

Sita put her arm around the girl's shoulders, then startled as an insect scuttled over her hand. She cried out in surprise, flinging it away. The creature landed at Karim's feet.

Zev rushed up behind them, skidding to a halt.

Together, the four stared.

The huge scarab beetle crawled across the sand, its shell gleaming green and gold in the sunlight. Scarabs were common in Khetara, so seeing one shouldn't have been a surprise—except this scarab was quite a bit larger than usual.

Another scarab erupted from the sand beside the first.

Then another.

And another.

"What is this?" Zev exclaimed, backing away from what was quickly becoming a writhing, crawling mass. "What wickedness have you brought upon us?"

Sita's attention was drawn to the head of the valley. Far in the distance, a dark shadow appeared against the lapis blue sky. Sita glanced away when a beetle skittered across her foot, and when she looked again, the shadow had vanished.

She shivered as Aya's warning echoed in her ears.

Something is coming.

16
RAE

Rae lay on her woven mat in the servants' quarters, surrounded by soft, sleeping bodies.

"Are you awake?" a voice asked.

Rae turned on her side. Tamerit lay next to her, her dark eyes luminous in the moonlight.

"I'm awake," Rae replied.

Silence stretched between them. They'd hardly spoken since the king's party the night before, since Rae defied Tam's wishes and blundered into a situation she wasn't prepared for. The experience left Rae feeling violated—her deepest desires exposed and exploited for the pleasure of that *snake*.

Rae had spent the morning working, still muddleheaded from the blue lotus wine. Then came the midday meal, and the news that changed everything.

And what of the Low Khetaran dogs?

They too must be prepared for the ritual.

They're the main event.

The exchange between the king and the high priest had given her confirmation that her father was alive.

It also told her that his time was running out.

Worse still, the king wasn't planning an execution, but a sacrifice. One that would curse all his enemies—including Rae.

As soon as the meal was over, Rae had pulled Tam aside and told her what she'd learned. The chill between them melted in the heat of urgency.

Tam had said, "Go to your father tonight. Tell him we're here and working on a plan. I'll cover for you in case you're missed. A little drink from the kitchens should keep the girls asleep in their beds."

They'd agreed and parted, only seeing each other again that night after their palace work was complete. Rae had sat by the window staring out into the city, while Tam delighted the other maidservants with the stolen wine, passing it around until the jar was empty. It wasn't long before the girls were all asleep.

Rae had lain on her sleeping mat next to Tam for hours, waiting for the right moment to steal away. She thought Tam had fallen asleep too until she'd spoken up.

Rae looked at the weaver, the gentle curve of her body aglow in the moonlight. A wave of remorse overwhelmed her.

"I'm sorry about last night," Rae whispered, her voice quavering. "I should have trusted you."

Tam reached for her hand and brought it to her lips, kissing Rae's calloused knuckles. "You're forgiven. But don't do it again."

"I won't."

Tam glanced out the window at the position of the moon.

Time to go, Rae thought.

Tam squeezed her hand. "We're going to save him," she said, the words a blessing.

Rae nodded, tucked a stray lock of Tam's curly hair behind her ear, and rose to her feet.

She slipped out of the servants' chambers and through the quiet palace, until she reached her hiding spot behind the column. Peering out, she looked to the stairwell leading down to the subterranean passage and was dismayed to see a different man standing guard. He was bigger than his predecessor, and he looked infuriatingly alert. If he didn't fall asleep or go off to make water, how was she going to get past him?

Rae watched and waited. Movement flashed on the other side of the wide hall, where the room opened to a series of windows that faced an interior courtyard, the sills decorated with fine objects—small statues and painted vases and such things. A cat had leaped onto one of the sills.

Nefermaat's cat.

The cat must have sensed Rae's presence, because she stopped and looked straight at her. Her tail flicked.

Stay away! Rae mouthed, as if the cat could understand. All she needed was a purring cat dancing around her ankles to attract the guard's attention. From behind the column, Rae waved off the cat with her hands. *Go on!* she gestured. *Go home!*

The guard burped.

Rae nearly jumped out of her skin at the noise.

The cat watched her with detached interest, her head tilted slightly. Then she turned to the ceramic vase next to her and delicately patted it with her paw.

Stop! Leave it! Rae whisper-shouted.

The cat looked at her once more, her gold eyes unblinking, and pushed the vase off the windowsill. Rae clapped a hand over her mouth as the vase shattered on the stone floor below with a resounding crash.

The guard's response was immediate. Hand on the khopesh

at his belt, he muttered, "What in Amun's name was that?" and stormed off to find the source of the disturbance.

Leaving the stairwell totally unguarded.

Astounded, Rae looked back at the cat, who—her random act of destruction enjoyed and then forgotten—was licking her paw.

"Thank you," Rae whispered, before racing through the dark portal and down the stone steps.

The dank, airless corridor below was lit by a few oil lamps. To the left, the corridor ended at a chamber covered by a red linen curtain.

That can't be it, Rae thought. Besides, something about the room made the hair on the back of her neck stand on end. To the right, she saw another corridor with several doors. Moving stealthily, she crept up to the first door and took a quick peek inside.

Closest to her was a table covered in a variety of implements: a leather flail, a jug of water, and a small bloody knife. A tall wooden post stood in the middle of the room, and a length of rope hung from a ring at the top. The stone floor around it was spattered with dark red stains.

Rae noted that the ends of the rope were frayed, as if sawed through. *What wickedness went on in here?* she wondered. Hopefully nothing to do with her father. She couldn't bear to think of the guards torturing him.

She grabbed the jug of water. *Someone might need it.*

Rae continued down the corridor, stopping in front of a heavy wooden door locked with a sliding bolt. There was a hole in the middle of the door, but nothing larger than a cat could have used it to get in or out. The window allowed a little light in, but even so, it was too dark to see inside.

Still, she recognized it for what it was. A cage.

Rae lifted one of the clay oil lamps from the wall in the

hallway. Then, taking care not to make any noise, she slid the bolt free and pulled the door open just enough for her to slip inside.

The smell hit her first. The stink of unwashed bodies, of excrement, of despair. It was so potent it nearly made her gag. She raised the oil lamp in front of her as she crept into the room, the small globe of light illuminating the prisoners in bits and pieces.

A skeletal woman curled into a corner, her feet in wooden fetters, shielding her eyes from the sudden glare. It was difficult to tell whether she was young or old.

A man lay on his side next to her, either sleeping or unconscious, his face lumpy with bruises, his wrists bound behind his back.

Another woman began to cry when Rae approached. Her feet were also in fetters, and she raised her hands in surrender. "Please don't hurt me," she moaned, her voice a dry rasp. "Please, please…"

The words transported Rae back to Sakesh, to the moments after she stabbed the traitorous brewer and watched him die, to the look of fear on his daughter's face when she saw Rae standing there, covered in blood—

Please don't hurt me, she'd said.

Rae gasped and dragged herself back into the present. She'd broken into a cold sweat. *Not now!* she told herself, shoving away the memory.

"I'm not your enemy," she whispered to the woman, and held out the jug of water.

The woman took it in disbelief, tears rolling down her dirt-stained face. "Oh!" she cried. "Bless you! Bless you!"

Rae nodded. "Drink, then share it with the others. I'm sorry I don't have more, but—"

"Raetawy?"

The voice came from the shadows. Heart in her throat, Rae carried the oil lamp toward the weak, familiar voice.

"Father?" Rae barely got out the word before emotion overwhelmed her. "Father?"

The light struck him, and he squinted into it. She watched his pupils constrict. His dry, peeling lips opened and closed, until finally he said, "Is this a dream?"

Rae found his hand and pressed his work-roughened palm to her face. "It's not a dream, Yati," she replied. "I'm here."

Ankhu stared at her for several seconds, his pale, withered face a mask of shock. Then, it crumpled. With surprising strength, he pulled her to him and wrapped his arms around her.

"I can't believe it," he murmured, his voice thick. "My girl. My beautiful girl. Thanks be to Ra. I thought I would never see you again. I thought...I thought..." He held her tightly, rocking back and forth on the filthy stone floor. Rae leaned into his embrace. In all her life, she had never seen her father cry.

"Did they hurt you?" Rae asked when he released her.

Ankhu sniffed and wiped his face, seemingly eager to put the uncharacteristic display of emotion behind him. "They only beat those who resisted," he said. "Besides that, they've simply left us in this chamber to starve."

"No one has interrogated you?"

Ankhu shook his head.

Rae's brow furrowed. Even if Meryamun planned to use the prisoners for his cursing ritual, why not question them? Why miss the opportunity to gather information about the southern rebellion straight from the source?

Rae went cold.

Back at the farm, when pestilence overtook a portion of the wheat, she and her father were forced to set fire to the entire area to ensure the disease wouldn't be passed on to the next crop.

Why bother rooting out the pest if you plan on burning the whole field?

"Sakesh…" she whispered.

"I don't understand how you got inside," Ankhu said, not privy to the workings of her mind. "This is the belly of the king's palace! There are gates and guards and—"

"Tamerit the weaver and I posed as High Khetaran commoners and were chosen to join the king's staff," Rae explained. "Omari and two others from Sakesh have made camp by the riverside and are using pigeons to send messages to the rebels back home. They're awaiting word on an escape plan."

Suddenly, the idea of leaving her father in that wretched place, of walking out that door without him, became unbearable.

"Perhaps I can get you out tonight," she said. "I could break the fetters on your ankles, knock out the guard at the door and run before anyone could stop us. We'd reach the river where the boat is waiting…" She trailed off as Ankhu shook his head, slowly, sadly.

"We cannot, Raetawy. You know this. What of Tamerit? Would you leave her alone in the palace to face interrogation? To face death? And what of the other prisoners? How could I live, knowing that I should have perished with them?"

Rae gritted her teeth. "Fine. Then I'll find another way."

"No." Her father's expression was resolute. He seized her shoulder. "There is no way out. You cannot keep me safe; you should never have made that promise. You need to leave while you still can. None of this is your fault, do you understand? I thank Ra that I got to see you one last time, but it is not your responsibility to save me."

He leaned back against the wall, his energy draining before

her eyes. "I may be hobbled like a donkey, but my ears work just fine. I have heard the guards speak of the king's cursing ritual. I know we are not long for this world, and I have made peace with my fate. I was already given a second chance at life when I survived the war. It is enough to have lived as long as I have, and to have had the opportunity to raise a woman like you."

His eyes shone in the lamplight. "I should never have forbade you from fighting for our freedom. That was wrong. But you must give up this madness. Leave now and return to Sakesh. Fight for our city, Rae. Fight the war that still has a chance of being won. Those of us here…we're already lost."

The heat of fury rose in Rae's breast. "As long as there is breath in your lungs, you are not lost."

Ankhu pressed his lips into a thin line. "Raetawy, *please*."

"I left others to defend the city, Father. Good men and women who work for the Low Khetaran cause. Say what you will, I will not allow you and our kin to perish here undefended. We must make a stand, before Ra and the pharaoh and everyone. I would rather die fighting for your right to live than to live with the knowledge that I walked away. Say what you will, I am not leaving without you."

Ankhu nodded, his lip trembling. He stroked her hair, as he had when she was a little girl. "I am so proud of you," he said fiercely. "*So proud*."

It took every ounce of Rae's willpower to rise to her feet. To let go of his hand. But she'd already been gone too long. The guard would soon return to his post, and then Ra only knew how she would get back to her chambers.

"Tell the others to be ready at any moment," she told her father. "I don't yet know when or how, but we will come for you. Listen for the call of the nightjar. When you hear its song, know that freedom is at hand."

Excited murmurs floated up from the shadows around them. The other prisoners had been listening, though she couldn't see them. She only had eyes for her father, the brightest sun in her sky.

Ankhu studied Rae's face as if it were the last time he'd see it. "We'll be ready."

Rae was quietly climbing the stairs to the main level when she heard a grunt from above, followed by the clatter of metal against the stone floor.

She paused. The guard had indeed returned to his post, and apparently someone else was fighting with him. But who? No one knew she was there besides Tamerit.

Rae's heart began to race. *No, she wouldn't…*

At the top of the stairs, Rae pressed herself against the wall and peeked out into the torchlit hall.

Two men were grappling outside the stairwell, both bent at the waist and locked in a battle for dominance, their arms gripping each other, turning around and around in a dangerous dance. One was the big guard. The other was a younger, leaner man Rae had never seen before. He wore only a bloodstained loincloth and was covered in nasty cuts, the wounds placed as if to cause the greatest suffering.

He's been tortured. Rae remembered the room with the wooden post, the dried blood, the cut rope. She hadn't checked every corner of that room. *Had he been hiding there, waiting to escape?*

The big guard bore down on the smaller man, forcing him to one knee. "Not so strong now, eh, Femi?" the guard grunted. "Did you really think you'd get out of here alive?"

The man called Femi didn't reply. Instead, he drove his

shoulders into the big man's hips while cinching his legs together. The guard toppled over sideways, his face hitting the ground with a crack.

That move looked familiar. *Two!* Rae thought with a smile.

But the fight wasn't over. Femi kept the guard pinned and crawled up the big man's body to a mounted position. As soon as he sat up, however, the guard thrust his fist straight into a fresh wound below Femi's ribs. On impact, the smaller man's eyes rolled up into his head, and he collapsed.

The guard shoved him off and stood, chuckling as he watched Femi's feeble attempts to move. The big man wiped his bloody mouth with a knuckle and spat a gob of pink saliva onto Femi's face.

Femi flinched, still struggling to rise.

The guard bent to retrieve his khopesh from the floor. Then he turned back to Femi, who'd managed to prop himself on an elbow and was pressing his other hand to his side, trying to stanch the blood flowing from his reopened wound. The guard nonchalantly flipped the weapon so that the blade was pointed down and stood over the fallen man.

With the guard's back to her, Rae had the perfect opening to sneak past the men toward the maidservants' chambers. Creeping out from the shadows of the stairwell, she pressed her back against the wall and began to shuffle by them, working hard not to make a sound.

The guard didn't notice her.

Femi did.

His eyes widened, and they sized each other up in an instant.

Rae froze, fearing he would expose her, use her as a distraction to escape the same way she was using him. Instead, he tipped his chin toward the corridor ahead, as if to say, *Run. Now. While you still can.*

Then the guard kicked Femi in the stomach.

He gasped but didn't cry out.

"To think you were one of us!" the guard said, shaking his head. "Now look at you! Pitiful. But what more can you expect from the princess's little whore?"

Rae stopped mid-step, her hands clenching into fists.

She knew she should run and leave the High Khetaran to his fate. His troubles were none of her business. She had her own battles to fight. Why should she risk it all for a stranger?

"Damn it all," she whispered, then turned and took a running leap onto the guard's back.

The big man barely had time to register the new attacker before Rae laced her arm around his throat. He made a startled choking sound as her arm tightened. He stumbled around like a drunkard, scrabbling at her arm with his fingernails. Then he fell backward, crushing Rae against the wall. She felt her ribs buckle, but she didn't let go.

The guard gurgled and then slumped to the ground.

Rae fell with him, trapped between his huge limp body and the wall. Gasping, she released her grip and tried to shove the guard off her, but to no avail.

Meanwhile, Femi staggered to his feet and stared at her in amazement.

"A little help?" she wheezed.

He darted to Rae's aid, dragging the guard aside and freeing her. Then they worked together to prop him up next to the stairwell, making it look as if he'd simply fallen asleep on the job.

That done, they stood panting and giving each other appraising looks.

"Who are you?" they asked in unison.

"You first," Rae said.

"You heard my name," Femi replied. He was pale and still

bleeding, but his expression didn't betray any pain. "I'm a—well, I *was* a palace guard."

"Why were they torturing you?"

Femi licked his lips. "I was protecting someone."

The princess's little whore, Rae recalled. So, this Femi was in league with Princess Sitamun. Tam had shared the rumors about the princess's disappearance, how people were saying that she ran away because the king intended to marry her, and that she was hiding from her brother somewhere in the kingdom. Meryamun was apparently quite keen to conceal the truth, but the palace was far from a watertight vessel. Secrets always found a way to leak out.

If Femi was the princess's ally, perhaps he could also be hers.

"Your turn," Femi prodded. "What's your name?"

"Raetawy," she said, distracted by her whirling thoughts.

She cursed herself. *Fool! You're supposed to give him your alias!*

"Well, Raetawy," Femi said, his words slurring slightly. "I have no idea what you were doing underground, but I appreciate your help." For all his show of courage, Femi's blood loss was clearly affecting him.

"Don't mention it," Rae replied. She knew she should head back to the maidservants' chambers and avoid additional conversation, but leaving Femi in his weakened state didn't sit right with her. *Besides, there's no rush to get back now. Tam is covering for me. I could take the opportunity to go to the riverbank and talk to Omari and the others about what I've learned.* "I expect you'll be fleeing the palace now, yes?" she asked Femi.

He nodded. "I'd best go quickly. There'll be a change of guard soon, and when they find him like this, there'll be a search. I know a back way…" He started toward the corridor leading to the main hall, but he stumbled after only a few steps.

Rae ducked under his arm and wrapped her own around his

shoulders to keep him from falling. "That sounds like a fine plan. But you're naked and bleeding, so maybe we grab you a tunic and find this back way together."

With effort, Femi turned to look up at her, his head lolling, his eyes unfocused. "You're very tall," he said vaguely, "has anyone ever told you that?"

Rae sighed and dragged him toward the main hall. "You know what, Femi? You're the first."

Femi directed Rae to the gardener's entrance at the back of the king's pleasure garden. From there, they were able to make their way down to the riverbank. Rae stood by while Femi drank his fill and washed the dirt and blood from his body. Thankfully, his wound had finally stopped bleeding.

"What are you going to do now?" she asked as he climbed out of the water. He'd stolen the khopesh and belt from the guard before they left, but other than that, Femi had nothing.

He slipped into the clean tunic she'd found for him in a laundry basket, then wrapped the leather belt around his narrow waist and cinched it tight.

"I have friends in the city I can trust," Femi said, taking the khopesh from her proffered hand. He sliced it through the air several times, testing its weight, before thrusting it into his belt with satisfaction. With a blade at his hip, Rae could see Femi's strength returning.

"This person you are protecting," Rae asked, hoping to pry more information from Femi before they went their separate ways. "She opposes the king?"

Femi looked at her sharply. He hadn't said it was a woman.

I'm going to need to give him more if I expect him to trust me.

Rae added, "If Sitamun opposes her brother, then she and I are in accord. As are many others, both in Thonis and beyond."

The guard searched her face for a long moment, considering her words. Finally, he said, "You're a spy."

Rae didn't confirm nor deny it. She waited to see what he would say next.

"You play a dangerous game, Raetawy."

Rae shrugged. "You risked your life to protect the princess. I risk mine for someone equally precious."

"I see," Femi said. "And I imagine you'd like something in return for saving my life? Something to aid you in your mission?"

"King Meryamun intends to sacrifice a number of political prisoners during a mass cursing ritual at the Thonis fortress in several days' time. This is dark magic. It will set all of Khetara down a path from which I fear there may be no return. I mean to free those prisoners before the ritual comes to pass."

Femi scoffed. "Then you mean to do the impossible."

"I got *you* out, didn't I?"

"I am but one man—and we barely escaped with our lives! Besides, the guards will redouble their number once they've discovered I'm gone. The prisoners you speak of, are they soldiers?"

Rae thought of the men and women huddled in that dark room, frightened and starving. She shook her head. "No, they're regular people. Farmers, merchants and the like."

"Then you would be lucky to visit them again, no less engineer their escape. I'm sorry, Raetawy, but that is the truth. Better to make your stand at the fortress, though that too is a suicide mission." He rubbed the hilt of the khopesh with one hand. "Still, I respect the choice to die for such a cause. Perhaps if you can disrupt this ritual, Meryamun will fail to gain the power he seeks—at least temporarily."

Frustrated, Rae began to pace. "Tell me about this fortress. Does it have any special attributes? Any vulnerabilities?"

Femi rubbed the back of his neck, thinking. "There is one thing..."

They spoke a bit more, Rae committing every detail to memory, before they both sensed they could tarry no longer.

"You should find shelter before first light," she told Femi. "I must go. There's something I need to do before returning to the palace."

"You mean to return?" Femi asked, incredulous.

"Of course." She'd already decided to wait until the servants began the kitchen work at dawn and slip in among them. Tam would vouch for her rising early to complete her duties in case anyone asked after her, not that they would. The maidservants were all but invisible.

Femi bowed his head. "You are a brave woman, Raetawy. May Amun be with you in the coming days."

"And Ra with you," Rae replied.

Femi looked at her askance as the full understanding of her allegiance became clear to him. "Why did you save me not knowing if I'd have done the same for you?" he asked quietly.

Rae shrugged. "Because I'm a fool."

Femi smiled. "A fool I won't soon forget."

With that, he turned and ran out of sight.

Sighing, Rae smoothed back her hair and hurried down the riverbank. Moonlight glimmered on the rippling surface of the Iteru. The night air was heavy with jasmine, which bloomed along the river like constellations of stars.

After a few minutes, Rae ducked into a dense thicket of papyrus and pushed her way through, the ground growing marshy beneath her feet. She was almost to the other side when an arm like a tree trunk burst through the reeds, grabbed hold of her tunic, and yanked her out into the open. An enormous man loomed over her, his fist pulled back, ready to strike.

"It's me!" she exclaimed, raising her hands in surrender. "It's Raetawy!"

Omari dropped his fist. "It's late," he said by way of greeting, and released his grip on her tunic. "I wasn't expecting you."

Rae peered around him at Kay and Buto, who slept huddled under blankets near the smoldering remains of a campfire. The fishing skiff was tied up nearby, bobbing gently in the water. *It must be Omari's turn to keep watch.* She glanced at him uncertainly, surprised that she hadn't received a warmer welcome. "You must really miss me," she said. "You look terrible."

Rae thought the jab might wrest a smile from her old friend, but Omari only grimaced. "I hope you come with good news. If I have to piss away another day sitting here doing nothing, I swear I'll go mad."

"I have news, but I'm afraid very little of it is good." For the next few minutes, Rae told Omari everything that she and Tam had learned about the king's political plans, the location of the Sakeshi prisoners, and the threat of their imminent demise at the cursing ritual. She repeated what she'd discussed with Femi, though she neglected to mention its source. Somehow, Rae imagined that Omari wouldn't be pleased to know she'd helped a High Khetaran guard escape from the palace, no matter what information the act had won her.

"There must be something more we can do besides wait until the final hour," Rae said when she'd finished. "But I can't think how to improve our situation."

Omari looked west across the river before answering. "What we need is leverage. Something to stay the king's hand."

"Like what?"

"Tell me more about this priestess you look after," he said. "You said the king is quite taken with her?"

Rae hesitated, uncomfortable with the direction of the conversation. "Yes, she's one of Meryamun's closest advisers. From what Tam told me, she had a premonition that saved his life and has been at his side ever since." She paused. "But she's just a girl, Omari. Barely more than a child. We can't—"

"Do you want your father back or not?" Omari retorted.

Rae felt a flush of indignation. "Of course I do! What kind of question is that?"

Omari scoffed. "The kind you must ask yourself when you decide what you can or can't do in order to stop these High Khetaran scum from slaughtering us where we stand. Or have you forgotten, during your cozy respite in the palace, why we came here? Have you gotten too comfortable eating their good food, sleeping on their plush beds?"

"No!"

"Then for the love of Ra, do what needs to be done!" He stepped so close that she could smell the beer on his breath. "This is no time to be squeamish. This is war."

Rae stared at him, unnerved by her friend's uncharacteristic aggression. Was prolonged inaction putting him on edge? "What's wrong with you, Omari?" she asked.

"Me? I'm thinking clearly. It's you who has your head in the sand. This Nefermaat could be the very thing we need to turn the tide. Can't you see that?"

"It's not that simple," Rae argued. "There's a chance that she and the prince might be plotting against the king as well. If she's on our side—"

Omari barked a laugh. "On *our* side? Now I know you've been in the palace too long. Do you seriously believe she would go against the very man who placed her at the seat of power? Who showered her with luxuries? She's manipulating you, Rae. That's what High Khetarans do."

Rae spun the gold bead on her swivel ring. Her mind turned to the friendly young girl who'd spared her from the guard's blade in the courtyard, who'd shared her breakfast that day in her chambers. Except now, Rae began to see those events in a different light. What if Nefermaat's actions hadn't been kind, but calculated? What if her vision had revealed Rae's true identity, and the priestess really had been deceiving her from the start?

Perhaps Rae *had* underestimated her.

When she put her feelings aside, she could see that Nefermaat was indeed the perfect target. The priestess was their best chance at shifting power in their direction, and Rae had easy access to her. Even if using Nefermaat as leverage forced the king to merely delay the cursing ritual, it would give them the opportunity to alert the rest of the rebels back in Sakesh and the time to transport more of their number to Thonis.

It was a good plan, and as their leader, Rae should have been the first to think of it. She felt a sting of shame. She glanced at Omari. He was watching her, waiting for her answer.

"You're right," she said. "The girl is no innocent. Every day she works to serve and protect the king, which increases his power."

"She is an accomplice to the murder of our people," Omari said. "Whatever comes to her, she deserves."

Rae repeated the words in her mind, knowing she'd need to come back to them later, when the time came to do the difficult thing. *Whatever comes to her, she deserves.*

Grimly, she said, "We need to plan—and quickly. I must return before dawn."

Omari took a step back, his tension falling away. "I knew

you'd see sense, Ay," he said approvingly. "This is going to work, you'll see. You wanted to send a message to Pharaoh, to bring the fight for Low Khetara to his doorstep. This is how we do it. This is how we start."

Her heart thus hardened, Rae agreed. "Let's begin."

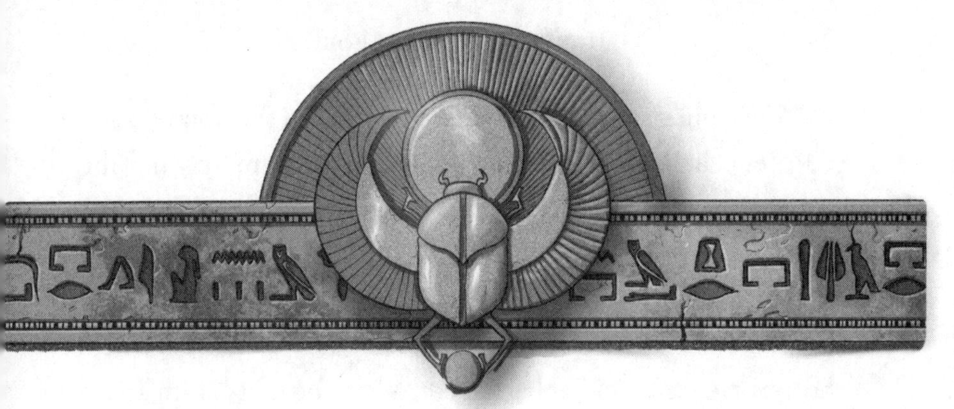

17
KARIM

Karim felt fate on the wind.

He felt it as soon as they emerged from the underground temple into the yellow blaze of day. A hot breeze dipped into the valley, ruffling his brown curls and filling his senses with that familiar, intoxicating scent. Even before Aya had shared her warning, he heard the words in the air, whispered with divine certainty.

Something is coming.

He hoped it was merely a figment of his imagination, the result of overexerting himself in the midday sun as he ran to the village for help.

When he saw the scarabs, he knew it was true.

"Where are they coming from?" Sita exclaimed in alarm as the beetles surged from beneath the desert floor to swarm all around them.

Aya started screaming, and Karim lifted the girl into his arms. She clung to him, shaking. "Don't let them get me!" she begged.

"*Shh*, young sena. I've got you." He watched the flow of black iridescent shells. They were not attacking them, merely moving past them—and in one direction. "They're all going toward the old palace!" he told Sitamun.

The breeze lifted the princess's mane of black hair off her shoulders and tossed it as she turned to Setnakht's palace, where the massive statue of Set beckoned. When she met Karim's gaze again, he knew they were sharing the same thought.

Handing Aya to Zev, Karim said, "Run to the village and raise the alarm, sen. Arm yourselves, quickly now. I fear these creatures are harbingers of what's to come."

"Why should I follow your orders?" Zev snarled. He was about to continue his rebuke when Aya pressed her cheek into the side of his neck.

"Please listen to him. Please!"

Zev relented. "This is your fault, I know it," he said to Karim. "You've brought this upon us." Then he hoisted the girl higher in his arms and ran.

Karim told Sita, "You should go with him too, Princess, where it's safe. Khetara needs you."

Sitamun lifted her chin and held the twisted serpent staff at her side. At her feet, the scarab beetles parted before her. Karim couldn't help but stare. Standing there, with her shoulders thrown back and the wind in her hair, the princess was magnificent to behold, the kind of woman who inspired men to take up paintbrushes and chisels, who soldiers traveled to the ends of the earth to fight for—to die for.

"I know my kingdom needs me," she said. "That's why I'm coming with you."

Karim nodded. "As you wish, sena."

He didn't believe in the Khetaran gods, but in that moment, he believed in her.

Together, they took off at a sprint, following the river of scarabs to the ancient palace.

They reached the large tree-lined courtyard in front of the palace in short order, though Sitamun was winded once they got there. Her staff must have been heavy, and Karim was impressed at how fleet of foot she was on her twisted ankle. As for himself, he was continually mystified at his inexhaustible stamina. He should have been tired after the run back and forth to the village, yet he felt as strong as ever. Perhaps his time among the Hudjefa had been more rejuvenating than he'd accounted for.

The scarabs had gathered and were crawling everywhere—up the trunks of the palm trees, the legs of the big statue, and the walls of the ruined palace, until every surface squirmed with restless excitement.

"Why are they all here?" Karim wondered aloud. "What are they waiting for?"

A thunder of hoofbeats answered him.

Karim's heart—still heavy, still strange—thrummed as he turned toward the sound.

In the distance, a dark rider appeared at the head of the road into Perset. He rode swiftly, growing from a black spot at the edge of Karim's vision to a defined silhouette within seconds. Karim watched the approach, enthralled, his mind desperately attempting to make sense of what he was seeing. He couldn't decide which was more forbidding, the man or his steed.

The man wore a crimson cape that sailed behind him, rippling like the current of a bloodred river. He was clad in gleaming bronze and black leather, and wore a helm boasting tall, blunted ears and the snout of an animal not known to nature but known to Karim.

The man's horse—if one could call it that—was so hideous, so foul, so utterly gruesome, that even to look upon it made Karim's stomach churn. It wore a glorious red-feathered headdress, a golden bridle, and a black leather saddle, but those pretty things did nothing to hide the horrors beneath: the eyeless, fleshless skull with its huge teeth gnashing at the bit; the black body, missing large patches of skin along its flank that revealed dark muscle, sinew, and bone beneath, moving in a ceaseless rhythm. And the worst feature of all: the heaving masses of insects flowing from those exposed, rotting places; the maggots and locusts and spiders and, yes, the scarabs. Insects writhed and dropped from the horse's desiccated flesh, only to follow in the beast's footsteps, both on the ground and in the air, a thousand flying, buzzing acolytes ushering their putrid god.

As the rider drew closer, Karim shook himself free of its spell and grabbed Sitamun by the hand. "We must take cover," he said.

The princess didn't take her eyes off the rider as they ducked behind a broken column to watch the man's final approach.

"Is that...?" she asked, leaving the question unfinished.

Karim's heart beat strongly, like a dog pulling at its lead, trying to return to its master. He felt panic rising inside him, threatening to flood all reason.

"No," he murmured. "No, no, no..."

The rider pulled back on the reins as he reached the courtyard, and the horse loosed a spine-chilling cry as it reared back and came to a halt in a cloud of red dust. Beetles wriggled around it, unfazed by the threat of the horse's stamping hooves. The rider reached up to lift his helm, exposing his face to the sun.

"Amun help us," Sita whispered.

A lordly, intelligent face took in the landscape, gazing upon the crumbling ancient palace with the pride of homecoming.

However, this was no ordinary man. His face was exceedingly long and narrow, giving him an unearthly quality, which was only accentuated by the greenish tinge of his skin.

The last time Karim had seen that face, it had been a grinning skull. But even in living flesh, he would recognize the creature anywhere. One does not usually get the opportunity to reunite with one's murderer, but that day, Karim did.

After a thousand years, Setnakht had returned to Perset.

"My city," Setnakht rumbled. His voice was deep and discordant, as if every utterance went against the law of nature. "How I've missed you."

The monstrous horse whinnied, and Setnakht reached out to stroke it until it calmed.

I think that's the mummified horse Djet and I saw inside the tomb, Karim thought. *He must have gone back there to get it, and his armor too.*

"What do we do?" Sita asked. She looked pale and frightened.

"I don't know..." The ancient pharaoh had been a formidable foe even before he'd taken Karim's heart. Now that Setnakht was fully resurrected, Karim hadn't the faintest idea how to stop him.

As if sensing their presence, Setnakht nudged the horse closer to the fallen column. Karim and Sitamun slid down low, pressing their backs to the stone. His pulse racing, Karim listened to the creature's slow, heavy footfalls approach them.

The sound stopped, near enough that some of the insects surrounding the beast crawled onto the stone column and skittered over Karim's shoulders and chest. He resisted the urge to brush them away, lest it betray them. Next to him, Sitamun suffered the same fate as insects swarmed over her body. When a spider crept across her throat, she covered her mouth with one hand to stop herself from screaming.

Once the swarm had scattered, Karim peered over his shoulder and saw Setnakht facing the enormous statue of Set.

"I have returned to you, Lord," the pharaoh said. "At long last, I have come to finish what I started."

With a frisson of dread, Karim remembered the words Sitamun had recited from the old map: *He shall not travel West, for his work is unfinished.*

"The heathen plague has infested Perset for too long," Setnakht continued. "They will be the first to feel the wrath of the Storm God." He paused, raising both arms to the sky. He held a black and crimson crook in one hand and a flail in the other. Then, in a voice that seemed to amplify a hundredfold, he spoke again.

"Heed me, O ushabti! Wake and hear my call! Your long sleep is now over, and as is your duty, you will rise to do great works in this land. Come, my ushabti! The sun rises once more on the reign of Set, the one true god! Rise from your slumber and say, 'Here I am,' so that I may count you among my number!"

"Ushabti?" Karim muttered, unfamiliar with the word.

"They're small figurines we place in royal tombs," Sitamun explained quietly. "To serve the dead as servants in the afterlife. We inscribe the name of the king on them so that when the ushabti comes to life, it will know its master. But why is he using an ushabti spell here? This isn't the underworld."

Karim thought of the army of tiny men he'd seen in Setnakht's tomb. Those must have been ushabti. They'd been arranged in front of a Set statue much like the larger one standing before them. It was as if that chamber of the tomb was a miniature replica of Perset's palace courtyard.

Karim swallowed hard. "I have a bad feeling about this..."

"Heed me, O ushabti!" Setnakht cried once more. "Wake and hear my call!"

The insects scattered.

Setnakht fell silent.

From where they lay concealed behind the column, Karim had a clear view of one side of the tree-lined courtyard. A bead of sweat trickled down his forehead and along the bridge of his nose, where it hung suspended for a long, long moment before it fell.

"Did you feel that?" Sitamun whispered.

"What?"

"The ground. It's shaking."

As soon as she said it, Karim felt it too. The earth beneath them had begun to quake, like something under the sand was clawing to get out. Then, like an unholy growth, a blackened arm sprang from the ground a few lengths in front of them, reaching for the sky.

First one, then three, then a dozen, then more.

There were copper spears, khopesh, and maces gripped in the hands, each one covered in a greenish-brown patina. As the sand fell away, heads and shoulders emerged after them. Karim watched in horror as men crafted of dark, pitted stone, their features either grotesquely distorted by cracks and fissures or worn smooth by time, rose from the ground. They'd been carved wearing Khetaran headdresses and false beards, and they were all identical aside from what the centuries had wrought upon them.

Then, one by one, they climbed to their feet and began to speak in voices as dry as the khamsin wind.

"Here I am," said the ushabti.

"Here I am."

"Here I am."

Setnakht's army, Karim thought with a shudder.

The ancient pharaoh wasn't done yet. Turning back to the statue of Set, he raised his arms and began again.

"Heed me, O Shesmu!" Setnakht commanded. "Wake and hear my call! You whom I name Butcher, Mutilator of Living

Flesh! You who I call the Dismemberer, who slays man and god alike, who makes the blood of the unworthy flow like wine! Wake, Shesmu, and remember that purpose for which you were crafted! Wake and lead my legion to glory!"

The shaking intensified, and the ground directly in front of the statue splintered, then exploded, sending a cloud of sand into Karim and Sitamun's faces.

Karim shielded his eyes from the stinging grit. Then he saw it, emerging from the reddish dust like a mountain from primeval waters.

Shesmu knelt before Setnakht, an enormous figure made from the same blackened stone as the ushabti but at least twice their size. He was sculpted in the image of a broad, powerful man clothed in scale armor, and he held two copper butcher knives crossed in front of his chest.

His head was a helm in the shape of a lion's skull, and as Shesmu looked skyward, red sand poured from the holes where his eyes would have been.

When the red dust had settled back to earth, Shesmu rose to his feet, brandishing the knives in a salute to the pharaoh. Karim noticed that the symbols for Setnakht's name—the cloth, the loaf, the jagged line, the vulture—were engraved on his chest.

The name of his master.

Shesmu moved to join the ushabti. The stone men stood at attention, waiting for their king's next command.

"I-I don't understand," Sitamun murmured. Her face was haunted. "Magic this powerful…it's not possible…"

Just then, a horn sounded from the village.

"Elyas is raising the alarm," Karim whispered.

In response, Setnakht wheeled his steed to face the city. His horse squealed and stomped the ground.

"Patience, imi-ib," Setnakht cooed, tugging on the reins. Then he shouted once more in that unnaturally loud voice: "Heed me, Shesmu! Heed me, my ushabti! I command you to cleanse this city of its human pestilence. Root them out to the last man and leave no survivors!"

With that, Setnakht kicked his horse into a gallop and thundered down the palace road toward the heart of the city. Shesmu and the stone men followed, weapons in hand, their stiff walk becoming a steady march as they cast off a thousand years of stillness. Karim tried to count them. Were there a hundred? Two hundred?

He waited until the last ushabti had passed before he stood, scouring his mind for a plan. "There are a lot of them, but they're slow," he said in a rush. "We could reach the Hudjefa first if we hurry, but what do we do once we get to them? How does one defeat an army of stone?"

Sitamun rose next to him, the serpent staff in her hand. "For now, we only need to get the Hudjefa out of the city. Khetaran magic is very literal. Setnakht's command was to kill every person they find in Perset. But if they aren't within the city limits..."

"Then there's no one to kill," Karim said, finishing Sitamun's thought. He nodded. "It's our best chance. Let's go."

He took off at a run. Sita sprinted by his side, her expression resolute—a far cry from the delicate princess he'd met in Thonis, who fatigued after only an hour of walking. They veered off the palace road to flank the ushabti, making their way through the winding city streets.

"Find Elyas," Sitamun told him, her chest heaving with exertion. "He will have assembled the men and will not want to abandon the city without a fight, but you must convince him that the threat is too great to make a stand here. I will go to the women and children and direct them to flee the valley."

"All right," Karim said. He hesitated. "Sitamun..."

"We will see each other again," Sitamun said, her voice catching with emotion. She reached out to press her palm to his cheek.

He put his hand on top of hers, suddenly desperate not to let the moment pass. Their brief respite from the turmoil of the outside world was over, he knew that. The little life they'd built there…that was over too. But it had been good.

So good.

He hated to let her go.

He dropped his hand, and she dropped hers. Fate was calling. They could not wait any longer to answer.

With one last look at Sitamun, Karim bolted toward the courtyard at the center of the village where Karim had first met the Hudjefa. He'd learned that it was often used as a meeting place, so he suspected it would be where Elyas and his men would assemble.

Sure enough, a crowd had already gathered when he arrived. Men were pulling weapons from their armory, albeit with less haste than Karim had hoped. Dumiya stood slightly apart from the rest, spear in hand. Karim found Zev and the tribe leader among them, engaged in animated disagreement.

"You've brought damnation upon us, Elyas!" Zev said, the scar on his face purpling with agitation. "We had peace before the outsiders came. You should have let me kill them while I had the chance!"

Elyas bristled at the accusation. "Get ahold of yourself, Zev! I have done as you've asked and prepared the men—but you still haven't explained what in god's name is going on!"

Zev was about to reply when both men noticed Karim.

"Take whatever you can carry and leave the rest!" Karim shouted to the crowd. "You cannot defend yourselves against what is coming. We must flee the city!"

The armed men stopped what they were doing and erupted

with protests and confusion. Elyas grabbed Karim by the shoulder and pulled him aside.

"Are you mad, sen? Raising an alarm is one thing, but fleeing the city? If this is a ploy to go back to your people and betray us, then I swear to you—"

"It's not a ploy," Karim broke in. "It's too much to explain right now. Please, for the safety of your people, we must go *now*."

Dumiya came over and watched the men's exchange with growing apprehension.

Zev shook his head, furious. "No. Absolutely not. The women and children can leave, but I am not going anywhere!"

Dumiya turned her head in the direction of the palace, her gray eyes narrowing and her body growing tense.

"Elyas!" Karim begged. "Listen to me!"

The old man's expression darkened like a thunderhead. "No, sen, you listen to *me*. Until you tell me what you're so afraid of, we aren't leaving."

The sound of barking joined the clamor of the crowd. Behkai came racing down one of the side streets and ran to Karim, his mouth foaming, his eyes wild. Then, a distant, terrified shout pierced the air.

"To arms!" the voice cried. *"To arms!"*

The crowd went still and silent.

In the quiet, Karim heard the rumble of many feet marching.

Elyas stared at Karim with growing unease. "What is it?" he asked. "What's coming?"

A second later, a man stumbled backward into view on the main road, his sword raised defensively.

"To arms!" he bellowed again, just as a great stone hand came down from above, grasped his head, and squeezed it like a grape. There was a pop, and a profusion of blood burst from between

the stone fingers. The man's body went still before dropping to its knees and toppling to the dust below.

Shesmu the Butcher's shadow fell over the crowd as he stepped over the body and into the courtyard. He opened his fist, releasing the wet wreckage of the man's skull before unsheathing the second knife from his belt.

For one shocked moment, not a single person moved or spoke.

Then came pandemonium.

Zev and a dozen others loosed war cries and charged the stone warrior, while others fled in terror down the side streets, only to be cut off by the ushabti marching toward them.

"Tell them to retreat!" Karim yelled, shaking Elyas by the shoulders.

The old man's gaze remained locked on the bloody corpse, his mouth agape.

"Tell them!"

"Retreat!" Elyas shouted, finally finding his voice.

It was too late.

No one could hear him over the screams.

Cursing, Karim pushed Elyas away from the oncoming horde and sprinted into the fray with Behkai galloping at his side. Up ahead, Shesmu's knives were slicing toward another Hudjefa tribesman, who was too distracted by the approach of the ushabti to notice the imminent danger. With a burst of speed that felt miraculous, Karim dove into the man, driving him to the ground before the swinging blades could cut him in two.

"Run for the desert, sen!" Karim told him.

Meanwhile, Behkai had bounded onto a barrel, then a rooftop, and started barking furiously at Shesmu, distracting the stone warrior so that the man could get away unscathed.

"Behkai, watch out!" Karim cried, and the dog leaped from

the roof as Shesmu's enormous fist crashed into the mud-brick house.

Karim was on his feet and caught the dog before he could hit the ground. *How did I do that?* he wondered. His resurrection had given him a second chance at life, but he'd begun to wonder if there was more to it than that.

Karim set the dog down, his body buzzing with vital energy begging to be expended.

With Behkai at his side, he dashed back into the crush of men and ushabti, following the dog's lead by jumping onto obstacles and using them to launch himself into the stone warriors, unbalancing some and toppling others long enough for the Hudjefa to escape. He caught a glimpse of Dumiya similarly bounding from one enemy to the next with fluid, silent grace, narrowly avoiding one fatal blow after another. Still, for many others, the damage had already been done. The ground was littered with bodies, the sand sodden with blood.

Karim had just landed on the ground in a crouch after having kicked two ushabti into each other, when he saw Zev sparring with another stone warrior across the way, their copper blades clashing. Karim could see the killing blow coming, could see the opening for a slash after the parry, but even he couldn't cross that distance in time. He was a mere arm's breadth away from Zev when the ushabti's sword sliced deep across the man's torso, disemboweling him.

Behkai rushed in from the side to attack the ushabti while Karim dropped to one knee beside Zev, lifting the man's head off the ground. Blood burbled from Zev's lips as he eyed Karim with fierce recrimination. "This is on you, sen," he said with difficulty. "Hudjefa blood is on your hands."

Then Zev's grimace relaxed, and he was still.

His chest burning with shame and despair, Karim set Zev gently on the ground and stood. Why did death follow him like a shadow everywhere he went?

The priestess Nefermaat's face appeared in his mind, her every word a premonition.

You had two shadows.

The oracle asked too much of him. He was nothing and no one, as Babu once said. What was he supposed to do with such a task? Such a burden?

Roaring, he threw himself into the nearest ushabti, shoving and kicking with reckless, careless rage. The stone men fell away from him like pawns on a game board, toppled but unharmed, some falling onto the corpses of men who lay beyond suffering's reach. He lost track of Behkai in the fray and prayed that the dog would have the sense to not get himself killed.

Then Karim heard the *clip-clop* of hooves approaching at a canter, followed by a booming command.

"Wait."

The ushabti stilled, stopping mid-battle as if transformed back to mere statues. Battered, his clothes torn, Karim whirled to see Setnakht astride his horse in the middle of the courtyard, taking in a scene of total carnage. The monstrous horse snorted and stamped, maggots dropping from its flanks to feast on the bodies below.

Setnakht removed his helm and set it on his knee, revealing his long, unearthly face. He eyed Karim with amazement. "Is it really you, my acolyte? You look quite well for my having killed you." The ancient pharaoh reached out toward him, and Karim felt the amulet pushing against his ribs as if it were trying to get out. Dizzy, Karim pressed a hand to his chest until the sensation faded.

"Apparently you did a poor job of it, sen," Karim replied through gritted teeth.

Setnakht dropped his arm back to the saddle, smiling. "So, you've taken my heart, as I've taken yours. Or rather...someone has given it to you. Very resourceful. I commend them. Still, it's irritating to find you here, interrupting the cleansing of my city. Perhaps the Lord of Chaos has chosen to set you in my path once more to test my will." He gave Karim a small nod. "So be it."

His next words were unnaturally loud, spoken in what Karim now recognized as his spell-casting voice: "Kill him, my ushabti. Make a home for your blades in his flesh, so that his body may better remember its demise."

Before Karim could react, before he could take a breath, he felt a jolt as a spearhead was thrust through him, sprouting from the middle of his chest.

Time slowed. The sounds of copper clashing with copper, of screams and shouts and wails of terror, grew muted and distant.

Karim staggered but remained standing. He took a lurching step toward Setnakht.

He sensed movement at his left as another spear lanced into him. His body jerked with the impact, and the pain took his breath away.

His vision grew dark. There was barking somewhere. Perhaps he was no longer on his feet but his knees. The weight of the spears made him heavy and unbalanced. He tried to rise, to move forward, and a third spear slid through his belly.

He fell.

18
SITA

Sita adjusted Sami's arm around her shoulders as she spoke to his mother. The boy could put a little weight on his injured leg, but not enough to walk by himself. "I've got him. You attend to Miri, all right?"

Sami's mother stared into the distance, while all around her, women and children ran in terror, carrying the few belongings they'd managed to gather before fleeing their homes. Nearby, Elyas's elderly wife, Miri, leaned against a house, her chest already heaving with exertion, her face gray.

Sita reached for the young mother's hand. "Look at me," she commanded. "You are going to lead Miri out of the city and join the others. Take shelter among the desert hills until the rest of the tribe rejoins you. Do you understand?"

Sami's mother shook her head in dismay. "I can't!" she cried.

Sita squeezed her hand. "You can, and you will."

The words seemed to steady Sami's mother. With a nod, she

went to the elderly woman and began leading her away. Sita and Sami followed at a slower pace, one labored step at a time.

"W-what's that?" Sami asked as the rhythmic stamp of footsteps grew louder behind them.

"Don't look back," Sita told him. "Keep walking."

Sita led him down a side street, hoping to get away from the approaching threat. In the shadows, the bodies of two women lay close together. A basket of figs had spilled from the arms of one, littering the ground with fruit.

"Keep your eyes ahead, Sami," Sita urged.

The boy nodded, tears rolling down his face.

The side street opened onto another main road, where they were nearly run over by a blood-drenched man tearing toward the city's limits.

"Thanks be to Amun!" Sita exclaimed when she saw it was not one of the ushabti. "Where are the rest of the men? Have they already fled?"

The man's voice was rough as gravel. "Only some got away," he said. "Others…"

Dread dropped into Sita's stomach like a cold stone. "What about Karim? Where is he?"

"He's still back there."

Sita tightened her grip on the serpent staff. *I must go to him.*

"Here," she said, transferring Sami's arm to the man's shoulder. "Follow the others and make sure he gets out of the valley safely."

Neither Sami nor the man made protest as she left them, taking off toward the village center at a run.

She dashed through the side streets, alternating from one to the next to avoid the ushabti marching through them, searching for survivors. Sita had almost reached the main courtyard when she saw a small, familiar form huddled in an alleyway.

"Aya?" she said, touching the girl on the shoulder.

Aya gasped, then burst into tears of relief when she saw who it was. She reached out for Sita, who gathered the girl into her arms.

"You're all right," Sita said soothingly, rubbing her back. "What happened to Zev? Why aren't you with him?"

Sniffing, Aya said, "Once he found Elyas, he told me to run home and join the other children. But the stone men came, so I've been hiding, and…and…" She became too overwhelmed to speak.

"Aya, you *must* get out of the city. The others went—"

"No!" Aya shrieked. "I'm staying with you!"

"Aya…"

The girl clung to Sita's arm. "Please."

Sita sucked her teeth in exasperation. "Fine," she said, not wishing to waste any more time arguing. She grabbed Aya's hand. "Come on!"

They had only taken a few steps when Setnakht's booming voice echoed through the alleyway. "Kill him, my ushabti," the voice said. "Make a home for your blades in his flesh, so that his body may better remember its demise."

Sita knew at once to whom the spell was directed.

Heart thumping, she ran as fast as she could, pulling Aya behind her.

Almost there, Sita thought. *Almost—!*

They arrived in the courtyard in time to see the first spear go through Karim's body.

Sita gasped.

No!

She collapsed against a wall, shielding Aya's face from the sight as the second spear struck its mark.

She felt the third and final spear in her own heart as it shattered to pieces.

She watched Karim fall to his knees and slump forward, the spear in his chest preventing him from tumbling to the ground.

"No…not again," Sita moaned. *I already lost you once,* she thought, despair claiming her. *Didn't I order you not to die?*

"Sabba?" Aya said.

The girl was peeking between Sita's fingers at the bodies strewn across the ground.

"Sabba!"

Before Sita could stop her, Aya ran into the courtyard and dropped to her knees beside Elyas's still form. In the courtyard, Shesmu and the ushabti continued to hunt and kill the men who remained. The girl's movement attracted Shesmu's attention, and he started toward her.

Sita rushed to Aya's side. The girl had her arms around her grandfather's body, her head on his chest as she sobbed, calling his name.

"I'm so sorry, little one," Sita whispered, softly, gently, each word suffused with sorrow. "I'm sorry, but we must go. We can't help him now…" Her words trailed off as Elyas's bloody, trembling hand lifted from his chest to rest on the back of his granddaughter's head.

"Shh." The sound from Elyas's lips shivered like an evening breeze through papyrus reeds. The old man's eyes were wide open, bright within his filthy, bloodstained face.

Sita was astounded.

Aya grasped her grandfather's hand, oblivious to the imminent danger they were all in. "See? He's only hurt! You can fix him like you fixed Sami!"

Sita should have been afraid. But the molten agony of losing

Karim for the second time hardened into ferocity. *Choose,* the voice of her soul demanded. *Will you fight? Or will you die?*

Aya pleaded with her. "We can't leave without my sabba!"

As the stone butcher approached, Sita set the serpent staff upright and stood to face him. "We're not going to."

Shesmu loomed over them, his blades awash in blood, the mottled brown-black stone of him spattered in gore. The face hidden within the lion-skull helm had a savage, leonine quality, but his expression was as placid as any Khetaran statue, unbothered by all the slaughter he'd wrought. He raised his knife to strike but hesitated when he noticed Sita's staff.

Sita felt the wood pulse in her hand like an extension of her body, alive and eager to perform. *You know the names,* it seemed to say. *Use them!*

Sita thrust the staff aloft and spoke in a voice that echoed through the streets of Perset.

"I name you, Shesmu the Butcher! Mutilator! Dismemberer!" she boomed. "I name you, and I say to you: By the power of Isis, you shall not enter this circle!" With that, she brought the staff down. When its tip struck the ground, a beam of white light burst from each side of the staff, encircling Sita, Aya, and Elyas within its brilliance.

The light closed around them as Shemsu's knife sliced down with terrifying force. There was a flash, and the next thing Sita knew, the butcher's blade flew backward through the air, clattering to the ground beyond Shemsu's reach. His orders unchanged, the butcher raised his other knife to strike.

The noise attracted Setnakht's attention.

The ancient pharaoh looked up from Karim's body, and his expression shifted from triumph to astonishment. More than that, his face shone with recognition.

"Anet?" he said.

Setnakht dismounted and walked toward Sita, the clash of man and stone parting before him, creating a clear path. Shesmu withdrew, lowering his knife.

"I watched you die," Setnakht said, his eyes locked on Sita's face. "I buried you in the Temple of Night. I sent your spirit across the Lake of Flowers to the Field of Reeds for an eternity of eternities. You cannot be standing here before me. You cannot, and yet you are no illusion."

Sita labored, trying to respond while concentrating on maintaining the protective magic. "This staff may have belonged to Anet," she said through gritted teeth, "but I am not your queen."

Setnakht said, "You may not have used blood magic as I did to rise from my tomb, but only Anet could wield that staff. The twin serpents obey only her." A pained, wistful longing crossed his face. "You are not my queen, but her ka lives on in you. I see her spirit, her fire, in your eyes." He reached for her, and to Sita's dismay, his hand passed through the circle of light.

The spell was directed at Shesmu, so it affects him alone, she realized.

The pharaoh caressed her cheek. His hand was as cold as death.

Summoning her heka voice, Sita cried, "I name you, Setnakht! I name you, heretic king! Within this circle, you can be only what you truly are: an abomination against the gods of this land!"

The circle of light intensified, shimmering from white to gold.

Sita watched in amazement as the flesh began peeling away from the ancient pharaoh's fingers, dropping from his bones as if a thousand years of rot were unfolding in an instant. The decay ate away at his hand and had reached his wrist when Setnakht recoiled, hissing with pain. Outside the protective light, the decay receded, and his greenish flesh returned, unbroken.

Setnakht flexed his fingers, his nostrils flaring with barely controlled rage. The next time he spoke, his voice was soft. "You could stand by my side again, Anet. Act as the sovereign's left hand, as you once did. Do you truly wish to waste yet another lifetime in opposition to your destiny?"

Sita frowned. "Opposing you *is* my destiny."

Setnakht closed his eyes and smiled bitterly. "Even after hundreds of thousands of sunrises, I see nothing has changed."

Sita's body trembled with the effort of holding the circle, yet she couldn't help but wonder at the pharaoh's words. *What does he mean, "nothing has changed"?*

Setnakht turned from her and began walking back to his mount. As he did, his spell-casting voice reverberated through the courtyard. His words to Shesmu held no mercy, and he did not look back at Sita as he spoke.

"She will weaken. She always does. When her power fails, kill her and throw her body into the Temple of Night where it belongs. Then follow me and the rest of the army north." He mounted his horse in a single fluid motion, his crimson cape flapping in the wind at his back.

"As for the rest of you," Setnakht said to the few remaining ushabti in the courtyard, "Ensure that this city is emptied; then stand at the gates to make sure none return."

With a whip of the reins, Setnakht drove his steed into a gallop and was soon flying down the main road out of the city.

Taking slow, deliberate steps, Shesmu repositioned himself in front of Sita.

She had never purposefully harnessed the power of heka before, so Sita didn't know how much longer she'd be able to maintain the circle.

Given how quickly the light was fading, it wouldn't be very long.

Behind her, Aya buried her face in Elyas's chest, heedless of the blood soaking his tunic.

It cannot end like this, Sita thought, staring at the green copper blade gripped in the butcher's hand. *Not after everything that's happened...*

The courtyard was still. The hopeless moans of the mortally wounded had gone quiet forever, and the other ushabti had left to root out any stragglers from the streets.

Sita gazed at Karim's body, held upright by the spears that had run him through. He was kneeling, as if frozen in a moment of supplication. *Where are the gods now?* she wondered. *Have they led us here only to abandon us to this fate?*

She remembered Karim's smile. His hand in hers as they danced. His kiss.

If she'd known it was to be their last, she would have told him—

Sita blinked. Was she imagining it, or had Karim's hand moved?

The interruption in her concentration caused the circle of light to flicker.

She focused on Karim, begging him to somehow do the impossible. "I need you," she whispered. "Come back to me."

The thief's arm hung at his side. Then, with what looked like immense effort, it lifted.

Sita watched, transfixed, as Karim reached for the spear in his side and tore it free, dropping it to the dust. Straightening his back, he gripped the haft of the spear in his chest with both hands and pulled it from his body with a grunt. Then, using it for support, he rose to his feet and turned to face her, the last spear still lodged in his body. His eyes flashed with that otherworldly light.

Sita gasped, the shock stealing away the last of her endurance. Her concentration broken, the protective circle pulled in on itself, the light receding and withdrawing back into the staff.

Shesmu raised his knife.

"Karim!" Sita screamed.

Spear in hand, Karim released a battle cry and sprinted toward them. Midstride, he pulled the final spear from his body, drove it into the ground, and used the momentum to vault himself into the air at the stone butcher.

Shesmu turned as Karim flew toward him, a spear in each hand. Karim's feet struck the butcher full in the chest, the force driving Shesmu back. The butcher fell to the ground and landed with an earthshaking boom that sent a tremendous dust cloud into the air. When the dust cleared, Karim was standing on top of the stone warrior, his chest heaving. Then he drove a spear through each of the stone man's shoulders with mighty force, pinning him to the dirt.

Karim jumped clear of Shesmu's slashing blade and bounded over to Sita. "Can you walk?" he asked. "We need to go quickly. Those spears won't hold him long."

Sita stared at him, agape. Karim's clothes were torn, but there was no blood. "I-I don't understand…" she stammered.

"I don't either," Karim admitted. "But now isn't the time to figure it out. You heard Setnakht. Shesmu won't stop until you're either dead or gone. Let's make sure it's the latter."

Over Karim's shoulder, Sita saw Shesmu writhing and tugging at one of the spears, levering it out of his body. Karim was right. If they didn't get beyond the city limits, Shesmu would hunt them down. And neither she nor Karim might have any strength left to stop him.

"I can walk," she said. "Elyas is injured but alive. Can you carry him?"

Karim beamed. "Sena, I'm pretty sure I can do anything!" He bent down. "Go with Sita," he said to Aya. "I will get your sabba to safety. I promise!"

Aya looked at him in wonderment and nodded. Sita took the girl's hand as Karim gently lifted Elyas and positioned the old man's body over his back.

"Time to go," Karim grunted, and gave Sita a nod before breaking into a sprint.

They tore through the streets of Perset, and what seemed like mere moments later, there was an earsplitting roar behind them, which Sita knew could only mean that Shesmu had broken free of his bondage and was in pursuit.

"We're almost there!" Karim assured them as they neared the edge of the city. Still, the thunderous footsteps and the sounds of wanton destruction were getting closer with every passing second.

"Don't stop, Aya!" Sita urged as the girl's steps began to falter. "Only a little farther!"

Aya screamed as part of a mud-brick house exploded behind them, sending debris flying through the air and into their backs. Sita glanced over her shoulder. Shemsu was at their heels, his fists leveling the ancient structures as he passed them.

Up ahead, Sita saw the last few ruined houses, and beyond them, the gentle slope of the valley rising to meet the Red Desert. Karim hit the slope first, with Sita and Aya close behind. Their speed decreased as they climbed, and more than once the loose sand sent them sliding down again before they recovered their footing.

Then Aya tripped and could not be coaxed to her feet. Sita stopped, panting and dripping sweat as the late afternoon sun beat down on them. She pushed the staff into the back of her belt, hoisted the girl into her arms, and continued forward.

When Sita risked another look back at the city, Shesmu was standing motionless at the perimeter. It was as she and Karim had hoped—Shesmu and the ushabti had no free will. They could only follow Setnakht's instructions, nothing more. Once Sita left Perset's borders, it was as if she no longer existed.

As they watched, Shesmu turned on his heel and made his way north through the city.

"We're safe, sena," Karim told Sita. "Stop and take a breath."

"He's taking the north road out of Perset with the rest of the army," Sita said. Her relief at their deliverance was momentary and fleeting. She turned to Karim. "Setnakht is leading them to Khetara."

After a brief respite, they continued their journey. They'd almost crested the slope of the valley and would soon find themselves back in the desert. With Aya still in her arms, Sita's pace slowed to a crawl. Even Karim, whose vigor seemed inexhaustible, was showing signs of fatigue.

After a few minutes of walking, Elyas stirred. "Put me down, I beg of you," he murmured. Karim stopped and opened his mouth to protest, but Elyas didn't give him the chance. "Please."

Karim relented and carefully set the old man on his feet. His tunic was a ruin from what looked like a stab wound to the shoulder, and his face had been battered. He wavered, holding on to Karim's arm.

"Here," Sita said. She set down Aya and tore a long strip of cloth from the bottom of her dress. She wrapped it under Elyas's arm and over his opposite shoulder several times, and then she tied it tight. "That should help stanch the bleeding until we reach the rest of the tribe."

Elyas raised a knuckle to his nose in thanks. "Who was that man, that rider?" he asked. "Was it he who created those stone demons?"

Karim nodded. "He was the founder of your city, a Khetaran

long since dead. Through magic and blood, he's returned to conquer this land once again."

"I swear, we will tell you all we know," Sita added. "But first we must get you to your people and tend to that wound."

"We can never go back, can we?" Elyas's voice was a whisper.

Sita and Karim said nothing.

Elyas breathed deeply. "Allow me to look upon our home one last time."

Together, they turned to face what was left of the city in the verdant valley below. The old man shook his head in despair. "I have failed them. I have failed my people. The very thing I feared most has come to pass, despite everything I've done to prevent it."

Sita placed a hand on Elyas's good shoulder. "The city may be lost, but the Hudjefa are not comprised of houses and land. The Hudjefa endure. They are flesh and blood, and they await you on the other side of this hill."

Karim said, "It's true, sen. Your people still need you."

Elyas stared into Karim's face with something like reverence. "I watched you die. Yet here you stand, unharmed." He looked over at Sita. "And you...that light... Are you god's messengers? If so, what have we done to deserve such punishment as this?"

Sita wondered at his words. Had Khnum, creator of the Oracle of the Lamb, intended for this desert tribe to be subsumed into an otherwise Khetaran crisis?

Or was it not a Khetaran crisis, but a *human* one?

She spoke, "Our gods do not share a name, but perhaps they share a desire for us to work toward a common cause. I do not believe the loss of your people is divine retribution, Elyas. I believe it must be the spark that lights an enduring flame—one that must not be extinguished, no matter how bitter the days ahead may be. You must not lose hope." She paused, feeling the steadying weight of the staff at her back. "In profound darkness, the smallest star can be a beacon."

Elyas gazed down at his city for a long time. Aya stood by him, then laced her fingers into his. "Come on, Sabba," she said. "We should go now. I'll walk with you."

The old man smoothed the girl's wild mane, his face tight with emotion. "All right, my dearest. We'll go."

"Are you certain you don't want me to carry you the rest of the way?" Karim asked.

Elyas shook his head. "My people must find me on my feet. If they see me standing, perhaps they too will have the strength to rise."

Sita had lived through her father's reign and had witnessed the birth of Mery's. But until that moment, watching the battered old man walk, straight-backed and undaunted, toward what was left of his once-mighty tribe, she'd never before seen true leadership.

They climbed over the ridge and spotted the remaining members of the Hudjefa gathered in the shadow of a tower of red stone. Sita scanned the congregation and counted roughly 140 people. Among them, a healer rushed to and fro, giving orders while tending to dozens of wounded, while a group of men tried to corral the donkeys, horses, and sheep they'd managed to get out of the city.

Among the frenzied activity, there was also a heavy stillness in the air. Many people simply sat in the sand and stared out into the desert, their faces creased with unfathomable sadness.

One by one, people in the tribe began to notice the group's approach and leaped to their feet, shouting and running to embrace them.

"Miri?" Elyas exclaimed as his wife hobbled toward him. *"Miri!"*

The elderly couple fell weeping into one another's arms as others surrounded them in a crush of joy and anguish both.

Sami's mother appeared at Miri's side. Sita met her eyes and gave her an approving nod. "You see? I knew you could do it. I knew you could get them to safety."

Sami's mother put a hand over her mouth, overcome.

Everyone asked a thousand questions at once—about where the stone men had come from, if there were more survivors, and when they could return home.

Elyas raised his hand for silence, and the crowd quieted.

"My people," he said, loud enough for all to hear. "A great calamity has befallen us this day. One that will be felt among us, our children, and our children's children. It is with the deepest sorrow that I tell you we were the last to escape the city, and we may never return to that place which we called home."

A wail of mourning erupted from the gathered people. Some collapsed in disbelief, some clutched each other in fear.

"What about food and water?" one of the men called out. "We have only what we could carry with us! How will we survive?"

His was joined by other cries of dismay.

Another man shouted, "It would have been better to die with our brethren than suffer a slow death in the desert!"

"No!" Sita exclaimed, surprising even herself.

The tribe, including Elyas, looked at her.

"No," she repeated. "It is always better to live. I know you are suffering. I know you are in pain. I, too, suffer the agonies that memory brings. But those who died today would not have wanted you to drink too deep of despair. They would have wanted you to *live*. To find a new land, and to tell their story."

"Even if we could survive a journey through the desert, where would we go?" a woman asked.

This time, Karim spoke up.

"I will lead you to my people, the Anen. They have also suffered strife and loss, and perhaps together, our two tribes can grow strong. That stone army will not stop at claiming Perset. They will march across the whole of this land, and none will be safe from their reach."

Sita was taken aback. *Journey to the Red Lands? What about Khetara? I must get home before Setnakht's army reaches Thonis.*

"Elyas, why do you allow these two outsiders to speak?" a woman shouted.

"Yes, why?"

"Aren't they to blame for what has befallen us?"

"Be silent!" Elyas commanded. "Without Karim and Sita's warning, none of us would be standing here! Without them, the Hudjefa would have breathed their last this day!"

Several of the wounded men had risen to join the rest of the tribe. One of them pointed at Karim with a trembling hand. "How is this possible? How are you here? I saw you die in battle!"

A murmur of confusion spread through the crowd.

"It's true!" another man said. "We were some of the last to escape the slaughter, and we saw the stone warriors spear him straight through! Not once, but three times!"

Sita saw Karim draw back. What might the tribe do to someone who was supposed to be dead? She stepped closer to him and reached for his hand.

"I witnessed this man's resurrection!" Elyas told the Hudjefa. "And now he stands among us—offering to lead us to salvation! Is this not a sign for hope? Is this not the hand of God reaching out to lift us from our tragedy?"

Sita scanned the faces in the crowd and watched in amazement as their expressions turned to wonder. Every eye was upon Karim. His hand trembled in hers.

Sita squeezed it. "It's going to be all right," she whispered, though the news of Karim's plan to take the Hudjefa to the Anen filled her with a mixture of pride and sadness.

"I'm just a thief, sena," Karim protested amid the people's exclamations. "I'm no divine messenger."

Sita held the staff at her side, the weight of its burden one she'd never planned to bear but was glad she now carried. "Aren't you?"

19
NEFF

She knew it wasn't a good idea. It would have been better to send another message with Ahura and arrange a safe time to meet Kenna, but that would have taken too long. With the king's cursing ritual only days away, Neff felt time slipping through her fingers like grains of sand.

Fortunately, it was supply delivery day at the Great Temple of Amun. So Neff managed to pass through the gate amid the vendors and donkeys and associated rabble unnoticed, as Karim had before her. Neff had learned at an early age that whether a person was a prince, a pauper, or a thief, there was always something to be learned from them.

She went straight to the embalming chamber, and sure enough, Kenna was there with an apprentice Sem priest, going over the proper way to lay out the tools of their trade.

"I cannot stress enough the importance of a sharp edge," he said, holding up an obsidian shard. "A dull blade may tear the skin and create an imperfect incision…" He trailed off as he caught sight of Neff at the doorway. Kenna cleared his throat. "I think that's enough for today," he said, his voice louder than before.

"But I thought—" the apprentice said.

"We will cover more tomorrow. I've just remembered that I'd planned to reorganize the storage room and I must get started."

"Oh! I can help with—"

"Much appreciated, but I'm afraid I'm *quite* particular about my methods, so it will be best for me to undertake the task alone."

Thus rebuffed, the apprentice bowed, then trudged out of the embalming chamber, past where Neff hid behind a pillar.

When the apprentice was safely out of sight, Kenna appeared beside her.

"Are you sleeping in honey, Nefermaat?" he muttered. "Do you realize how dangerous it is to show up here like this? If someone saw you—"

"No one saw me," Neff assured him. "I'm sorry, brother, but it couldn't wait. I need to speak to you."

Kenna studied her. "You don't look well. You haven't been sleeping."

Neff touched her face. She thought she'd done a good job masking the dark circles under her eyes with kohl, but Kenna was too observant to be fooled. He'd probably also noticed the subtle drop in her posture and the paleness of her skin. In truth, she hadn't slept well since she'd concluded her study of the Book of the Red Lady. Its final spell had thrown her mind into turmoil, and she'd been grappling with indecision ever since.

"I'm fine," she said, not wanting to be distracted from her goal.

Kenna sighed, running a hand through his wild hair. "All right. Let's go to the storage room. We shouldn't be disturbed there."

Neff nodded and pulled the hood of the white robe she wore closer around her face so she wouldn't be recognized. As they walked, Neff gave Kenna an appraising look. He wore his standard white tunic, but he had added a small amulet to his costume: an Eye of Horus carved from malachite, strung on black cord.

"Where did that come from?" she asked. Kenna usually spurned any type of adornment.

He quickly tucked the amulet under his tunic. "It was a gift from Sitamun. A long time ago."

Neff peeked over at him. "You miss her."

The prince kept his eyes forward and said nothing.

"She's alive," Neff said.

Kenna turned to her sharply. "How can you know this?" Then he scoffed, as if he'd asked a question he could easily answer himself. "You've had a vision."

"A dream, actually. Of two snakes, as in your father's vision. Except this was different. The snakes were entwined with one another and suffused with light. The divine message is clear: Sitamun lives."

Relief washed over Kenna's face before he hid his emotions out of sight. "That is very good news," he said evenly. "Though it makes me wonder what she's been doing all this time. The world is a stranger to her outside the palace walls."

Thinking of the oracle, Neff replied, "Perhaps fate has delivered her a friend."

When they arrived at the storage room, the same chamber where Kenna had collected his mummy wrappings when they'd first met, Kenna ushered her inside. The room was small and dark, the only light filtering in from the door. Rolls of linen wrappings were piled on the floor along with sacks of natron, jars of various sacred oils and resins, and baskets of incense pellets. The smell of it was so intense that it made Neff's eyes water.

Kenna peered out to check both ends of the corridor once

more before speaking. "This is about the Book of the Red Lady, isn't it? I went back and forth about sending it to you."

"Don't worry. I have a lookout in case someone comes this way," Neff said.

"A lookout?" Kenna's brow furrowed. "You mean that servant girl? I didn't see her with you."

"Not Ahura. She doesn't know I'm here. Something else."

"Some*thing*?"

Neff licked her lips. "The book isn't the only reason I needed to see you. Do you remember that spell I cast, summoning a minor god named Medjed?"

Kenna's eyes narrowed. "You said it didn't work."

Neff made an apologetic face. "Well..." Removing a small folded cloth from the pocket of her robe, she turned and flung the fabric into the air beside her. It fluttered and came to rest on a child-sized shape beside her. "I was wrong."

Kenna jumped back, nearly tumbling a pile of wrappings. The dome-like creature didn't move. It simply hovered there, watching him with its painted eyes.

"That's...Medjed?" Kenna exclaimed.

"I think he must be," Neff replied. "He can't talk, but he's been helping me stay out of trouble. Within reason, of course."

"Of course," Kenna repeated, still staring at Medjed.

"Go on, now," Neff said to the little spirit, gesturing toward the corridor. "Let me know if you see anyone coming."

Medjed bobbed in assent and slipped out from beneath the cloth, leaving it behind on the floor.

Neff turned back to Kenna. "I wanted to show him to you, because it proves I'm ready to cast the spells in the Book of the Red Lady."

Kenna shook off his discomfort and composed himself. "I agree. As much as I wish we didn't need to delve into malicious magic, I cannot see that we have a choice. Mery's execration ritual must not be allowed to succeed. A curse of such magnitude would render my brother's enemies defenseless against him. Swords would crumble and rust in their scabbards, and even the strongest men would fall before him. We must act against him with the most powerful magic available to us." He bent closer. "Perhaps we consider the blinding spell, or 'To Loosen a Bowstring.'"

"No. We cannot afford to wait until the day of the ritual to act," Neff said. "If we fail, it may be too late to stop him."

"What are you suggesting?"

The idea that had been keeping Neff awake at night sat on the tip of her tongue. "Mery has been teaching me to play Mehen," she began.

"The snake game. He used to play that with Sita all the time. What of it?"

"He is a ruthless opponent, but I learn fast. I've beaten him a couple times now. The only way to win is to think like he thinks—and always be one step ahead." She thought of the Mehen board and the winding coils of the snake, upon which one can either kill or be killed. "If we want to beat Mery at his own game, I must curse him before he can curse us."

"Curse the king? You can't mean..."

Neff recalled the words written in red ink. The final spell in Sekhmet's book.

To Make a Man Die.

"It's the only way," Neff said.

Kenna was incredulous. "Are you mad, little sister? You'd be caught and executed before you could succeed, and even if you *did* somehow manage to complete the curse, your life would be forfeit. You're the only one with knowledge of heka who has access to Mery. Everyone would know it was you."

Neff licked her lips. "Forgive me, my prince, but I have

thought long and hard about this. You are a man of the temple. You of all people must agree that the gods placed me at Mery's side for a reason. I have earned his trust. He suspects nothing. I am the only one who can do this. I am *meant* to do this."

"You can't know that!" Kenna said angrily.

"I have faith. I feel rightness in this. It will be simple, you'll see. Tomorrow morning, the servant will come to apply the king's makeup. First, she will shave him. I will take her place, claiming that I wish to attend to him instead. Mery will think it all a bit of fun, but I'll cut him with the blade—just a little, just enough—and catch the blood on a square of cloth. It will look like an accident. After all, I'm a novice at such things, and it will soon be forgotten. I have already finished gathering the other ingredients I need for the spell. Once I have the king's blood, the rest will be easy."

"Simple and easy, eh? Like adding a bit of poison to a honey cake?"

Neff's cheeks flushed with heat. "That's different! I am doing this to save the kingdom!"

"Oh, yes?" Kenna shot back. "I'm fairly certain that's what Mery thought he was doing too."

The words struck Neff like a knife to the gut. She was silent, her soul at war with itself. *Was I not a child just yesterday?* she wondered. *And now, instead of dolls and skipping stones, I'm toying with murder? What's happening to me?*

She shook away her doubt.

"I won't fail," she said.

Kenna's face was a mask of hopelessness. "Perhaps not. But what will you lose? Neff, please. Listen to me before you make up your mind!"

The discarded cloth rose up once more, and Medjed rushed toward them, nudging Neff with urgency. Neff and Kenna looked at each other in alarm.

"Someone's coming!" she whispered. In a flash, she pulled the cloth off Medjed and ducked behind the pile of natron sacks.

Seconds later, a shadow fell across the doorway.

"Looking for something, my prince?"

Huddled on the floor, Neff felt the blood drain from her face. *Montuhotep.*

"Oh! Erm, yes, High Priest," Kenna said. Neff heard him fumbling with the jars. "I need more pine resin for my embalming mixture. Ah! Here it is."

"I'm surprised at you, Bakenamun," Master Montuhotep said.

"Excuse me?"

"Endangering yourself for the sake of a common whelp. I thought you were smarter than that."

"I'm sure I don't know what you're talking about."

"Show yourself, Nefermaat. I know you're in here. I tasked one of the Wab priests to keep track of your movements outside of the palace. I knew you were on temple grounds the moment you arrived."

Neff froze, suddenly cold with sweat. *If he heard what we were saying… If he knows…*

"It will be worse for you if I have to root you out."

She let out a shuddering breath and rose to her feet.

Montuhotep stood by the door with Kenna, who clutched a jar of resin, stricken. The high priest smiled. "There you are." He clucked his tongue. "My little apprentice. How far you've come. One day you're vomiting on the floor of my chambers, the next, you're conspiring against the king. At least, I assume that's what you two are doing in here."

He didn't overhear us, Neff thought, relieved. He doesn't know my plans. She still had a chance to salvage the situation.

"Absolutely not, Master!" she protested. "I only came to visit the prince. We'd become close during my time here, and I missed him. I'm lonely at the palace. I came in secret because the king wouldn't approve. That's all."

"Do you take me for a fool, girl?" Montuhotep sneered. "If you think you can come into these sacred halls straight off the streets of Bubas, wrest my preordained position out from under me, and lie to my face, then—"

"High Priest!" Kenna broke in. "I suggest you take care before making unproven accusations against the king's closest adviser."

Montuhotep whirled on the prince. "Bakenamun, during Amunmose's reign I wouldn't have *dreamed* of going against either of his sons' wishes—but this is not your father's Khetara. Not anymore. And there isn't a single person in Thonis I wouldn't throw to the lions to regain my place at the king's side. Not even you."

Kenna swallowed, then squared his shoulders. "Don't touch her. If you try, you'll have to go through me first."

Neff's heart swelled as she watched the diminutive prince stand up to her old master, who towered over him. *I knew he had it in him.*

The high priest looked down at Kenna and sighed. "I suppose I must draw the line at striking a royal prince." He turned back to Neff. "No matter. As soon as I get an audience with Meryamun, I will make your betrayal known. If you're lucky, he'll simply send you back to your village. If not, well, perhaps you'll find yourself back in Bakenamun's embalming chamber sooner than you think."

A chill ran down Neff's spine. "He won't believe you," she said.

Montuhotep shrugged. "A seed of doubt is all I need. And time for it to grow..." He stepped back and pointed at the door. "Now get out of my temple."

Clutching Medjed's cloth to her chest, Neff pulled up her hood and strode to the door with a confidence she did not feel in her heart. Kenna met her gaze, shaking his head as if to say: *Don't do it, Neff. Think about what I told you.*

She gave him a sad, apologetic smile before hurrying off. Montuhotep's threats only made her more committed to her plan. The days she thought she had left had suddenly turned to hours.

The truth was, she'd already made up her mind about the plan before she arrived. She hadn't come to ask for Kenna's advice or his permission. She'd come because she wanted to see him one last time before the end.

The cat was waiting for her when she returned to her chambers. She wound around Neff's ankles and meowed continuously, as if enumerating her grievances about Neff's absence. Paying the cat little mind, Neff sank into the chair by the table and wrapped her arms around herself. Her body shook uncontrollably, and as her tears fell, she wished with all her heart that the arms around her were her mother's.

I'm so sorry, Mamet, she thought as she rocked back and forth. *I'm so sorry I left you. I'm so sorry I'm causing you pain.*

She gritted her teeth and forced herself to stop crying.

But I must take action.

The lamb had returned to her dreams, its dolorous voice insistent. So many of its predictions had already come to pass—the river of blood, the abundance of lies, the chaos brewing in every corner of the kingdom. How soon before the crowns were broken? How soon before the coming of sorrow and ruin that could never be undone?

Kenna had put the weapon in her hand—for the Book of the Red Lady was a deadly weapon indeed—but the gods themselves had given her the power to wield it and placed her within striking distance of its intended target.

Meryamun.

The man whose life she'd saved from the crocodile was the same life she now intended to take.

Would the curse work quickly? she wondered. *Or slowly, like poison?* The Book of the Red Lady had been hidden away in the House of Life for untold years, so neither Kenna nor anyone alive knew exactly how its spells might work. She would have to find out for herself.

Kenna's words stuck in her mind like thorns, and Neff struggled to dislodge them. *It's not the same!* she thought. *Mery killing his father is different from me casting this curse!*

Maybe it was different. Or maybe she'd learned to play Mery's game a little too well.

The cat jumped onto the table and bumped her chin against Neff's face, purring. The sound soothed her, as did the cat's tender ministrations. Slowly, her muscles released their tension, and Neff found herself leaning forward onto the table and resting her head on her arms. She was so exhausted that she could barely keep her eyes open. Outside her window, the sun had begun to set in a bloody pool of light. The cat curled up next to her, and Neff reached out to stroke her warm, soft neck, wishing that the day would not end, so that tomorrow—and the task that lay before her—might never come.

Soon, she was asleep.

The threads of dawn had just begun to filter into her room when Neff woke to a gentle rustling. She blinked into the murk, not ready to raise her head from the table. Her neck ached. Had she really slept through the night like that?

The cat had disappeared, probably off hunting. In the corner of her eye, she saw a tall female figure approach carrying a large, lidded laundry basket—much like the one she'd hidden inside in the underground hallway.

"Is it time to get up already, Ahura?" Neff murmured groggily. She yawned and stretched.

Ahura stopped. Her face was cloaked in shadow.

"I left the laundry piled by the door," Neff went on, wondering why her maidservant felt the need to come into the room at this hour. Then she spied Medjed's cloth discarded on the floor. It must have fallen out of her pocket when she returned from the temple. Perhaps Ahura thought it was a soiled rag that needed washing?

"Oh, that's not—" Neff began, but she never got a chance to finish.

She was so confused by the rag over her mouth that she didn't even think to scream. It wasn't until she felt it pulled tight and tied behind her head that panic set in, and by then, it was too late to cry out. Neff tried to throw herself from the chair and away from her assailant, but Ahura was very strong. She held Neff's head against the table while she grabbed her wrists and tied them behind her back with another rag.

Except that wasn't possible. Ahura only had two hands.

Someone else was in the room with them. It was too dark for Neff to make out who it was, but it looked like another woman. Another maidservant. Within seconds, they'd bound her ankles too.

Neff's heart raced. She screamed into the gag, though the sound was so muted that it made no difference. Suddenly, she was lifted straight out of her chair as if she weighed nothing at all and placed inside the laundry basket. After that, the two servants quickly packed the empty spaces around Neff's body with her own laundry, taking care to leave enough room around her face for her to breathe, then covered her head with a light cloth to shield it from view. Finally, the lid was replaced on top of the basket, casting her into total darkness.

No, no, no! Neff thought as the basket was hoisted into the air. *Don't you understand? Today is the day I curse the king! You can't take me now! You can't!*

She felt herself being carried and heard voices pass by her.

"...furious that Femi escaped. He's sent the guard out to look for him, but so far, no luck..."

"...I heard the king's already sent messengers to Tash with an ultimatum: Swear fealty to Khetara, or Prince Harsi's head will be displayed at the end of a spear by the palace gate..."

"Greetings to you, Ahura, Herit. You're up early this morning."

The voice was female, elderly, and familiar. The movement stopped.

"Greetings to you, Nebet," said a young female voice.

That must be Herit, Ahura's accomplice. Neff pictured the round-faced, curly-haired maidservant that she'd seen Ahura talking to in the corridors.

"Yes, we wanted to get a head start on the laundry so that we might have time for swimming later on."

The older woman spoke again, her voice filled with profound sadness. "Mm, yes. Sitamun used to love swimming in the afternoons."

Neff screamed into the rag again and thrashed wildly in her bonds. She felt Ahura struggle to keep hold of the basket, nearly dropping it.

"Are you all right?" Nebet asked.

"I'm fine," Ahura replied, getting a better hold on the basket. "A lot of laundry this morning. We'd better be going. Have a good day, Nebet."

The movement resumed.

Exhausted and nearly suffocated by her exertions, Neff gave up and lay still. *Where are they taking me? And who are they, really?* she wondered. She'd had her doubts about the veracity of Ahura's story from the start, but she thought they had built a rapport. She hadn't expected to be kidnapped. Then again, she *was* the king's closest adviser…

Inside the basket, Neff felt a change in the air. It was fresher and cooler, and a slight breeze wafted through the weave.

We're outside, she realized, which of course, made sense. If they were pretending to do the day's laundry, they'd be taking her down to the river.

Soon, the gentle burble of the Iteru filled her ears along with the distant chatter of women.

"We're clear," Herit said quietly. "The other servants are facing away from us. Go! Go!"

Neff bounced uncomfortably in the basket as Ahura's pace quickened. The flow of water was joined by the dry sound of reeds brushing against the basket. *They're carrying me through the marshes.*

Then, a man's voice: "Did you do it? Is she in there?"

"Yes," Ahura said, though she didn't sound pleased.

"Put it here."

The basket was set on the ground, and a moment later, opened.

The light cloth over Neff's head was lifted away, and she blinked into the sudden light.

The sun had risen since her abduction and blazed from the eastern horizon, throwing her kidnappers into silhouette. Still, she could see that there were three men and two women standing around her, and the largest of the men appeared to be the one who had spoken. He dragged her roughly from the basket and set her on her feet.

"Careful with her, will you?" Ahura said. "She's loyal to the king, but she's still just a girl, Omari. She's scared."

Neff cowered under the intense gaze of the men and women. She *was* scared, but she was also angry. Whoever these people were, they'd interrupted her from carrying out her divine mission.

The man called Omari scoffed. "High Khetarans don't feel emotion the way we do. Not even their children."

"Omari!"

"Rae, will you stop worrying about the girl and rejoice? You did it! You landed the first strike against the pharaoh. Now that we have leverage, we can finally fight back! We can fight for your father! For Sakesh!"

Neff turned sharply to look at Ahura—no, not Ahura. Her name was Rae.

So I was right! Neff thought. *She is the woman Karim met by the river in Sakesh! She is the fourth figure from the Oracle!*

As if sensing Neff's gaze, Rae turned to look at her, and sunlight lanced across her face. Her eyes shone with triumph, but there was another emotion there too.

Doubt.

She and these others must be part of the southern rebellion, Neff thought. *She doesn't know about the oracle. About the four of us. About any of it.*

The lamb whispered in Neff's ear, louder and more insistent than ever before.

Take heed, Thonis, Great House of Amun!

Take heed, Sakesh, Great House of Ra!

Beware! Sorrow and ruin comes to the Children of the Two Lands!

Neff's body relaxed, despite the dark portents whispering in her mind.

She doesn't know...

Yet.

Perhaps she hadn't veered off the path after all. Perhaps once again, she was right where she was supposed to be.

20 RAE

Put her in the tent, Buto. Quickly now." Omari tipped his chin toward the young priestess. She'd stopped struggling in her bonds and stared at Rae with an intensity that was deeply unsettling.

Rae tried to look away but found that she couldn't. Had the girl cast some kind of spell on her? She'd never witnessed heka before but knew from her father's stories that it was real—a magic reserved for the rich and powerful. Still, Neff had been gagged before she could have uttered a curse. They'd made sure of that. Then why did Rae feel like she was falling into the girl's gaze? Into a deep well where a fearsome power lurked?

Beware…

"Rae?" Tam's voice sounded far away.

The lamb.

Someone shook her by the shoulder. "Rae!"

The lamb.

Buto slung the girl over his shoulder, and the connection was severed. Rae blinked rapidly, stumbling back as she watched Buto carry Neff into the rebels' tent.

"Are you all right?" Tam studied her with concern.

She felt chilled, struck by the memory of a blind old soldier on the streets of Sakesh, muttering words that at the time, she'd thought were only ravings.

The lamb, the lamb, the lamb…

"I'm fine," Rae replied, her mouth dry. "A little shaken up, I guess."

"I know. I didn't like it either," Tam whispered. "But hopefully Meryamun agrees to release the prisoners in return for his priestess, and we can wash our hands of all this."

Hopefully, Rae thought. "We'd better return to the riverbank before we're missed," she said. She bent to repack the soiled laundry into the basket.

"We're going, Omari," Tam called out.

Omari nodded but didn't meet the weaver's eye. "Be careful," he said to Rae. "Come back as soon as you have news."

With a final uncertain glance toward the tent, Rae turned to the marshes.

"Omari doesn't like me very much, does he?" Tam said as they pushed through the reeds.

"He's worried, that's all," Rae said.

"Is it?"

Rae didn't reply.

She and Tam were walking through the main hall of the palace when the guards came for her.

"Are you Ahura?" the head guard commanded. "Where have you been?"

"Doing the washing on the riverbank," Rae replied, indicating the empty basket in her arms. "Why? Is something wrong?"

"Have you seen your mistress today?" he asked.

Rae glanced at Tam and shook her head. "Nefermaat leaves her laundry by the door every morning, so I simply pick it up and move on. I assumed she was still asleep."

The head guard grimaced. "Come with me."

Rae bowed her head and passed the basket to Tam, who gave her hand a secret squeeze before hurrying away. As Rae followed the guards through the corridors, she did her best to calm her racing heart.

This is all part of the plan, she told herself. *We knew I'd be questioned about the priestess's disappearance. I'll simply say I don't know anything, and that will be that.*

They arrived at the door to the throne room and were approached by an attendant.

"I'm afraid that Pharaoh is engaged at the moment," the man told them. "You'll have to wait."

The head guard shoved the attendant aside. "Not today I won't," he grunted, and pushed through the door.

King Meryamun looked up as Rae and the guards entered the throne room. Rae barely had time to register the extravagance of the chamber—the vividly painted walls and columns illuminated by sunlight—before the pharaoh was addressing them.

"What's the meaning of this?" Meryamun demanded.

A priest was in the room with the king, along with two attendants bearing ostrich feather fans. Rae had seen the priest once before during a meal she'd serviced, the one when she'd learned of the plan for the prisoners. What was his name?

It took her a moment to remember.

Montuhotep.

"Humblest apologies, my king," the head guard said. "But there is a matter of urgency I must bring to your attention. It concerns the seer Nefermaat. She is missing."

Montuhotep's eyes widened. "Ah! You see? You see?" he said to the king. "The girl knew she was about to be exposed, so she's fled in the night. It is as I said, my king! Just as I've said! She's been conspiring with your brother, working against you all this time!"

"Silence!" Meryamun snarled. He turned back to the guards. "Explain."

"When Nefermaat's attendants arrived at her chambers this morning to help her dress, they found their mistress gone and the room in shambles. A chair was overturned and items were strewn about. And there was this." The guard held up a scrap of papyrus.

"Give it here," the king said, rising from his throne and descending from its platform. The guard advanced just close enough for the king to snatch the note from his hand.

Rae watched Meryamun's expression darken as he read the words scribbled in the common script. She knew what it said because she'd written the note herself.

Release the Sakeshi prisoners or you'll never see the priestess again.

"It's a blessing that she's gone, really," Montuhotep said as Meryamun crumpled the note in his hand. "Though I'm sure you'll want to send the guards to search for her. Perhaps she'll have run back to her parents in Bubas? They should be questioned, to be sure. But you'll have me at your side, my king, as it should be! A high priest of Amun! Not some commoner from the—"

With the speed of a cobra, Meryamun whipped a dagger from the guard's belt and slashed it across the priest's throat. The priest stared at the king, mouth agape as blood trickled from the gash onto his pristine white robes.

Montuhotep looked down at the spreading stain, and with a disgusted, choking sound, he dropped like a stone.

Rae's heart leaped into her throat.

The king thrust the knife back into the guard's belt and sighed. "By Amun, that was a long time coming. I thought the man would never shut up." Then he ascended the ramp to his throne and slouched into it with the grace of a panther.

"Remove that filth from my sight," he said to his attendants. They rushed to obey, lifting the priest's corpse between them and whisking it into a back room. "Can you believe the audacity of that man? He'd say anything to regain his old position—though accusing a child of political intrigue is certainly a creative effort." He paused as the attendants returned to wipe the blood from the blue and green tiled floor. "I suppose I can't fault Montuhotep for his ambition," Mery mused. "For some of us, there is little we wouldn't do to get what we want. Isn't that right, Ahura?"

Rae's stomach lurched at the use of her alias.

"My king?" she said as the guard shoved her forward.

"That day in the courtyard. You wanted to work in the palace so much that you risked touching my arm to keep me from overlooking you. Isn't that right?"

Rae nodded.

"I can respect that. And so could Neff, I suppose, which is why she chose you. You're here, I imagine, because as her maidservant, you were one of the last to see her. Is that correct?"

Rae nodded again.

"And? What say you?"

"All seemed well when I attended her at yesterday's midday meal. She was in a hurry to return to her studies, and she told me she didn't wish to be disturbed until morning. She said she would be fine with some leftover bread and fruit."

Rae paused and took a steadying breath. She'd heard from

Tam, Neff, and many other palace servants that the young pharaoh was notorious for being able to sniff out lies. It was part of his heka, they said, part of the innate magic that comes with having royal blood. So she had to be careful not to lie, to tell the truth and tell it convincingly, albeit only part of it.

"This morning, Herit and I went to the priestess's chambers earlier than usual, as we had other plans for later in the day. The priestess's soiled garments were by the door as usual, and we gathered the laundry and proceeded to the riverbank."

The king studied Rae's face over his tented fingers. "And that is all? You didn't see anything else?"

Perspiration began to bead at Rae's hairline as her mind searched for an answer that was truthful but not damning. "As I said before, it was only a little past dawn and very dark. We saw very little. Only shadows."

Meryamun frowned and, to Rae's immense relief, turned his attention back to the note. "You care for your mistress, do you not, Ahura?"

"I do," Rae said without thinking.

Meryamun nodded.

Rae swallowed hard. The king didn't question her response, not because it was a lie he missed, but because it was true.

Damn you, Omari, she thought. *I hate it when you're right. Foolish as I am, I do care about the girl.*

The king went on. "Then tell me, what would you do if a bunch of savage dogs from the south threatened to kill your beloved mistress unless you released a dozen traitors to the crown?"

Taken aback by his question, Rae struggled to speak. "B-but my king, I'm only— I'm not—"

"Don't stand there gaping like a fish out of water. You're the only other person in this palace who owes their life to Nefermaat the way that I do, so I've asked you the question. Now speak!"

Rae bit back a hundred angry responses, a thousand curses upon his wicked house, and instead replied with another truth. "I would give them whatever they asked to ensure the safe return of my mistress. No prisoner, no conquest, is worth the life of my beloved."

King Meryamun raised his eyebrows and tilted his head appreciatively. "Beautifully put. Particularly for a commoner such as yourself. The heart of a lion and the soul of a poet, quite a combination. Little Herit must thoroughly enjoy her revels with you—in fact, I *know* she does." He traced a long finger across his bottom lip, his eyes knowing.

Rae's cheeks reddened. She wanted to rake her nails across his face and tear the flesh from it.

Beneath her feet, the ground seemed to tremble.

Rae dug her fingernails into her palms, forcing herself to focus. She couldn't afford to lose control. Especially when there was a chance that she could convince the king to release her father and the others. She tilted her head in a bow.

"It is a sweet sentiment," Meryamun went on. "But it's also very wrong."

Rae went rigid.

"You see, when you love someone, as I love Nefermaat, you do not express that love through submission. You do not show your devotion by groveling before cowards and malefactors, begging for her freedom like some common peasant. No. A lion does not submit to jackals, dear Ahura. You of all people should know this. What does a lion do?"

Meryamun smiled, and his handsome, striking face was transformed. Despite herself, despite everything, Rae could feel the pull of his spell. His radiance was as fierce as the sun.

"He roars," Meryamun said with relish. "He roars and shows them tooth and claw, the likes of which they have never seen nor felt. And thus, the jackals will discover they've been dead since the moment they decided to touch her."

Rae's heart dropped.

With sudden, painful clarity, Rae recognized that they had underestimated the young king. Catastrophically underestimated him.

"Guard, send a message to the battalion we shipped down to Sakesh to support the tax collections," the king said. "Brief them about the situation here, and let them know that for every day the priestess is not returned to me, they are to take a hundred hands. One for each enemy slain in the name of my dear Nefermaat. Let it be known throughout the land that every hour of her confinement is awash in Sakeshi blood."

The head guard bowed. "It shall be done."

Rae could not mask her horror, and Meryamun laughed.

"Worry not, sweet lioness. I do not blame you for your soft heart, nor will you be punished for your honesty. Honesty is rare within these walls. The last thing I want is to snuff it out."

Rae struggled to reply. She had not been worried about her own life, but the others… "Thank you, my king," she managed. She hoped Meryamun wouldn't notice the hate in her voice.

He didn't. He'd already moved on.

"Ah! Sabni. Just who I wanted to see," Meryamun said to the little man who'd come skittering into the throne room after the head guard left with his commands. "Tell me, is there any word from the delegation we sent to Tash? I'm curious to hear their thoughts on my proposals. Harsi has his own ideas about how their queen will respond, but honestly, what wouldn't a mother do for her beloved son?"

"I'm afraid we lost contact with the delegation," the man called Sabni replied as the remaining guard led Rae from the chamber. "We expected a message from them yesterday, but so far, nothing. I'm concerned something may have happened..."

The throne room doors closed behind them, cutting off his response. Away from the king, Rae's breath quickened.

I must speak with Omari, she thought.

The situation was bad before, but they'd just made it much, much worse.

It was midafternoon by the time Rae was able to get away from her duties and return to the riverside camp. She burst through the reeds without announcement and found Omari, Buto, and Kay roasting fish over a fire and tearing into some loaves of bread from the market.

"Well?" Omari asked.

At the sight of his face, Rae's fear and anger found a target. "I *told you* this was a bad idea, Omari. *I told you!*"

With exaggerated control, Omari handed his skewer of fish to Kay, brushed the grit from his hands, and stood. "Tell me what's happened."

Cursing, Rae kicked at a rock and sent it sailing into the river. She wanted to scream.

Omari grabbed her by the shoulders and shook her. "For the love of Ra, will you get ahold of yourself? You're going to bring the entire palace guard down on our heads if you keep carrying on like that!" Squeezing her hard enough to cause pain, he leaned in so his face was nearly touching hers. "Now," he said in a low voice, "*tell me* what's happened."

Rae jerked away and rubbed her shoulder. Again, she was struck by how much her friend's behavior had changed since they'd left Sakesh. He'd always been passionate about their cause but never violent. And never toward her.

"They found the note," she said. "The head guard brought it

and me before the king. There was a priest in the throne room when we arrived, and he claimed the young priestess and Prince Bakenamun were conspiring together against the king. As I had suspected!"

Omari's eyebrows rose. "I see."

"Meryamun didn't believe it, though. In fact, he killed the priest right in front of me."

Buto nearly dropped his fish in the fire. "He *killed* a priest?"

Rae nodded. "The king has total faith in Nefermaat and will do whatever it takes to get her back."

"That's good news, then," Omari said, folding his arms.

"No, it isn't!" Rae exclaimed. "Because Meryamun's idea of doing 'whatever it takes' involves his men killing a hundred civilians in Sakesh for every day the girl isn't returned!"

The two rebels at the fire jumped to their feet in chagrin.

"What?" Buto exclaimed.

Omari's face turned scarlet. Then he turned back to the men. "Buto, finish cooking those fish. Kay, come with me. We need to send a pigeon to Sakesh to warn them. I'll write the message, and you make sure the bird is ready. If he flies fast enough, he might make it there in time."

Omari moved to leave, but Rae caught his arm.

"We should free the girl now!" she said. "If she shows up at the palace unharmed, no one has to die. We can come up with another plan to free the prisoners."

Omari chuckled humorlessly. "Ay, have you learned nothing about war? Someone *always* has to die." He glanced back at the tent. "The girl knows our faces. Our names. If we let her go now, we'll be dead before sunset. The girl could still be useful. Guard her until I get back, will you?"

Nodding vaguely, Rae watched the men go about their business. To Buto, she asked, "Has the girl gotten any food or water?"

Buto shook his head. "Omari didn't think it was safe to remove her gag. He said she'd probably put a curse on us. Make us smell bad or never get it up again."

Rae rolled her eyes. "Give me that, you fool," she said, snatching the bread from Buto's hand. "A curse would be wasted on you. You already smell bad." Then she grabbed an empty clay cup, dipped it into the river, and carried both items into the tent.

She found Nefermaat slumped in the corner, her eyes closed.

Rae hurried over to her, worried that the priestess might have fainted from the heat. It was stifling and airless inside the little tent.

"Neff," she whispered, sliding a hand behind the girl's bald head and lifting it gently. When she didn't stir, Rae loosened the gag and pulled it out of her mouth.

Let her curse me if she wants, Rae thought. *My luck couldn't get much worse.*

"Neff," Rae said again. "Wake up. I have some food and water for you." She lifted the cup to the girl's lips and poured a few drops into her mouth.

The girl's throat bobbed as she swallowed, and then she was leaning toward the cup and drinking greedily.

"Not so fast," Rae cautioned. "You'll get sick."

Neff nodded and licked her lips, taking deep, labored breaths. Then she looked at Rae with those dark, haunting eyes and—inexplicably—smiled.

"Now I understand," she said.

Rae blinked. "Understand what?"

"Why he didn't warn me about you. Why he didn't try to protect me."

"Who?"

"Medjed."

"Who?" Rae repeated.

"He knew that we were supposed to meet. He knew that you wouldn't really hurt me."

Rae felt the earth tilt beneath her feet. The girl was doing it again. There was something about her that unnerved Rae. Something that made the hairs on the back of her neck stand on end.

"You're wrong," Rae said. "You're in great danger, Nefermaat."

"I am. But not from you."

Rae swallowed and decided to change tack. "What do you mean, 'supposed to meet'? We've already met."

Neff shook her head. "I met Ahura, but you're not her. You're Rae. Greetings to you. You're not the only one with secrets. Our goals are not as different as you think."

Rae felt a flash of satisfaction. *I knew it.* "So the priest was right. You and the prince really are conspiring against the king."

Neff looked surprised. "You saw Montuhotep?"

"I did, in the throne room. He was going on and on about what a devious child you are. He only ended his rant because the king slit his throat. He won't be spreading rumors about you any longer, I can tell you that much."

Nefermaat's eyes bugged. "Montuhotep is dead?"

"Very much so."

Neff slumped back against the wall of the tent.

"It wasn't your fault. The rat obviously had it coming."

"Still." The girl's gaze settled on the loaf of bread. "Could I...?"

Rae gave her a stern look. "I'll untie your hands, but you must promise not to try to escape."

"I'm not going anywhere," Neff replied. "I'm exactly where I need to be."

Another thrill of energy crept up Rae's spine as she unbound Nefermaat's hands. *Why does she speak in riddles?*

"I still don't understand," Rae said as she watched the girl devour the bread. "You're just a child. Why would you risk your life to work against the king?"

Neff swallowed a bite of food and looked straight at Rae. "Because of the lamb."

Rae straightened. "The lamb?" The words whispered through her mind like the wind, full of smoke and honey and wine.

"Yes. The Oracle of the Lamb."

The little priestess told her everything. About her dreams, her visions, her journey from Bubas to the Temple of Amun to the royal palace. She recited the words of the lamb and their connection to four very special individuals: Nefermaat herself, the princess Sitamun, a Red Lander named Karim—

"And you."

Rae scoffed. "You've got to be joking."

"I'm not," Neff replied.

"You want me to believe that a thousand years ago, Khnum, the Divine Potter, decided that a High Khetaran princess, a thirteen-year-old girl, some desert tribesman, and a Sakeshi rebel were supposed to meet and somehow save the kingdom from… what? A tyrant king? Is Meryamun the cause of the 'sorrow and ruin' your lamb speaks of?"

"Yes and no," Neff mused. "Stopping Meryamun is part of our calling, but I'm certain there's more to it than that. I don't know yet exactly what, but I have a feeling that we'll find out very soon."

Rae tilted her chin and stared at the top of the tent, where early evening light filtered through the weave of the canvas. "This is madness. Come on, you've finished eating. I've got to tie you up again and go find Omari."

Neff shook her head. "No, don't! You must listen!"

"Enough! Now stay still."

The girl began to struggle as Rae attempted to bind her wrists. "Please, Rae! I know you're a good person! I can see it in your eyes! You want to do what's right for the kingdom!"

"Be quiet!" Rae snarled. She could feel her anger growing. It was all too much.

"You met him! Karim! By the riverbank! Isn't that right?"

Rae froze. *She couldn't be talking about the Jackal, could she?*

"You remember him, don't you?" the girl went on, seemingly encouraged by the confusion on Rae's face. "He saw you on a farm by the side of the river. He had curly hair. Stubble. Big smile. You gave him fish to eat, and he gave you gifts in exchange."

Neff squeezed her eyes shut, as if straining to recall the memory. "When I met him, he said he gave you a…a ring, I think, and something else." Then she gasped. Before Rae could stop her, the young priestess reached out, looped her finger under the cord around Rae's neck, and pulled the lion amulet from its hiding place beneath Rae's dress.

"This," Neff said with triumph. "He gave you this Sekhmet amulet. For the one who wields the scepter."

Thunderstruck, Rae jerked the amulet out of the girl's grasp and tucked it back beneath her dress with a trembling hand. The hand wearing the very ring that Neff had also mentioned. The ring featuring four symbols: a snake, a feather, an eye, and a scarab. She glanced at the packs piled up in the corner of the tent, one of which contained her sekhem scepter. "You can't know all that…" Rae muttered, her mind whirling. "You can't! This is some kind of High Khetaran magic. Some kind of trick!"

"It's not, and you know it!" The little priestess didn't raise her voice, but the strength in her words shone through nonetheless. "Look inside you, Rae. Look into your soul and tell me you don't believe!"

Rae scanned Neff's face, searching for deception or guile, but found only a young girl begging for someone to share a burden she'd been carrying alone.

Rae growled in frustration. "Fine! I'll...consider what you've told me. Now I must return to the palace. I'll come back soon. All right?"

Mollified, the priestess simply said, "Thank you."

"I need to tie you up again, but I'll make the bindings looser this time."

The girl didn't move a muscle as Rae retied the rags around her wrists and mouth, and she seemed at peace when Rae gave her a final glance before stepping out of the tent. "I'm not saying I believe you. I'm only saying I'll think about it."

Neff didn't need to reply, her eyes said it all. *You may not believe yet, but you will.*

Rae gripped the rough canvas and shut the tent flap. The memory of the Jackal's thoughtful face filled her mind, profiled against the sun as he gazed out onto the Iteru.

The river gets its way, in the end.

She cursed.

21
SITA

It was early evening by the time they'd helped the Hudjefa tend to their wounded and set up camp for the night. It was also when Sita noticed Behkai was missing.

Karim must have had the same realization, because he came running over to her, his expression frantic.

"I can't find that cursed dog anywhere," he said. "No one has seen him since we fled the city. What if he didn't get out? What if...?"

He didn't need to finish his thought. Sita knew full well that Behkai—stupidly, wonderfully brave Behkai—wouldn't have hesitated to attack one of the ushabti if it had been hurting an innocent person. The dog couldn't have known that the stone men were impenetrable. But he would have broken all his teeth trying to bite them anyway.

"Come on," she said, handing the pile of makeshift bandages she'd collected to another woman. "Let's go look for him while there's still a little light left." If the dog was alive, he could have been anywhere by then, but they had to try.

They walked back toward the valley, careful to keep an eye out for any movement as they scanned the horizon. Sita knew that the only ushabti still in Perset were there to guard the city as Setnakht had commanded, but she didn't want any more surprises.

"Behkai!" she called for the twentieth time.

"It's no use," Karim finally said, leaning against a boulder. "He's gone."

Karim had stayed busy helping the bereaved and making plans with Elyas, but Sita could see the strain of the day and its grief had finally caught up with him.

"Let's walk a little while longer," she said.

Karim nodded but said nothing. They continued in silence.

Sita snuck a glance at him. *Is it really possible that he cannot die?* She wondered what he was thinking and how he must feel, and she desperately wanted to ask him—except this wasn't the time. The experience was still too fresh, too raw. Besides, she feared his answer. She bore the responsibility for his newfound immortality. The sight of him that morning at their campsite in the valley, his body soaked in blood, his eyes glinting strangely in the dawn's light, was seared into her memory.

Sitamun, what have you done?

She shivered and asked a different question instead.

"Do you think it's wise? Bringing the Hudjefa across the desert in the hope that the Anen will take them in?"

"Do you have a better idea?" Karim asked.

"No, I just thought you weren't on good terms with your tribe. What makes you think they'll agree?"

"The Anen's numbers have been dwindling ever since the

Shass began besieging us every chance they got. There are good fighting men among the Hudjefa, and their women are skilled too. Dumiya's abilities alone make her more valuable than ten common fighters. An alliance between the tribes would be fruitful for both, especially as Setnakht's army rides on Khetara. The Red Lands must be protected."

Sita frowned. "I wish you luck. In my experience, simply because a plan makes perfect sense, doesn't mean people will agree to it. But I'm certain you will find a way to convince them."

Karim regarded her warily. "Why do I get the feeling you aren't coming with me?"

Sita tried to meet his gaze but found that she couldn't. "Because I'm not," she said evenly. "I must return to Thonis."

"What?" Karim said, suddenly furious. "You can't! We barely made it out of there alive! And now you're going to march right back into your brother's house? He'll kill you! Or worse—marry you!"

Sita glanced at the twin serpents that wound around her staff and held it a little tighter. "Things have changed. I'm no longer afraid of Mery. And I'm one of the only people in the kingdom who knows what's coming. It's my duty as a princess and a Khetaran to warn the palace of the oncoming horde. My brother will have no choice but to put aside our differences until Setnakht is no longer a threat."

Karim raised an eyebrow. "In my experience, simply because a plan makes perfect sense, doesn't mean people will agree to it."

Sita scoffed.

After a long moment, Karim said quietly, "I thought we were supposed to do this together, sena. Until the end."

"I'm sorry," Sita replied. "You have a duty to your people, and I have a duty to mine."

Another silence washed over them, this one heavier than the first.

Sita turned northwest, toward the river, toward home, a mixture of excitement and dread churning in her veins.

She squinted.

A black animal galloped toward them.

Sita grabbed the thief's shoulder and pointed. "Look!"

Karim laughed. It was the first truly joyous sound Sita had heard that day. "I can't believe it," he said.

Behkai did not stop running until he'd reached them, and then he leaped straight onto Karim, knocking him flat on his back.

"Get off me you great oaf!" Karim complained as the dog stood atop his master, his long, thin tail wagging furiously. "What is that? What's in your mouth?"

"I think it's a rabbit," Sita observed with amusement.

As if on command, Behkai dropped the dead hare onto Karim's chest.

While Karim struggled to extricate himself from both dog and rabbit, Sita chuckled. "You should be grateful! He's brought you dinner. Look at him. He's so proud of himself."

Behkai sat on his haunches and looked between them, panting gloriously, tongue lolling.

A grin crept into the corner of Karim's mouth. He reached out and gave the dog a hearty pat. "It's good to have you back, boy."

Sita bent down and placed a kiss on top of the beast's head, right above the white handprint on his face. "It is." Her gaze met Karim's as they fawned over Behkai, and Sita felt a sharp sting in her heart.

I am going to miss this, she thought. *I am going to miss this very much.*

Sita and Karim hardly spoke for the rest of the evening, busy as they were helping build a fire and ration out the water the tribe had managed to bring with them during their flight from the city. They only had enough water to last a day or so, and it would take more than that to reach the river on foot, especially with the wounded in tow.

"We will make it," Elyas said to Sita as she worried over the meager water jars. "I have faith."

Elyas wasn't the only one who felt that way. Karim and Sita's presence seemed to inspire the Hudjefa. None were smiling that night as they ate the roasted rabbit Behkai had caught along with some other wild game, but Sita noticed there was a calm among the survivors. A feeling that despite their terrible plight, they were in the hands of a power greater than their own.

Sita wished she felt the same. On one hand, she couldn't wait to set her eyes on Thonis, to smell the jasmine on the breeze, to walk through the yawning, vivid halls of the palace, and to see those she loved, especially Nebet. On the other, she knew full well the danger she was walking into. If Mery didn't believe her story about Setnakht—for it was a fantastic story indeed—all of Khetara might be doomed. And that's if Mery didn't kill her first.

He wouldn't, would he? He loves me—tainted though that love might be.

She thought back on what Setnakht had said when he'd mistaken her for his wife, Queen Anet, a woman whom he'd obviously loved deeply. When Sita rejected his advances, he'd told his soldiers to kill her and throw her body into the mortuary temple. The experience taught her an important lesson: Mery's enduring love for her was not a shield. If anything, it was a poison.

I must be prepared for him, she thought. *For his cunning. For his games. I must see the board in front of me and all the players upon it.*

It was hard to imagine confronting her brother, but it was easier than thinking of Karim.

When had she fallen for him? There hadn't been a single

instance she could pinpoint, but a constellation of tiny moments that amounted to love: sharing his meal with her that first day on the riverbank; the way he looked while washing in the river, his lean body glistening under the sun; how he'd gently tucked the blanket around her when he thought she was sleeping; the way it felt living as husband and wife in Perset, far away from their troubles and their true identities.

Could she ever feel that way again? Or was their fantasy doomed to end with their parting?

Late that night, after Sita finished changing her last bandage on one of the wounded, she was sitting by the fire, gazing into the flames. Behkai had bedded down with the children, treating them like his pups and making sure they were all fully licked before going to sleep. She sensed Karim come up beside her to sit on the blanket Miri had provided.

The fire hissed and crackled, illuminating their faces with a golden glow. It was a long time before either of them spoke.

"Will I ever see you again?" Sita asked.

Karim turned to her and chuckled without humor. "Given my penchant for eternal life, sena, I expect you will."

"Perhaps you can't die, but I can," Sita murmured.

She felt Karim's body tense. "I wish I could come with you," he said softly. "But I know this is a battle you must fight alone."

Sita's focus hadn't left the fire. She was so afraid to look at him, so afraid the emotion on his face would be her undoing. Except he was like the river's current—irresistible, inevitable. She turned to him.

How could she have ever thought he had a common face? One like any other in a crowd? How had she neglected to see the rugged beauty of his stubbled jaw, his roguish smile, his earthen skin, and the waving, windblown glory of his curls? Perhaps they'd started out as ordinary features, but now they were inexorably attached to the memories she had of him.

Each extraordinary moment they'd shared had transformed a stranger into her beloved.

With terrified desperation, she wondered if he felt the same. What if he didn't? What if all his affection had been him playing the part to fool the Hudjefa? He hated Khetarans, after all, and he cared nothing for her status or her royal blood.

Perhaps it would be better if he didn't love me, she thought, a lump rising in her throat. *It would be easier to leave him.*

"Sitamun, you *will* see me again," Karim said, mistaking the source of her consternation.

Sita shook her head, not trusting herself to speak.

Tentatively, he lifted a hand to her face, cupping her cheek with his calloused palm. She leaned against it, despite herself.

"Do you remember what you said, when you called me back from the dead?" he asked.

Sita recalled kneeling beside Karim's mutilated body with the scarab amulet in her hand. *You can't die, tomb robber,* she'd said. *I can't bear another death on my conscience.* The memory gave her a jolt. The amulet hadn't given him immortality, she realized. *It was me.*

The amulet's magic had brought him back. Her command made it permanent.

The word is the deed.

"You said you needed me," Karim went on, fire in his voice. "You ordered me to come back to you."

"I'm sorry," Sita whispered, her tears threatening to overflow. "I didn't realize… I didn't mean to…" She couldn't continue. She'd only meant to save him, not to burden him with a life without end.

"You Khetarans," Karim broke into her thoughts, his voice husky but suffused with good humor. "Always so imperious. Telling people when they can and can't die. What will you think of next, hey?" He paused, his face growing serious. "Sena, you have told me much about your magic, this 'heka.' You say that with object, word, and action, you can make your wishes real."

"Yes."

"Then hear me now. Let me cast my own spell this night." He took her hand and pressed it to his chest. "Do you feel my heart beating?"

Sita nodded.

"That is the object. These are my words." He licked his lips. "No matter where you go, Sitamun, no matter what darkness befalls us in the days to come, I will always come back to you. I owe no fealty to your king or your kingdom, but your command called me back to this earth and to your side. I intend to obey it."

"I don't want you to be bound to me because of this magic," Sita broke in. "It was never my intention to enchant you."

Karim leaned closer, smiling. "Wasn't it?" He laid his hand over hers, pressing it to him. "You gave me this heart, Princess. It is yours, magic or no."

Sita felt her breath grow shallow. Her belly tingled with the closeness of him, the smell of his body, and the heat of his skin beneath her palm.

"Your action," she murmured.

"What?" His lips were so close to hers that she could taste his breath with every word he spoke.

"The spell you're casting…" she said, feathery soft. "You have your object and your words. Spells have three parts. What is your action?"

Karim eyes were filled with the sight of her and her alone. "Only this," he said, and pulled her lips to his.

They'd kissed before, but that kiss was different. There was a hunger behind it, a desperation. This kiss was one to last for days, weeks, centuries.

There was suddenly too much between them—too much space and too much fabric. They struggled to free themselves from their clothes, tossing them aside and nearly into the fire in their haste to entangle their bodies under the midnight sky.

She pulled him on top of her, eager to feel his weight pressing her into the sand, holding her fast to the earth that seemed to be spinning more and more out of control. He was lean and lithe, the dark hair of his body pleasantly rough against her smoothness, his every movement creating friction that set her senses aflame.

He tore his lips from hers and traveled down her throat, then her collarbone, forging a path of kisses along her body. She gasped as he traversed her curves with his hands like some wondrous, unexplored country. She wove her fingers into his hair, clutching its waves and guiding him down to her belly, her hips.

She lifted her head to watch him, the muscles of his back and shoulders flexing as he moved, serpentine; as he drank her in, open-mouthed, like wine.

Every thought was driven from her mind as sensation flooded her body. When she could stand it no longer, she reached for him, coaxing him back into her arms, pulling him to her.

Karim hesitated, his face flushed with desire. "Are you sure?" he asked.

Above them, the sky was dazzling with stars. It was said that Nut, the sky goddess whose starry body arched over creation, had once been so entwined with her lover, the earth god Geb, that the sun had no space to rise between them. The sky and the earth could not bear to separated, but they were forced to part in order for another day to come.

Never had Sita felt that story so deeply, nor the fierce need to savor a moment that was destined to burn away in the light of dawn.

"I'm sure," she whispered into his mouth as she kissed him. "I'm sure."

Sita felt the earth and sky collide. Not even a single mote of light could possibly shine between them, because there was no between. There was only fire and breath and passion, and a yearning to stop the night from ending, stop the sun from rising, to remain together and together and together until all the imperishable stars went out.

They held each other, wrapped in a blanket and nothing else, until the dawn came.

Then she wept.

Sita refused to take more than the barest minimum of provisions for her journey back to Thonis, despite how fervently Miri and the others tried to send her with more. She accepted only two gifts: their fastest horse, one of five the men had rescued from the city, and a traveling companion.

"You cannot undertake such an expedition alone," Elyas had insisted. "It's madness, even for you!"

Aya appeared by her grandfather's side. "I'll go!"

"Hush, child," Elyas scolded.

"This is *my* fight, Elyas," Sita said. "The Hudjefa have suffered enough." She was about to say more when someone gripped her shoulder, and she turned to find Dumiya standing beside her. Unlike the other warriors, the older woman looked no worse for wear and sported nary a bruise nor a scrape from her battles with the ushabti.

Dumiya put a hand to her chest, then pressed her two fists together and pointed to Sita. Her message was clear.

I am with you.

Sita relented. "Thank you," she said. It was obvious the woman had already made up her mind and would not be dissuaded.

Elyas watched the exchange with satisfaction. "Dumiya will be an excellent escort—a good rider and even better in a fight. You are wrong to say this is your fight alone, Sita. The fight against those accursed creatures belongs to us all."

It didn't take long for them to finish packing the supplies and readying Sita and Dumiya's horses. In fact, it all happened far too quickly.

Karim said, "You should go while it's still early. Try to get some ground under you before the hottest part of the day." He adjusted the black hood around her face. She could see that every word pained him. The worst was yet to come. They both knew it.

Many of the Hudjefa came to say their goodbyes. They, too, were preparing to set off toward the Iteru, where Karim hoped to barter with a trading ship for passage to the western riverbank. From there, they wouldn't be far from the Anen's herding route.

"My tracking skills have yet to fail me, sen," he assured Elyas. "We'll find them. My nose will lead me home."

"Once a dog, always a dog," Sita teased.

She looked down at Behkai, who seemed to sense that the time of their parting was close at hand. His long black tail was tucked between his legs, and his pointed ears drooped.

"It's all right, boy," Sita said, placing a kiss on his head as she always did. "You take care of that thief while I'm away, all right?"

Behkai whined.

"Do both dogs get a kiss?" Karim asked.

Sita chuckled. It was better than crying. She kissed him, lingering long enough that the young women standing nearby tittered. They still believed Sita and Karim were married—she hadn't had the time nor the energy to admit the truth. Her eyes were wet when she pulled away, and she quickly dashed the tears from her face, eager to move past the pain.

Turning from Karim, she tangled her fingers in the black stallion's thick mane and hoisted herself onto his back. Dumiya was already astride a large silver mare. Sita checked that the packs were secure, and Karim handed her the serpent staff, which he'd fitted with a strip of leather so that she could more easily sling it across her back.

When her fingers slipped from his, she knew it was the last time they'd touch.

She bit her lip, willing herself to be strong.

The oracle meant for the four of us to be together, she thought. *Maybe the little priestess and the warrior are together already. The lamb's prophecy can't come true until we're all in the same place, so I* will *see him again. I must.*

Still, she didn't know that for a fact, nor if the oracle would actually come to pass. After all, what if they'd made choices to alter the foretold course of events in some way?

No. There was no point in that line of thinking. It would only lead to chaos. She, like the Hudjefa, needed to have faith. She needed to believe she was on the gods' path.

"Here," she said, removing the green scarab amulet from her neck and tossing it to Karim. "I want you to have it."

Karim examined the necklace. "I can't take this. Didn't you say your father gave it to you?"

Sita glanced at his chest, where she could just make out the edge of his scarab-shaped scar. "You can return it when you come back to me."

Karim's jaw tightened, and he looped the amulet around his neck. "Very well, sena. Until I see you again."

With that, she spurred the horse with her heels and held on

tight as the stallion broke into a gallop. Dumiya followed at her side with the wind at her back.

Together they rode into the Red Desert, their horses kicking plumes of sand into the air as they went.

Sita looked back at the tribe as they crested a dune and left them to their own long and treacherous journey. Then she turned her gaze toward Thonis.

You can stop searching for me now, Mery, Sita thought. *I'm coming home.*

22
WINGS

A jackal stalked a heron on the riverbank, and the ibis roosting on a tree nearby was the only one to notice. The heron was napping, her neck tucked in on itself, and the ibis could tell she was old from the bedraggled state of her plumage. The jackal approached her slowly, his belly low to the ground.

Fly away, quick-quick, the ibis's instincts told him. *Be glad it's the heron and not you.*

Then the ibis remembered the net that fell upon him and his brethren while they hunted in the marshes. How different it might have been if another bird had called out a warning!

The jackal stopped, muscles tensing, ready to pounce.

Oh dear, oh dear, the ibis thought, then swooped down toward them, yelping like a puppy.

The jackal and the heron both took notice. The jackal looked up, hackles rising, and the heron unfolded herself and stood. The jackal reared back in surprise, for the bird was at least twice as large as a common heron. Her plumage, which the ibis would have sworn had been dingy and faded, radiated with color—her breast pure white, her back, wings, and head the variegated green-blue of the river itself. She towered over the jackal, her golden beak long and sharp, and the predator shrank under her imperious gaze.

With a snarl, the jackal turned tail and ran. He'd been looking for an easy meal, not a battle with a giant.

Even after the jackal had gone, the ibis was hesitant to alight. Herons were usually friendly, but this was no typical heron.

The bird eyed him, and let out a deep, guttural sound. *Be not afraid, little ibis. I am grateful for your warning. I am old and not as watchful as I once was.*

The ibis blinked. The heron's plumage had faded again. Had he simply imagined its brightness? She no longer looked as formidable.

The ibis fluttered down and landed in front of her. *Heron, you are big!* he squawked. *Very big! Never have I seen your equal!*

I am no heron, the bird said, shaking her great head indignantly. *I am Bennu. I was here before the sand, before the sky, before the light. It was I who flew over the endless waters, whose call announced the birth of this world.*

The ibis crooked his head. He had known other birds with delusions of grandeur—storks, mostly—but none quite like this one.

It has been too long since I hunted, the Bennu bird went on, sinking back to sit. *Fending off that creature has taken my strength. Be a dear and get us some fish, would you?*

The ibis could not believe the gall of this "Bennu bird." First, he saves her life, and then she orders him to bring her food? Still, she was the first friend he'd made since the death of his flock. Perhaps, at her age, the Bennu had earned the right to make such demands. And besides, the ibis was hungry too.

Fine-fine—a fish, a fish. I'll do what I can do, the ibis said.

Thank you, the Bennu bird said, and craned her neck to gently touch her golden beak against his black one.

An odd, pleasant warmth flooded the ibis's body, and he felt happy for the first time in a long, long while. He flew south.

The ibis flew toward marshlands he'd seen near a city on the horizon, but when he reached its outskirts, the river was clogged with ships. Many of the sails sported ram heads painted in black and red, and the ibis wondered what they meant. Thinking he might have better luck scavenging from people than fishing, the ibis wheeled east, coasting over the tops of the buildings clustered there. Unlike the white shining city up north, this city seemed to be falling into disrepair—and into bloodshed.

As the ibis drew closer, cries rose from the streets. Below him, people were running this way and that, while swords clashed and carts overturned, spilling food everywhere. The ibis thought to dive down and grab a meal, but when he saw the bodies, he decided against it.

Disturbed by what he saw, the ibis descended to perch on the roof of a large house on a grand estate. It was quiet, untouched by the violence, and seemed a useful spot for a brief respite. A small hunched man with a red nose sat at the back of the house on a wide patio, lush with potted flowers and small trees. He was chewing rhythmically, like cattle do, and staring out into the desert beyond. Another man came out of the house and approached the smaller one.

"We've collected fifty hands so far, Nomarch," the man said, "And we've piled the bodies of the dead in the marketplace for all to see."

The nomarch snorted. "Only fifty? It's been hours. Are the

king's reinforcements not enough to handle a bunch of old soldiers and shopkeepers?"

"It's not that we can't handle them. We can't *find* them. People have gone into hiding. It's as if they knew we were coming."

The nomarch sighed. "Ever since Ankhu's girl put a knife in my spy, that brewer, there has been unrest." He clucked his tongue. "I should have killed her when I had the chance."

"Humblest apologies, Nomarch, but it appears the people of Sakesh have a spy of their own."

The nomarch slammed a fist against the arm of his chair. "I don't care if they've got Sekhmet herself. King Meryamun expects us to deliver—so *deliver*! Fifty more hands, do you hear? Make it sixty, for good measure!"

The noise startled the ibis, and he launched back into the air. It was time to keep looking for food.

At the southern edge of the city, past blackened fields and grazing zebu, the ibis spied another large building, crumbling but still grand. An older woman was running toward it with half a dozen others, glancing over her shoulder as she went. "Faster, girls, faster now. Don't wait for me," said the woman, panting and red-faced.

The younger girls looked at her with concern. "We won't leave you, Mamet Mut," one of them said.

"Ach, I'm too old for rebellion," Mamet Mut grunted, but it was clear even to the ibis that she didn't mean it. She was, in fact, the perfect age for rebellion—the age when a woman no longer cares what anyone thinks and does exactly as she wishes.

The girls each looped an arm around the older woman's and helped her along the road, a small loaf of bread and two fish slipping out of one of their packs as they went.

What luck, yes-yes! The ibis descended and grabbed the fish in his beak. He was about to take off, back to the ailing Bennu bird, when a large man caught his attention.

"More, Mamet?" asked the man with remarkably large ears. "I'm not sure how many others we can fit in the underground tunnels." He quickly directed the group inside the building, where it appeared other men were waiting to greet them.

Mamet Mut stopped, hands on hips, trying to catch her breath. "They had nowhere else to go, Menk. But I think that's the last of them. Everyone else has either found their own hiding places or…"

The ibis thought of the piled bodies.

"Thank goodness Omari's message got to us when it did. If we hadn't had advance notice, we never would have been able to save so many," Mamet Mut said.

Menk turned to the sturdy old woman. He spoke quietly, "That wasn't all his note said."

Mamet Mut's eyes widened. "What else?"

"Omari says that our people, Ankhu included, will be sacrificed in a cursing ritual that King Meryamun intends to hold at the Thonis fortress in a few days' time. The pharaoh intends to use heka to curse all his enemies—including us."

"Blood magic," Mamet Mut breathed.

Menk nodded, his expression grim.

"Did Omari say anything else?"

"That we should marshal our army and prepare for war."

The old woman's brow furrowed. "Nothing about a rescue mission? What about Rae? What are her orders?"

"He didn't mention Raetawy. I thought it odd, but then again, they are quite close, so perhaps her word and his are the same." Menk looked troubled. "Though it didn't sound like her. She wouldn't give up on her father, not without a fight." He tugged on one of his oversized ears. "I don't know what to do. I'm used to following orders, not giving them."

"Leaders are made, not born, Menk," Mamet Mut told him. "You said so yourself. We chose Raetawy to lead us because she has the heart of a lion that always points to justice. All we need to ask ourselves is: What would she do?"

The two fell to silence.

The ibis's stomach growled. He took to the air, having satisfied his curiosity but not his appetite. With the two fish clamped in his beak, he wheeled back toward his aging companion.

The Bennu bird swallowed her fish in one gulp, then set to preening herself.

The ibis took his time with his meal. Despite his great hunger, he'd given her the larger fish. If she noticed his generosity, she didn't mention it.

Once she was done arranging her feathers, the Bennu bird stood.

Ah, she said, clacking her beak. *I feel much better now. So, tell me, where is your flock, sacred one?*

No one had ever called him that before. The ibis stood a little taller.

Dead, he replied. *Taken for tokens by the men of this land.*

The Bennu bird stretched her great blue wings, which were so large that they blotted out the sun. *Perhaps our meeting was not by chance after all. I am old and have little time left on this earth before I must sing another song. I know not what will happen, only that there will be a great tumult, and that I must announce the end of this world and the beginning of another.*

The ibis had never met such a philosophical bird. Still, her words were interesting and seemed important.

I see, I see, he said encouragingly.

It would be nice to have company, the Bennu added, glancing at him with those bright, yellow eyes.

The ibis considered this. He, too, was tired of being alone.

The ibis said, *Yes-yes, I will come. But where are we going?*

North. To the shining city. We must be there to witness what is coming.

The ibis shivered. What would it be like to go back to where his troubles began? What would it be like to go home?

Come, come, the Bennu bird said. *Be not afraid. You wear the face of a god.*

A god? The ibis had no reference for the word.

Men can be terrible creatures, but in their struggles for meaning, they sometimes stumble upon truth. The truth is, there is magic in you, little ibis. There is a reason you survived, a reason you met me, a reason we must embark on this journey together. There is a reason for everything, if only you look hard enough.

The ibis did not understand all the Bennu's words, but he liked the sound of them. They made him feel brave.

In a flurry of black and white feathers, they launched themselves into the sky and flew side by side, following the river's current.

23
NEFF

Between that morning's ordeal and the heat inside the little tent, Neff could only hold off sleep for so long. The bread and water that Rae had brought her had satiated the worst of her hunger and thirst, and eventually she nodded off.

The next thing she knew, something was poking her in the shoulder. She snorted and woke, stiff from the awkward way she was bound. When she opened her eyes, though, she was alone in the tent.

Then she saw the little footprints in the sand.

Neff managed to shake the loosened gag from her mouth. "Medjed!" she whispered. "You're here!" She pushed a piece of loose cloth toward him with her toe. "Look—I managed to keep hold of your shroud when they packed away the rest of the laundry."

A moment later, the cloth rose up from the ground with Medjed's diminutive form beneath.

"Your eyes are on backward."

After some shifting, the painted eyes rotated to face her.

"That's better. You knew I needed to be with her, didn't you? Rae? That's why you didn't try to stop her from taking me."

Medjed nodded.

"Part of me really wants you to help me escape, because I'm scared, but... I know I can't leave yet. I need her to trust me. The oracle wants us to work together, I'm sure of it. Rae needs to believe that we're on the same side."

Neff thought about the young woman she'd known as Ahura, and how different she was after she'd dispensed with the pretense of being a servant. It was as if she'd been making herself small to fit into palace life. Away from there, she seemed to exhale, to expand—proving to be someone very powerful indeed.

Without warning, Medjed turned to face the tent flap and dropped out of sight. The little cloth had only just settled on the ground when someone bent low to enter.

It was the big man, the one Rae called Omari.

Of all the Low Khetaran rebels, he was the one who really frightened her. Neff quickly nuzzled her face back into the gag so Omari wouldn't think anything was amiss.

When he stood, Omari's head brushed the top of the tent. He glowered down at her. "So, what do you think, eh? Is your life worth a hundred of our people?"

Neff had overheard Rae telling him that Meryamun had ordered a hundred Sakeshi citizens slaughtered for each day she was missing. It was horrific, but not surprising. If they'd asked her, Neff could have told them their kidnapping scheme wouldn't work. Meryamun didn't negotiate. He destroyed.

Neff shook her head, the gag preventing her from saying more.

Omari scoffed. "Of course. You'd say anything to save yourself. You may *look* young, but I've heard of your power. You cannot trick me." He bent, seizing her arm in his thick, calloused hand. "I know what you're trying to do with Rae. Do you think I'm stupid? You've put a spell on her to make her think you're her friend." He paused. "She and I were great friends once. I hardly know her anymore." A look of anguish crossed his face. "She was keeping secrets from me! All this time!"

His grip hurt her. Tears sprung to Neff's eyes, but she made no sound.

"I thought she wanted... I thought we would..." He didn't finish. He took her chin in his hand, forcing her to look up at him. "Your king wants to send a message to Sakesh, does he? Fine. Then Sakesh will send her own message."

When he stormed through the flap, Neff curled into a ball, trying to calm herself. Did Rae know what darkness lay in her friend's heart?

And what might happen before she found out?

24 KARIM

For two days and two nights, Karim led the Hudjefa through the eastern desert. Some people stumbled along the way and had to be carried. A few fell and did not rise again. When finally, on the third day, they saw the Iteru glittering on the horizon, nearly all of them sank to their knees and cried.

"I want to see!" Aya clambered onto Karim's shoulders to get a better view. There was a scattering of palm trees and scrubby bushes ahead, and their vivid greenness was welcome to the Hudjefa's weary eyes.

"It's so pretty!" Aya exclaimed.

She's never seen the river before, Karim realized. *None of them have.*

The sight of it must have felt like a miracle.

Kicking off their sandals on the riverbank, the people ran into the water, cupping it in their hands and pouring it over their faces and into their mouths. They smiled and laughed—a sound Karim hadn't heard since before the attack on Perset.

Aya joined them, shrieking with delight as she splashed the other children.

Behkai was excited too, galloping into the water then out again, stopping to shake himself all over and spray Karim with a combination of dog-water and slobber. Karim retaliated with a string of curses, though he had to admit the dog's shower *was* quite refreshing.

Elyas watched it all, his expression equal parts exhaustion and relief. He was doing remarkably well given his injury, a testament to the old man's stubborn nature. He gave Karim a grateful pat on the back. "What now, sen?"

"Once all our waterskins are filled and the animals are watered, we can hail a trading ship to help us cross. Some of your embroidered linens and a sheep or two should be enough payment. Once we're on the west side, we'll set out for the Anen's camp. They move the flock north this time of year, so I'm hoping we won't have too much trouble finding them."

Elyas nodded. "And you think your tribe will embrace us?"

Karim licked his lips. "I plan to make the decision clear to them, sen—if you take my meaning."

Elyas shifted uneasily and crossed his arms. "I will not force myself upon another tribe, no matter how desperate our situation. I trust you, Karim-sen, but I have seen enough bloodshed. I will not be the cause of more."

"I understand." It was Karim's turn to be uneasy. Babu would be on the other side of that river. The big man wouldn't have forgotten his promise to slit his throat from ear to ear if Karim ever showed his face again. He still believed that Karim had murdered Djet in the tomb so he could take all the treasure for himself. It would not be a happy reunion, and more than his own life was on the line.

"I'll shed as little blood as possible," he told Elyas.

In fact, if I strangle Babu, he won't bleed at all.

It was only after they'd been wandering the Red Lands for several hours that Karim had his first doubts about finding the Anen. His keen sense of direction had never led him astray before, and being back in his native land only sharpened his senses. Yet, he could have sworn he'd seen that very same tree an hour earlier…or had he?

"You aren't leading us in circles, are you, dear?" Miri asked. Her tone was sweet, but it had an edge to it. "If God is truly leading you, perhaps you could ask him to do it with a bit more haste? My knees aren't what they used to be."

"They should be here," Karim muttered. "I swear, they should be right over this—"

Then he heard the unmistakable sound of a bleating lamb.

Excited, Karim turned to Miri and Elyas. "Stay here. I'll be right back."

He hurried to the top of a tall hill, a grin spreading over his face at the sight of a herd of sheep grazing in the scrub. A hooded man walked among them, a shepherd's crook in his hand.

"Greetings to you!" Karim shouted, waving his arm. "Don't be alarmed! I come in peace!"

The man looked up, his hood dropping back. The face beneath was lean and puckered with blemishes, his hair dark brown and curly.

The young man's brow furrowed. "Brother?"

Karim couldn't believe his eyes. "Gamil? Is that you?"

It can't be. When I left, I could have sworn he was still just a boy!

Karim sped down the hill while the shepherd shoved his way through the herd toward him.

"My god, it *is* you!" Karim cried.

Gamil nearly knocked him over with his embrace. "Karim-sen—where have you *been*? Babu and Hager came back saying the most terrible things, and when you didn't return, we thought you were dead!"

Karim stuck out his lower lip and tilted his head. "Well, you weren't far wrong…" Instead of launching into what would have been an extremely long story, he held Gamil at arm's length and studied him. "Let me have a look at you, sen. What is that on your face, hey?" He poked at the patchy beard growing on his brother's jaw. "A bit of dirt?"

Gamil swatted his hand away and gave Karim a shove. "You're just jealous because I'm taller than you now."

It was true. In a matter of weeks, Gamil had shot up like a reed. He was gangly and his face still hadn't quite grown into his mouth and nose, but Karim could clearly see the man his brother would become peering back at him. A man who looked remarkably like their father. Karim swallowed. *Half his childhood was stolen when Father died, and the other half I took when I abandoned him.*

Shame struck him like an open palm.

Once a thief, always a thief.

It had been easy to forget about his family in the face of oracles and magic and monsters. Perhaps a bit too easy. He'd barely spared a thought for them—in fact, he'd tried his very best to avoid thinking of what might have happened to his family during his absence. He was too afraid of what he'd find when he returned.

Gamil looked all right—though Karim was surprised to see him holding a shepherd's crook instead of a blade. Karim dared to hope that perhaps the rest of his family was fine too.

"Come! Come! We must tell the others that you're back!" Gamil tugged on his arm, his face bright with childlike excitement.

Karim smiled. *There's my little brother.*

Gamil led him past the herd before Karim remembered the Hudjefa. "Wait a minute, sen," Karim said. "There's something I have to tell you."

Gamil didn't seem to hear him. "Dima! Faiza! Look who I found!"

A large tent stood nearby, one that Karim recognized instantly. Two girls looked up from their work milking a pair of ewes in front of it. When they saw the brothers coming toward them, they jumped up in astonishment.

Twelve-year-old Faiza screamed. As the youngest sibling, she did a lot of that—regardless of whether an event was good or bad. She raced over to them and threw her arms around Karim's waist, her round cheeks already streaming with tears. Karim reached down to pat her wavy hair.

"It's all right, sena, it's all right," he said, trying in vain to calm her.

Faiza continued to wail as if a jar had been unstopped and its contents were pouring out.

Dima, who was thirteen but behaved as if she were twice that, did not approach them. She was an ample-figured, serious girl—much like their mother. Instead, she crossed her arms and leveled Karim with a critical frown. "So? Did you?" she asked.

Karim cocked his head, trying to hear her over Faiza's ceaseless blubbering. "Did I what?"

"Did you really kill Djet for treasure?"

"Dima!" Gamil chastised.

"It's a fair question."

"It's not!" Gamil retorted. "How can you ask our brother if he would do such a thing? He loved Djet! We all did!"

"The brother I know wasn't a murderer," Dima said, her voice low. "But the brother I know also wouldn't have left us." To Karim she said, "At least when we thought you were dead, you had a good excuse for being away."

Dima's words speared him, and Karim welcomed the pain. It was the least that he deserved. Still, he didn't want them to think he had anything to do with Djet's death. "I tried to save Djet, I swear it. Babu wouldn't believe me, and he said he'd kill me if I ever returned." He sighed. "But you're right, Dima. I should have come back sooner."

For a long moment, no one moved or spoke. The only sound was Faiza's sniffling. Finally, Dima closed the space between them and leaned her forehead against Karim's chest, nudging the tear-soddened Faiza out of the way. "I built a barrow for you, sen," she whispered. "Next to Father's."

Karim grimaced. *I've been so selfish and stupid to think they would simply forget about me.* "I'm so sorry, sena. For everything. Can you ever forgive me?"

"Maybe. Did you meet any pretty girls while you were roaming the kingdom?"

A grin quirked at Karim's lips. "Well…"

Faiza perked up, wiping her snotty nose on her sleeve. "Oh? What's her name? Did you kiss her? What color dress was she wearing?"

"Wait a minute," Gamil broke in. "Saved Djet from *what?*"

Suddenly there was a clatter, and they all turned toward the sound. A woman stood beside the tent, a pile of branches and twigs dropped at her feet. She was not much taller than Dima and wore a dark brown robe that had seen better days. The three younger siblings took one look at the woman's expression and backed away from Karim.

Karim gulped. "Greetings to you, Omma."

From the way she looked at him, he might as well have burst into flames.

Before he could attempt to explain himself, Karim's mother stepped over the firewood, strode toward him, and slapped him across the face.

Karim's cheek stung, and he rubbed it. "Would you believe you're the second woman to do that recently?"

The next thing he knew, his mother grabbed him and dragged him into a tight embrace. "You stupid, stupid boy," she said, her voice muffled as she pressed her face into his hair. "Don't you *ever* do that to me again."

He hugged her back, feeling a little weepy himself. "I won't, Omma. I promise."

His mother, known to the Anen as Nour, held him at arm's length, as he'd done to Gamil. "You've changed," she said, studying his face.

More than you know, Karim thought.

Her gaze dropped to his chest and the large scarab-shaped scar that peeked out from his robes. Her eyes widened in alarm. "What is this? What's happened to you?"

"He still hasn't explained Djet," Gamil said.

"Or where he's been," Dima added.

"Did you bring me a present?" Faiza asked, tugging at Karim's pack.

"Everyone wait a minute!" Karim raised his arms for quiet. He'd forgotten just how overbearing his family could be. "I promise to answer all your questions, but there's something I must do first. I haven't come alone, you see. During my travels, I crossed paths with the Hudjefa tribe."

His mother looked confused. "The Hudjefa? They don't exist. At least, not anymore."

"The stories were wrong, Omma. They have been living in a forgotten Khetaran city, far out in the eastern desert. They've been expelled from their home and lost many of their brethren in battle, and now...now they need our help."

"That's not going to go over well with Babu," his mother said.

"Babu..."

Perhaps I'll snap up one of your little sisters, hey? They're nearly ripe for the picking.

Remembering the Jackal's threats during their fight, Karim whirled to face his sisters. "Tell me, did Babu ever...touch you since I've been gone? Did he hurt you in any way? Because if he has, I swear I'll kill him!"

Faiza crinkled her nose. "Touched me? Eugh, no!"

Dima said, "He's mean and rude, and he pinched my bottom once. I kicked him really hard, and he never did it again. He probably knows Omma would bite his head off if he tried."

Karim exhaled in relief, though Babu would have to pay for the pinched bottom.

"He forced me to take over shepherding the old leader's herd after he died," Gamil grumbled. "I told him I wanted to fight, but he wouldn't listen."

"The old tribe leader is dead?" Karim asked.

His mother nodded. "Passed away in his sleep soon after you'd gone. Babu leads the Anen now."

"You're joking." Karim cursed under his breath. *Of all the people in all the world, why did it have to be Babu?* "I need to get back to the Hudjefa before something terrible happens," he said.

"Something like what?" his mother asked.

Just then, angry shouts erupted from the other side of the hill.

Karim grumbled in exasperation. "Like that."

The five of them took off running toward the sound.

Karim reached the top of the hill and saw Babu and Elyas

in a heated argument, while a dozen armed Anen and Hudjefa warriors stared down their opposition. Hager was beside Babu, looking as lank and spidery as ever, glancing between the two men as if he were hoping they'd come to blows.

"And how do I know you're not all a bunch of Shass waiting for us to let down our guard, so you can slit our throats in the night, hey?" Babu snarled. His savage demeanor hadn't softened in his new position as tribe leader, though his beard was certainly longer. The brute towered over Elyas, his hands curled into fists at his sides.

Elyas's reply was strained. "As I've already told you, we are the Hudjefa, not the Shass. We were led here by one of your own tribesmen, though I'm not sure where he's gone to…" The old man scanned the landscape and found Karim atop the hill. He pointed. "Ah! There he is."

Babu turned, and his face purpled with rage. *"You!"* he snarled.

Karim sucked his teeth. *Well, shit.*

Babu unsheathed his dagger. "I *told* you what I'd do if you ever showed your face here again!" With a roar, the big man charged toward him, a hippopotamus on the rampage, enormous and much faster than one expected. All Karim's old instincts kicked in, telling him to run away—but he didn't.

Omma was right. I have *changed.*

Karim loosed a guttural cry and ran down the slope toward Babu. He had no reason to be afraid of the Jackal's dagger, nor his fists, nor his rage. He had no reason to be afraid of anything.

Babu lifted the dagger in his meaty hand, ready to finish the job he'd started that day in the valley. Karim didn't give him the chance. Without slowing, he sprinted forward and rammed into the big man, toppling him onto the ground. Once Babu was down, Karim scrambled on top of him and began punching him in the head, over and over again.

How dare he even think *about touching my sisters!*

Karim kept punching. He wasn't tired. He could do it all day.

If it weren't for Babu, maybe we could have closed that tomb before Setnakht got out! He could have helped me! He could have listened!

The next punch landed with a wet crack.

He's a pig and a liar and he deserves to—

"Karim!"

Panting, sweating, his blood thrumming in his veins, Karim heard his mother's shout and paused, his bloody fist raised to strike again. She looked down from the hill with the rest of his family, her arms crossed over her chest, disapproval clear on her face.

Karim sagged. Babu stared up at him through a mask of blood, eyes wide and nostrils flaring.

He's afraid of me now. I could kill him with my bare hands. It would be easy. The thought was both exhilarating and a little frightening. If Karim wasn't careful, this newfound power of his could turn him into a monster.

Faiza screamed.

Again.

This time, though, she pointed at Babu's dagger, which was buried in Karim's shoulder. He hadn't even felt it.

Sighing, Karim reached up and yanked it out—eliciting screams not only from Faiza but other onlookers as well. Somebody fainted.

"I thought you said, 'as little blood as possible!'" Elyas hissed at him.

Karim shrugged. "*I'm* not bleeding."

Elyas rolled his eyes.

Karim looked back down and stabbed the blade into the ground beside Babu's head. "There," he said. "Leave me and my family alone, and we'll call it a truce." Feeling that he'd made his point, he stood up and brushed the dust from his bloodstained hands.

Babu scuttled away, his lip curled in loathing. Hager darted forward to try and help him to his feet, but Babu swatted at him. He refused to take his eyes off Karim. "W-what are you?" he stammered.

"He is a messenger from God!" Elyas announced. "And you should treat him with the respect he deserves, lest you feel his wrath upon you!"

Karim winced. He would have preferred a less ostentatious defense, but he couldn't blame Elyas for trying to be supportive.

Karim glanced around the assembled tribes. More members of the Anen had come to see what all the fuss was about and watched him warily. He knew they'd been told he was a traitor and a murderer, and now he'd proved to be capable of even more extraordinary violence. The Hudjefa, on the other hand, beheld him with a kind of reverence.

Karim wasn't sure which of the two opinions disturbed him more.

"How do you know he's not a demon? They, too, have powers," Babu countered.

"A demon would not have fought the accursed monsters that slaughtered half of my tribe. I saw him slain! Saw him sustain wounds that would kill any man! Yet Karim-sen survived. And he was strong enough to lead us across the desert, over the great river, and here, to you."

Babu struggled to his feet, and Karim was satisfied to see that the Jackal still limped a little from the leg wound he'd given him. "Monsters, eh?" Babu said with mockery. "Would that be the same kind of beast as the one that supposedly killed Djet?"

Karim advanced once more, his anger rising. "The creature that killed Djet escaped the tomb, as I said it would. And after following me across the kingdom and trying to kill me, it came to the city where the Hudjefa were living and raised an army of stone men to fight on his behalf."

At this, the Anen erupted into alarmed chatter. Babu snorted. "You speak in riddles, sen. Stone men?"

"I mean exactly what I say. The kingdom now faces a foe that cannot be killed with blades nor arrows. These creatures are powered by magic—what the Khetarans call 'heka.' And until we discover how to defeat them, they will spread across this land like a pestilence and destroy everything in their path."

The crowd fell silent.

"Since when do you know so much about Khetaran sorcery?" Babu asked.

Karim thought of Nefermaat, the little priestess with the haunting eyes, and of Sitamun. Beautiful, brilliant, intoxicating Sitamun. "Since I made some interesting new friends."

Babu crossed his arms. "Really, sen? You're the last person I'd expect to break bread with the Khetarans. Why should I care if this stone army slaughters them in their plush little beds? It serves them right."

"Do you really think those unholy creatures will be satisfied when they've conquered Thonis? I've seen them with my own eyes—most of the Hudjefa have too. They won't stop until we are all dead or under their thrall. If we fail to fight evil when it threatens our neighbor, then we will have no allies left when it comes for us."

Karim caught sight of his mother in the corner of his vision. She and his siblings had come down to join the group, and she stood listening, her lips parted, one hand pressed to her chest. Unlike the others, there was neither fear nor reverence in her eyes. Her earlier disapproval had vanished too. There was only pride, as if she were seeing her eldest son for the first time.

Karim's heart warmed.

Has this strength always been within me? he wondered. *Or is it simply what happens when you no longer fear death?*

Perhaps it didn't matter.

"Hear me," Karim said to Babu. "If you can't promise to leave our quarrel behind, you and Hager must leave and never return."

Babu wiped the blood from his face and growled in frustration. "Have it your way," he said. "But I'm still the leader here, understand? While you've been fooling around with Khetarans, I've been keeping the Anen alive. That includes your family as well as my own."

"Fine," Karim said. As much as he hated to admit it, Babu was right. The Jackal was a cruel, vicious swine, but he had managed to keep the tribe safe, and that counted for something.

Babu went on. "Not that we have enough food for all the extra mouths you've brought us. First, they're too good to roam the Red Lands, and now that they're kicked out of their paradise, suddenly we owe them refuge?"

Elyas's expression darkened.

Karim was quick to interject. "You don't have to worry about the Hudjefa. They've brought some of their animals, along with skilled artisans, laborers, and warriors too. Isn't that right, Elyas?"

The old man crossed his arms. "My people are not paupers come to beg for charity, especially not from a brute like you." To Karim, he added, "If I had known we would be received in this way, we would have set up camp on the eastern riverbank. Are you certain this alliance is wise, sen?"

Karim wasn't sure. In fact, the whole plan might have been a huge mistake. There was no divine voice whispering instructions in his ear. There was only his gut instinct, and the tug that usually led him where he was supposed to go. But maybe that wasn't enough anymore.

Babu and Elyas glared at each other with open contempt. The others shifted uncomfortably from foot to foot and eyed Karim, waiting to see what he'd do next.

Why did I ever think this was going to work? Karim wondered miserably.

He was so focused on the two men that he didn't see Aya break away from her grandmother and approach Faiza, who clung to their mother's side. It was only when Aya spoke that Karim took notice.

"Here," the little girl said, producing a small bouquet of flowers bound with twine. The white lotus blossoms, grouped with a spray of red poppies, were limp and bruised from traveling in the pocket of Aya's robes. She offered them to Faiza, who looked at the flowers uncertainly.

Aya explained, "I picked them by the river. They're a little sad now…" She shrugged and nudged them toward Faiza again.

By that time, everyone else had fallen silent watching the two girls.

Faiza stepped away from her mother's side and accepted the flowers from the younger girl. "They, um, might be better if we put them in some water. What do you think?"

Aya nodded enthusiastically.

"And perhaps you'd like some milk and a little bread?" Faiza added.

"Oh, yes!" Aya clapped her hands. "Then maybe we can play a game? I love games. Do you know how to play sheeza?"

Faiza smiled. "Yes, but I'm not very good."

"I can teach you. I'm very good. I beat Sabba *every time*."

"All right," Faiza said warmly, taking the little girl's hand. "Teach me then."

Karim felt a swell of emotion as Faiza led Aya toward the family tent. *Bless that girl,* he thought. For all Faiza's screaming and carrying on, she'd always had the biggest heart.

The playful exchange between the two girls seemed to have sucked the tension out of the air. People in the crowd murmured approvingly, and some even smiled.

Elyas stared after them. "While the men sow discord, the children water flowers," he said, then turned back to Babu. "You are not the kind of man I prefer to break bread with, but you would probably say the same about me. Karim is right—the Hudjefa bring with us many skills and resources that we are willing to share with the Anen if you are willing to share yours with us. We can weather the dark days ahead more easily if we join forces. We *were* brothers once, though so long ago that only the old stories remain as evidence of it. Perhaps it would do us good to remember that."

Babu's jaw worked as he considered a response.

Come on, you fool, Karim thought. *Do something good for once in your life!*

Finally, Babu said, "You say you have fighters? Weapons too?"

"You don't remain a secret from the world for generations without a good defense system," Elyas told him.

Babu nodded. "Good. We'll show the Shass what's what the next time they decide to raid us. They'll think twice before doing it again, won't they?"

Elyas chuckled gruffly. "They will, sen. They will indeed."

At that, it was as if the crowd exhaled as one. Weapons lowered, conversations erupted, and wounded men and women were brought forward and attended to. As the business of living started up again, Karim hoped peace would hold, especially considering what he knew was coming.

Through the moving crowd, he caught sight of his mother. She regarded him with a look: *We need to talk.*

Karim cringed. He had, it seemed, a lot of explaining to do.

The first thing his mother did when they returned to sit in front of the family tent was demand to see the knife wound in his shoulder. When he removed his robes and she saw that it was already healing, she slumped onto a milking stool and shook her head.

"I don't understand," she said. "Is what that man said true? Are you really…a messenger from God?"

"It's a bit more complicated than that," Karim replied.

"*More* complicated?"

It took until the sun was melting into the horizon for Karim to relate all that had happened since he'd left the Jackals. He didn't tell her *everything*, but enough for her to understand the magnitude of the situation they faced. His mother went about her daily chores while she listened. When his story was finished, Karim expected Nour's first reaction to be about the oracle, or Setnakht and his army, or his own newfound powers. Instead, she asked, "You really love this girl?"

Karim scoffed. *Leave it to my mother.*

He considered the question. He and Sitamun had never spoken so baldly about the subject and never said the words—they'd expressed it in, well, *other* ways. He couldn't speak for Sitamun, but his own answer came easily.

"I do."

Nour blew out her cheeks. "A Khetaran…and what's more, a *princess*! If only your father were here. He would have the shock of his life!"

Karim took up the scarab amulet Sitamun had given him and rubbed it between his fingers. "I suppose Father would have forbid it. He hated the Khetarans even more than he hated the Shass."

His mother shook the sand from a blanket and folded it with care. "I think he would have come around. If Babu can see the sense in making peace rather than war, then I should think your father would have been capable of that too."

It was a comforting thought.

"Do you know which girl Djet admired?" he asked after a long moment.

His mother sighed, heavy with sadness. "Yes. She still mourns his loss. Sweet thing."

Karim rummaged in his pack and pulled out a fine golden bracelet studded with lapis. "Could you give her this? Tell her it's a gift from Djet. Tell her…that he wanted to give her the world."

His mother accepted the bracelet. She ran her fingertips over the blue stones, thoughtful, before asking, "What will you do now? I'm guessing you aren't staying."

Karim grimaced. *How does she always know?*

"You want to go to her, yes? This girl you love?" She poked at the fire she'd started in preparation for the evening meal. "I assume you'd like my blessing. And my forgiveness."

Karim gazed into the distance, where he could see Gamil, his sisters, and a few of the Hudjefa children playing what had to be the seventeenth round of sheeza with little stones in the sand. Already he could feel the rope tugging him, urging him to keep moving. He felt bad about leaving them again, but that didn't make the feeling go away. "Yes."

Nour sighed, the firelight catching on new lines that had developed on her face. "You may have both—on one condition."

"What's that?"

She gave him a hard look. "This power of yours, this…invulnerability. Don't let it turn you into someone I wouldn't recognize. Something came over you today; I saw it. The way you struck Babu again and again. If I hadn't stopped you, would you have stopped yourself?"

Karim didn't reply.

"However this power has come to you—whether it be through Khetaran magic or God himself—it has a cost." She laid her small hand over his. "Promise me you won't forget who you are. No matter where this journey takes you."

"I promise," Karim said, giving his mother's hand a reassuring pat.

He made the vow honestly. He just hoped he wouldn't have to break it.

25
RAE

"Well, what do you think?"

Rae studied Tam's reflection in the surface of the water, dimly lit by firelight from the braziers at the entrance to the palace's pleasure garden. They sat next to each other by the fishpond, whispering so that the guards who passed by at intervals wouldn't overhear their conversation. Below the floating white lotus, luminous in the thickening dark, Rae could see the silver flash of fish swimming through the water.

Tam wrinkled her nose, perplexed. "You're sure there's no way Nefermaat could have known about your chance meeting with that Red Lander back in Sakesh? You didn't mention it to anyone since we arrived?"

"I know I'm a bad spy, but I'm not *that* bad."

"It could be a trick of some kind. The other servants told me that the young priestess has been given access to magic scrolls from the House of Life. Who knows what she's capable of?"

"Yes, I thought of that too…" Rae trailed her fingers in the water, blurring her own reflection. A flame-orange fish came to nibble at them.

"You believe her, don't you?" Tam said, reading the message beneath Rae's silence.

"It sounds ridiculous, but I think I do."

"Why?"

It took Rae a full minute to come up with an answer. "It's as soon as she spoke of this prophecy, this 'Oracle of the Lamb,' everything I've done in my life suddenly fell into place. Like every choice I've made has been leading me to this moment." She shook her head. "Do you know what I mean? Have you ever felt that way?"

Tam licked her lips. "The day I met you."

Rae reached up to tuck a loose curl behind Tam's ear, her fingers lingering on the weaver's cheek. "What do you think? Am I a fool for wanting to trust her? For thinking I might have some grand destiny?"

"All great men are fools," Tam replied. "They have the audacity to believe in their own potential so deeply that they actually reach it."

Rae grinned wryly. "So, you're saying I *am* a fool."

"Oh, absolutely," Tam agreed. "And you have the potential to be a *great* one." She leaned forward, placing a single kiss on Rae's lips. "I am with you, Raetawy. If you think this is the path forward, I will follow wherever it may lead. If putting your trust in the priestess saves lives, then you must take the risk. We don't have many options, and time is running out."

At the mention of saving lives, Rae felt a chill come over her. She thought of her father down in the belly of the palace, and the attack on Sakesh that the king had promised as retaliation for

Nefermaat's abduction. "Do you think they're all right—Menk, Mamet Mut, and the others? Do you think they got the message in time?"

"I pray they did."

Rae stood. With the decision made, the urgency of the situation descended upon her. "I must talk to Nefermaat again so we can figure out how to prevent Sakesh from enduring another day of slaughter."

Tam rose as well, then cast a sidelong glance at the guards in the main hall. "I'll cover for you here. Just…be careful."

With a nod, Rae snuck through the dark to the gardener's entrance and made her way to the riverbank.

She found Omari alone at the moonlit encampment, sharpening his knife by the riverside with a smooth gray stone. His broad back was hunched over the task, and he reminded Rae of a bull standing alone against the night. When she emerged from the reeds, he straightened. "You came alone?"

"Tam is covering for me at the palace," Rae replied. "Have you received any word from Menk?"

Omari looked down at the knife and slid the blade over the whetstone. He shook his head.

"Where are Kay and Buto?"

"Fishing. We need to trade for more supplies at the market tomorrow. Speaking of tomorrow, I need to talk to you."

"Yes, I need to talk to you too. I must see Nefermaat first."

Omari stopped sharpening. "Why?"

Rae swallowed. A nervous prickle at the back of her neck told her not to tell Omari about her intentions, not yet. "I just need to see her."

"Do not let her speak," Omari said. "She'll curse you."

"Not with her hands tied. Spells require an object and action in addition to words to work."

Omari narrowed his eyes. "You're an expert on magic now?"

"I was her servant. I paid attention. That's all."

Omari spit on the ground and resumed his sharpening. "Well, I wish you luck getting anything useful out of her. As far as I'm concerned, there's only one thing she'd good for now."

His tone was ominous, but Rae was too focused on speaking with the priestess to question him. "Look, we can talk more in a minute." She ducked into the small tent.

Nefermaat was sitting up, her bound hands pressed together in a prayer position, looking for all the world like a tiny goddess waiting for a supplicant to arrive. There was no fear in her eyes as she followed Rae's approach, nor surprise when Rae pulled the gag from her mouth.

Neff was the first to speak, though her voice was ragged and dry. "You believe me, don't you?"

Rae shivered, unnerved. "Yes."

Neff's huge eyes glimmered, and for an instant, she looked like she was going to cry. Rae had begun untying her wrists and ankles when she reached for Rae's hand and squeezed it.

"So..." Rae said once she was done. She suddenly felt too big and too awkward in the intimacy of the little tent. "You said the man I met—Karim—is part of this oracle?"

Neff nodded. "He came to the Temple of Amun searching for information about a pharaoh named Setnakht, who had been erased from the king's lists. It's got to be connected to the oracle, I just don't know how yet."

"And the last person is Princess Sitamun? I figured she'd be a lot like her brother."

"Sitamun and Meryamun are alike in many ways, but different in all the important ones. You know she ran away from him."

"Why?"

"Because he wanted to marry her. And because he murdered their father."

Rae's eyebrows rose. Bedding his sister? Patricide? *The king is even worse than I thought!* "Do you know where she is now?"

"Close," Neff said, staring into the middle distance. "And getting closer." She blinked and focused back on Rae. "Listen. The cursing ritual will take place in two days. If we are going to stop the king and save your people, we must move quickly."

"I agree. I will explain everything to my friends. It's going to take a little convincing..." Rae helped Neff to her feet and moved to leave the tent, but the girl stopped her.

"The big man, Omari. He is not your friend."

Rae scoffed, incredulous. "What are you talking about?"

The young priestess hesitated. "There is darkness in him. I fear you will not be able to convince him to go along with this plan." Rae noticed Neff's hand move to rub her upper arm, where a lurid bruise had formed.

"Wait. Did he do this to you?" Rae asked. Upon closer inspection, she found purple marks on the girl's neck as well.

Neff didn't reply.

She didn't need to.

Rage kindled inside Rae's belly, greeting her like an old friend. Perhaps it burned hotter because she'd been keeping herself under such tight control for so long, or perhaps it was the thought of someone harming a defenseless young girl. Either way, she wasn't exactly in control of herself when she stormed out of the tent, straight to where Omari was sitting, and shoved him.

"What is wrong with you?" she exclaimed. "What did you do to her?"

Omari stopped, knife in hand, and slowly turned toward her. "Calm down, Ay," he said warningly.

"No, I won't calm down. I thought we were fighting for freedom. For the greater good. Since when does that include torturing *children*?"

Omari slipped the whetstone in the pocket of his tunic. "Since the king gave us no choice but to retaliate in kind. His men are in Sakesh right now, killing our people in droves. Or had you forgotten?"

Rae said, "Of course I haven't forgotten! But if we aren't careful, we will find ourselves making excuses for atrocities, each one more heinous than the last, until it will be impossible to tell the difference between our enemies and ourselves!"

Omari gripped the knife so tightly his knuckles turned white. "If you think this rebellion has any chance of success without spilling innocent blood, you're a bigger fool than I thought."

The insult was fuel to her fury, and Rae was about to shoot back when she sensed movement behind her. Nefermaat emerged from the tent. The girl looked unsteady on her feet and glanced warily between them.

With a roar, Omari dashed toward the girl and grabbed her by the wrist. "Why would you untie her?" he asked, seething. "She'll run right back to the palace and tell them where we are! Are you *trying* to get us killed?"

"She's not going to run away, Omari! That's what I wanted to tell you." Rae paused and took a deep breath. She didn't wish to dispel her rage, but she had to control it long enough to explain the situation. As succinctly as she could, she told Omari about Neff's plan to stop Meryamun and about their connection through the Oracle of the Lamb.

When she was finished, Omari was stupefied into silence. Finally, he said, "You're not serious."

Rae gritted her teeth. "I am. And she hasn't put me under a spell, if that's what you're thinking."

"I wish she had. It would be an excuse for you believing this nonsense."

"Curse you, Omari, will you just listen for a minute? Even if the oracle does not come to pass, it remains true that Neff has a plan to take down Meryamun. If we release her, the slaughter in Sakesh will cease, and she and I can work together to ensure the cursing ritual doesn't take place. She has more access in the palace than I ever could." When it looked like Omari still wasn't convinced, she added, "I already told Tam about it. She believes me."

Omari's lip curled. "Of course she does."

"What's that supposed to mean?"

"It *means* that Tamerit is predisposed to swallow your nonsense because apparently you've been bedding her every night." Omari spoke with such venom that Rae momentarily forgot about everything else.

Heat rushed to her cheeks. "Is this about you walking in on us that day back in Sakesh? You're *still* upset about that? Look, I'm sorry I didn't tell you how I feel about her, and I'm sorry you had to find out the way you did. But it's not fair to suggest Tam would blindly follow my orders no matter what. She's brilliant, and if she thought it was a bad idea, she would say so."

Omari shook his head in disbelief. "You think I'm angry because you didn't share your gossip about having a lover? Really, Rae? After all these years, you *really* don't know?"

Rae blinked. "What are you talking about?" Then, slowly, realization dawned on her, turning her entire world on its head. "Omari, you're not suggesting… You didn't think *we* would…"

Omari's face was an open wound, bleeding years of pain and

frustration and anguish. "Of course I did! I loved you, Rae!" he exclaimed. "I've loved you since we were children! Since the day your mother died, and we sat by the river and promised everything to each other! I thought you understood! I thought you felt the same! Then, when everyone around us spoke as if our union was inevitable, you acted like it was a joke! And every time it was like a knife in my heart!"

Rae put a hand to her mouth in dawning horror. "Omari…"

Omari was shaking, his breath coming in short bursts. "I joined the Horizon because I wanted to do something important, to rise in the ranks and become a leader in the community. I'd hoped that if I did, you'd finally see me for the man I am, a man deserving of your love.

"But then you had to drag the truth out of me too early, force yourself into that first meeting, and made such an impression on Asim that it took all the attention off me and put it on you instead. Suddenly *you* were the leader, *you* held the sway, and I was simply there to clean up your mess.

"But at least we were working together, I thought. We could connect during this mission to Thonis. There was still time for me to show you who I really am. I hadn't given up hope. And then I saw you with *her*."

Rae had forgotten to breathe. Her gaze flicked to Neff, whose face had gone deathly pale. Throughout his tirade, Omari hadn't slackened his grip on her wrist.

"If it had been another man, it would have been painful enough. But a woman? It was proof that all those years of my pining and hoping and striving for your love had been a total *waste*. I never had a chance. You made me into a fool. An utter, complete fool."

Rae worked to get her thundering heart under control, to slow the whirl of her mind enough to choose her next words. "I am sorry you suffered so long in silence, Omari," she said. "If you had only *told me* about your feelings, all of this could have been avoided."

"So, this is my fault, is it?"

"I'm not saying that."

Omari was squeezing Neff so hard that Rae could see he was hurting her. She was angry, but she knew that anger would only make things worse. *I need to ease the situation. Say whatever is necessary to get Neff away from Omari until he calms down.*

"Look, I want things to be right between us, Omari. You're my best friend, and I never intended to hurt you. But we don't have time to settle our differences now. We must get Neff back to the palace and make a plan to liberate our people before it's too late. I promised my father the Horizon would come to their aid."

Omari barked a humorless laugh. "Ah yes, your father. I'm sorry to tell you this, Ay, but he was dead the moment he was taken."

Rae went cold. The ground beneath her trembled.

"Take it back, Omari."

"It's true, and you know it. This entire rescue mission was pointless from the start, not that the rest of the Horizon seemed to understand that. They were so dazzled by your feats of heroism they were willing to look past the fact that a small group of rebels have exactly zero chance of saving prisoners from inside the king's palace. I only came to conduct reconnaissance work for when we eventually invade this city—and to ensure you didn't do anything monumentally stupid." He swept an arm before him, encompassing their current predicament. "And it's a good thing I did."

"You were the one to suggest abducting Nefermaat in the first place!" Rae retorted. "Why would you do that if you thought the plan would fail?"

Omari shrugged. "There was a chance the king was soft enough on the girl to release one or two of the prisoners in exchange for her safe return. But I wasn't surprised when he raised the stakes instead. It was the obvious choice."

"You *predicted* that he would attack Sakesh? And you said nothing?"

"Do you remember what you told me in Baki's barn? The night you killed the brewer? You said we can't force everyone in Sakesh to join us in this fight. They have to come to it willingly. 'Not every mind works as yours does,' that's what you said. And you know what? You were right. Besides dealing with the king's taxes and the rule of the nomarch and the Medjay, most Low Khetarans are too busy living their lives to dedicate themselves to the cause. What they needed was to find their fury. Their passion. They needed an event that would unite the whole city under the Horizon's banner."

"An event like a massacre?" Rae asked. She felt sick.

Omari smiled grimly. "Now our people know the pharaoh's true nature. When we arrive on their doorsteps and ask them to sail north with us, to take every city and village along the way for Low Khetara, they will come gladly. So, you see, this was really your idea all along."

"No," Rae said, her fury rising, brighter and hotter than before. "You've taken my words and my intentions and corrupted them. You used me, undermined me, *lied to me*..."

"Oh, give it up, Ay. I don't care about your sanctimony. We've wasted enough precious time." He tilted his head toward Neff. "We need to finish our business here and get back to Sakesh to start amassing our forces."

Rae felt a frisson of dread. "Finish our business?"

Omari yanked Neff toward him and shifted his grip to her shoulder. Then he lifted the freshly sharpened knife to her throat. "Yes. We kill the girl and leave her on the riverbank outside the palace for the guards to find in the morning. Like I said, she's seen our faces, Rae. She knows our names and our plans." His lip curled. "The king wanted to send a message to the Low Khetarans. I intend to send one back."

Neff gasped as the blade pierced her skin.

"Stop! Stop!" Rae held up both hands as blood pounded in her ears. She scanned the ground for a weapon and saw the handle of her sekhem scepter sticking out from the tent. It must have fallen from the pile of their belongings and slipped through. She snatched it up and hefted the scepter into a two-handed grip. "Let her go," she commanded.

Omari looked unfazed. "Or what? Her throat will be slit long before you reach me."

Curse him, he's right. Not knowing what else to do, Rae raised the scepter over her shoulder. "I'm warning you, Omari," she said. "Stop this madness now."

Neff cried out as the knife dug deeper into her flesh.

Omari narrowed his eyes. "I'm done taking orders from you. For all your unchecked rage and recklessness, you've never had the courage to do what really needs to be done."

Rae's heart was in her throat as Omari's forearm flexed, ready to deal the fatal wound—when his hand inexplicably stilled. It was as if an invisible force had grabbed hold of the weapon and refused to let go.

"What in the name of Ra?" Omari exclaimed, straining until the knife slipped out of his sweaty palm and skittered across the ground. With a frustrated growl, he clamped both hands onto Nefermaat's neck. Omari was strong. Strangling the girl would take mere seconds.

Rae thought only to stop him. To deliver a blow that would make him let go, stand down, back off.

But in moments of crisis, finesse often falls by the wayside.

She closed the distance between them and brought the stone head of the sekhem scepter hurtling down. Rae was too frightened, too horrified by Omari's cruelty to lessen the force of her swing.

Her best friend, whom she'd known all her life, whom she loved—though not in the way he'd wanted her to—was a monster. She didn't want to believe it, but the truth had its fingers wrapped around a young girl's throat.

"Let her go!" Rae cried.

The scepter crashed into the side of Omari's face, crushing it like an egg.

His hands went limp and dropped from Neff's neck, and his body slumped to the ground.

Neff looked down at him and screamed. Despite the dark, Rae could see there was blood everywhere. Omari didn't move or make a sound.

The scepter slipped from Rae's hands as she fell to her knees. "Omari?" she whispered, staring at his body. "Omari?"

Suddenly there was shouting by the riverside, and Buto and Kay appeared, staring at the gruesome tableau in shock.

Buto ran up to her, thinking she too might be hurt. He hauled her to her feet. "Raetawy, what happened? Was there an ambush? Is he dead?"

Rae's body shook. Kay had gone to Nefermaat. The cut on her throat was bleeding but not dangerously so. Still, the girl looked as if she might faint.

"I hit him," Rae admitted. There was no point in lying to them. "He tried to kill the girl, and I stopped him." In as few words as she could, she related the events to the two men—omitting the part about Omari being secretly in love with her.

Buto and Kay were astounded.

Kay said, "Omari *wanted* the king to attack Sakesh? So our people would agree to open war with High Khetara?"

Rae nodded. "I didn't intend to hurt him so badly, I swear it. I only wanted him to stop—"

"For the love of Ra, he might still be alive!" Kay exclaimed. "If he still breathes, there's a chance he could survive."

The four of them turned back to where Omari lay in the dirt.

He was gone.

The only evidence of what had happened was a pool of dark blood and a small papyrus scroll. Rae picked it up, dumbfounded. "I don't understand. He was out cold. I thought he was dead! How could he have gotten up and walked away?"

Buto shrugged. "Omari's a tough fellow. Maybe the injury looked worse than it was."

"I don't think so. It was bad."

Kay said, "Maybe he's heading back to Sakesh without us."

"Maybe," Rae murmured, unconvinced.

She went to check on the little priestess, who was sitting on a rock, catching her breath.

"I'm so sorry for what happened," Neff said, sniffling, her eyes wet. "I know you two were close, and if it wasn't for me—"

"If it wasn't for you," Rae broke in, "I would not get the chance to save my father. Omari chose his fate, and I've chosen mine."

Rae had a feeling there would come a time when she'd have to reckon with the repercussions of her actions. When the horror of her clash with Omari would come back to haunt her.

She lay a gentle hand on Neff's shoulder and forced a confident expression onto her face. "Let's talk about how we get you back to the palace where you belong."

Neff nodded gratefully and gestured to the tiny scroll in Rae's hand. "What's that?"

"I don't know. It must have fallen out of Omari's pocket when he collapsed." She unrolled it. In the dim moonlight, she squinted at the words written in the common script. Her eyebrows lifted.

When she was done, she handed it to Neff. "What do you think of this?"

Neff read the note and a little color returned to her face. "I think our chances of success just improved."

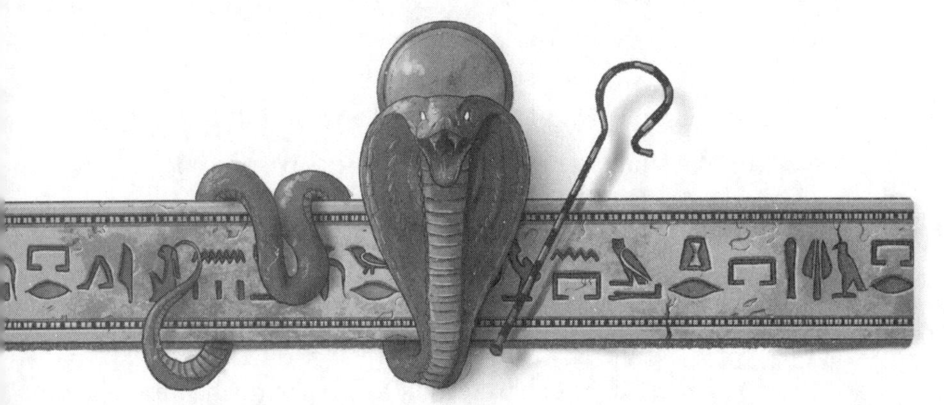

26
SITA

After so many hours on horseback, traveling past nothing but rocks and sand, Thonis and the Iteru were a welcome sight. Not wishing to be discovered, Sita and Dumiya skirted the city, only approaching when they reached its northern edge, near the Temple of Amun. Once there, they directed the horses to the riverbank, where the animals drank their fill. Sita patted her mount appreciatively. It had been a long, arduous journey, and they'd pushed the horses hard.

"Good boy," she whispered to the stallion, then left him to graze.

She turned to Dumiya, who stood overlooking the city with her spear at her side. The silver-haired warrior appeared undaunted by the trek—on the contrary, she seemed energized by it. Sita moved to take in Dumiya's view and spied some kind of activity going on at the temple. There was a large crowd assembling, many of them carrying baskets of grain, grapes, and other provisions.

"They're probably celebrating the Festival of Renenutet," Sita guessed. "It's a bit late, but with my father's passing and the coronation, it was likely delayed."

Dumiya gave her a questioning look.

"Oh—right, sorry," she said, remembering that Dumiya was a Hudjefa tribeswoman and had no knowledge of Khetaran festivals. "Renenutet is the cobra-headed goddess of the harvest. She's also the pharaoh's divine nurse, who cares for him from birth until death. Every year during the harvest, people bring offerings of food to honor her." In an attempt to communicate more clearly, Sita used hand gestures to illustrate what she was saying.

Dumiya nodded with polite interest, though Sita sensed that the older woman's opinion of those who worshipped gods with snake heads was low at best. Then Dumiya made two quick motions with both hands, first a pinching gesture, then an opening movement with palms up. Dumiya accompanied this with another questioning expression. It took Sita a moment, but then she understood.

What do we do now?

Sita replied, continuing to use hand gestures as she spoke, "I can't thank you enough for your help getting me here, but we must part ways. I don't know how the palace guard would react to seeing a Red Land tribeswoman on their doorstep, and I will not put you in any more danger than I already have. I will leave the horses with you and continue on foot. My advice is that you patrol the outskirts of the city and watch for Karim."

The mention of his name brought fresh yearning to Sita's heart. "I don't know when he might arrive, as he will secure your tribe's safety first, but once he does, he'll be able to tell you where to go to rejoin them."

Dumiya dipped her head in understanding, then tilted it toward the growing crowd at the temple, her eyebrow raised.

What about them? The warrior clearly thought it would be difficult for Sita to make a stealthy approach with so many people about.

"Oh, that's no problem," Sita explained. "In fact, it's perfect. I want to make a grand entrance. The more people who see me, the better."

Dumiya gave her a small, roguish smile. Then she lay a sinewy, freckled hand on Sita's shoulder, squeezed it, and turned to leap astride her horse. Grabbing the reins of Sita's black mount, Dumiya led both horses back south and away.

Alone on the riverbank, Sita removed the serpent staff from its harness and held it before her. It was large and would attract quite a bit of attention, and although she intended for her return to be noticed, she didn't want Meryamun—or anyone else—to see the staff and guess at her newfound powers. Then again, leaving it behind was out of the question.

"What to do, what to do..." she muttered, tapping her lip. "If only it were smaller, I could hide it away and always have it at hand."

As if the staff heard her plea, it began to glow.

Eyes wide, Sita watched as the wooden staff shrank in her hand until the two metal serpents contracted to the size of worms, one red and one black. She shrieked as the little serpents slithered up her arm, her neck, and onto her left ear, curling around it like a fanciful piece of jewelry. There, the serpents settled and froze in position, their heads bent over the shell of her ear as if they might whisper into it.

Once the shock wore off, Sita touched the serpents gingerly. They were cool like metal. If she combed her hair over top of them, they would be completely hidden. "Yes," she said with a satisfied smile, "that will work just fine."

"And through your bounty, O Renenutet, the kingdom will flourish. Through your mother's milk, we, the children of Khetara, will grow strong."

Meryamun's prayer floated over the gathered citizens, the words recited in a monotone as if by rote. To Sita, standing at the back of the crowd, it sounded as if he wanted to get the ceremony over with, that he had something more pressing on his mind.

He's about to get a lot more to think about.

Sita wore the same plain black robes that she'd stolen from the palace storeroom the night she fled, and she had pulled the wide hood over her head, shielding her face from view. Gathering her resolve, she stepped into the empty aisle leading up to the dais where her brother stood in a blaze of sunshine at the temple gate. She approached slowly and steadily, past the ram-headed sphinx that flanked her on either side. She knew that the statues were meant to represent Amun—not Khnum—yet Sita couldn't help but feel the oracle's divine lamb was watching her through their eyes. People began to murmur as she passed them.

"Who's the woman in black?"

"What is she doing?"

"She's going toward the king!"

By the time she reached the front of the crowd, Sita had stirred such a hubbub that the guards took notice. She scanned the guards' faces and saw with dread that Femi wasn't among them. *Just because he's not here, doesn't mean he's…*

She didn't allow herself to finish the thought.

Mery lowered the basket of bread and grapes he'd been holding aloft and searched the area for the interruption, annoyed. He was dressed in a rich scarlet schenti and a bejeweled cobra-themed collar, with the double crown on his brow.

When she saw her brother, Sita had an irrational urge to rush to him and fall into his arms. Maybe it was the familiarity of someone she used to love—

My twin. My mirror.

She smothered the feeling as soon as it came, like snuffing out an errant spark before it caught fire.

Remember what he did, what he wants *to do,* Sita told herself. *Don't let yourself fall under his spell.*

"Guards! Stop that woman!" Mery commanded. "Who dares interrupt a sacred ritual?"

Four guards charged toward her. The crowd fell silent, cowed by the king's wrath.

Sita stood between the first two sphinx, threw back her hood, and said: "I do."

There was an audible gasp from the crowd, and the guards all stopped in their tracks the moment they saw her face. Sita watched as Meryamun's face flit through a series of emotions in quick succession—shock, relief, fury—before compelling itself into a guise of rapture.

"People of Thonis!" he announced, again raising his arms to the heavens. "Today is a truly blessed day! Our beloved Princess Sitamun has returned! Thanks be to Amun for keeping her safe from harm and delivering her home! Thanks be to Renenutet for rewarding us with the greatest bounty of all!"

Having been given permission to respond, the crowd roared.

Mery set down the basket and strode forward to pull Sita into his arms, drawing her into a bittersweet, cassia-scented embrace.

"Where have you been?" he whispered harshly in her ear. "I've scoured the entire kingdom for weeks, making excuses for why you vanished, and now you reappear in the middle of a festival to embarrass me in front of my people?"

Mery pulled back to study her face. Then he smiled, that same blazing, heart-stopping smile. When he spoke again, his voice was warm honey—sweet and intoxicating. "Oh, I see. You didn't do this to embarrass me. You were afraid that if your return wasn't witnessed publicly that I might…what? Kill you?"

Sita kept her face passive. "Let's just say I see the board now."

Mery chuckled. "Do you? Do you really think so?"

"We must talk, Mery. It's urgent."

His dazzling smile dimmed. "Oh, we'll talk. We have much to discuss. There is greatness on the horizon for us, dear sister. Come to my chambers tonight after you've gotten yourself cleaned up and dressed in something decent. You smell like horse."

Sita wanted to stop him from walking away, to command him to listen to all she'd planned to say, everything she'd rehearsed in her mind during those long, silent hours riding through the desert. Instead, she watched him pick up his basket of fruit and resume his prayer as the guards led her onto the Royal Road to the palace. After all that had happened, after all that she'd done to take control of her life, the familiar sense of powerlessness came over her again. She felt the old terror rising within her. The impulse to make it better, to make him happy.

No! she told herself. *That's not who I am anymore. I will make him listen, no matter what it takes.*

Her traitorous heart, however, made no promises.

As Sita had hoped, news of her reappearance traveled fast. When she arrived at the palace, an attendant was already waiting for her.

"Nebet!" Sita exclaimed, wrapping her arms around her beloved nurse.

"Oh, thank you, thank you," Nebet cried, kissing her on each cheek and on the backs of her hands, as if making up for lost time. "I prayed to Isis to bring you back to me, to bring you home, and she did. She did!"

She examined Sita all over. "Are you hurt?"

"No."

"Hungry?"

"Actually, yes. Famished."

"Of course you are. I'll have the servants bring a meal to your chambers. We'll prepare a bath, a fresh dress, get your hair in order, and—"

"Nebet." Sita knew that her attendant was happy to see her, but she didn't have time for her ministrations. With a meaningful glance toward the guards hovering nearby, Sita whispered, "You are one of the few people I can trust. Walk with me. There are things I must ask of you."

Nebet's well-rehearsed smile didn't falter. "I understand, my princess," she said, and they began slowly making their way toward her rooms, nodding at inquisitive courtiers and officials who greeted the princess along the way.

On the surface, the palace hadn't changed much since Sita left, but there was an undercurrent of tension and violence—like fingers wrapped around a throat—that pervaded the gilded halls. Mery's influence, no doubt.

"Where is Femi?" she asked quietly. "Tell me he's alive."

Nebet cast a glance at the guards following behind them and said, "I can't say for sure. I was told the king's men were interrogating him for information about where you'd gone, and that afterward he fled and hasn't been seen since. They said he must have had help getting away, but no one knows who it was."

Sita nearly collapsed with relief. It was terrible to think what Mery might have done to him, but if Femi had been able to escape, she knew he'd be all right. *What will I do if I see him again?* she wondered. "And what of my mother?"

"The queen has not been the same since your father's death," Nebet said with sadness. "She has been spending a great deal of time alone in the pleasure garden. According to the gardeners, she has developed a keen interest in plants. Perhaps it is her way of coping with the grief."

That's strange, Sita thought. *Mother always hated anything involving dirt.* Before she could inquire further, Nebet called out to two maidservants who were hurrying down the hall toward them with empty food trays in hand.

"Ah, Herit! Ahura! Just who I wanted to see. Quite a day we're having—first one precious girl returned to us, now two!"

Sita didn't recognize either of the servants, so they must have been new. The shorter one, a curvaceous young woman with curly black hair, paused before seeming to recognize who she was greeting.

"Princess Sitamun!" the woman exclaimed and dipped her head in a bow.

The other servant, who was unusually tall and broad, stared at Sita in astonishment. The shorter girl nudged her with an elbow several times before she too dropped into a clumsy bow. When she looked up again, it seemed like she wanted to speak but decided against it.

"Ahura, is it?" Sita asked. "Is everything all right?"

Ahura gripped the tray so hard that the muscles in her arms and shoulders flexed.

She looks more suited to wrestling lions than sweating over a washbasin, Sita thought. She'd never seen a more intimidating servant girl in her life. *Strange, she's not Mery's type.*

"It's...good to have you back, um, Princess," Ahura said.

Her companion, Herit, chimed in. "Yes, so very good," she said smoothly. "What can we do to help, Nebet?"

"Put together a tray for Sitamun and bring it to her chambers right away," Nebet replied. "Bread, fruit, some jute mallow leaf soup, a bit of roast duck if you've got some..."

"Wine?" Herit inquired.

Nebet replied without hesitation. "No wine. A jug of fresh water will do."

Sita pursed her lips. *I suppose I deserve that.*

Nebet turned to her. "Is there anything else you need, Sitamun?"

"Can one of you go to the temple and find Prince Bakenamun?" Sita said. "I didn't see him at the ceremony for Renenutet, and I need to speak to him at once."

Ahura perked up at this request. "He's already in the palace. We just picked up his empty trays."

"What? Where?"

Ahura pointed to one of the bedchambers that Sita remembered having been unoccupied when she left.

The guards were watching her every move, and she was parched, half-starved, and covered in sand, but Sita couldn't wait another second to see the brother she'd neglected for so long. She didn't know what tomorrow would bring, but that day, she vowed to make things right between them.

"Nebet, please keep the guards occupied for a little while," Sita said, and before anyone could object, she walked to the chamber and pushed through the thick curtain.

Kenna sat beside a slight, bald-headed girl who was tucked into bed. The bedchamber was messy, with an odd assortment of objects strewn across every surface—piles of scrolls, tiny alabaster jars, bundles of dried leaves, feathers, and animal bones tied in twine. Either the girl didn't care to keep her room tidy, or someone had turned the place upside down.

Kenna and the girl spoke quietly, their heads bent close together. The girl had bruises on her arms and a fresh bandage around her neck, and her brother's face was creased with worry. They both looked up in alarm at Sita's arrival.

"Sitamun?" Kenna exclaimed, jumping up so abruptly that he knocked over the stool he'd be sitting on.

The girl gasped and sat up in bed. There were wadjet eyes tattooed on each of her shoulders, marks usually reserved for a high priestess. But this girl couldn't have been older than thirteen.

Sita frowned. The girl was familiar. *Very* familiar.

"You've returned!" Kenna wove around the clutter to reach her, stopping short of an embrace. "I was worried." He paused, gathering himself. Sita had never seen him so flustered. "I…I didn't know if I'd ever see you again."

"Kenna—" Sita began.

Kenna raised a hand. "Wait. Before you continue, there's something I need to say to you. When you came to the temple that day, you were trying to tell me about…about what was going on with Father. And with you and Mery. I understand that now. I was a fool not to see it, not to have put the clues together."

"Kenna, please—"

"I belittled you. I turned you away. And when you disappeared, when no one could find you…I thought that Mery had…" His face crumpled.

"Kenna."

Sita knew Kenna didn't really like being touched, so instead of pulling him into her arms the way she wanted to, Sita tried to put all her affection into the sound of her voice. "I'm sorry too," she said. "If I had taken the time to understand you better, to visit your domain instead of always expecting you to come to mine, then you wouldn't have had so many reasons to doubt my word. You deserve better. Especially from me."

Gratitude smoothed the worry lines on Kenna's face.

"You know the truth about Father, then?" Sita asked.

Kenna nodded. "I deduced the likelihood of death by poison

during the mummification process." He tilted his head toward the girl on the bed. "Nefermaat supplied the rest."

Sita froze. "Nefermaat," she whispered.

The lamb.

"You're the girl I saw at the Festival of Bast," Sita said in awe. "You're the girl who had a vision of the Oracle of the Lamb. You're here!"

Nefermaat gave a small nod. "Greetings to you, Princess Sitamun. I've been praying for your safe return. I'm so happy to see you."

Sita swooned.

Kenna darted forward to help her into a chair and pushed a cup of fresh water into her hands. She gulped it down and asked for more. A familiar striped cat that had been dozing on the windowsill came to nuzzle at Sita's hand.

Sita's head still spun, but the water was helping.

Kenna asked, "Are you all right? From the condition of your skin and the odor of your garments, you've had quite the journey through the desert. Red sand granules mixed with gold…hmm, yes. *Quite* the journey! And given the hairs stuck to the bottom of your robes—on horseback! I'm curious about the stone dust in your hair, though…"

Nefermaat cleared her throat. "Perhaps you can continue your deductions once your sister has had a chance to rest?"

Kenna's cheeks flared pink. "Ah. Yes, of course. When's the last time you've had anything to eat, Sitamun?"

"Yesterday, I think," Sita said, scratching the purring cat behind her ears. "I broke my fast with Karim before we parted ways."

Nefermaat beamed. "You were with Karim?"

Sita nodded. "He told me about you. He said you met at the temple."

Kenna was perplexed. "You mean that mouthy Red Lander? How in the world did you cross paths with *him?*"

"The oracle made it happen," Nefermaat said. "It's as I told you, Kenna!"

Kenna glanced between them, wonder in his eyes. "There are great and terrible things afoot, Sitamun. Great and terrible things." Briefly, he and Nefermaat shared Meryamun's plans for the cursing ritual that would take place the next day.

"He's planning to sacrifice Low Khetaran prisoners during this ritual?" Sita said, aghast.

"More than a dozen of them."

Sita set down the cup and stood. "He'll reconsider further alienating the south when I tell him that Khetara is at war."

Nefermaat's brow furrowed. "War?"

"With whom?" Kenna asked.

"Do you remember the ancient pharaoh Karim asked you about? Setnakht? It may be hard to believe, but he's returned—resurrected from his tomb through powerful heka. And he has raised an army of enchanted ushabti to help him retake the kingdom. They're on the march to Thonis as we speak. We haven't a moment to waste."

There was a long, shocked silence as this revelation sank in. Then Nefermaat murmured, "'A secret shall rise from beneath the earth, and the Red and White crowns will be forever broken.'"

"That's why I came back," Sita went on. "To warn Mery and everyone else. I will speak with him in his chambers tonight."

Kenna shook his head. "Sitamun, please. He won't listen to you, not after what he's done. You are only putting yourself in danger. I'm exceedingly glad to see you, but you never should have returned to the palace."

"I'm not the weak, frivolous girl I once was," Sita insisted. "If he won't listen, then I'll *make* him listen! He must act for the safety of the kingdom!"

Kenna studied her with his deep, penetrating gaze. "Yes, you have changed. I see it plainly. If anyone can get through to him, it would be you, Sitamun. For all our sakes, I hope you succeed."

Sita said, "I can't stay any longer, there are guards outside waiting to escort me."

The young priestess' lips tightened like she wanted to interject, but—seeing that she was between a prince and a princess—decided to hold her tongue.

"Know that if something goes awry, Neff and I have other plans," Kenna said.

Sita was about to push through the curtain when Kenna's voice stopped her again.

"Be careful."

Sita gave a small smile and whispered, "I love you too."

They came for her at sundown.

The head guard arrived at Sita's chambers, sidestepping an attendant leaving with a basket of soiled linens.

"The king has called for you, Princess," he said.

Sita looked up from the meal she'd just finished and nodded. Dressed once more in her usual fineries and smelling of cyprinum oil, Sita felt much like her old self again.

Too much.

She hadn't considered what it would be like to be home, surrounded by the artifacts of who she'd been before. She hadn't thought how easy it would be to slip into old habits, like the rut of a well-trod but ill-fated path. It had been simple enough to remake herself in Perset where no one knew her original form—but in the palace, she had a mold into which everyone expected her to fit.

She rose, and Nebet's worried eyes followed her to the door.

In the hallway, they were joined by the two guards who'd been stationed in front of her rooms. As she strode toward the king's chambers with this new entourage, Sitamun spoke.

"There's no need to accompany me. I know the way."

"King's orders," the head guard replied. There was no deference, no warmth, no standard formality of "my princess."

It was not a good sign.

The guards stopped outside the king's chambers, and two took up positions on either side of the door. The head guard gestured for her to enter.

Taking a deep breath, Sita pushed through the heavy curtain into a room transformed. The last time she'd been in the pharaoh's chambers, her father had been on his deathbed. The room had been nearly empty, odorous, pitiable, much like Amunmose himself. That had all changed. Mery had packed the space with luxuries—fine furniture, rugs, ornaments—until each surface was spread with fur, anointed with gold, and bedecked with every rare and beautiful thing that could be found along the Iteru.

Mery stood beside a copper bathtub in the back of the room, tearing petals from a bouquet of blue lotus blossoms and scattering them into the filled basin.

"Come in," he said without looking up.

Sita took a few steps inside, but no more.

"Mery," she began, not waiting for her brother to make the first move. "There is no time to contend with what happened between us. I did not return for revenge nor forgiveness. I am here because you are king now, brother, and as pharaoh of this land you must know there is an imminent threat to Khetara. An army rides for Thonis as we speak. It is one of supernatural strength led by an equally powerful foe. His name is Setnakht, and he was once—"

"Get in the bath."

Sita was so stunned, she didn't know how to respond. "I've already washed in the basin. I don't need a bath. Besides, you're not listening to what I'm—"

"Get in the bath."

Sita clenched her fists. "This isn't a game! The kingdom is in grave danger. I swear it upon Amun himself! Do you think I would have placed myself back in your grasp if the situation wasn't dire? Do you? Look at me!"

Mery stared at the water, fragrant and steaming.

"Look at me, Mery!"

He turned toward her. The glint in his eyes frightened her, but she pressed on.

"You've always known when people are lying to you. Ever since we were children. Can you not see that I'm telling the truth?"

Mery chuckled without humor. "I cannot, Sitamun, no. I thought I could see through people's lies, no matter who they were. But I was wrong. I know that now. I allowed my affections to cloud my judgment. The lies piled up around me, putrid and rotting, yet I smelled only flowers."

Sita's forehead knotted in confusion. *Is he talking about me or someone else?*

"Frankly, dear sister," he said, striding forward until they were only a breath apart, "it doesn't matter if you're telling the truth. If this army you speak of is a ploy to deceive or distract me from your true aims, I will root you out. And, in the unlikely event that you have come with honorable intentions, I have no fear of this threat.

"Tomorrow, I will bring such a curse upon each and every enemy of this land that none shall challenge me, lest I soak the earth with their blood. If you'd been at my coronation, you would know that I promised as much in my first address as pharaoh. I won't settle for merely being as great a king as Sematawy; I aim to surpass him. And nobody—not some phantom, not even you—is going to stop me. Now…" He paused and then added, his voice chillingly soft: "Get in the bath."

The blood began to pound in Sita's veins. "I'm not getting in the damned bath, Mery."

Mery's expression didn't change. "Oh yes, you are." He snapped his fingers and two of the guards reentered the room, marched straight over to Sitamun, and seized her by the arms.

Sita cried out in disbelief. "Release me at once!" She wrenched her body away from the two men. They didn't react to her struggles. They dragged her to the bathtub, lifted her by her arms and legs, and lowered her into the water.

"Now, are you going to behave?" Mery asked.

Sita roiled with impotent fury. It was clear Mery wanted to punish her, shame her, and if she tried to fight back, he'd only make it last longer. "Yes," she said, her lip curling.

Mery dismissed the two guards with a wave of his hand.

Sita's white kalasiris clung to her body in the bath, making her feel heavy. The water was warm and sweet-smelling, and the room around her glinted with gold in the soft lamplight. When Mery stood over her, his handsome face was bisected by shadow.

"There you are," he said. "Isn't that better?"

Sita said nothing.

Mery reached out and threaded his fingers through the damp tresses of her hair. "My beautiful, sweet sister. Do you know, there wasn't a moment that went by that I didn't think of you while you were gone? That I didn't long for the day that you'd stand by my side as queen?"

The blue lotus petals clung to Sita's skin, exuding a heady, dizzying scent. "That's never going to happen," she said, recoiling from his touch. "It's wrong, Mery. I'd die first."

Mery clucked his tongue. "Those are ugly words for such a

pretty mouth. Tell me, Sitamun, did you not spare a thought for your dear brother while you were away? Or were you too busy enjoying yourself with your new friend?"

Sita froze.

"Oh, yes. I know you were not alone. Not only because a girl like you couldn't have survived beyond these walls without help, but because I can *smell him on you*."

His fingers tightened in her hair.

Sita gasped in pain. She tried to call on the serpent staff, still coiled around her ear, but her mind had grown fuzzy at the edges and would not respond.

"You reek of his touch, sweet sister," Mery snarled, dragging her up until her ear was at his lips. "And it's going to take a long time to wash it out." With that, he plunged her head under the water.

A wave of terror jolted Sita's body as she screamed into the bathwater. She flailed, tearing at the hand that held her down, to no avail. Water sloshed over the edges of the tub as she thrashed, and her lungs burned hotter and hotter as they begged for air.

Just as she thought her chest would burst, Mery dragged her head above the surface.

Sita coughed up a gout of sweet-smelling water, then retched. She gasped in tortured, ragged breaths. She wanted to scream for help, but she knew the guards wouldn't respond.

Mery watched her struggle with obvious pleasure. "Lucky for you," he said when her breathing began to stabilize, "I can do this all night."

And he plunged her beneath the water again.

Sometime later, Sita lay on the stone floor of Mery's chambers, soaked and shivering in her thin, ruined dress. She wanted to move, but she couldn't. Her mind floated on a river somewhere out of reach, too afraid to return to her body. Even in her state, though, she understood why her brother had chosen that specific punishment. Unlike a lash, a fist, a rope, or a blade, the water would not leave a mark.

At least, not on the outside.

Dimly, she saw Mery cross the room to the door and draw the curtain aside. A demon stood on the other side, or what looked like one in the murk of midnight.

"Herihor," Mery greeted the man with a ram's face. "The princess has proved to be intractable, as I feared. Proceed with the plan. I've gathered the necessary items." He handed over what looked like a bloodstained cloth and a lock of black hair. "You can do it tonight?"

The demon nodded and melted back into the shadows without a word.

Mery let the curtain fall and returned to where Sita lay. She stared silently at his golden sandals, the water from her body pooling beneath her.

"Tomorrow, Sitamun," he said. "Tomorrow is the big day. Tomorrow everything changes."

27
Neff

Neff took no rest that night.

She sat in her chambers through the hours of thick darkness, working at the table by lamplight. She sliced strings of woven sinew and packed the pieces into a tiny linen bag along with splinters of birchwood, then tied it tightly with twine.

Next, she dropped twigs from a juniper tree into an alabaster bowl, along with pebbles of myrrh resin, four drops of wine, and a swirl of honey. That done, she used the lamp to set the mixture aflame, letting it all burn to ash. When it was cool, she poured the contents into a tiny clay jar and sealed it.

She referred to the Book of the Red Lady often, checking and rechecking her work to ensure perfect accuracy. She would have liked to look over her notes as well, but she'd not seen them since returning to the palace. Before her abduction, she'd copied nearly the entire contents of the scroll in her own hand—both to help her memorize it and to add notes and questions in the margins. It was frustrating that her copy was missing, but then again, her chambers were in total disarray. There was no time to look further, so she made do with the original.

Every detail of every quiet hour that passed felt significant. The dry scrape of her finger against the scroll as she read. The purr of the cat as she dozed nearby. The slow gray creep of morning as sunlight poured over the horizon. Neff peered out the window to watch the coming of day and wondered if it might be her last.

Neff intended to visit Sitamun's chambers as soon as she finished her morning meal, before her attendants arrived to dress her for the king's ritual at the Thonis fortress. She hadn't had enough time the day before to share the details of their plan, and she wanted to prepare the princess to act in concert with her, Kenna, Raetawy, and the rebels. Being that the palace was a flurry of activity, Rae brought her tray a bit later than usual. The rebel-in-disguise looked as if she hadn't slept either, but there was an excitement radiating from her too.

"Everything ready?" Rae asked when she set down the food.

"Yes, and you?"

Rae nodded grimly. "For Khetara," she said.

"For Khetara."

Neff didn't have much of an appetite, but she managed to eat a little bread and beer, which reminded her of home. *What will Mamet and Yati think if I die today? Will they hear my story and think me a traitor? Will Yati's pride turn to shame? Will he be driven out of the market, out of Bubas, because of me?*

She spared a moment to send two prayers to the gods. One to Bast, to ask for protection for her home and her mother; and another to Maat, to beg the goddess of justice to carry the truth to her father's ears. *May he know everything I do, I do in your service.*

She left the rest of her breakfast for the cat.

After ensuring that the materials she'd prepared in the night were safely hidden away, Neff pushed through the door covering and nearly ran straight into someone on the other side.

Her heart leaped into her throat.

"Greetings to you, Nefermaat," said Meryamun. His voice was as gentle as a caress. "It seems you've made a miraculous recovery. Thanks be to Amun."

"Thanks be to Amun," Neff repeated, and bowed her head. She'd only seen the king briefly upon her return to the palace. The Festival of Renenutet and Princess Sitamun's appearance quickly overshadowed her arrival, preventing Meryamun or anyone else from asking too many questions. As they'd agreed, Rae and the other servant—whose real name was Tamerit—had left Neff bound and blindfolded outside the gates of the palace the night before, so that she would be found in the daylight. When the guards discovered and questioned her, Neff told them a story about how the Low Khetaran rebels had released her in order to prevent another day of slaughter in Sakesh, and that they'd kept her blindfolded for the entire duration of her captivity, so she never once saw their faces or knew the location of their camp.

She made the most of her injuries and had feigned weakness to avoid further interrogation from the king's men. They sent a messenger to bring a healer from the temple, and one of the guards had transported her to her chambers.

Meryamun intercepted them when news of her reappearance reached him. "I knew you would be returned to me," he'd said. "I always knew."

Neff had hoped to avoid seeing him again until the ritual began, but apparently Meryamun had other plans.

"Going somewhere?" he asked.

"I wanted to take a short walk in the pleasure garden," Neff answered. "My legs are still stiff from being tied up for so long." The second part, at least, was true.

"Of course." His gaze poked and prodded her much like the healer had, testing her, seeing what made her flinch. "You shouldn't tire yourself though. You have a big day ahead of you."

Neff remembered Kenna appearing shortly after Mery's healer had bandaged her neck, and how he'd thrown the poor man out, saying he would attend to her himself. Despite Kenna's calm demeanor, his trembling hands had betrayed him. He'd been so frightened that the story of her abduction had been a fabrication, that Mery had found out about Neff's plans to curse him and killed her. It haunted him that the last words they'd shared had been in anger.

"Tomorrow is our last chance to stop him," she'd told the prince.

"I know," Kenna had replied.

And so, they'd made new plans in hurried detail until Sitamun arrived.

It was all coming together, just as the oracle said it would.

"Yes," Neff said to Meryamun. "It's a big day for us all."

The king nodded, releasing her. She headed toward the pleasure garden, but once Meryamun was safely out of sight, she doubled back to Sitamun's chambers.

Half a dozen servants streamed in and out of the princess's rooms, carrying empty food trays, various jars of oils and cosmetic palettes, and fresh linens. The guards stationed by the door didn't pay Neff much attention when she slipped in among the busy attendants.

She wondered what the king's response had been to Sitamun's warning about Setnakht and his army. Had he believed her or even listened? Considering his calm demeanor moments before, she had little hope that he'd taken the threat seriously. *It's even more important now that we stop this ritual and unseat him from the throne. It's not only the lives of the Low Khetaran prisoners that are at stake—it's everyone in the kingdom.*

Neff stepped inside Sitamun's bedchamber as the last attendant finished her duties and departed. Neff thought she was alone with the princess until she heard a voice speaking from the second chamber, which held the bath and dressing area.

"You've always had the most beautiful hair."

Queen Bintanath. Neff moved closer to the portal dividing the two rooms.

"I remember when you were little," the queen continued, "I would sit and brush cyprinum oil into your hair before you went to bed, just as I'm doing now. One hundred strokes, until it shone like the river under moonlight." She sighed. "I should have done it more. So often I left the responsibility to Nebet. I left so much of your care to Nebet."

Sitamun did not respond.

"Have I been a good mother to you, Sitamun?"

After a long pause, the princess said, "Yes, Mother."

"There was always so much to handle—managing your father, keeping the palace running, making sure you and your brothers had the best of everything… You needed to be taught to carry the burden of your birth. Nebet was the best. Your tutor was the best. The artisans who made your gowns and your jewelry were the best. And I…I thought that was enough." Her breath became uneven.

Was she crying?

Sitamun remained silent.

"There," the queen said. She sniffed and cleared her throat, making her voice strong again. "You look lovely. Though perhaps the attendants could add a little more rouge to your cheeks. You're pale." The next words were so quiet that Neff almost couldn't make them out. It was as if the queen had bent close to whisper in Sitamun's ear. "It will be all right. I promise."

Neff dove behind a chest when Queen Bintanath strode from the dressing room and out of the princess's chambers. She waited a full minute before emerging from her hiding place and hurrying back to the portal.

"Princess?" she called softly, poking her head through.

Sitamun sat on a stool in front of her brass mirror, gazing at her reflection. Her black hair rippled down her back, and she wore a simple gold circlet upon her brow that was fitted with an obsidian-eyed cobra. Her gown was long and of the darkest green, with two wide straps covering her chest. An ornamental pendant hung down over her legs, decorated with blue lotus.

"Hello, Nefermaat," she said to her in the mirror. "Is there something you need?"

Neff bowed awkwardly, suddenly feeling much less familiar than she had when they'd met the day before. There was a new formality in Sitamun's voice, and it unbalanced her.

"I'm sorry to disturb you like this, but I wanted to make sure you were all right."

Sitamun cocked her head. "Why wouldn't I be?"

"You were going to talk to the king last night, and I…I…" Without Kenna there, Neff felt the difference of their station keenly. Sitamun had been much less intimidating in filthy robes than she was in her full royal regalia. "I wanted to know how he responded to your news."

Sitamun considered this, her eyes drifting back to her own reflection. "He responded exactly as expected."

Neff didn't know what to make of her answer, but she was afraid to inquire further. The princess could be worried about being overheard, so it made sense to speak in abstracts. *Kenna expected Meryamun to ignore the threat, so she must mean for us to disrupt the ritual and stop him.* Abandoning her idea of sharing more details, Neff settled for asking, "So, we are to proceed as planned?"

Sitamun grimaced and touched her left ear, almost as if she'd been bitten. After a moment, her expression relaxed once more. "Yes, everything is going to plan."

There was a commotion outside the chambers, and one of the guards announced, "Princess Sitamun, your palanquin is ready. It's time to go."

Sitamun rose and made her way toward the door.

"Princess!" Neff called to her.

Sitamun stopped and turned.

"When the time comes, you'll know what to do?" she asked.

"I'll know exactly what to do," the princess said, and left the room.

Neff closed her eyes in silent prayer. *Amun be with her,* she thought. *Amun be with us all.*

28
RAE

"There's something I need to tell you."

Rae glanced at Tam, who walked beside her as they approached the fortress. Neff, Princess Sitamun, and Queen Bintanath were at the head of the procession, held aloft on palanquins carried by male servants. Select courtiers and attendants followed on foot, carrying baskets of offerings. A tall, broad-chested Tashan that Rae recognized from the king's party, Prince Harsi, walked with them too, though he was notably flanked by half a dozen guards.

"What is it?" Rae asked, distracted. The fortress, located along the riverbank slightly north of Thonis, was a massive structure of towering stone ramparts topped with battlements and wide bastions built at intervals all around it. Rae craned her neck to count the guards stationed atop the high walls. *Are there more men than we estimated?* she wondered. Her confidence flickered like a flame in a sudden breeze.

The sight of the fortress, so much larger and more imposing

than it had been in her imagination, sent a shiver of dread down her spine. *Did we plan for the right contingencies? Is this going to work?* She swallowed, her throat parched from the long walk in the hot sun.

"Rae, are you listening?"

Rae turned to Tam, who, like her, wore a loose-fitting green gown, pleated in a way that better concealed the items they'd hidden beneath. A headband beaded with green faience and bone held back Tam's curly hair, which had become unruly in the heat.

"Yes, sorry," she said.

Tam licked her lips. She looked nervous, but it seemed there was more on her mind than their current predicament. "Listen, the sun rose on one world and may set on another, and I don't know what our part in it will be. I hope that you and I will leave this place as we entered it: together and whole." Her voice trembled. "In case we don't, I want to tell you I—"

"Tam."

Rae steadied her basket on her hip and reached out to give Tam's hand a squeeze. "Tell me after. I will fight that much harder, knowing your words are waiting for me on the other side."

Tam took a shaky breath and nodded.

Rae released her hand and refocused on the fortress, her courage renewed. *You can do this,* she thought. *You* must *do this. For Father. For Sakesh. For her.*

They passed between two cedar flagpoles flying the black and red banners of Thonis and followed the royal procession onto the drawbridge that crossed a narrow moat fed by the Iteru. Being that it was still the dry season, the moat was shallow and appeared free of crocodiles, but both still provided additional defense for the fortress.

After crossing the drawbridge, the procession approached the gatehouse—a formidable structure comprised of three sets of huge wooden doors leading to the interior. Rae followed the group through each set of doors, her nervousness threatening to resurface.

For the love of Ra, I hope Femi was telling the truth, she thought. The success of their mission hinged on it. If he'd led her astray, all would be lost.

Rae squinted as they emerged from the shadows of the gatehouse and into the light of a wide interior courtyard, alive with people and the sound of beating drums. Rae could imagine small armies amassing there to train, receive commands, and defend the kingdom from invading forces. The place looked a bit sparse and underused, but Rae had a feeling that was changing. She knew Amunmose had allowed the size of Khetara's military to decline during his reign—so assured was he of their superiority over neighboring kingdoms. It was clear that Meryamun intended to change that. About a hundred armed guards and soldiers were stationed around the courtyard, with the majority gathered on either side of the procession.

In front of them, a large flat-topped stone citadel stood at the center of the courtyard, a stronghold containing administrative chambers, soldiers' barracks, and a temple devoted to Horus, the falcon-headed god of war. Femi had told her that much, though there hadn't been time during their escape for further detail. Aside from the crucial one, of course.

Behind them, starting with the outermost set, each of the gatehouse doors swung shut with finality.

One, two, three.

Rae swallowed. *Here we go.*

At the base of the entrance to the citadel, a raised platform had been erected and draped with billowing red and black fabric. Tall bronze braziers burned on each end, framing the three masked priests who stood there, chanting words Rae couldn't hear while the procession found their places. There was a surreal, grotesque quality to those men, their bodies hairless and barefoot, shining with oil, their faces hidden beneath sneering animal masks—a ram, an ibis, and a falcon.

In front of the platform, a great trench had been dug into the earth, more than fifty arms' lengths long and deep enough that Rae could not see the bottom from her position. A dozen white-clad priestesses moved at the rim of the trench, some beating goblet drums and shaking sistrums, others dancing while carrying vases of red clay. The vases were painted with sacred words in spidery black symbols that seemed to shiver with the sway of the dance.

The air was taut with anticipation, magic building within it like sparks ready to catch fire. Rae fought to keep her expression passive, though her chest tightened and her stomach roiled with every step.

Neff, the queen, and the princess's palanquins were lowered to allow them to ascend the platform, each of the women carrying a bundle of blue lotus blossoms. Meanwhile, Rae, Tam, and the other servants and courtiers approached the trench with reverence, all carrying baskets of offerings in their arms. One by one, they spilled their contents into the pit.

Rae waited her turn, mesmerized at the sight of colorful linens, bunches of grapes, fragrant sacks of incense, and all manner of prosperity cascading down into the earth. Her own basket carried a sheaf of golden wheat, and as she watched it fall into the deep trench, she reminded herself why she was there.

I'm here, Father. I've come.

Once the baskets were emptied, the assembled gathered before the trench, leaving ample room for what was about to unfold.

The priestesses ceased their drumbeat, filling the courtyard with a pregnant silence before starting again, louder and faster than before. As if racing to match them, Rae's pulse quickened as the door to the citadel was thrown open. The king emerged into the light.

Meryamun gazed out at the assembly, his eyes piercing beneath the double crown, which dazzled with gold and diamond and electrum. He wore a knee-length black schenti and, over his bare chest, a wide falcon-shaped collar studded with emerald and obsidian. A long green cape was fastened over his shoulders, which rippled behind him as he descended the steps toward the platform.

The drums beat louder and faster still.

When Meryamun reached the platform, the three masked priests raised their hands, and the priestesses carrying the red vases—whose movements, like the music, had been growing more and more frenetic—all stopped at the edge of the trench.

The priests dropped their hands, and the music ended.

In perfect unison, the priestesses hurled the vases into the pit, and Rae flinched as they shattered on the ground below. The priestesses withdrew in silence.

Rae scanned the figures on the platform. The princess looked positively reptilian in deep green embroidered with gold; Neff was in sacred white and wore the same short wig she'd had on when Rae had first seen her. The queen was also garbed in green, her gown accompanied by an amethyst-studded vulture collar around her neck.

Where is Prince Bakenamun? Rae wondered. He was not on the platform, and though she stretched to look, she could not spot him among the congregation of priests.

Meryamun stepped forward, his arms crossed over his chest, the royal crook in one hand and the flail in the other. "My people," he said, his voice carrying across the vast space. "When my father lay dying—may he live forever in the West—I promised him I would restore Khetara to its former glory, the glory envisioned and realized by King Sematawy, who gave his life to unite the Two Lands under one crown.

"But great deeds come at a high cost, and not everyone has the fortitude to pay such a price. Some may even go so far as to attempt to undermine this sacred work, to allow their weak hearts and simple minds to guide them to annihilation." He paused, his eyes hawkish. "That ends here."

Rae's hands balled into fists.

"Modern pharaohs have been satisfied with a tempered version of execration. They have burned their enemies in effigy; they have broken the red pots. Well, we have burned, and we have broken. We have made our offerings to the gods of war. But today, I say to you: That is not enough!" His shout rang across the courtyard. "It has *never* been enough. When our resolve weakened, the fissures in our once-formidable kingdom appeared. Today, we strike a blow against our enemies, both within and beyond our borders. We lay a curse upon the heads of all who oppose Khetara and its king, wherever they may roam. Today, we armor ourselves in blood."

A side door opened in the citadel, and a parade of ragged prisoners emerged, their heads hooded and their wrists bound behind their backs. Guards prodded them toward the pit, hoisting them back to their feet when they stumbled and fell.

Red-hot fury poured through Rae's veins, and as she watched the men and women stand in front of the trench, it was all she could do not to issue a war cry and launch herself toward them.

Not yet, she told herself. *Wait for the signal.*

The prisoners were silent as they faced the assembly, though Rae thought she could hear one of them sobbing. She scanned the line, trying to discern which one was her father, but without being able to see their faces and with their arms bound behind them, she couldn't be sure. Their time in the dark had hollowed them, made them all pale and shrunken and knobby-kneed.

Rae flicked her gaze to the sky and measured the angle of the sun.

She prayed.

"Traitors stand before you," Meryamun declared. "These Sakeshi men and women stoked the fires of rebellion in Low Khetara. Not only will their deaths channel the old magic that my father and his predecessors were too feeble to employ, but it will send a message to all who mean to betray the sanctity of the crown. The might of the gods themselves will come thundering upon their heads should they raise a weapon or a word against me."

Rae's muscles twitched. The guards stationed along the ramparts were all turned inward, watching the ritual. It was almost time.

"I do not speak lightly of betrayal," Meryamun continued, descending the steps from the platform and making his way toward the prisoners. The ram-masked priest followed him, taking the crook and flail from the king and passing him a ceremonial mace. "I know betrayal both broadly and acutely. It is one thing to be betrayed by a hundred faceless peasants, but quite another to find treachery at the heart of your own house."

Rae and Neff's eyes met. Something wasn't right.

Meryamun stopped beside the first prisoner, a slight, stooped figure in a dirty white tunic. "It brings me back to what I said about the necessity of fortitude. Great sacrifices must be made to steer this kingdom back to glory, and I will spill that blood. Even if it is my own." With that, he removed the prisoner's hood with a flourish.

The crowd gasped, and Rae's stomach twisted.

Standing before them, his angular face bruised and battered, was Prince Bakenamun.

29
NEFF

An instant.

That's how long it took for Neff's carefully laid plans to disintegrate. The instant she saw Kenna's face, she knew it had all gone completely, terribly wrong.

Meryamun silenced the bewildered chatter of the crowd. "Yes!" he cried. "It was a shock to find that my own brother, a Man of Anubis, was plotting to remove me from the throne."

"Mery," Kenna said weakly. "For the love of Amun, don't do this. Blood magic—it's strong, but it is wicked, Mery. It will bring damnation upon us!"

Meryamun seized Kenna by the hair, clenching his fist until pain stole the rest of Kenna's pleas. The king continued to address the crowd. "Not only that—he did not do it alone." The king turned toward the platform and gave Sitamun a nod.

Before Neff could grasp what was going on, the princess fell upon her, driving her to the ground and kneeling on her back.

"What are you doing?" Neff cried, struggling in vain while

Sitamun bound her wrists. Had she so wildly misjudged the princess? Had she always been on Meryamun's side? Was her disappearance and the story about Karim and the resurrected pharaoh all part of an elaborate ruse? *It can't be! The oracle told me to trust her!*

Neff felt hot tears spring to her eyes as she sent a message to the heavens. *I did everything you asked. Why have you abandoned me?*

With her cheek pressed to the wooden platform, Neff stared at Meryamun, whose face was now level with hers. She knew there was no point in trying to deny her duplicity.

"How did you know?" she asked dully.

Meryamun cocked his head to the side to look at her straight on. "When my men searched your quarters, they found the Book of the Red Lady stashed with the rest of the heka scrolls. The priests denied ever giving it to you—in fact, they denied knowledge of its very existence. Which told me it found its way there through different means." He clucked his tongue. "So, Montuhotep was telling the truth. Ah, well, it's not such a loss. Even if I hadn't killed him then, I'm sure I would have done so eventually. He was a terrible pest."

Neff said, "I don't understand. If you've known the truth since I returned, why wait until now to reveal it?"

Meryamun moved in close, so close that she could feel the heat radiating off him. "Because I wanted to see it."

"See what?"

"That expression on your face. The one you're wearing right now. And I wanted you to watch. You've given me a perfect excuse to crush my brother's skull, just as I've always wanted to."

Neff wanted to beg the king for mercy, to offer anything and everything to spare Kenna's life, but she knew that was useless. In the end, despite all her attempts to hide her true intentions, Meryamun saw her. He saw everything. Like the eye of the sun, his unforgiving light illuminated all her lies.

"You did well, sweet sister," the king said to Sitamun when she pulled Neff back to her feet. "Now leave her with the guard and come take your place by my side, where you belong."

Sitamun dipped her head and relinquished her grip on Neff's arm.

"Help us, please," Neff whispered to her, hoping the princess might change her mind, that perhaps she was acting out of fear. *Had the king hurt her? Threatened her?*

Sitamun didn't respond. She simply gave Neff a blank look and turned away, leaving her in the hands of a palace guard. Yet, in her eyes, Neff noticed something strange. Sitamun's pupils were huge and black, as if the princess were staring into a dark void, not the glare of the noonday sun. There was a fizz of energy around her too, the same kind of energy Neff felt after casting a spell.

That's it! she realized. *She's been enchanted!*

Suddenly, a particular spell from the Book of the Red Lady came to mind.

To Enthrall a Man: Take a lock of hair from the man you wish to enthrall and soak it in blood from your own hand for one night. Fasten the hair to a waxen figure inscribed with the man's name and burn it in sacred fire while speaking the words below...

Meryamun had used the spell.

He said his men found the book when they searched my room. They must have taken my copy and left the original so I wouldn't notice it was missing. He probably shared it with the Heka priests and had them curse Sitamun when she met with the king last night.

It was a relief that Sitamun hadn't betrayed them, but that didn't improve their situation. Neff knew how to cast spells, but breaking them? That hadn't been part of her lessons. Worse still, the Heka priests had possession of the rest of the spells in the Book of the Red Lady too.

Held fast by the guard, Neff watched helplessly as Sitamun followed the king to the line of prisoners. Kenna, the only one without a hood, looked bewildered when he saw his sister, but to his credit, it took only seconds for understanding to dawn on his face. The prince was too observant not to notice what Neff herself had seen in Sitamun's eyes.

Neff fought back the wave of hopelessness that threatened to consume her. *There's still a chance for us to prevail. It all hinges on Rae.*

"Kneel," Meryamun commanded, and the prisoners—some of them simply too weak to stand any longer—dropped to their knees. "Don't worry," he said to Kenna, "I'll save the best for last." With that, he strode to the other end of the line.

The three Heka priests began to chant from atop the platform.

Meryamun opened his arms, and his green cape spread out behind him like a great wing, its underside threaded in gold that sparkled in the sunlight.

"Today, I am Horus the Falcon!" he boomed. "I am he who perches upon the gate of the Primeval, who overlooks all and flies beyond the reach of gods and men."

"The word is the deed," the priests intoned.

Come on, come on, Neff thought anxiously. *What's taking so long?*

"Today I am the Great Sun Disk, soaring above the horizon on golden wings!" Meryamun continued. "I see every enemy in every land, and I curse them with my words, my blows, and the blood of many rivals! Let none who oppose me escape my Eye, and let all suffer the scourge of Horus, Son of Isis, Avenger of the Great Father, the Morning and Evening Star!"

"The word is the deed!"

With one swift strike, Meryamun brought the stone mace down upon the head of the first kneeling figure.

A sickening crack cut through the quiet.

The prisoner arched, stilled, and then slid lifelessly into the pit.

The three priests remained silent. There was no wind in the courtyard, not even an exhalation.

Horrified, Neff stared into the pit, then at Meryamun. Did he look brighter than before?

Neff found Rae in the crowd again, and the rebel's face blazed with anger and despair. *For the love of Amun, what if that man was her father?* Between the hoods and shapeless rags the prisoners wore, it was nearly impossible to tell one from another. For Rae to come so far and do so much, only to lose the very person she came to save!

Either way, an innocent person had just been executed, and another would soon follow.

The king stepped up to the next prisoner in line, and the priests resumed their chant.

"Please!" Neff cried out. "Stop!"

Meryamun raised the mace—

"Wait."

The muffled voice came from the prisoner himself. It was deep, calm—the voice of a man who'd accepted his fate with grace.

Meryamun paused, curious. "Speak."

"If I am to die," the prisoner went on, "I wish to do it with my eyes upon Ra, with His glorious light upon my face."

The king considered the request. "Very well," he said, and pulled off the hood.

It was then, as Meryamun raised his mace once more and the older man lifted his sun-bronzed face to the sky, that Neff noticed his arms bound behind him. He had only one hand.

30
RAE

Rae's peripheral vision vanished. All she saw was her father's serene, emaciated face, turned up in reverence to a god who had forsaken him.

Rae didn't care that the signal hadn't come. She didn't care that if she ran to him, if she tore a bloody hole through the crowd standing between them and leaped over the yawning pit, she would be cut down long before she reached him. She would do it. Even if she couldn't save him, she would die trying.

Kroo! Kroo!

To the crowd, it was simply the call of a nightjar. But to Rae, it was salvation.

She reached back to grasp the neck of her dress and tore it from her body with a flourish. Beneath was the golden armor, stolen first from the court of King Rahotep and again by Rae herself when she reclaimed it from the Medjay. The armored wings folded over her short tunic, each feather glittering. Then she reached for the sekhem scepter strapped to her back and pulled it free.

She held the scepter aloft, its long stone head pointed to the sky.

"For Khetara!" she roared.

The king froze, and every eye in the courtyard turned to her, as the rebels hoped they would.

"What in Amun's name is she doing?" Meryamun said. Beside him, Sitamun gazed toward her, emotionless.

I knew we shouldn't have trusted her, Rae thought. *Doesn't matter. We don't need her.*

"For Khetara!" she roared again. She didn't attack, she merely stood there, a resolute colossus gleaming in the sun.

The crowd withdrew in confusion, erupting in noisy chatter. Tam vanished among them.

The head guard called to his gawking men. "What are you waiting for?" he shouted. "Take her down! She's disrupting the ritual!"

"For Khetara!" Rae shouted a third time as the guards closed in.

A thunderous wave of sound came crashing toward them, the clamor of running feet and war cries from more than fifty throats. Rae turned to see a horde of Horizon rebels charging from the far side of the courtyard, weapons raised—the same weapons they'd taken from the Medjay in what felt like another lifetime. She saw Buto and Kay the fisherman, and at the front, leading the charge, she saw Menk.

Rae smiled as she recalled the words written on the scroll she'd found after Omari disappeared. A note from Menk himself.

The Horizon sails for Thonis, it said. *Come what may, we are with you.*

The royal guard, who had been focused on Rae, lost precious

seconds to prepare to meet their attackers. While the courtiers fled screaming, the guards barely had the chance to unsheathe their khopesh before the Low Khetarans crashed into them at full force.

The courtyard fell into total mayhem.

Rae brought the sekhem scepter swooping down into a guard's forearm as he reached for his blade. The guard shrieked as the bone shattered on impact, then rounded on Rae, head down, barreling into her like a raging bull. Rae sidestepped nimbly and kicked the guard in the back as he passed, sending him sprawling. Her neck tingled as she sensed movement behind her, but when she whirled around, she found Menk pulling a spear from a guard's chest—one who had been about to run her through with his khopesh. The guard collapsed.

Menk grinned and waggled his enormous ears.

"That was cutting it close, don't you think?" Rae asked as the battle raged around them.

Menk scoffed. "That's a funny way of saying 'thank you.' I speared him as rapidly as I could!"

"Not that! The break-in, you goose! A second longer and it would have been too late!" She pressed her back to his, and they circled around, weapons at the ready.

"Oh, because breaking into a fortress is so easy!"

"You found the conduit on the riverbank?"

"It was exactly where you said it would be."

So, Femi's information had been accurate. After she'd helped him escape the palace, the former guard had told her about an underground stone channel that ran from the Iteru under the fortress wall and emptied into a cistern that supplied water to those stationed inside. Since it was the dry season, the channel wasn't flooded and could be traversed on foot. When she'd first suggested the plan to Neff, the young priestess had brought up a serious concern. There would be archers positioned along the ramparts who could easily pick off the rebels with arrows as they climbed out of the cistern.

"We need a distraction," Neff had advised. "Something to hold their attention long enough for your people to get their feet on the ground."

"I can do that," Rae had assured her. "I'll tell them to send a signal when they're ready. There's still a problem, though. Once the fighting breaks out, the archers will start shooting from above. It won't be as easy for them to target us amid courtiers and guards, but there are still a lot more of them than there are of us."

"That's where I'll come in," Neff had said with a smile. "I know just the thing."

"What's the plan now?" Menk shouted over the din, jabbing with his spear when a battle between a guard and a rebel got too close for comfort. "I thought the young priestess was going to make a move!"

Rae dodged a swinging blade and kicked out at her attacker, doubling him over. "Yes, well, somebody's got to free her first! The situation got a little out of hand before you showed up."

"Go!" Menk told her. "Get your father and release the girl! The boys and I will try to hold them off until you do!"

Rae nodded and turned toward the platform. Rae could see through the fray that Meryamun hadn't moved from his position. He still stood over her father, his face purpling with rage as he surveyed the chaos.

"Keep going!" he commanded the Heka priests.

After a nervous pause, the three men resumed their chanting.

He means to finish the ritual!

Rae shoved a dueling pair aside, trying to forge a path through the crush of people. Another man hit the ground in front of her, and she vaulted over him.

Meryamun adjusted his grip on the mace.

I'm not going to make it! Fighting men jostled her from every side, blocking the way.

Ankhu watched the scene in amazement, seemingly unaware of the blow about to fall upon him. Then his eyes met Rae's, and his lips formed her name.

"Father!" Rae screamed.

Fury rose within her, steaming up from her belly and into her extremities, filling her with reckless abandon. It was the same fury that Omari always urged her to resist. The same fury that had led her to join the Horizon as a way to channel her emotions. Ever since she'd come to the palace, she'd done everything she could to make herself as small as possible, suppressing her true self for fear of exposing her intentions. She'd felt constrained, her emotions begging for release.

What if Omari had been wrong? What if that rage wasn't a weakness, but her greatest strength?

She remembered the tahtib match with Asim. That unforgettable moment of intense, focused energy, like channeling a swath of sunlight into a concentrated beam of blinding radiance.

Let go, a voice inside her whispered, a voice that sounded a lot like Neff's. *Let go and embrace your destiny.*

Wind gusted through the courtyard, and Rae's golden scale armor chimed with a haunting melody.

She let go.

"You will not hurt him!" Rae cried and struck the head of the scepter against the ground with breathtaking force. Upon impact, a deep fissure cracked the earth and raced toward the king, throwing men off their feet as it went. Meryamun saw it coming, but too late. The fissure erupted beneath him. He tripped and fell, the mace slipping from his hand.

Rae sprinted toward her father, the path before her now clear.

Also thrown off-balance by the quaking around him, Ankhu teetered on the edge of the pit.

Rae slid across the ground and wrapped her arms around him, pulling him from the brink. "I've got you!" Rae said in a rush. "I've got you!"

They lay together in the dirt. Rae didn't want to let go.

"Rae," Ankhu said, his voice full of wonder. "What did you—*how* did you—?"

"Perhaps the gods are listening after all," Rae replied, sitting up to untie the bindings on his arms. Her body crackled with energy, and she felt more herself than she ever had before. She wasn't sure exactly what had happened, only that it felt *right*. "Come on. We have to get you and the others to safety."

Rae surveyed the situation. Meryamun had scrambled behind the platform in the shadow of the citadel and was surrounded by palace guards. Meanwhile, arrows rained down from the battlements, and even as Rae watched, two more rebels went down. She could already count six Horizon dead on the ground.

They were losing.

Despite successfully rescuing her father, none of them would survive if they didn't find a way to turn the tide. And soon.

"Buto! Watch out!" she shouted as she saw one of the archers take aim.

It was too loud. He couldn't hear her.

Buto took the arrow full in the chest and dropped.

"Buto!"

Ankhu said, "Rae, the prisoners can't defend themselves if they're bound. Help me free them, quickly!"

Trembling with shock, Rae tore her eyes from Buto's body and tried to focus on the knots in the ropes as men screamed and died around her.

"We need the priestess," she said, glancing up at the platform where Neff still cowered beside the guard. "We need her help or else we're all going to die here." She considered mounting the platform herself to free Neff, but she was hesitant to leave her father and the other prisoners undefended.

Rae scanned the area for the curly-haired weaver. "Tam, I need you!"

31
NEFF

Neff had never seen a person die before. She'd been at her grandfather's bedside the night he passed, but that was different. In the fortress, she witnessed Meryamun crush a man's skull. She heard the wet crack as the stone mace connected with the prisoner's head, saw the blood spatter through the thin hood. The gruesome sight reminded her of the day she'd cried tears of blood.

You must make your own mistakes, Nefermaat, the High Priestess had told her. *You may doubt yourself, but never doubt the goddess. You are on this path because she deemed it so. Stay on it, no matter where it leads.*

Neff knew the path would be difficult. Still, she never imagined it would lead to this.

When the dead man slumped and fell into the pit, something inside Neff broke. All remaining vestiges of her childhood died in that moment, along with the innocent man. She neither cried nor screamed. The contradiction of being both empty and overwhelmed left her numb.

It took Rae's war cry to tear her from that stupor.

Even then, what could she do? With her hands tied behind her back, she couldn't reach the tiny linen bag tucked into the folds of her dress. The guard's grip on her had only tightened as the battle broke out, and although she'd hoped he would be tempted to join the fight, he stayed at her side.

When Rae cracked the earth with her scepter, Neff felt a surge of triumph. *It's starting.* Her certainty was bone-deep and primal. She knew it the way her fingers would recognize the contours of her mother's face among a sea of women.

Rae couldn't carry the fight on her own, though. Arrows fell like rain all around the courtyard, and the rebels were dying.

I've got to get free! Neff thought.

Rae shouted something in her direction. A moment later, the guard next to her yelped. Neff turned to see him land hard on his back before he was dragged off the platform and onto the ground below by a rope looped around his ankle. Then came a hard thump, a cry, and then nothing.

Neff peered over the edge of the platform to find Tamerit, Rae's companion, standing over the guard's unconscious body.

"I hope I hit him hard enough," she said to Neff. Then she hoisted herself onto the platform and got to work on Neff's bindings.

"Hurry," Neff said as another rebel took an arrow in the back. The second the ropes loosened, Neff yanked her hands free and pulled the tiny linen satchel from her dress. Before she could speak, a hand closed around her ankle. The guard had recovered himself and snarled up at her, trying to pull her down.

Tamerit cursed and lashed out, trying to dislodge him. "Let her go!" Tamerit shouted.

Suddenly, a discarded black hood rose from the dirt, as if by some unseen force. All at once, the floating hood launched itself at the guard's back. The guard gasped as the air was knocked from his lungs. His grip on Neff's ankle slipped, and Tamerit gave him a kick square in the temple. "Now, stay down!" she yelled.

He did.

The floating hood rose up to the platform and settled at Neff's side, bobbing gently. Tamerit stared at it in wonder.

"What in Ra's name is *that*?" she asked.

"That's Medjed," Neff replied, giving the hood an appreciative pat on the head.

Tamerit blinked, waiting for an additional explanation that didn't come.

Ripping the wig from her head, Neff raised her arms to the sky. "I call to you, Neith, Goddess of War! Heed me, Fierce Hunter, and unmake the weapons of my enemy! Weaken the sinew and splinter the bow, so that they are useless against me! For I, too, am a creature of war! The word is the deed!" With that, she threw the satchel into the burning brazier.

The fire flared and turned a deep crimson.

All along the ramparts, one archer after another exclaimed in dismay as their bows disintegrated in their hands. The volley of arrows stopped.

The rebels noticed and raised a cheer. They were still outnumbered, but at least now they had a chance. Rae and the one-handed man—who Neff assumed was her father—had managed to free the rest of the prisoners.

They need a way out, Neff thought, and pulled the little clay pot she'd prepared from the hidden pocket in her dress.

"Herihor, with me!" came a shout from behind her. Neff whirled to see Meryamun, surrounded by a phalanx of palace guards, heading to the entrance of the citadel. The ram-faced Heka priest peeled away from his brethren to follow the king.

"You two!" Meryamun continued, gesturing to the other Heka priests. "Don't let them escape! Use the spell!"

Once Herihor joined them, the head guard led the group up the steps and into the citadel. As they went, she saw two of the guards struggling to control a smaller figure held captive between them.

Neff gasped.

"Rae!" she screamed, pointing. "They've got Kenna!"

The rebel warrior turned away from the battle to see the doors of the citadel slam shut.

Neff said to Tamerit, "He brought the priest with him to continue the ritual! He'll gain immense power from spilling his own brother's blood!"

Neff choked back a sob. She couldn't bear to lose Kenna.

"Please, Rae! Please help him!" she cried out.

Rae shouted, "We have to get the prisoners out first!"

The two remaining Heka priests began to chant, each pulling long black cloths from their belts, which appeared to have been inscribed with sacred words written in red. In unison, the priests wrapped the cloths around their eyes and continued chanting, their hands reaching out toward the battle before them.

Neff recognized the spell. *To Make a Man Blind to His Brothers.*

"Oh no," she whispered.

Tendrils of black smoke rose from the priests' hands and drifted toward the fighting men. Neff watched as a thin finger of smoke fell upon one of the rebels' eyes, turning them black. The man had been about to engage one of the guards, but he began attacking one of the other rebels instead. His fellow warrior took a blow before defending himself, clearly confused by the turn of events.

The smoke continued snaking toward its next victim.

"Ra preserve us," Tamerit said as the battle turned against them once more. "Quick, Nefermaat! The spell!" she urged.

Nodding, Neff went to unstop her little clay pot when there was a flash of movement at the end of the platform.

Sitamun barreled toward them, snarling, and shoved a surprised Tamerit off the edge. She slapped Neff's hand, knocking the clay pot out of her grasp, and struck her hard across the face.

Neff cried out, her cheek burning as stars leapt in front of her eyes.

Sitamun lunged for her, but Neff ducked out of the way, scrabbling after the clay pot. It rolled across the platform, just out of reach.

Sitamun lunged for her legs, and Neff collapsed flat on her belly. The princess, her full weight pinning Neff, chuckled in a way that reminded her of the king. Neff's fingers brushed the side of the pot but could not get purchase on it.

"It's already too late, little seer," Sitamun said. "Even if you could give them a way out, there will be no one left to run." Neff craned her neck to look at the princess. Her smile wasn't her own. It was Mery's.

"Give up now, Nefermaat," she said. "And perhaps he'll let me keep you as a pet. Do you know the punishment for betraying a king? It's *quite* severe."

Sitamun's words were like an echo of a nightmare. They wormed into her heart, breaking her resolve, manipulating her spirit. *They're Meryamun's words. Meryamun's power working through the enchantment.*

Neff moaned, squeezing her eyes shut against despair.

"It's over," Sitamun purred, crawling up her body like a serpent consuming its prey whole.

"No!" With a final, desperate heave, Neff lunged toward the

pot, and her fingers closed around it. She flipped off the seal with her thumb and shouted as the breeze pulled the ash from inside and set it flying. "Winds of the east! Heed me, for I am Shu, your god and ruler! I command you to blow as you once did when the earth was new, before my sister Maat tamed you! Blow so that no man nor edifice can stand against you, so that all must fall before your power!"

Men exclaimed as a sudden wind buffeted the courtyard, a wind scented with myrrh and smoke and honey. Neff dropped the pot and shielded her eyes as a swirl of sand peppered her face. She focused on the great door to the fortress, which was guarded by half a dozen soldiers.

Concentrate, she told herself. *Look for the darkness at the center of the light.*

The princess shouted at her, shaking her, but Neff kept her eyes on the gatehouse door.

Let it surround you. Let it become your world.

A resounding boom echoed across the courtyard. Neff felt the platform tremble beneath her, but still, she did not break her gaze.

"What was that?" she heard someone shout.

One.

Then again, *boom*. Closer now.

More than half the fighters had taken notice, pausing their skirmishes to try and determine the source of the sound.

Two.

Neff felt herself weaken, her head growing light. It was hard to breathe with Sitamun's weight crushing her. *Just a little longer.*

She thought of Kenna.

You can call me brother, if you wish.

With a cry of effort, she concentrated all her remaining strength at the gatehouse door.

Boom.

The final door burst open in a flurry of blowing sand, causing every man in the courtyard to shout.

Three!

When the dust settled, a man astride a black stallion stood in the doorway with the wind at his back. His dark, wavy hair danced in the breeze.

The lamb, the lamb, the lamb…

He wore a rough, dark schenti, with sheepskin leather spaulders and bracers. His chest, however, was bare, and bore a scarab-shaped scar over one side.

The horse pawed the ground eagerly, and the man pulled the reins taut. His eyes met Neff's across the courtyard, glinting with an otherworldly light.

Neff's heart soared.

"Advance!" Karim commanded, and from behind him, a host of Red Land tribesmen charged into the fray.

32
KARIM

Focus your efforts on driving out the soldiers and the royal guard!" Karim shouted to his men. "Kill only when necessary! Protect the prisoners and secure the fortress!"

Shouting their accord, warriors from both the Anen and the Hudjefa tribes flooded the courtyard, adding fuel to an already raging battle.

Where are you, Sitamun? Karim scanned the area. The courtyard was littered with bodies and ringing with the bellows and screams of those fighting for their lives. A thrill of dread coursed up Karim's spine as he considered the possibility that something terrible had happened to the princess.

"Now you're going to tell me that you *knew* that was going to happen," said Gamil.

Karim looked down at his younger brother standing by his side, armed with a leather shield and staff. "What, the doors? Of course I did!"

"Liar."

Karim absolutely did *not* know that the three gatehouse doors would blow open, allowing him and the small army he'd assembled to storm the fortress. In fact, when they'd arrived and saw the immense structure before them, Karim's confidence had faltered. Dumiya had intercepted them in the desert and relayed how she'd delivered Sita to the temple and seen her taken into her brother's custody, and how she'd learned about a cursing ritual that would involve human sacrifice, which Sita would likely attend.

Upon their approach of the fortress that day, Karim spied several large empty vessels moored on the riverbank alongside the fortress. From that, he got the sense that they might not be the only ones looking to disrupt the ritual.

Unlike whomever had come by boat, however, Karim hadn't had a plan to get inside the fortress. It was only when his hair began to twist in the wind and he smelled the notes of magic in the air that he thought: *Maybe I don't need one.*

The streams were converging; he could feel it.

The river was about to flood.

Gamil moved to enter the fray, but Karim nudged the horse in front of him.

"Not so fast, sen," he said. "Mind yourself in there, hey? Omma will have my hide if anything happens to you."

"Don't be such a goose," Gamil replied. "I've been training all my life for this!"

Karim snorted. "You've been training for about as long as you've been growing that mouse pelt you call a beard." When Gamil scowled, Karim gave him a reluctant smile. "Just be careful. Oh, and Gamil—"

"Yes?"

Karim lay a hand on his brother's shoulder. "Father would have been proud."

Gamil's upper lip trembled slightly. "I hope you find her, sen," he said, and ran inside.

Dumiya rode up next to him, astride a silver mare. The Hudjefa warrior was clad in leather armor similar to Karim's, though hers covered her whole chest and extended over her hips. Under that she wore a short gray tunic, as gauzy and ephemeral as smoke.

Karim gestured toward the battle before them. "Well, is it everything you'd hoped it would be?"

The older woman's sunbaked face crinkled as she grinned, her dark eyes flashing. She urged the horse into a gallop and charged ahead.

Karim shook his head, whipped the reins with a *"Yah!"* and followed.

His stallion charged into the crush of fighters, and Karim directed him around the battle, working toward the citadel. *Is that Sita on a platform ahead?* There was a loud grunt beside him, and Karim looked over to find a familiar face. A face that had recently taken a heavy punch, given the state of her bottom lip.

Karim sidled up to her opponent, a brute who was thicker than he was tall, and brought the butt of his sword down on the top of the man's skull. The soldier slumped to the ground.

Raetawy swiped a bead of blood from her lip, then squinted up at him. "I could have done that, you know."

Karim scoffed. "I know. I just thought—"

"You thought you'd ride in on your horse like the big hero?"

"It's nice to see you again, too, Raetawy."

Raetawy smiled. "Greetings to you, Jackal. You and your people are most welcome here." She tilted her chin toward the gatehouse. "We're focusing on getting the prisoners out. They'll be taken on the boats back to Sakesh. The rest of us will stay until the battle is won, though I fear the war is only beginning."

A vision of Setnakht and his horde of stone men flashed in Karim's mind. "You're quite right, sena," he said.

Just then, a soldier came screaming toward them, his spear aimed directly at Raetawy. An arm's breadth before the spear-head could reach her, a snarling black beast leaped at the attacker, knocking him sideways. His shouts turned to shrieks of pain as Behkai tore into him before chasing him off.

"Still tolerating that dog, I see," Raetawy commented.

Karim shrugged. "He's grown on me." Then his tone turned serious. "Sena, where is the princess? Is she here?"

Raetawy's expression darkened. She cast a glance toward the platform near the entrance to the citadel. "The traitor? Oh, she's here."

"Traitor?"

"The little priestess and I had a plan to stop this ritual and take down the king. When Sitamun returned to the palace, Neff said she needed to be involved. I didn't like the idea, but the priest-ess swore it was in service to some oracle, so I went along. Then Sitamun turned on us the first chance she got! She's up there fighting with Neff right now! She must be stopped!" Raetawy hoisted some kind of stone hammer over her shoulder and started to run.

Karim prodded the horse to follow. He was thunderstruck. "Why would Sita do such a thing?" he called out. "It makes no sense."

"How would you know? You don't know her."

"Actually… I do."

Rae swung the hammer into a soldier's stomach as she passed him and glanced back at Karim with a skeptical expression. "Did you steal her jewelry or something?"

Karim grumbled and drove the horse faster, overtaking Raetawy and reaching the platform first. What he saw confirmed what he'd been told: Sita had an arm slung around the young priestess's shoulders and was violently wrenching the girl to her feet.

Alarmed, Karim pulled the horse close and dismounted onto the platform. He moved to separate the two women, exclaiming, "Sita! What are you doing?"

"Get back!" the princess shouted, brandishing a dagger. "Don't come any closer! I'll kill her! I'll slit her throat!"

Raetawy vaulted onto the platform beside Karim. "You see?"

It was strange to behold Sita dressed in finery, her lips rouged, her eyes lined in black kohl. She looked so different from the girl he'd met in the market and had grown to love. Combined with her bizarre behavior, she seemed like a stranger.

Exactly the kind of woman I'd once expected a Khetaran princess to be.

"She's under a spell!" Nefermaat cried out. "The king's priests cursed her, and I don't know how to break it!"

"Shut your mouth!" Sita said.

"What are we supposed to do?" Raetawy muttered. "If Neff can't undo the spell, we don't have a chance!"

I know only one person powerful enough to break such a curse, Karim thought. He stepped forward, his hands held empty before him to show he meant no harm. "Sitamun. Please, listen to me. I know you're in there. I need you to fight, sena."

"She can't break the heka herself!" Neff exclaimed.

"Yes, she can," Karim said, and took another step.

"Don't come any closer!" Sita screamed, her dark eyes fierce.

"Do you remember when we met, sena?" Karim asked, his voice calm and even. "You taught me how to eat a pomegranate. We sat with Behkai on the riverbank, and you were so hungry that you had seconds."

"Stop talking!"

"Do you remember all those days in Perset? Sharing that little house and playing at being husband and wife?"

Sita's hand holding the dagger began to tremble.

"Do you remember lying together beside the fire, the night I gave you my heart?"

A ragged, tortured wail escaped Sita's lips, and Karim saw her grip on the knife falter. Without warning, he darted forward and pulled Nefermaat free of the princess's grasp.

Sita roared with fury.

Pushing the girl behind him, safe into Raetawy's arms, Karim turned to catch the princess's wrist as she slashed at him with the dagger.

"You are nothing to me!" she snarled. "Nothing but a dirty, stinking *thief*!"

He grappled with her, holding back the blade. He could overpower her, but that would do nothing to break the spell. The curse had weakened, but his words weren't enough. He needed something drastic to bring Sita back to herself.

The answer broke over him like the dawn.

"If that is so, then do as you wish," Karim said and released her wrist. His resistance gone, Sita plunged the dagger straight into his chest.

Nefermaat screamed.

Sita stared at the knife in astonishment. Her pupils dilated and constricted, as if a war was waging within her.

"Perhaps I am nothing to you, sena," Karim said, his voice husky with pain, "But you are everything to me."

And with those words, he pulled her into a kiss, the press of her body pushing the blade into him to the hilt.

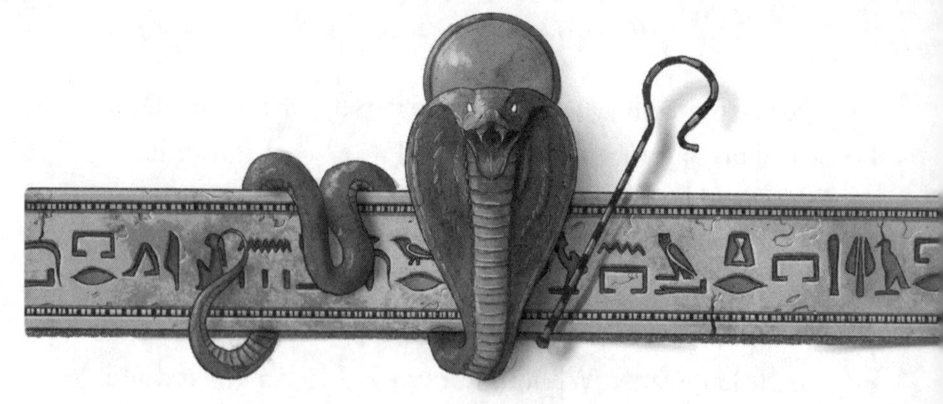

33
SITA

Sita drifted within a deep, blue-green pool. The world was out there, somewhere beyond the surface, but she could not reach it. Lights and shapes flickered in her vision, fractured by the ever-moving current of her mind.

She didn't know how long she'd been down there. It might have been an eternity.

She reached out, tried to speak. Every time, the waters filled her mouth with silence.

She was drowning in herself.

Even the serpent staff, which nipped at the edges of her consciousness, could not free her from Mery's cage.

Then, words sliced through the water, clean and clear and full of heat.

"I need you to fight, sena."

Strength began returning to her limbs. She pushed at the water and found purchase. She began to swim upward, though it was slow and hard going.

A face hovered beyond the surface, brown and warm and familiar, and she worked to reform its rippling pieces into a whole.

She was reminded of gold and silver fish, their scales flashing in the sun, their mouths open and nibbling at her fingers. She remembered the carnelian Isis-knot amulet she'd worn since she was a girl.

With this amulet, the blood of Isis, the spells of Isis, and the magic words of Isis shall protect you from those who would do you harm.

Isis.

The name buoyed her. She recalled a bright face lit by torchlight, paired with another like it, somber and kind.

Perhaps you are capable of unimaginable things too.

With renewed vigor, she fought toward the surface, but she still could not penetrate it. She grew weak, and the weight of the water began dragging her back down.

I can't, she thought. *I'm sorry...*

That's when the shock wave hit. A blast of horror and anguish caused the silent waters to explode with noise. The wave launched her up, up—until she burst through the surface and into the light.

Sita gasped as her consciousness breached. Karim's arms were wrapped around her waist, his lips pressed against hers.

War raged around them, cacophonous, dizzying.

Someone was screaming.

She pulled away from the heat of the kiss and found her hand wrapped around the hilt of a knife buried in Karim's chest.

Then Sita was screaming too.

Karim grunted and jerked the dagger free.

"What are you doing? Don't pull it out!" A horrified Neff stood with a tall, muscular woman who was shouting at Karim. Sita recognized her as one of the new servants she'd met upon her return to the palace.

"It's all right," Karim said through gritted teeth. Sure enough, his skin began knitting itself back together before their eyes.

"What in the name of Ra..." the tall servant said. "I don't understand. You should be dead!"

Karim gave her a wry grin. "Raetawy, you have no idea how right you are."

Sita threw herself into Karim's arms, hugging him tightly and tangling her fingers in his dark, sandy hair. "You came back to me," she murmured in his ear.

When she pulled away to take in the wonder of him, Karim reached up to remove the scarab necklace from around his neck and place it over her head. "I told you I would."

Sita smiled, then furrowed her brow at the servant girl. "Raetawy? I thought your name was Ahura."

The servant scrutinized her. Only then did Sita notice that the woman wore golden scale armor and carried a sekhem scepter, its stone head spattered with blood. Both seemed to fit her far better than a white kalasiris and a food tray.

"You're no servant girl," Sita said.

"Correct, Princess," Raetawy confirmed. "I'm not."

Sita gazed at the three of them standing in a circle on the platform. The wind picked up, its intoxicating fragrance so potent that the air was alive with it.

The lamb, the lamb, the lamb...

"Something's happening," Sita said in awe.

Air swirled around them, lifting Sita's hair and Neff's dress and making them dance. The noise of war seemed to grow distant and muted, and the whispering wind began to shout.

The lamb, the lamb, the lamb!

"We're all together," Neff said, her eyes dark and strange, as they'd been when Sita had first seen her in the temple. "The princess—"

Neff pressed a hand to her own chest. "The priestess—"

She turned to Raetawy. "The rebel—"

Karim's eyes flashed as they met Nefermaat's. The girl smiled. "And the thief."

Sita felt a surge of energy as the wind raged, her mind filling with a rapid succession of images and sounds, memories of decisive moments, of choices, of meetings that had seemed incidental at the time. She remembered…

She remembered standing before the goddess Bast: *I wish to be free.*

Drowning her guilt and shame in wine and passion and delay…

Murder is an exciting game, dear sister, and now you're playing it with me.

Stepping over the threshold from the pleasure garden into the unknown…

I don't know who I am away from this place.

Commanding Karim back to life…

When the time comes, remember the word is the deed.

Bringing method and magic to bear to save an injured boy…

I trust that the Lord has put her in our path for a reason.

Dancing with Karim around the campfire…

Tomorrow is not promised! Tomorrow is not certain! There is only tonight!

Finding the serpent staff down in the depths of the necropolis…

I am the Candle in the Darkness, and the Shadow in the Dawn!

She remembered telling Karim that she no longer believed in stories, which was a lie, because she never stopped believing, never stopped seeing meaning in every encounter, the patterns everywhere hinting at a grand design.

The lamb, the lamb, the lamb…

She remembered everything she'd done since she'd prayed for

freedom, and how it had all led her to this moment, this place, and these three people.

She remembered...

34
NEFF

She remembered a dream of being alone in the desert, listening to the words of a bloody god…

Beware! Sorrow and ruin to the Children of the Two Lands!

She remembered staring at a painting of Isis after the Wabet cut her hair and transformed her into a stranger…

Who am I now? If you know all the names, can you tell me mine?

Hovering before the face of the Invisible One in the Holy of Holies, hearing his sacred words in her mind…

Amun created everything, even himself. And all while no one was watching.

Standing before a sea of faces at the king's coronation and finding her mother and father among them…

They'll come to see me from all over Bubas, from all over Khetara, to hear your story.

She remembered meeting each of the three people from her visions for the first time:

Sitamun, beautiful and full of secrets, approaching the goddess during the Festival of Bast.

Karim, all charm and mischief, sneaking into the temple alongside a merchant and a donkey.

Raetawy, a force of nature barely contained, kneeling in the palace courtyard.

The lamb, the lamb, the lamb…

Neff had feared the responsibility the gods had placed upon her, feared that she was unprepared for the task, yet she'd never questioned the validity of the oracle, never once doubted that all the pieces would fall into place, and that Khnum's word would lead them here.

One wore a crown, another carried a scepter, the third had two shadows, and the last…she was small.

She remembered…

35
RAE

She remembered her hands curling into fists as she watched the nomarch spit his gum at her father's feet…

Don't you ever wonder why you're so angry?

She remembered the crack of the whip on her back the day her purpose was born…

Find another way, Raetawy.

Clacking her asa against Asim's as they sparred in the Garden of the Dead…

My dear girl, you've gone and sparked a rebellion.

Killing one of the Medjay during the raid, and feeling the weight of his corpse upon her…

Violence changes you. Once you visit that bleak country, there's no coming back.

Praying over the dead rebels after the ambush…

Hear me, Ra, Maker of Hours, Lord of Days—hear me and cast your light upon this man.

Tamerit kissing each of the scars on her back…

I would take a hundred more for you.

Striking Omari with the stone scepter, their secrets shattering the bond between them forever…

You've never had the courage to do what really needs to be done.

Rae remembered the hypnotic way that Tamerit spun raw fiber into thread, and the *shh, clack!* of the looms in the weavers' workshop. The threads wove over and under, creating pattern and design. She thought of a chance meeting on the riverbank, of being chosen from a crowd by a stranger, of being asked to fight alongside a sworn enemy in a war far greater than she'd ever anticipated.

Over and under the threads go, the warp and the weft, *shh, clack!*

Slowly a pattern emerged.

The lamb, the lamb, the lamb…

She remembered…

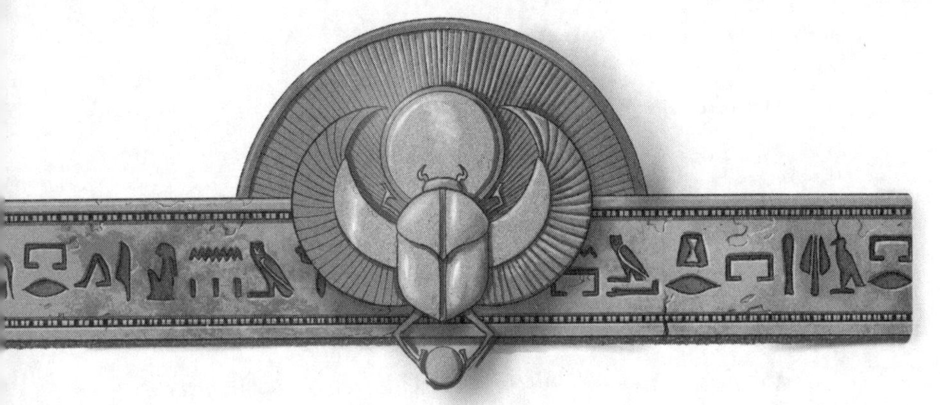

36
KARIM

He remembered the tug of that invisible rope around his chest, pulling him toward a forgotten tomb…

It's not a wall. It's a door.

He remembered the knock of a monster awakened, and the voice of a boy left to die in the dark…

If anyone can find it, you can!

Sweeping the floor of a forgotten temple, and finding his own image rendered on an ancient wall…

The oracle only foretells the beginning of the story. It's up to us to decide how it ends.

Traversing the kingdom with Behkai, a deathless creature in relentless pursuit, then facing his fate…

You can't die, tomb robber. Your story is not finished. This kingdom needs you.

Searching for the lost city with Sitamun, philosophizing and falling in love…

You really think we get to choose our fate?

Witnessing the birth of an infernal army…

Heed me, O ushabti! Wake and hear my call!

Surviving three spears to lead a lost tribe home…

Is this not a sign for hope? Is this not the hand of God reaching out to lift us from our tragedy?

Finding unity among division…

While the men sow discord, the children water flowers.

Karim remembered the way he felt when he met Raetawy on the riverbank, and she showed him kindness when others had not. He remembered telling her about the river, how its current seemed to pull him toward a destination not of his choosing. He could pause on his journey, he could fight the pull of the water and the pull of fate, and perhaps alter his course. But the current *wanted* him to find his place, wanted him to follow the path set out for him. Like the streams and tributaries that all flow to the great river, he was one of many, and the many were but one.

The lamb, the lamb, the lamb…

He remembered.

He remembered and he knew that, somehow, whether by choice or courage or divine intervention or mortal foolishness—or each of those things at once—they had all arrived in the place where they were truly meant to be.

"Greetings to you, Princess, sena, young sena," he said, speaking to each of them in turn as the winds of fate swirled around them. "As lovely as it is to see you all, I believe we have a battle to fight."

37
SITA

Three soldiers advanced toward the platform with spears. Sitamun whirled on them, her voluminous green gown following like an ocean wave. By the time she registered the attackers, they'd already let their spears fly.

The thick fog that had clouded her mind while she'd been enchanted had given way to a crystalline clarity. Without hesitation or forethought, she unfurled her left arm, and the two tiny serpents that had been curled around her ear came to life. They slithered down her neck and along her arm, growing all the while, and then curled themselves in her hand, one red and one black, stretching, straightening, twisting into each other along a band of white light. In the blink of an eye, the light developed shape and texture. A length of twisted wood now in her hand, the serpents twined around it went still.

Sita slammed the base of the serpent staff on the platform.

Next to her, Neff shrieked as the three spears sliced through the air toward them. Rae stepped in front of the girl, while Karim raised his arms to try and shield them both.

Twin beams of white light surged from the serpent staff and encircled all four of them with sudden radiance. The spears struck the light and bounced back, clattering to the ground.

The three soldiers stared at Sita, aghast.

They ran.

Sita exhaled, and the ring of light faded. She turned to the others. "Are you all right?"

She saw Neff peer out from under Rae's arm, and at the sight of the girl, the memory of what she had done while under Mery's curse came flooding back to her.

Shame rose in Sita's throat. "I'm so sorry, Nefermaat. I hurt you, didn't I? Can you forgive me?"

Neff's expression was soft. "It wasn't you who did those things. It was him."

Even as the battle thundered around them, Sita felt more at peace than she had in a long, long time. The little priestess had given her the absolution she hadn't known she'd needed.

Sita nodded in thanks as the air crackled between them. She felt the power of the oracle, and from the determined expressions on the others' faces, she could tell they felt it too.

"Princess, we must go to the citadel," Neff said. "Meryamun took Kenna inside. He's going to kill him!"

Sita blanched. A season earlier, she never would have believed her brother capable of such an atrocity. Now, she didn't question it. She leaped off the platform and made for the citadel.

"Wait!" Karim exclaimed, coming after her. "You're not going in there alone. We go together!"

"Fine, but we must go *now*!"

The woman called Raetawy jumped to the ground and grabbed Sita by the shoulder.

"Hey! What about my men? Those priests cast some kind of spell on them, and they're out there killing each other! They're the ones who put a stop to this barbaric ritual in the first place. Are you going to leave them to die? The prince's life isn't the only one at stake here!"

Sita glanced at the hand on her shoulder and the rebel's face with exasperation. "I can't lose my brother! Don't you understand?"

Nefermaat stepped between them. "I think the priests are maintaining the spell through concentration, which is why they're wearing the blindfolds." The two Heka priests stood in the shadow of the citadel, chanting and releasing the tendrils of black smoke. "If we can break it—"

Before Nefermaat could finish her thought, Raetawy launched herself toward the two priests. The rebel whipped the scepter she carried in a low arc, striking a devastating blow to one of the priest's knees.

The man howled in agony and collapsed to the ground, curling around his shattered joint and screaming. The other priest stopped chanting and started to remove his blindfold. Tossing the scepter into her other hand, Raetawy landed a heavy punch to his temple that knocked him out cold.

"Like that?" Raetawy called back at them.

In the courtyard, the black smoke dissipated, rendering a dozen men stunned. They looked at each other in confusion, then turned their weapons from ally to enemy once more.

Nefermaat blinked. "Um, yes. Exactly like that."

Sita ran up the citadel steps and wrenched the brass ring affixed to the large wooden door. It wouldn't budge.

"Allow me," Karim offered, and took a turn, but to no avail. Even with Raetawy adding her own strength to the task, the door remained firmly shut.

"It must be braced from the inside," Sita said, frantic.

Beside her, Nefermaat bent to pick up a wooden arrow that hadn't found its target.

"Let me try something," she said, and stood at the door holding the arrow in both hands. Her brow furrowed, and her lips moved silently before she cleared her throat and spoke.

"Hear me, Bes—protector of women and children, guardian of the threshold! I am both woman and child, and I ask you to break the barrier that prevents me from entering this place! Help me repel evil from this door, as you would every door upon this earth!"

With that, the young priestess snapped the arrow in half.

Sita heard a distinct splintering noise on the other side of the door, then the *clunk! clunk!* of two objects hitting the ground. Incredulous, she gave the door another tug.

It creaked open, revealing a broken wooden brace beyond the threshold.

They all stared at Nefermaat, who blushed with pleasure.

"How could you know such a specific spell?" Sita asked her.

"I didn't. I made it up. I can't believe it worked!"

Sita scrutinized the young priestess. She hadn't studied a lot of heka, but she knew that spells were sacred, written only by the sagest of priests, who often spent lifetimes in trial and error, combining objects, words, and actions to create a successful result.

Yet this girl had done it on a whim.

Truly, the gods must be at her ear, Sita thought.

They rushed inside the citadel, Raetawy and Karim at the front, Sita and Neff following behind them. Inside, they faced an empty antechamber, with long corridors stretching to the left and right.

"Which way?" Karim asked.

Raetawy pressed her ear to the wall and held up a hand for

silence. After listening intently for a few seconds, she said, "Left," and turned down the corridor.

They'd only gone a few steps before they heard a strident shout and half a dozen armed guards poured out of a doorway ahead, charging toward them.

"You take three and I take three," Raetawy said to Karim.

Karim grinned, then ducked as a khopesh blade sailed over his head. "Your generosity, sena, it is boundless." The guard took the full force of Karim's attack as he rammed into the man's hips and slammed him—and the guard behind him—into the stone wall.

Meanwhile, Raetawy blocked a guard's first strike, dealt him a punch to the gut, and spun out to kick another man into the opposite wall, bashing the sword from his hand with her scepter as he bounced back. It all happened in a whirl of flashing blades and bellows while Sita looked on, holding Nefermaat behind her and her serpent staff as a shield.

After thirty seconds of frenzied fighting, Karim and Raetawy stood over the unconscious guards, panting.

"You said *three* each, sena, and yet you took four," Karim complained.

"You hit that last one first."

"Yes, but you took him down, so I hardly think that counts."

"Can we please argue about this later?" Sita said, rushing past them both to the doorway ahead.

When she reached the portal, Sita found a smaller chamber within, boasting high ceilings, tall windows, and a line of cold braziers terminating at an austere wooden throne. Near the throne, the ram-masked priest chanted, his arms raised to the heavens. Kenna knelt before him in a pool of sunlight, dust motes floating around him.

Kenna looked up when Sita entered the room, and when their eyes met, she saw a slight brightening in his pale, somber face.

Then Mery stepped out from the shadow of the throne behind him. "Goodbye, brother," he said, and hefted the stone mace into the air. His face alive with malice, Mery brought it crashing down upon Kenna's head.

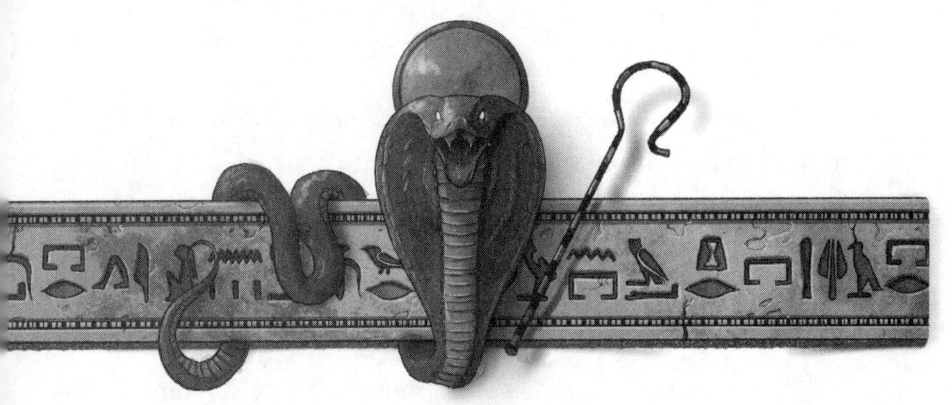

38
SITA

The staff's beam of protective light was halfway across the room when the mace connected with Kenna's skull. It didn't reach him in time.

Blood spattered Mery's bare chest as Kenna jerked with the impact of the blow. His eyes, which had been focused on Sita, rolled up into his head and he slumped to the floor.

"No!" Sita screamed, running to him. She dropped the staff and fell to her knees beside her fallen brother, heedless of the sibling who loomed over them both.

"Kenna, please! Stay with me, please!" she cried, gathering him into her arms. Blood leaked onto her dress as she put pressure on his wound, her fingers slipping in the wet tangle of his hair. Behind her, Nefermaat released a choked sob, and Sita fought back her own tears as she looked down at Kenna's face. It was slack and gray.

"No."

We were finally together again. We'd finally put the past behind us, and now, and now…

The pain in her heart was too much. She held his thin body to her chest and began to rock back and forth, weeping.

She was so deep in her sorrow that it barely registered when Mery spoke.

"Do not grieve for him, sister," he said. "I've given him what he's always longed for: A journey west. Our brother has been fixated on death since the moment he was born."

"How could you do this?" Sita whispered, not looking at Mery.

"I can feel it already," Mery went on. "The blood magic doing its work, draining the strength from my enemies and siphoning it into me. Kenna's life wasn't worth much, but his death is priceless."

Sita gently laid Kenna's body on the floor and brushed the blood-drenched locks from his face. Trembling, she stood to confront the king.

"I'm going to kill you, Mery."

There was silence, then Mery laughed with delight. "Oh, Sitamun," he said, his smile dazzling. "You don't have it in you."

Sita flinched. They'd dispatched Mery's guards, and the priest Herihor looked like he was on the verge of flight. There was no one to protect her brother, but could she really do it? For all her fury at the horrible things Mery had done, could she really take his life with her own hands?

Suddenly, a deep sense of calm filled her.

"You're right," she said evenly.

Mery's brows furrowed. This was a move he wasn't expecting.

Sita went on. "I am a betrayer, and a coward, and a fool. But I'm not a killer. Not like you." The serpent staff glowed faintly. "You don't need to die for me to ensure you never hurt anyone else, ever again."

Mery scoffed. "Don't be silly. As long as I'm alive, I will find you and I will break you, that's a promise."

Another figure moved out of the shadows, looking almost like a shadow herself, the amethyst-studded wings of her favorite vulture collar sparkling in the pale light.

Made to honor the goddess Nekhbet, Sita thought.

Mother of Mothers.

Mother Night.

Mery noticed the new direction of Sita's gaze and turned to Queen Bintanath.

"Mother? What are you doing here?" Mery asked with an almost imperceptible note of alarm.

Queen Bintanath said nothing, her attention on the body of her youngest son. "You killed him, Mery," she said, her tone and expression unreadable.

The bloody mace still hung loosely from Mery's right hand. "He betrayed me, Mother. He and the little priestess. Sita too. They all betrayed me." There was a hint of childishness in his voice. "They're all trying to prevent me from what I was born to do: return Khetara to glory!"

The queen did not respond.

"You understand, don't you, Mother? You know what it takes to rule. I watched you grit your teeth while Father let the kingdom fall to ruin, watched you hold your tongue a thousand times when all the while it was you who put him on the throne in the first place, you who were the clever one, the one with an ear to the ground, the one who knew everybody's secrets. You always told me that I would put things right. That one day, a thousand years from now, our descendants would tell stories about a great prosperity, about how Khetara's finest days were those under my reign."

Still, Queen Bintanath was silent.

"I did what needed to be done!" Mery suddenly raged. "There are traitors behind every door! Don't you see that? In Tash, in Sakesh, *in my own house*! The gods placed a serpent upon my brow and divine power in my blood. Why would they give me such gifts if they didn't mean for me to use them?"

The queen looked at Mery with a sorrow that did not sit comfortably upon her severe, imperious face. Walking up behind Mery, she wrapped one arm around his chest and held him close, her chin resting on his shoulder.

"My boy," she said softly. "My beautiful, brilliant boy."

Mery relaxed in her arms.

"The gods didn't give you that crown. You took it when you killed your father."

The king's eyes widened.

"Did you really think I wouldn't find out?" the queen asked. "I might have forgiven you for that, you know. Perhaps. With time. But I can't forgive you for Kenna."

In a blur of movement, the queen's other arm wrapped around her son's body and pulled him into a sudden, tight embrace.

Mery's handsome face opened wide with shock, and he coughed. A glut of blood poured from his lips and down his chin. He looked at his chest as Queen Bintanath released him, at the hilt of the dagger she'd buried there.

Sita gasped in horror.

"Mother?" Mery said, the word wet and choked. He stumbled back, tripping over the voluminous folds of his cape, and collapsed into the wooden throne.

As he fell, the double crown slipped from his brow and tumbled down, breaking in two when it hit the ground. The crimson-gold circlet rolled along the stone floor, coming to rest near Sita's feet.

Time stopped.

Sita's heartbeat seemed to vibrate the floor beneath her, the walls, the ceiling high above. She watched Mery's blood pulse in his throat.

Once.

Twice.

No more.

The room was still.

Finally, Sita let out a sob that was part anguish, part relief. She looked to her mother.

The queen's face was a ruin. In an instant, she had aged a hundred years.

Herihor the priest took one look at the scene in front of him and ran from the room.

Queen Bintanath fiddled in the folds of her dress, as if searching for something. She turned to Sita, Kenna's body between them on the floor.

"I see it all clearly now," she said quietly. "I tried to give you the best of everything, and I failed to give you the very things you needed most."

Sita regarded her, tears streaming down her face, unable to respond.

The queen went on. "I know it's too late to fix what I've broken. But at least…at least I could do this." Her gaze fell on Mery. "So you don't have to."

She pulled a small clay pot from the folds of her dress and flicked the stopper open with her thumb.

Sita didn't need to ask what it was. Nebet's offhand comment about the queen's activities came rushing back to her, heavy with newfound significance—

She's been spending a great deal of time alone in the pleasure garden. According to the gardeners, she has developed a keen interest in plants…

"Mother, no!"

The queen's smile bore the pain and enormity of maternal love. "You know the punishment for killing a king, Sitamun." She raised the pot to her lips and drank.

Sita stepped over Kenna to dash the pot from her mother's hand. It shattered on the stone floor—empty.

"Mother!"

Karim ran to her side, looking between the two women helplessly.

With no one to stand in her way, Neff ran to Kenna, her hands roving over his face and chest, begging him not to be dead. Raetawy stood at a distance, solemn and silent.

The queen's skin began to turn an odd shade of purple as she coughed convulsively.

"What was it?" Sita demanded. "Hemlock? We can find an antidote if we hurry! We can stop it!" She shook her mother by the shoulders. *"What was it?"*

The queen only stared at her, foam gathering at the corners of her mouth.

I'm going to be alone, Sita thought, her grief sudden and crushing. *They're all gone. Father, Mery, Mother, and—*

There was a sudden cry behind her, and Sita whirled to find Neff holding Kenna, radiating unimaginable joy. "He's alive!" she wailed. "He's breathing! He's alive!"

"What?" Leaving Karim to support her mother, Sita dashed toward them and knelt on Kenna's other side.

Her brother blinked up at her through a curtain of blood. "Sitamun?" he whispered, his voice hoarse.

Sita laughed, overwhelmed, hysterical. "It's a miracle!" she said through tears.

Neff collapsed onto the prince, wrapping her arms around him as she sobbed.

Kenna patted the girl. "There, there," he said awkwardly, seemingly uncertain how to react to such an outpouring of love. He peered around the room in growing dismay. "What happened?" he asked Sita.

"Mother thought Mery killed you, so she..." Sita couldn't finish the words. "He's gone," she said instead. "And now she's taken some kind of poison. She's dying, Kenna."

Kenna's brow furrowed, shock driving the fog from his eyes. She felt his muscles constrict as he tried to rise.

"What are you doing? Your head! You're bleeding!"

Kenna ignored her, straining to move despite his injury.

Seeing that he would not be dissuaded. Sita helped move him closer to their mother. Karim had laid the queen on the floor in front of the throne. Her breathing was shallow, her eyes closed.

"Mother," Kenna said.

The queen's eyes opened and focused on the prince's face, bloody but very much alive.

"Bakenamun?" Her voice was feathery and barely audible.

"Mother," Kenna repeated. Like Mery, he seemed to be reduced to a child before her. "You didn't need to do this... Why did you do this?"

The queen reached for him, her hand trembling, and caressed his cheek. "My boy. You never asked for anything. Never caused me any pain—even at your birth."

Kenna's face was awash with grief.

The queen coughed again, each word a struggle. "Yet I caused you...so much. Made you feel that you were not enough."

"Mother..."

"I should have loved you better."

"Please, don't—"

The queen's face, which had always been so stern and full of tension, relaxed.

Sita clapped a hand over her mouth and cried.

Kenna bowed his head as they knelt together beside the dead queen, silently honoring her final bloody gift.

Then they stood, Sita helping her injured brother to his feet and slipping an arm around his shoulder. She looked at Mery, seated in the wooden throne. Only a little blood dripped from the knife wound down his chest, staining his fine green schenti. His head was tilted to the side, exposing his chiseled jawline, and he'd thrown one of his hands over the arm of the chair, as if he were holding a cup of wine in it. Even in death, he was the picture of elegance.

Bitterly, Sita said, "All he ever wanted was to save the kingdom. How could he go so wrong?"

"Mery never cared about the kingdom, Sitamun," Kenna replied. "He only cared about the crown."

The double crown of Khetara lay at Sita's feet, broken, no longer dazzling, and with no head to bear it.

Sita clung to Kenna as the enormity of what faced them fell upon her. "You're all I have left," she said through her tears.

Kenna scanned the room, his gaze pausing on the thief, the rebel, and the little priestess. He said, "Oh, I don't know about that."

39

NEFF

Neff faced the bloody tableau, her heart in turmoil. The horror of what she'd just witnessed was seared into her mind like a brand.

Rae moved to stand beside her, a strong, reassuring presence. When the rebel spoke to the group, her voice was gentle but firm. "I'm sorry, but now is not the time for mourning. The battle still rages."

Reluctantly, Sitamun turned away from the corpses. "You're right." She bent to retrieve her serpent staff from where she'd discarded it on the floor. "I'm needed out there."

"Not only you," Karim corrected her. "All of us."

They walked out of the throne room and through the corridor past the still unconscious guards. Karim and Sita were hand in hand, and Rae supported Kenna with what looked like no effort at all. No one walked with Neff, but a strange displacement in the air beside her reminded her that she did not walk alone.

“Thank you for your help,” she whispered, and hoped that Medjed heard her.

Kenna stumbled and would have fallen if not for Rae setting him back on his feet.

“How did you do it, brother?” Neff asked him. “I know you’re hardheaded, but that blow should have killed you.”

Kenna offered her a crooked smile. “A fine joke, little sister—though you should already know the answer to that question.” He pulled the Eye of Horus amulet from underneath his tunic and dangled it in front of her.

Neff squinted. A tiny square of papyrus covered in carefully written gods’ words had been fastened to the back of the amulet. “What does it say?” she asked.

“‘Hear me, O Ptah, divine craftsman!’” Kenna recited. “‘Should a heavy blow fall upon me, sculpt my head as if from stone, so that it remains whole and unbroken.’”

“A protection spell!” Neff was impressed.

“Indeed. One that is only triggered by a specific situation, as I taught you.”

“But how did you know this was going to happen?”

“When I first heard of your disappearance, I assumed your quarters would be searched, and that the Book of the Red Lady would be discovered. Mery was no fool. He would deduce I was the one who’d given it to you, which would alert him to our clandestine activities. Knowing that, I assumed that he would conceive of a public display during which to execute me for treason. Given the imminence of the cursing ritual, it seemed likely he’d do it there and use the same method of a blow to the head. Therefore, a spell to magically enhance the durability of my skull was the natural choice.”

Rae chuckled. “See, I knew you were clever.”

Kenna tilted his chin to indicate Rae's armor. "I'm glad to see you found a vocation for which you're better suited."

Rae twirled the scepter in her other hand. "I suppose I have."

As they neared the entrance, Rae's curly-haired companion and a black dog with a white mark on its face came dashing into the citadel.

"Tam!" Rae called out. "Oh, thanks be to Ra! You're all right."

The dog raced up to Sita and Karim, greeting the princess first.

"After everything I've done for him," Karim remarked wearily, giving the dog a pat on the rump, "Still, I manage to be second-best."

"What's going on out there?" Rae asked her companion.

"Many casualties on both sides, and the fighting continues. And Rae, there's something else." There was fear and confusion on the woman's face.

"What do you mean?" Rae asked.

Tam wrung her hands. "You'll have to see for yourself."

A chill crept down Neff's spine as she followed the others out the citadel doors. The scene in the courtyard was no less terrible than the one they'd left—bodies were scattered across the ground, and many rebels, tribesmen, and royal soldiers were still engaged in brutal warfare.

A young man ran toward them as they descended the steps, followed closely by a fierce-looking older woman with silver hair.

"Karim-sen!" the young man said, crashing into the Red Lander with enough force to nearly knock him off his feet. It was then that Neff noticed the familial similarity between them.

"Gamil, thank God," Karim said, giving the young man a slap on the back. "You're not hurt."

The older woman pointed to her eye and then at Gamil. *No, because I kept an eye on him,* she seemed to say.

Karim touched a knuckle to his nose in thanks.

"We're winning, sen," Gamil said, oblivious to the exchange. "The Khetarans are few in number, and soon we will prevail!"

Rae stared out onto the battlefield and focused on a particular dead young man who lay by the trench with an arrow in his chest. "Perhaps," she murmured thickly. "But the price was high."

Sitamun pushed past them toward a tall man with deep brown skin, clothed in emerald green robes that must once have been exquisite. He was battered and bruised, and he held a bloodied khopesh in his hand. "By Amun—Harsi? Is that you? What are you doing here?"

The man called Harsi stopped short and stared at Sitamun, bewildered. "Your brother abducted me and has been holding me ransom, Princess. I assumed you knew that, since you appear to be on his side!"

"I'm not on his side," Sitamun countered.

"Then where is he?"

The princess's nostrils flared. "He's finished. As is the queen."

Harsi lowered his khopesh. "Finished?" He turned toward the screaming, dying men. "Then who are they fighting for?"

Neff saw something change in Sitamun's expression. Saw resolve grow there and harden. Without another word, the princess strode past the man in green and mounted the platform. The serpent staff at her side glowed with sudden white radiance.

"Hear me!" Sitamun shouted, her voice reverberating across the courtyard. "Lay down your arms, for this battle is over!"

Weapons stilled mid-swing as every man and woman stopped and turned toward her.

Sitamun's next words rolled over them all like a great flood. "The king of Khetara is dead!"

There was a moment of stunned silence, followed by the dull

sounds of spears and swords and hammers falling to the ground, one by one.

Neff took in the scene and realized something about it wasn't quite right. The courtyard had been awash in afternoon sun when they'd entered the citadel. They hadn't been inside very long, and yet the light outside was different. Darker despite there not being a single cloud in the sky.

"Something's wrong," Neff said.

Tam nodded as she pointed west.

A black circle was sliding in front of the sun. It had already obscured half of it, and it was advancing before their eyes. The light around them was fading rapidly, transforming day into night.

Around the courtyard, there were gasps, shrieks of terror, and confusion as people turned their faces to the heavens. Sitamun jumped down from the platform to rejoin them and grabbed Karim's hand.

"What is it?" he exclaimed. "What's happening?"

Neff gazed at the spectacle above her, as if she were staring into the darkness at the center of a flame. The noise around her melted away and was replaced by an insistent whispering.

"Beware, for soon the Great River of Khetara will turn to blood," she said, adding her own voice to the chorus of whispers.

Sitamun, Rae, and Karim looked at her, their faces pale with wonder and fear.

"Lies will grow fruitful as wheat in the fields, and where once there was order, chaos will reign. A secret shall rise from beneath the earth—"

Visions of an infernal army marching toward Thonis filled Neff's mind, stone soldiers leaving slaughter in their wake, along with a name that sounded more like a curse.

Setnakht.

"—and the Red and the White crowns will be forever broken."

She saw the broken crown, the empty throne.

"Take heed, Thonis, Great House of Amun! Beware of what is unseen among you! Take heed, Sakesh, Great House of Ra! Beware of what burns and destroys you!"

Neff felt the power of four streams converging into a river, its inexorable current rushing toward a precipice, toward the unknown.

"Beware! Sorrow and ruin comes to the Children of the Two Lands!"

EPILOGUE
WINGS

Perched on the fortress rampart, the ibis cocked his dark head to peer at the black disc that moments ago had been the sun. A nimbus of light radiated from its edges, as if the sun was waving its golden fingers, reminding the world that it was still there.

Below, the people made a harrowing noise, like the screams of herons in flight. The sight of their dead reminded the ibis of his own flock, their soft bodies broken on the riverbank.

The great Bennu bird perched beside him, tall and solemn. *Are you afraid?* she asked after a while.

The ibis saw no point in pretending to be brave. *Yes-yes. Very much.*

Good. Fear sharpens the mind. It encourages us to focus only on what is most vital. Following his gaze, she bent her long white neck to observe the scene below. *Many stories have ended this day, but another story, perhaps the greatest of them all, has only just begun. And you, sacred one, are part of it.*

The ibis's feathers bristled in confusion. *I am one bird. One of millions, all of them the same.*

Not true, the Bennu countered. *You survived when all your flock perished. You warned me of the jackal when I was but a stranger. You entered willingly into peril and found enlightenment. You are not just one bird. You are singular. And now, you will stay with me until the end.*

The ibis felt a surge of pride. Perhaps despite his wrinkled head and jumbled tail feathers, he was meant for something special.

Besides, the Bennu bird added, launching into the air, her blue wings bright in the darkness, *You gave me the bigger fish.*

The ibis hurried to follow, stretching to catch the updraft and soar after his strange new friend. And as the wind—warm and fragrant—filled his wings, he thought that perhaps he liked a bit of adventure after all.

SERIES GUIDE

SETTING

KHETARA [KEH-TAH-RAH]: The united kingdom of two lands, High Khetara in the north and Low Khetara in the south. High Khetara consists of the delta region, and Low Khetara the more mountainous, arid region.

THE ITERU [IT-ER-OO]: The great river of Khetara that runs south to north in the middle of the kingdom, emptying into the Great Green Sea, feeding the crops on either side of its banks and acting as a trade route to other kingdoms.

THONIS [THON-ISS]: The capital of High Khetara and location of the royal palace.

BUBAS [BOO-BAHSS]: A small village southeast of Thonis, sacred home of the goddess Bast and her temple.

SAKESH [SAH-KESH]: The capital city of Low Khetara, and the center of the southern rebellion against the crown.

THE RED LANDS: The western desert outside of the borders of Khetara, where nomadic tribes live, and where the Khetarans build tombs for their sacred dead.

PERSET [PURR-SET]: The ancient capital city of King Setnakht located in the eastern desert, which was abandoned upon his death.

CHARACTERS
(IN ALPHABETICAL ORDER)

FROM THONIS

PRINCE BAKENAMUN A.K.A. "KENNA" [BAH-KEN-AMIN]: Seventeen-year-old son of Amunmose and Bintanath, brother to Sita and Mery, and a Sem priest in the House of Amun.

QUEEN BINTANATH [BINNA-TAH-NETH]: Great Wife to the late Amunmose, and mother of the triplets Mery, Sita, and Kenna.

FEMI [FEH-MEE]: A young palace guard.

PRINCE HARSI [HAR-SEE]: An ambassador from the southern kingdom of Tash.

HERIHOR [HERRY-HOR]: Head Heka priest at the Temple of Amun.

MEDJED [MED-JED]: A small, invisible guardian deity with unknown origins.

KING MERYAMUN A.K.A. "MERY" [MERRY-AMIN]: The newly crowned seventeen-year-old pharaoh of Khetara, son of Amunmose and Bintanath, brother to Sita and Kenna.

MASTER MONTUHOTEP [MON-TOO-HO-TEP]: High priest of Amun and Hour priest.

NEBET [NEH-BET]: Attendant to the princess.

SABNI [SAHB-NEE]: Meryamun's head vizier.

PRINCESS SITAMUN A.K.A. "SITA" [SIT·AH·MIN A.K.A. SEE·TAH]: Seventeen-year-old daughter of Amunmose and Bintanath, sister to Mery and Kenna.

THE WABET [WAH·BET]: Priestesses at the Temple of Amun.

DECEASED

KING AMUNMOSE [AMMON·MOHZ]: Late pharaoh of Khetara, husband to Bintanath (among many other Lesser Wives), father of the triplets.

MAET [MAH·ET]: The six-year-old daughter of one of Amunmose's lesser wives, and half-sister of the triplets.

KING SEMATAWY [SEM·AH·TAH·WAY]: The Great Uniter—the High Khetaran king who preceded Amunmose. Went to war with Low Khetara during his reign and slaughtered the southern king, King Rahotep, in order to unite the Two Lands under the double crown.

FROM BUBAS

AHURA [AH·HOOR·AH]: Neff's mother.

MISTRESS KARO, THE HIGH PRIESTESS OF BAST [KAH·ROH]: Powerful priestess in charge of the Temple of Bast.

NEFERMAAT A.K.A. "NEFF" [NEFF·ER·MAH·AHT]: A thirteen-year-old common girl who was conscripted into the priesthood at the Temple of Amun by Mistress Karo, then taken to the palace to be Meryamun's personal seer and adviser.

PEPI [PEH·PEE]: Neff's father, a spell vendor.

FROM SAKESH

ANKHU [AHN·KOO]: Rae's father, an ex-scribe and wheat and cattle farmer who lost a hand in the Great War with High Khetara.

BAKI [BAH·KHI]: A local shepherd and Horizon rebel.

BUTO [BOO·TOW]: A street fighter and Horizon rebel.

KAY: A fisherman and Horizon rebel.

MAMET MUT [MAM·ET MOOT]: Head of the weavers, town gossip, and Horizon rebel.

MENK [MEN·EKH]: Friend of the late Asim, and high-ranking member of the Horizon rebels.

THE NOMARCH [NO·MARK]: Sakesh's governor, elected by King Amunmose and currently serving under Meryamun.

OMARI [AH·MAH·REE]: Rae's best friend, a nineteen-year-old carpenter and member of the Horizon rebels.

RAETAWY A.K.A. "RAE" [RAH·AH·TAW·EE A.K.A. RAY]: Nineteen-year-old farm girl, street fighter, and newly appointed leader of the Horizon rebels. Daughter of Ankhu. Uses the alias "Ahura" while acting as a spy.

TAMERIT A.K.A. "TAM" [TAH·MER·IT]: A twenty-year-old weaver and member of the Horizon rebels. Uses the alias "Herit" [HAIR-eet] while acting as a spy.

DECEASED

ASIM [AH·SEEM]: The first leader of the Horizon rebels.

KING RAHOTEP [RAH·HO·TEP]: The last king of Low Khetara before the war of Unification. Slaughtered by King Sematawy along with most of his court.

FROM PERSET

THE HUDJEFA [HOOHD·JEFF·AH] TRIBE:

AYA [EYE·AH]: Elyas's eight-year-old granddaughter.

DUMIYA [DOO·MEE·YAH]: Deaf, middle-agedwarrior and guardian of the tribe.

ELYAS [EE·LIE·YASS]: Elderly leader of the Hudjefa tribe.

MIRI [ME·REE]: Elyas's elderly wife.

SAMI [SAM·EE]: A fifteen-year-old boy.

SHESMU THE BUTCHER [SHESS·MOO]: A warlike deity associated both with the winepress and with slaughter; his spirit is called forth into an enormous stone man.

ZEV: A warrior.

FROM THE RED LANDS

THE ANEN [AH-NEN] TRIBE:

BABU [BAH-BOO]: Twenty-one-year-old leader of the Jackals.

BEHKAI [BEH-KHAI]: Karim's black dog, who acquired a white handprint mark on his face from Setnakht's touch.

DIMA [DEE-MAH]: Karim's sister.

FAIZA [FAI-ZAH]: Karim's youngest sister.

GAMIL [GAH-MEEL]: Karim's younger brother.

HAGER [HAH-GER]: A member of the Jackals.

KARIM [KAR-EEM]: A nineteen-year-old tomb robber and ex-Jackal, recently resurrected.

NOUR [NOOR]: Karim's mother.

SETNAKHT [SET-NAHKT]: An ancient pharaoh whose name was erased from history—only to be rediscovered a thousand years after his death and resurrected through dark magic.

DECEASED

DJET [D-JET]: A thirteen-year old boy and member of the Jackals.

PASENHOR A.K.A. "PA" [PAH-SEN-HOR]: An old priest of Khnum.

GODS
(IN ALPHABETICAL ORDER)

AMUN [AH·MOON]: The blue-skinned, invisible creator god of air and mystery—also known as the Hidden One. Like Khnum, he is sometimes depicted with a ram's head.

ANUBIS [ANU·BISS]: The jackal-headed god of funerary rites and guide to the underworld.

BAST/SEKHMET: The cat-headed goddess of pleasure and women's secrets. She can also appear with a lioness head as Sekhmet, goddess of war—to represent her more savage aspect as a defender and protector from evil.

BENNU BIRD: A creator god, Bennu is a large heron-like bird who is said to be the soul of Ra. According to legend, Bennu alighted on the primeval mound and released a call that announced the beginning of creation.

GEB: Primeval god of the earth.

HORUS [HOR·ISS]: The falcon-headed son of Isis and Osiris, who avenged his father's murder by defeating Set in battle. The eye of Horus (the wedjat) is considered to be a protective symbol.

ISIS [EYE·SIS]: The Great Mother, goddess of magic and kingship, protector of the kingdom. She is sister to Nephthys and wife to Osiris.

KHNUM [KAH·NOOM]: The ram-headed Divine Potter who is said to have molded man from clay on the Great Wheel. He can sometimes be represented as a lamb.

NEITH [NEETH]: Creator goddess of war, hunting, and weaving.

NEPHTHYS [NEFF·THISS]: Protector goddess of darkness, childbirth, funerary rites, and magic. Sister to Isis, wife of Set.

NUT [NOOT]: Primeval goddess of the sky.

OSIRIS [OH·SIRE·ISS]: The green-skinned god of the dead, Judge and Lord of the Underworld. Husband to Isis, who resurrected him after he was killed by his brother Set.

RA [RAH]: God of the noonday sun, order, and kings, and thought to be Khetara's first pharaoh. He is portrayed in many different forms, including a falcon, a scarab, a man, and, while in the underworld, a ram.

SET: The god of chaos, storms, the desert, and the color red. Portrayed with the head of a strange, canine-like black animal.

SHU: Primeval god of the air and wind, known for creating space between the sky and the earth in order for life to exist.

THOTH [THOH·TH]: Ibis-headed god of wisdom, writing, knowledge, and magic who plays a prominent role in maintaining order in the universe. As the scribe of the gods, Thoth is also involved in divine arbitration and judgment of souls in the afterlife.

TERMINOLOGY

AY: Nickname meaning "donkey."

DUAT [DOO-AHT]: The Khetaran underworld, located in the West.

EXECRATION RITUAL: A cursing ritual meant to bring malicious magic upon one's enemies.

HEKA [HEH-KAH]: Khetaran magic; alternatively, a god of magic (i.e. Heka the Child)

HEKAT [HEH-KAHT]: A Khetaran measurement, as in for crops.

IMI-IB [EH-MEE EEB]: Sweetheart or darling.

KA [KAH]: A major aspect of the human soul, namely their spiritual essence or divine, creative force.

KALASIRIS [KAH-LAH-SEER-ISS]: A type of simple close-fitting dress.

KHAMSIN [KHAM-SEEN]: A hot, dry desert wind.

KHOPESH [KO-PESH]: A sickle-shaped Khetaran sword.

OMMA: The Red Lander word for "Mama."

MAMET AND YATI [MAH-MET AND YAH-TEE]: Khetaran for "Mama and Papa."

MEDJAY: The police force in Khetara.

MUTU: A spirit who does not move on to the afterlife and is left to wander the earth.

NUNU: A very young child or toddler.

SABBA: The Red Lander word for "Grandpa."

SCHENTI [SHEN-TEE]: A short pleated skirt worn by Khetaran men.

SEN/SENA [SEN/SEN-AH]: Brother/sister.

SHEMSU HOR: An event during which the pharaoh travels throughout Khetara to visit the people and assess the kingdom.

SISTRUM: A rattle-like instrument used for sacred ceremonies and rituals.

TAHTIB [TAH-TEEB]: Khetaran art of stick-fighting.

USHABTI [OO-SHAB-TEE]: Small figurines placed in tombs to represent servants who can magically come to life and serve their masters in the Duat.

WEDJAT [WED-JAHT]: The protective Eye of Horus.

ZEBU [ZEH-BOO]: Humpbacked Khetaran cattle.

TYPES OF PRIESTS

HEKA [HEH-KAH]: Those who use spells, wands, and rituals for magical purposes.

HOUR [OUR]: Those who interpret dreams and make predictions about the future.

SEM: Those who conduct funerary rites and embalming for the dead—otherwise known as "Men of Anubis."

WAB (WABAU/WABET) [WAHB]: Lower-rank novice priests/priestess, sometimes healers.

AUTHOR'S NOTE

I hope you have been enjoying your time in my ancient Egyptian–inspired kingdom of Khetara. Although writing these books is awfully hard work, when they're finished, I find myself very reluctant to leave them. I have spent so many hundreds of hours in this world that it's come to feel like home.

As in *His Face Is the Sun*, certain elements of *She Knows All the Names* were inspired by true stories from ancient Egyptian history. Setnakht and his city of Perset, for instance, are loosely based on King Akhenaten and his capital city of Akhetaten, known to us today as Amarna. Like Setnakht, Akhenaten rejected polytheism in favor of worshipping one god—in his case, Aten, the sun disk. Upon Akhenaten's death, his son—a young boy by the name of Tutankhamun—eventually abandoned Akhetaten and reinstated Memphis and Thebes as the administrative and religious capitals of the kingdom. Obviously, Setnakht and his cult of Set is a very different story, but I really enjoyed creating something that was a fusion of truth and fiction. Akhenaten was seen as a heretic, but today he is also recognized as one of the world's first monotheists—which just goes to show that stories are often more nuanced than they seem. Even the oft-maligned god Set isn't just a simple baddie, an idea I aim to explore in the final book of this series.

Perset's Temple of Night is another element of this book that was inspired by history. The Labyrinth of Egypt, located at Hawara, is a vast, incredibly complex structure with many subterranean levels and thousands of rooms, which is why it's often compared to a maze. First described by Herodotus in ancient times, what remains of the structure is buried deep underground and, to this day, is still a source of mystery and intrigue. As soon as I learned about the labyrinth, I just knew I had to incorporate it into the adventure somehow!

Finally, I am grateful for everything I have learned about ancient Egyptian magic. Throughout this experience, I felt buoyed by many of the same sensations I was writing about. Like Neff, I felt the crackle of energy in the air as I wrote about the power of heka and the inexorable pull of fate that directs us toward our greatest potential. I learned that unlike many magic systems we read about, ancient Egyptian magic is not supernatural; it is nature itself. It is magic found in the world as it is, and it's that power, combined with our words and our actions, that creates wonders. I cannot tell you how much that concept fueled me throughout the writing process and how much hope it brings into my life.

I am so thankful for the knowledge, wisdom, and magic these books have brought me and so grateful to you, the reader, for choosing to be a part of it.

Michelle Jabès Corpora
September 2025

ACKNOWLEDGMENTS

When I wrote the acknowledgments for *His Face Is the Sun*, it was months before publication, and I had no idea how the book would be received. One always hopes for the best, of course, and I'd felt a spark of magic for *HFITS* that I hadn't felt for any of my previous books, but you never know. Publishing is a roller coaster in the dark—it's impossible to know what's coming next.

Summer is ending as I write these acknowledgments, and *HFITS* has been out in the world for almost exactly four months. In that time, it has received a starred review, a Junior Library League Gold Selection, and has become both an indie and *New York Times* bestseller. Needless to say, these months have been the most amazing, humbling, and mind-boggling time in my entire life. As I prepare to release this second book, I am overwhelmed with gratitude for the countless people who made all of this possible and who continue to support me and this series with their whole heart.

First, I'd like to acknowledge the contributions of my amazing readers. Never have I felt such closeness to people all around the world, who spent their time, their money, and their energy supporting my work. I have received heartfelt messages, read incredibly insightful and thought-provoking reviews, and met warm and kind people who have given me the strength and the will to continue this work. Thank you all so much—it is for you that I will always strive to be better and to give you the reading experience you so richly deserve.

In a similar vein, I want to thank all of the hardworking booksellers and librarians who I have met in my adventures promoting the series across the country. I have been continually inspired by your dauntless dedication to literature and so thankful that you embraced this story with open arms.

To everyone at Sourcebooks and Sourcebooks Fire…what can I say? I have never met so many incredible, dedicated, and wonderful people all in one place. If you have touched this book in any way, please believe this message is for you. Thank you for being my publishing *family*, in the truest sense of the word! Dominique, you really created something special. I am so proud to be a part of it.

And to all my publishing partners at Stimola Literary Studio, the International Literary Agency, Schlueck Agency, The Dravis Agency, Hachette UK, Saxo, Rizzoli, Rocco, Karibu, PRH Spain, Lira, Metaixmio, Recorded Books, and Lizzie—thank you all for helping to bring Throne of Khetara to the world. And once again thank you to the incredible Tom Roberts and Micaela Alcaino for creating two more showstopping cover designs for *She Knows All the Names*, to Gerralt Landman for his beautiful map and chapter headers, and to the extremely talented Suehyla El-Attar Young for her performance of the audiobooks. And thanks so much to Egyptologist Dr. W. Raymond Johnson for both reviewing the manuscript of *His Face Is the Sun* and for assisting me with pronunciation for all the ancient Egyptian names and terms. This series is truly a *team effort*!

Thanks as well to my incredible team at Crazy 88 MMA for supporting me through this journey, for treating me like a celebrity every time I come to the gym, and for still beating me up during sparring so I stay grounded.

To my wonderful friends, especially Nathan Allen, Heather Allen, Mike Delaney, and Tom Poovan, thank you for all the love and laughter you've given me throughout this process, which I desperately needed to stay sane. Whether we were fighting vampires in D&D or deep-frying everything in my pantry while listening to classic rock, those nights really kept me going, and I love you for sharing them with me.

To my wonderful family, thank you for always showing up and for being my cheerleaders! It's been the wildest year of my life, and I couldn't have done it without you.

To my editor, Annette Pollert-Morgan: As my daughters would say, you "saw the vision." Your brilliant editorial observations and suggestions made it possible for this story to reach its potential, and I have grown so much as a novelist because of you. Thank you so much for your partnership—I cannot wait to finish the last leg of this race hand in hand!

To my agent, Allison Hellegers—what a ride, hey? I'm so incredibly thankful that fate brought us together the way it did. I know you don't believe me when I say this, but without your nurturing, your pushing, your faith, none of this would have happened. Thank you, thank you, thank you.

My two daughters make me so proud every day, and I want to thank them both for their support and their love throughout this very tumultuous season of our lives. I love our walks with Charlie, our nights watching *Gilmore Girls* and *Supernatural*, our hangouts in the sunroom, and of course, our BuzzFeed personality quizzes, because it's really important to know what kind of potato you are. I love being your mom. Thank you for being such wonderful human beings.

And to my husband, Adam—whose reaction to my getting on the *New York Times* list has now been watched by more than six and a half million people—is it any wonder that we went viral for how wonderful a partner you are? Thank you for your endless support and love, for your advice, for playing *Elden Ring* while I read this book out loud to you for hours and hours and hours and cursed like a sailor after every other sentence. You are cute and fun, and I like your new hat. Thanks for being my forever person and for riding this roller coaster with me. I love you, dear!

ABOUT THE AUTHOR

Michelle Jabès Corpora is the author of eleven novels for young readers, including the Holly Horror duology and five ghostwritten novels in a world-famous mystery series. A lifelong bibliophile, Michelle has worked as an editor and concept creator in children's fiction for nineteen years. In her spare time, Michelle trains as a blue belt in Brazilian jiu jitsu at Crazy 88 MMA and plays Dungeons & Dragons with her friends. She lives in Maryland with her husband, two daughters, and a dog named Charlie. Learn more at michellejcorpora.com.

THE RED LANDS
THE ANEN CAMP
THE ITERU
SAKESH
SETNAKHT'S TOMB
THE TEMPLE OF KHNUM
PER-ABU
THE KINGDOM OF TASH
HURWAR